FOR JULIE LEE, IT WAS A NIGHT OF TERROR . . .
AND THE BEGINNING OF THE LONG ROAD TO
FREEDOM.

Julie Lee trembled and unconsciously fingered the talisman swinging by a string around her neck. Jeddah had
given her the charm a few weeks earlier with a promise
that it would protect her from bad spirits. Now Jeddah was
sleeping peacefully in her cabin unaware that Julie Lee
was on the first leg of her flight toward freedom. . . .

Julie Lee sprinted between the open spaces separating
one cabin from another. Occasionally she would pause to
look over her shoulder. There was no one behind her.

In the dark, everything seemed to be alive—creeping,
crawling or screeching out. Every shadow loomed big and
ominous, and phantoms lurked everywhere, waiting to
reach out and grab her.

As the night wind blew sharply around her face, she
tried to push thoughts of Hannibal out of her mind. She
didn't want to see her brother's disapproving frown, his
accusatory eyes.

Hannibal would never understand that she was leaving
not out of selfishness but out of love for him, Dancer and
little John. She wanted for all of them what she wanted for
herself—*freedom*. The simple freedom of coming and going
as they pleased.

She had never had that freedom, and she hungered for it
as for nothing else. . . .

THE AFRICANS

BETTY WINSTON

THE AFRICANS

A Dell/Banbury Book

Published by
Banbury Books, Inc.
37 West Avenue
Wayne, Pennsylvania 19087

Dell ® TM 681510, Dell Publishing Co., Inc.

ISBN: 0-440-00076-9

Printed in the United States of America

First printing—July 1983
Second printing—September 1984

To my parents, George and Betty Winston

PART I

Prologue

Fourteen-year-old Homer Pennyfeather rolled his trouser legs up above his knees. The sun was blazing. Sweat poured from his armpits and down his hairless chest. It was the hottest day of any in the three weeks they'd been on the Guinea coast. The boy plunked himself down on the beach. Absently he sifted the clean white sand through his fingers while he stared off in the direction of the big ships anchored a few miles off the coast. Soon the ships would be loaded down with cargo and made ready for their journey to America.

The thrill and excitement of accompanying his father on a slaving expedition had by now worn off for Homer. He longed to return home. He missed his mother, his brother and his sisters terribly. Before this trip, Homer had had no idea that slaving was so brutal. The truth about his father's business had turned out to be quite unlike the colorful stories he'd always heard over the years. All he'd ever thought about until this trip was the fun he could have seeing different countries and meeting other boys his age who spoke different languages and wore clothes unlike his own.

As he sat deep in thought, Homer was oblivious to the activity around him. He'd grown used to the pitiful sounds of black men crying and rattling their chains in the dust as they were being transported from one side of the camp to the other. The Africans always seemed to be in motion. They had to be examined, counted, separated by age group and sex, and divided into groupings for deployment to the various ships. After all that, they had to be counted again.

Homer's father, Amos Pennyfeather, was a loyal employee of the Royal African Company. He had been a slave trader for many years and had been to Africa countless times. The man had often boasted to his son about the hundreds of Africans, black gold, as he called them, whom he'd delivered out of Africa to ports of call in America and the Caribbean. The elder Pennyfeather had attained the rank of captain when Homer was two years old, and since that time, he had commanded his own ship, the *Genesis I*.

Amos was not unaware of his son's unhappiness. He adored the boy. "Tomorrow we leave, son. Then we'll be off to America, and after that, home to England."

Homer was not impressed. Father had said the same things two days earlier, and two days before that, but there had always been some reason for them to stay a little longer.

Amos cupped the boy's face in his hands. "I know how it is, son. You're homesick. I was the same way the first time I came here, but if you're going to make your living as I do, you have to get used to being away for long periods of time."

Amos wanted the boy to enjoy his first trip away from home. He smiled down at him tenderly. "Just think, Homer, the longer you're away, the better the homecoming is.

4

Some people make their money on the land, but me, I love the sea, and I love the money I can make bringing these savages here to civilization. There's nothing wrong with what we do. Maybe you're just too young to understand that we're saving these people from themselves. Why, if we didn't bring them out, they'd be eating each other up alive. Wait until you see how much I get paid for just this one trip, then you'll agree that it's all worth it.''

Homer looked away. He hoped his father would not read the disgust on his face. After all, he had begged to be permitted to join the trip. All his life he had dreamed of following in his father's footsteps. But now that he was in Africa the dream had died. He didn't have the heart to tell the elder man that he never wanted to come back again, and that he wasn't proud of what his father did for a living.

Several miles away, a thirteen-year-old African girl snuggled down deep on her pallet. The village of Mwamko was quiet, and all the men except for the very elderly were away. They would be gone for three days and two nights while the women celebrated the rites of passage for the young girls who had seen their first blood that year.

Zuri could not contain her excitement. Tomorrow she would be a woman. She hoped that the night would pass quickly. Then Mother Safiya would come to her house and prepare her for the ceremony. In the morning Zuri would put on her beautiful white robe and Mother Safiya would place around her neck the gold amulet of the Bayaro clan.

Every family of Mwamko had its own emblem, representative of some heroic deed accomplished by one of the clan's ancestors. The Bayaro emblem was a great, two-headed bird, with talons as long as its body. The old storytellers said that Zuri's great-great-grandfather Tutu had slain such a bird with a slingshot when the Kitano-trained predator had swooped down on his village intent on capturing infants for sacrifice on the altar of the Kitano tribe, Mwamko's arch enemies, who lived on the other side of the river.

Zuri had never seen a Kitano, but like most of the other children of Mwamko, she feared them. Often when young boys and girls disobeyed their parents, they would be told that they would be sent off to the land of the Kitanoes, where they were sure to be eaten alive.

Grandfather Tutu, as Zuri and all the other Bayaro children had been made to understand, had been a brave warrior and a great hero to his people. "We have much to live up to, my children." Zuri's father Tinnibu had always said, "Our family is a proud one. There are no cowards in this clan."

Father Tinnibu was the most handsome man Zuri had ever seen. He was the color of the darkest tree in the forest, and his hair had been bleached to a coppery brilliance by the hot sun under which he toiled much of the time.

Tinnibu was loved by all his wives. He was strong, yet gentle and kind. He never scolded the women publicly like some of the husbands did. He tried to share himself as equally as possible among all four of his wives, including Zuri's mother, Ayodele, but village law required that Mother Safiya receive the greatest attention, since she was the first wife and the mother of Tinnibu's first-born son.

Zuri's young limbs tingled with excitement. In the morning, Mother Ayodele would comb and dress her hair with multicolored beads. Once ready, the girl would join her three half sisters, Nia, Hasani and Taji, who had also

6

seen their blood for the first time that year. Their father would be proud of his daughters, for now they were ready to extend his clan.

Zuri fell off to sleep after a while, but even in her sleep, she dreamed of nothing but the ceremony. She would walk up the three steps to the altar, where Mother Ayodele would be standing with a bowl of clear water with which to wash her daughter's feet. For the three days of the rites, there would be singing and dancing and the old women would teach the young women what they needed to know to make their husbands happy.

She had hardly been asleep an hour when she heard a loud, cracking sound she'd never heard before, followed by shouts from outside the hut. There was the loud blast again and soon a piercing scream. Next she heard the sound of her mother's voice—a frantic whisper. "Zuri! Zuri! Come here to me, child. Come here!"

The girl was only half awake and she huddled close to her mother's chest in the darkness. "What is it, Mother? What is it?"

"I don't know, child, but be quiet. We must listen."

"Perhaps it's Father and the other men come home early."

"Oh no, daughter. The men would never come back before the ceremonies are over. It's bad luck. Be still, child. Let me listen."

The girl pulled closer to her mother. She could feel the woman's heart beating quickly. Mother was afraid too. "Mother Ayodele, what are we going to do?"

"Hush, my daughter, and listen. Only listen."

They could hear the sounds of footsteps rushing past their house, when Zuri recognized a voice. It was Mother

Safiya. "What do you want here? We are only women, children and old people here."

Then another voice followed. It was a man's voice, but Zuri couldn't understand his words.

"Stay, daughter," her mother commanded as she sprang up in the darkness and made her way to the other side of the house. She pulled down from its place on the wall the long, sharp knife Father Tinnibu had left for them to protect themselves should there be any danger in his absence.

"Get behind me, child," Ayodele said in a tone that Zuri had never heard. Her voice was strong and fierce.

The two crept toward the door. When Ayodele peeked out, she could hardly believe what she was seeing.

Outside there were men. Some were black, but many more were of a complexion that she had never seen before. They were almost colorless, and some had hair that looked yellow like the sun. The men were holding long, black sticks in their hands, and they had gathered many of the women in a semicircle in the middle of the village. Instinctively, her eyes wandered in the direction of her sister Ife's house. Ife was dragged outside. Her sleeping gown was over her head and the men laughed as they dragged the woman, kicking and screaming, through the dust. Ife's daughters were weeping and were being pushed behind their mother. Ayodele watched in mute horror as one of the men took the blunt end of his stick and struck one of the girls in the middle of her face.

Mother Ayodele backed into the cabin. "Get back, child! Get back!" she commanded Zuri. She poised herself near the doorway, holding Tinnibu's knife in both hands, prepared to bring it down on the head of the first man who poked his way inside. Minutes later such a man arrived. Both Ayodele's arms came down with all her strength, but not soon enough. The man wrestled the knife from her and Zuri's scream died in her throat, for when the man aimed his long stick at Mother a bright light flashed, and a loud noise crashed. Mother fell to the floor of the house. Without thinking Zuri leapt on the man's back. He hadn't seen her in the dark. But the girl wasn't strong enough, and in seconds, the man had grabbed her around her waist and was dragging her toward the door. "Zuri. Zuri," she heard her mother say feebly. Her continued blows on the man were like a feather going up against the wind.

"Mother! Mother!" she screamed.

In an hour the carnage was over. The women who had been left to die moaned softly as they lay in red pools of their own blood, which mixed with the dust and turned to mud. The pitiful moans of the dying combined with the wails of the helpless elders, who had been spared. They had lived long but had never seen anything like that night's assault.

The other women, Zuri among them, were being marched two by two away from the village of Mwamko. They were tied to bamboo poles. There was a great deal of crying and weeping.

One of the women, Mother Afua, of the Olamede clan, caused herself to fall to the ground, pulling down the other woman on her pole with her. One of the intruders, who Zuri was now convinced were the dreaded Kitanoes, kicked Mother Afua unmercifully as she lay on the ground. He yanked her back onto her feet and shoved the long stick-instrument that made a lot of noise into the woman's face. Zuri could not understand what he said, but she knew that he meant to hurt Mother Afua. In moments several other women fell to the ground just as Mother Afua had done. The noise frightened poor Zuri nearly out of her skin when two of the men aimed their instruments at the women and let out the blast of light. The women lay still after that.

Zuri's feet ached after walking many miles. The tears had dried on her face, and all she could think about was the revenge she wished against the Kitanoes. She knew they would be sorry when her father and the other men of Mwamko found out what had been done to their wives and children. Father Tinnibu would kill them all with his knife. Zuri was sure he would.

The daylight, for which she had prayed only hours earlier, finally came. In the light, she caught sight of her sister Nia, who was tied to another pole. Nia was sobbing hysterically. They were close enough to talk to each other.

"Don't cry, sister," Zuri said. "Father Tinnibu will come and save us. You'll see."

But Nia never stopped sobbing. "We'll never see our father again, Zuri. We'll never see our father again," she cried.

The sun was high in the sky when they finally reached the camp. Once there, Zuri saw that she and the women of Mwamko were not alone. There were many others, from other tribes, and there were many men as well as women, and other girls and boys her own age. All were chained or tied together. They all appeared to be confused and dazed.

When Zuri looked and saw all the small boats sitting at the water's edge, and then the larger ones far off in the distance, she realized that the worst fate of all had befallen them—they were going to be taken to the land of the Kitanoes, where they would surely be eaten alive.

When her time came to be loaded into one of the small boats, Zuri turned her head. Her eyes searched desperately for her father and the other men of Mwamko, who should have found them by then. She wailed out loud, "Oh, Father, where are you? Don't let them take me to the land of the Kitanoes! Where are you, my father?"

Even as the water slapped up against the sides of the small boat, and as the taste of salt filled her mouth, Zuri never stopped looking back at the shore.

Zuri's land of the Kitano turned out to be America, and before long her name had been changed to Cissie. And as hard as she tried to remember, the memories of her mother and father faded as the years went by.

Zuri became the mother of a girl child named Nellie, who would bear a girl child named Roxie, who would then bear a girl child by the name of Julie Lee.

Chapter 1

Little Julie Lee was awakened by the sound of her brother Hannibal's loud snoring. He was lying right up next to her on the straw pallet, with his face turned toward the cabin wall. Julie Lee shivered. A strong draft was blowing over her. She rose up on one elbow and shook her head in exasperation. Hannibal had done it again: he had pulled all the covers over to his side sometime during the night. Lord, she thought as she yanked a corner of blanket back over herself, ain't I ever gonna get one night's sleep without being woke up by the cold, or his snoring, or heaven knows what all? Nothing don't ever change around here. Cold in the night and hot in the day. Sometime just maybe I'm gonna get myself free of this place.

This place. The Lorelei. A plantation in Virginia, in a county called Henrico, near a river called the James. Hundreds of acres of Virginia soil, and on it, the big house with its twenty rooms on three levels. Stately white columns out front majestically supported a second-story verandah that wrapped around the house and onto which opened several sets of French doors.

The Lorelei. Dozens of other smaller buildings that

circled the main house—the carriage house, the barns, the smokehouse, the stables and the long, low rows of shacks where hundreds of slaves lived and died, where Julie Lee had been born, a mulatto, a slave.

The Lorelei, the only home, the only world Julie Lee had ever known. But she imagined other places and longed to see them, to go exploring in the lands beyond the fences. She fell back to sleep and, as always, dreamed about those other places.

The next sound she heard wasn't Hannibal's snoring, but the snakelike hissing of their mother's old leather belt zinging through the air above their heads.

"Hannibal! Julie Lee! You children better get up, and get up now."

The young girl didn't want to move. She opened one eye slowly. It was still dark outside. She squeezed both eyes tightly shut, hoping that her mother would go away.

"I can see I'm going to have to burn some behinds this morning," her mother said menacingly. "You know Old Massa got company coming today, and I ain't aiming for us to be late on the job."

Mama was a copper-colored woman, and tall, just under six feet. Her height came courtesy of her slave mother. Her hazel eyes and straight brown hair came courtesy of her white father. Mama. Her name was Roxie. She was not quite thirty. Born a slave on the Lively plantation, she would surely die one here on the Lorelei plantation.

Julie Lee eased the bottom half of her body off the pallet and onto the floor. "Oooooh weeee, Mama. This floor sure is cold this morning."

"And it's gonna stay cold too if your brother don't

14

hoist his little black ass out of that bed and fetch some wood so I can start this fire.''

Julie Lee shook the sleeping boy beside her. "Hannibal! Hannibal, come on, get up, boy.''

He pushed her hand away. "Leave me alone, Julie Lee. It ain't time to get up yet.''

Their mother strode back to the pallet again and Julie Lee rolled out of her way. Roxie snatched the covers off the boy and let the tip of her belt tickle the back of his long, skinny legs.

"I'm going to give you one more minute to get up, boy, and if you don't get to moving, I'm going to sting your little behind like it ain't never been stung before.''

The touch of the belt and the tone of Roxie's voice worked like magic. Hannibal poked his head out from beneath the cover, which he had managed to pull back over to his side. He sat up and began to blink his eyes. "All right, Mama. I'm getting up.''

A half-hour later all three were dressed. Roxie sat down in her old, squeaky rocker and said, "Girl, bring me that comb so I can fix your hair.''

Julie Lee obliged her mother and sat down on the floor between the woman's legs. The fire had taken the chill off the cabin and she was glad for the relief. It got plenty cold in that valley in the wintertime.

"Hannibal, bring me my Bible,'' Roxie said after she'd combed the tangles out of her daughter's auburn hair. She opened up the ragged book and directed the children to sit down facing her. "We gonna read the verse.''

Mother could read even though she wasn't supposed to know how. She'd learned from her former master's wife, Miss Belle Lively.

"I sure do miss that Miss Belle," she would often say. "She was as fine a white woman as ever was born. She was good to me and my mama, and when I was a very little girl she taught me to read, though she made me promise I wouldn't tell nobody. Miss Belle said she could get in a heap of trouble if her husband found out that she had taught some of us niggas to read."

Hannibal squinched up his face. "Mama, why we always got to read from that old thing? I don't even think there is God. If there is, how come He don't make us free?" He gave her an arrogantly challenging look.

Instantly Roxie's hand flashed out and found its target in the middle of his face. Hannibal howled in pain.

"Boy, I can see you trying to test my patience this morning. You must be aching to feel my strap. Don't let me ever hear you say there ain't no God." She took his face in one of her hands and held it tight so that he had no choice but to look directly into her eyes. "There is a God, and when He see fit, we gonna be free."

Julie Lee, however, had never been one to let an argument go so easily. "Looks to me like He ain't never gonna see fit," she said in defense of her brother. "In all my fourteen years I ain't never seen no nigga set free. Maybe Hannibal's right and there ain't no God after all." The words were no sooner out than she regretted them, for her mother grabbed her by the earlobe and pulled her toward the door.

"Don't you give me none of that talk," her mother scolded. "I won't hear it from your brother, and I won't hear it from you. Maybe you got light skin like a little white girl, but you *ain't* no little white girl, so don't you go sassin' me like you was." Roxie's voice grew more shrill with every word. "You be no less a nigga than me."

16

"Why you always be saying that, Mama?" Julie Lee snapped back through her tears. "I know I ain't no white child. I didn't mean to sass you neither . . ."

But Roxie was too enraged to listen. "Don't you backtalk me! Outside now," she shouted and opened the flimsy cabin door, then gave her daughter a quick shove into the crisp morning air. "You cool off and don't come back in until you're ready to mind your manners, you hear?" With that she slammed the door shut.

Hannibal stared mutely at his mother. Roxie put her hand to her head as if to soften the ache she felt. Julie Lee was right. There was no call to be blaming the child for her light skin. That wasn't nobody's fault but the young massa's. Still, it wasn't right for no child to talk to her mother that way, neither. Lord, if Julie Lee forgot herself that way with one of the massas, she'd find herself on the wrong end of a bullwhip. The girl had to learn.

"Mama," Hannibal ventured, "you gonna let her freeze out there?"

"She ain't gonna freeze, boy," Roxie replied with guilt and annoyance. "It ain't that cold out." But a moment later she threw up her hands in dismay at her son's accusing stare and opened the door to bring her daughter back in.

Julie Lee wasn't there. Her mother shook her head and went looking for her.

Julie Lee. Her honey-colored skin, auburn hair and sea-green eyes the same as her slave master daddy's. She was tall, and like her mother she was high-spirited and proud.

With angry tears in her eyes, she had run from the cabin and out of the slave quarter to the top of a bald hill

17

overlooking the tobacco fields up along the northern boundary of the plantation.

There she sat on the ground and pulled the shoes from her feet. She squeezed her toes into the soft dirt. It was cold and damp. She yelled up to the sky, "Why me, God? Why me? If You really be there, why'd You do this to me? Why couldn't You make me like all the other colored people? Why'd You put me inside this white body and let me straddle between and betwixt?"

She closed her eyes and allowed her hands to hang at her sides. Then her fingers clawed at the dirt until finally she'd pulled up two handfuls. She smeared the black stuff on her face, her arms and her legs, crying all the time, "Why me, God? Why me?"

Then she felt a gentle arm go around her shoulder. Roxie, kneeling next to her, held her in a warm embrace. Julie Lee snuggled her head to her mother's bosom and sobbed as if her heart would break. They knelt there for a long time on that hill. Not a word was spoken between them. Not a word was needed.

Chapter 2

Young Massa Andy never seemed to care that Roxie and most of the other quarter women obviously didn't enjoy his attentions. He took any of them whenever and wherever he wanted—in the fields, in the barns and in the cabins as the women's children looked on. He'd slapped away more than one child who had jumped up on his back, believing that he was trying to hurt his mother.

The young master's friends had dubbed him Randy Andy because they believed his tall tales about his sexual exploits down in the quarter, and he was fond of the nickname. But he might have been quite taken aback if he knew how the women there made fun of him. Some would get out their hanky rags to wipe away tears of laughter when Cleola talked about him. Cleola, a sassy-mouthed woman with finely sculpted features, was one of the house slaves.

"I ain't kidding. That man's thing ain't no bigger than *that*." She would pinch off a small part of her finger to measure what she estimated to be his size.

"Aw, come on, Cleola," some of the women would say, "you know you be liking it."

"Like it? I hates it. When that man leaves my cabin some nights, I'm just about ready to run up and down the quarter looking for one of them fine young bucks to come on in and take up where that white boy done left off."

Everyone but Roxie laughed. She rarely participated in the humorous exchanges, for there was nothing amusing about the young master as far as she was concerned. She detested the man, especially since he'd made his father sell her Harvey away.

Harvey was Hannibal's father and the love of Roxie's life. She'd cried many a night since he'd gone. She loved him so. He was a strong, handsome man, and she often recalled how, when she was in his arms at night, she'd felt like nothing could ever come between them.

She could still picture him so clearly. He had a birthmark shaped like a rose that took up nearly one whole side of his face. Harvey had often said the mark was ugly, but she didn't agree. She would trace it with her finger and say, "This mark is the prettiest thing that I ever did see. It means you is real special, Harvey. It means that you is one of God's special children."

"I ain't no such thing," Harvey would protest. "This mark only makes me stand out among niggas, and everybody knows that a nigga what stands out gets beat the worst."

When Hannibal was born, Harvey had been as excited as he could be. He wasn't just studding with Roxie. She was his woman. He intended to ask the master for permission to jump the broom with her so they could be truly married up.

Life had gone well for several months after Hannibal's birth. Harvey would come to her cabin almost every night. They would put the baby to bed and make love. But it all changed once the young master decided to have Roxie for his own.

Young Massa had come to Roxie's cabin one evening after midnight. Harvey had followed him and had watched through the window as the young master pushed her down on the pallet, then roughly spread her legs open. The more Roxie fought, the more Young Massa seemed to want her.

Harvey cried and pounded his fists into the ground until they were bloody. Before he knew what was happening to him, he had burst into the cabin and yanked the young white boy up off Roxie.

"Get off my woman. Get off!"

Young Massa, startled by the intrusion, tried to get off Roxie, but didn't move quickly enough. Harvey grabbed him around his waist, and spun him around and threw him to the opposite side of the cabin.

Roxie, scared to death, tried to make Harvey stop. "Harvey. Harvey, please! It ain't nothing. Please, Harvey."

But Harvey pushed her over to the side and advanced once again on the white man. He was right over him when the young master came up with a knife from his pants pocket and jumped to his feet. The blade of the knife was gleaming in the fire's glow. "Come on, nigga," he beckoned. "Let me stick this here knife in you. I'm gonna kill you, nigga, I swear I am."

Harvey jumped out of the way as the white man lunged at him. "Please, massa sir," he backed off. "I ain't aiming to fight no more. I just want you to leave Roxie alone. Why you got to have Roxie when you can pick and choose whatever one you want? Roxie's my woman, and she got my child. Please, massa, sir. Please."

21

The black man's pleading seemed to make the young master only angrier. *"Your* woman? What you talking about, nigga? Ain't you come to know yet that everything around this place, including you, Roxie and that pickaninny over there, belongs to me and my daddy?"

The ruckus caused Hannibal to awaken with a scream. Roxie let the boy cry, her heart was beating so fast at the scene going on before her.

The two men circled each other like gladiators. The young master lunged again, but this time Harvey caught his arm and squeezed it until the knife fell to the cabin floor. During the struggle that ensued, Roxie managed to pick the knife up, and she tossed it into the fireplace.

Harvey had him down on the floor, and his hands were tight around his neck. The master's face was starting to turn blue. No matter how hard he tried, he couldn't pry Harvey's hands loose.

"Don't kill him, Harvey. Don't kill him," moaned Roxie.

The sound of Roxie's voice seemed to bring Harvey suddenly to his senses. He eased his grip. The white boy quickly rolled away and grabbed his pants from the chair. "You're gonna pay for this, nigga," he screamed on his way out the door. "You're gonna pay. Just you wait and see."

Harvey's shirt was hanging off his back. He was sweating and crying.

"Oh my God, Roxie. What have I done? I didn't mean to hurt Young Massa, but I just couldn't stand to see him doing what he doing to you. I just couldn't stand it."

He fell into her arms. "Harvey, don't cry; please don't cry. You done what any good man would have done. You tried to protect me."

22

"But I ain't any man, Roxie, and you ain't any woman. We're just niggas, and everybody know that we ain't supposed to sass back white folks. I guess I'm gonna get hung." Harvey's eyes searched the room widly. "I thinks maybe I should try to run away."

She shushed him by putting her fingers across his lips. "Ain't got to run. Old Massa knows that you my man. First thing in the morning, I'm gonna tell Old Massa what went on 'tween you and his son. Old Massa, he likes me, and he won't let nothing happen to you. You just wait and see."

Roxie wiped the blood from Harvey's lips and sent him back to the men's dormitory. She spent a restless night wondering if Old Massa would indeed do anything to hurt Harvey. Of one thing she was certain: if Harvey were caught trying to escape, he would be hanged.

The next morning, right after breakfast and before the old master, Andy's father, headed out to the field, Roxie asked to speak with him, but before she could say more he raised his hand to silence her. "Ain't no need, Roxie. Andy Jr. told me all about it. He told me that you'd come and try to plead for the nigga's life, but it won't do no good. Can't have no niggas around this place disrespecting white folks."

"But, massa sir, Harvey was only just . . ."

"Silence, woman. I said I can't have none of my niggas doing what Harvey done. If the word gets around, then every one of these niggas will be challenging my authority."

"But, massa, sir," she pleaded, inadvertently grabbing his hand, "please, massa sir, don't hurt my Harvey. Please, he didn't mean no harm."

He yanked her hand away from his with a force that threw her off balance. "My mind's made up. Harvey has got to go."

"What you gonna do, massa? What you gonna do? You gonna kill my Harvey? You ain't gonna kill him, is you, massa?"

"Listen here, woman, I ain't got to tell you nothing. Now you get on back to your chores and I'll take care of your Harvey."

Roxie couldn't concentrate on her work that day. Late in the afternoon she slipped down to the quarter, only to be told that Harvey had been locked up and chained in the beating house. She went to see him, but a big slave standing outside wouldn't let her near the place.

Old Massa gonna kill my Harvey, she thought in agitation. What am I gonna do? Oh Lord, it's my fault. What am I gonna do?

Three days passed and Harvey remained locked up in the beating house. So far he hadn't been whipped, however, just left to languish and imagine what his ultimate fate would be. In all that time Roxie had not been able to see him.

On Saturday a peddler came up to the big house. He was looking to buy cheap slave flesh. Such peddlers made their living buying up slaves who were cast off because they were sick or because their masters considered them too ornery to be tamed. The man's appearance was a vindication to the old master, who had decided Harvey was too valuable a piece of property to be beat half to death. His son had wanted to hang the slave as an example to the others, but his father wouldn't hear of it.

Harvey blinked in the sunlight after having been locked up for so many days. His heart was beating nearly out of his chest. He had no idea what was going to happen to him. He prayed silently as the two slave guards dragged him up to the porch of the big house.

"Here he is, Old Massa," one of the slaves said. He pushed Harvey forward so violently that Harvey fell down on his knees.

Andy Jr. came out on the porch behind his father. He looked at Harvey with a wicked smile on his face. When he caught sight of the white man, Harvey felt an urge to run up onto that porch and this time to make good on his attempt to kill him.

"Harvey, I done decided that you got to go," Andy Sr. said. "You done violated one of the primary rules around here. You know a nigga can't go putting his hands on a white man and get away with it. Now what you think I ought to do with you, boy?"

Harvey was frightened, but he shook his head. "Don't know, massa. Don't know what you should do with me. All I know is that it wasn't all my fault. I was just—"

Andy Sr. came down off the porch and slapped Harvey's face as hard as he could. Hot blood spurted out of the side of Harvey's mouth. "Shut up, nigga. You're lucky I'm not going to have your black ass killed."

The peddler came forward. Until then Harvey hadn't noticed him standing there. The peddler stepped down off the porch and ordered Harvey to stand up. He didn't move fast enough and the two slaves who were on either side of him yanked him up onto his feet.

He patted Harvey's back and felt his rump, then turned his attention to the old master. "This nigga's solid

25

as a rock. Open your mouth, nigga, let me examine your teeth.''

Harvey grimaced, but did as he was ordered.

The peddler seemed quite satisfied. "How much you want for this nigga?"

Andy Sr. decided to bargain a bit. "How much you think he's worth?"

The peddler acted as if he were thinking hard. "I guess I could give you three hundred dollars. The nigga is ornery, and it's gonna cost me extra to care for him until I can sell him."

Andy Sr. came down off the porch and squeezed Harvey's biceps. Harvey flinched and the two men at his side drew him tighter so that it was impossible for him to move around.

"Three hundred dollars," the old master snorted contemptuously. "Now you and I know that this nigga is worth more than that. Give me five hundred dollars, and you can take the nigga free and clear."

"You got a deal," the peddler said, believing all the time that he could sell Harvey for a thousand dollars.

Andy Sr. turned toward Harvey. "Take that nigga back to the dorm and put some decent clothes on him. Bring him back here in fifteen minutes, you hear me?"

"Yes, sir, massa," the slaves replied. They yanked Harvey around and headed him back down toward the quarter.

Within a half-hour the papers were signed and Harvey was dressed and ready to go. The guards chained up one of Harvey's legs to the wagon in which the peddler had been riding.

Roxie was hysterical. She begged, "Massa, please!

26

Massa, please! Please don't sell my Harvey away. Please, massa. He's Hannibal's daddy.''

She reeled when the old master reached out and slapped her so hard that she fell down to the floor. "Get out of my sight, woman, or I'll swear I'll have you sent down to the beating house."

She ran out the door past Andy Sr. and over to Harvey. Crying and pleading, she grabbed the peddler by one of his legs. "Please, sir. Please don't take my Harvey away."

She wasn't prepared for the vicious kick the peddler gave her, which sent her down into the dust. "Let me go, nigga bitch. Let my leg go. This buck belongs to me now. Bought him fair and square."

The peddler climbed up on his wagon and began driving away. She followed them up the road. "Harvey! Harvey!" she screamed.

He turned around and yelled back, "Go on back to the house, Roxie. Don't worry, baby, I'll be back one day, and then I'm gonna get you and my mama. Go on back, Roxie."

She kept pace with him. Her heart felt like it was breaking in half. "I love you, Harvey. I always will. Please come back, Harvey. I'll be waiting."

She was still screaming when the two men grabbed her and dragged her back up to Andy Sr. who growled, "Put her in her cabin and keep her there."

The weeks after Harvey's departure were empty for Roxie. As if it weren't bad enough that Harvey had been sold away, Andy Jr. came to her cabin regularly. But the light in her soul had been snuffed out and she submitted to

27

the young master without a whimper, learning to hate him more and more.

After a while she began to throw up nearly every morning, and the tea made for her by Katy, the cook from the big house, was no help. Roxie knew what was wrong: she was pregnant. She could only hope against hope that it would be Harvey's baby, and not the young master's.

When Julie Lee was born, she was as fair as the early morning sun and obviously no child of Harvey's. Roxie, who couldn't find it in her heart even to take the baby to breast, tried to kill herself, but Katy, who after nursing Roxie through months of morning sickness had grown especially fond of the young woman, intervened.

"Now, Roxie," the plump, ebony-colored woman said, trying to coax her to hand over a tin spoon laced with rat poison, "if you kills yourself, what's gonna happen to Hannibal? And what am I gonna tell Harvey if he comes back for you?"

It was the slight hope that Harvey would return some-day that stayed Roxie's hand. Still, she would have nothing to do with the child. In fact it was Katy who finally named the baby girl and who kept after the distraught mother day after day with arguments on the child's behalf: "Roxie, you can't keep blaming that innocent little thing. It ain't none of her fault who her daddy is. She's just as innocent as you. You don't want Young Massa for your man, but you can't do nothing about it, can you? Well, it's the same for that baby. She ain't to be faulted."

After a week of this Roxie grudgingly nursed the child, and in time, without her even being aware of it, her feelings toward the baby began to change.

One night, as she held the little girl tightly in her

arms she whispered in humble contrition, "I'm sorry, baby. Mama's sorry for what she done to you. I know it ain't none of your fault. Me and you, we is in the same boat. Mama promises that she won't be mean to you no more." And she tried her best to keep her word.

Chapter 3

Julie Lee closed the door to the linen closet with the heel of her foot. Her arms were loaded down with a pile of fresh pillow cases and sheets. It was her regular day to change the linens, but even so Miss Clementine, the old master's wife, made a fuss about it being done since she was expecting company to stay over night.

The linens were piled so high that Julie Lee couldn't see in front of her. It didn't matter though, because she'd made a game of counting the number of steps in the staircase leading down to the second floor, where all the bedrooms were.

She hummed as she went about her work that morning, excited that she was finally going to be permitted to serve the guests at the dinner party that night. In the past, Julie Lee had looked on wide-eyed at all the white people who came to these parties. She loved the clothes the white women wore. Her mother had already taught her to sew. If only there were decent material to be had, Julie Lee was certain she could make clothes for her own use that would be just as fine.

In her excitement she'd forgotten that there was already one guest in the house, Charles Lightfoot. Whenever old Lightfoot was around, there was resentment aplenty among the house slaves. They hated the way he ordered them, as if *he* were master of the plantation. As far as anyone could tell, he was a freeloader and a ne'er-do-well, without property, means or pride.

Sometimes Lightfoot's visits stretched out for weeks, though no one could figure out exactly why the old master liked having him around. When he would leave, few people on the plantation were happier than Katy, since Lightfoot had the awful habit of hanging around in the kitchen and tasting food directly from the pots while it was still cooking.

Julie Lee, humming as she worked, was startled when she pushed open the door to Lightfoot's room and found him standing there half dressed.

"Oh, excuse me, Mr. Lightfoot, sir," she said, backing out of the room. "I didn't know you was still about. I'll come back later."

"That's all right, little girl. I'm just about dressed anyhow. I'll be out of your way momentarily."

She tried to avoid looking but couldn't help it. Lightfoot's chest was covered with long, grey-blond hair. She thought to herself that he was just about the hairiest man she'd ever seen.

"What's your name, little girl?" he asked, disturbing her thoughts.

"Julie Lee, Mr. Lightfoot, sir."

"That's a real pretty name. I seen you around here before, but I never realized how pretty you are. Why, you're almost as fair-skinned as me."

There was something in his eyes that frightened her. She backed away a small step and said, "I'll just come

31

back later, Mr. Lightfoot, sir. I got me some other beds to make.''

"Oh no, don't leave. Go on and finish up in here.''

"All right, sir,'' she said, but only because she was afraid to disobey him.

As she pulled the soiled linen from the bed, Julie Lee could feel his eyes following her around the room. Why don't he hurry up and go on about his business? she thought.

She had her back turned when Lightfoot suddenly came up behind her and took hold of both her arms. His face was close to her neck, so close that his hot breath made the small hairs on the nape of her neck stand on end. She tried to break away, but he only held on tighter.

He pulled her around and made her face him. "How old are you, girl?''

"Please, Mr. Lightfoot, sir, I got to finish up my work or Miss Clementine gonna be mad at me. Old Missus, she likes for all the beds to be made up early.''

He would not let her arms go. Fear began to creep up her body. He pushed his face right up into hers. "I said, how old are you, girl?''

Her eyes ached and strained with fear. "I guess I'm about fourteen years or so.''

Lightfoot laughed. "Well, I think you is just old enough to learn when you done went and got a man all excited. Looks like you don't know much about what pleases a man. Ain't your massa ever tried to do something to you?''

She tried to pry her arm loose, but he wouldn't let go. "No sir, Mr. Lightfoot. I ain't never done nothing. What for you talking to me like this?''

He squeezed her arm so tightly that it turned red.

"I'll talk to you or any other nigga the way I want to. Ain't nobody ever told you that you ain't supposed to sass back white folks? It don't matter none to me that you is damned near white. You ain't nothing but another nigga to me. A half-white little nigga bitch."

"Ain't meaning to sass you, Mr. Lightfoot, sir. I swear I ain't. I just want to do my work. Please, sir."

He pulled her tightly to him. She could feel the bulge in his pants.

"Maybe I should just pull your dress over your head and paddle your behind till you learn not to sass white folks. I'm sure your massa won't mind one bit, 'cause he and I agree that sassy niggas ain't to be put up with."

She pushed herself back against the wall. "I ain't sassing you, sir. Please, Mr. Lightfoot, sir. I don't want no trouble."

He pinned her flat up against the wall. "You don't want no trouble and I ain't aiming to give you none. I just want to make you feel good. Don't you want to feel good, little miss white nigga?"

Lightfoot's breathing was getting heavier and the heavier *it* became, the more frightened *she* became. She had heard some of the other girls talk about what happens when a man starts to breathing hard.

She tried to dart away from him, but he was too quick. He grabbed her by the hair and yanked her back, then pushed her down onto the bed. She opened her mouth to scream, but before any sound could escape, his heavy hand came crashing down to silence her. She thought for sure he was going to smother her.

"You gonna be nice to me, ain't you, girl? I ain't had no woman in quite a spell, and I thinks you just fit the bill. You so damned near white that maybe I can pretend you is one of them white girls up in Richmond.'' His voice dropped real low. ''Now if I take my hand away, you promise me you ain't gonna scream. 'Cause if you do, I'm gonna have to hurt you real bad, and I don't want to do that. Don't want to bloody up that pretty little face of yours. I just want to make you feel real good.''

He removed his hand slowly. She kept her silence. He pushed his full weight down on her, pinning her to the bed. With his free hand he stroked her hair, and whispered hoarsely in her ear. He was saying things that she had never heard before, sickening things. She closed her eyes, hoping that she would wake up and discover this was all a bad dream.

The more he talked, the more excited he seemed to become. The bulge in his pants was growing larger. It was pressing down into her stomach. He was hurting her with his grinding motions. She wanted to scream, but she was too afraid.

''You just lay still and quiet, little girl, and let old Lightfoot make you feel real good.''

Ignoring her tears, he pushed his fingers up between her legs, and eased up off her just enough to undo the buttons on his pants. He wasn't wearing underwear, so the hard thing just popped out. She caught a glimpse of it. It looked like a mushroom, she thought, but it was all red and swollen.

''Please, Mr. Lightfoot, sir,'' she said. ''I don't know what you aiming to do to me. Please, sir . . .''

He was too excited to hear her protests. If anything, her pleading only heightened his passion, for he pushed her legs apart. She closed her eyes, waiting for the terrible thing to happen. There was nothing else she could do. Her mother and Katy were right downstairs, but she couldn't call out to them unless she wanted Lightfoot to kill her.

Lightfoot had edged his way toward the top of the bed, and into a position where the dreaded weapon was aimed directly at her face.

She felt a small wet drop of something dribble down her face. "Please, Mr. Lightfoot, sir. Please don't."

"Shut up, girl. Open up your mouth. I want you to put it in, and then I want you to suck on it like it was a piece of candy."

"Oh no, sir, please. I ain't wanting to do that. It ain't right. It just ain't right."

She hadn't seen his hand draw back and she was shocked when it came crashing down on the side of her face. The blow stung her. She whimpered like a small animal.

He was still talking low, but his voice had turned mean. "Goddamnit, girl, I said put it in your mouth before I kill you."

His eyes were closed and he was trembling. She kept her lips tightly shut. She'd heard the girls talk about how the boys pestered them, but she'd never heard anybody talking about folks putting nothing in their mouths. The thought of it sickened her. She felt as if she would vomit.

He yanked her again. This time, as her head bumped hard up against the wall, her skull exploded in pain.

"Open your mouth, bitch!" In his excitement Lightfoot hadn't realized how loud his voice was.

Suddenly the door to the room crashed open. It was Andy Jr. and his face was contorted in anger. "What the hell is going on in here?" he screamed, and without waiting for an answer, he yanked Lightfoot off Julie Lee and onto his feet.

35

Julie Lee started to cry. "Please, massa sir, I ain't done nothing. I just come in here to change the sheets, and Mr. Lightfoot, he . . ."

"Get the hell out of here, Julie Lee!" the young master barked without giving her a chance to explain.

She ran from the room directly down to the kitchen where her mother and Katy sat snapping green beans. Roxie's heart stopped when she saw the big red welt along her daughter's face.

"Oh my God! What happened, baby? What happened?" Roxie cried out, dropping a handful of beans to the floor.

Julie Lee fell into her mother's arms. She was crying hysterically.

"What happened to Mama's baby?" Roxie sobbed along with her.

Julie Lee was so embarrassed that she didn't want to tell her mother what Lightfoot had tried to do.

"Come on, baby, ain't nothing too bad to tell Mama."

Before it was all out, Katy was on her feet pacing. "I knew it. I knew it all the time. That man ain't never been up to no good. An old geezer like him trying to pester a child like Julie Lee. Why she ain't even hardly developed yet. She ain't none of them field wenches that knows what to do for a man."

Roxie held the sobbing child in her arms. "Oh my poor, poor baby. You go on back to the cabin, and Mama's gonna be there real soon."

"But what about my work?" the girl asked.

"Don't worry none about that, I'll get your beds made."

Julie Lee went out the door and Roxie watched her run toward the quarter.

Before Roxie could say a word, Katy signaled her to be still and inched toward the end of the kitchen ramp. She wanted to hear what the loud voices were saying on the floor above. Before long Lightfoot came storming down the stairs. Andy Jr. was close behind.

"You've taken advantage of our hospitality for the last time, Lightfoot. I never want to see your face around this place again, and I don't care how long you knowed my daddy."

"Aw, I wasn't doing anything, Andy. Just having myself a little fun."

"Just a little fun, huh? If you want fun, then you go out and buy your own whores. You abused our hospitality, Lightfoot."

"But what will your father say when he finds me gone? We had business to discuss."

Andy Jr. was hissing fire now. "Don't you worry about my daddy, Mr. Lightfoot. Any business you got with him is done, I'll see to that. Believe me, I'll give him a good explanation of your sudden and most rude departure."

Katy clapped her hands. "Thank you, Jesus. I think that'll be the last we'll see of that Lightfoot man around here. Thank you, Jesus."

The young master strode into the kitchen and went directly to Roxie. "Where's Julie Lee?"

"I told her to go on back to the cabin."

"Come with me," he demanded, pulling her by her hands out the door.

By the time the two of them reached the cabin, Julie Lee was stretched out on the pallet. She was still sobbing, but she kept her face turned toward the wall. Her cheek still burned from Lightfoot's slap, though maybe it was

37

just burning from embarrassment. She wasn't sure which. Inside herself she worried that perhaps she had done something bad, had done something to encourage Lightfoot's attack.

"You talk to her," ordered Andy Jr. "You tell her that Lightfoot is gone and won't be back no more. You tell her that what happened to her ain't right and that it ain't never gonna happen no more. Tell her, Roxie, that she ain't got nothing to be ascared of."

Turning to face him, Roxie summoned up courage from some place deep down inside of her. Without much passion in her voice, she said, "What am I supposed to tell my child? That it ain't gonna happen to her no more? You know I can't promise her that, because it would be a lie. Me and her ain't nothing but niggas, and you and your friends can do with us as you please. If any man want us, especially if he's white, he can have us with or without your say-so."

He shook her at that. "What the hell are you talking about, woman? Don't get me any more riled than I already am."

Wet tears ran down Roxie's cheeks. "You remember Harvey, massa? Do you remember Harvey?"

He tried to turn away from her hard stare.

"You didn't answer me, massa. I said, do you remember Harvey? I do. I remember what happened to Harvey too. Why don't you tell Julie Lee how she come to be born? Why don't you tell her who her daddy is? Remember, massa? You ain't asked none of my permission. You just come and took me, just like old Lightfoot tried to take her."

"Oh, Roxie, all that is nothing but water done already gone under the bridge. That was then, and this is now.''

She sat down on a chair and listened to her daughter's sobs. "It don't seem that way to me. Ain't nothing changed. I don't want nothing to hurt my child. God knows I don't, but maybe it's better this way. Maybe it's good that she's learning what being a nigga girl is all about. She's just there for the taking. It was Lightfoot today and tomorrow it might be some other man.''

Roxie was beginning to get hysterical. The young master appreciated her grief and so tolerated her insolence. He didn't respond to what she'd said. Instead he just turned around and walked out of the cabin.

When he was gone, Roxie pulled her daughter into arms. She rocked her.

"What you was trying to tell Massa, Mama? What did you mean?''

"One day I'll tell you the whole story, baby. Not now, but soon.''

Roxie kept rocking the girl. They were both crying. "Don't fret, now. We niggas ain't supposed to have no love, child, but your mama has love for you.''

"I love you too, Mama,'' Julie Lee sobbed and hugged her mother so tight that Roxie thought nothing could ever tear her away.

Chapter 4

When the sun had crept behind the clouds and the moon had risen in its place, the flickering lamplight from the big house cast a quiet glow over the landscape. Shortly after eight o'clock, the first of fifty invited guests arrived at the Lorelei. Ornate barouches, kicking up clouds of dust in their wakes, paraded single file along the drive that led up to the big house.

Each time a carriage passed, the crowd of slaves that had gathered along the lane sent up a loud cheer. They pushed and shoved each other, stretching and strain-ing to get the best vantage point from which to see the rich white people. Every once in a while a pale hand would push back one of the carriage's heavy curtains and wave. The slaves, most of them youngsters, waved back enthusiastically.

An air of festivity everywhere enlivened the planta-tion. When the white folks in the big house threw a party, the slaves outside had their own good time. Old Jebediah, the most elderly black man on the plantation, plucked furiously on the strings of his nearly worn out banjo, while to the beat of the music some of the young children shook their hips in a lively dance as the older folks urged them on by clapping.

Inside the kitchen, Katy was clucking like a nervous hen. She ran up and down the line of house slaves she'd assembled, inspecting their attire and giving them last minute instructions. She straightened the men's ties and the women's aprons and she pushed her hammy fists into protruding bellies. "Hold that stomach in, boy, before you pops them buttons on that uniform. If you gets any fatter, you ain't gonna be able to work the parties no more."

"And you, Ginny May, you push that hair up under that hat. Just 'cause you got hair like some of them white women, ain't meaning they wants you flaunting it in their faces. All we needs is for one of them to start hollering about hair in their food.

"Did y'all wash up good like I told you?"

"Yes ma'am, Miss Katy, we did," the assembly chorused.

"Y'all better had. Ain't nothing white folks hate more than some stinky nigga leaning over and serving them food."

Just then Miss Clementine strolled into the kitchen to make sure that everything was ready. Upon seeing her, Katy grew even more stern in her warnings, trying hard to impress the woman and to give her no excuse to tarry long.

"Katy, do we have enough glasses?" Miss Clementine fretted. "Is the meat done just right? I don't know what I'm going to do, I'm just so nervous."

Katy rolled her eyes at the woman. "Everything is gonna be all right ma'am, so don't you worry about a thing. You just go on and have yourself a good time.

Don't old Katy always take care of everything? I ain't let you down in all these years, and I ain't about to start now.''

Katy literally pushed her mistress out of the kitchen. She sucked her teeth as she said to others, "Lord, if that woman don't leave me alone I'm gonna go screaming down the road. What would any of these white folks do without us? Sure would be a sad world then. Seems like they can't do much of nothing without some help.''

"Ain't that the truth," Roxie put in, only to be joined by a chorus of amens.

Julie Lee was terribly excited. She asked her mother to let her comb her own hair. "Oh please, Mama. Let me make my own style," she'd begged her mother before they left the cabin for the big house.

Roxie said, "I don't know what kind of style you think you're going to wear. You know Katy's just gonna make you push it up under your cap like all the other serving girls.''

"I know, Mama. I just want to make pretend.''

Roxie laughed at her child. "All right, honey. Have it your way.''

Julie Lee ran down the ramp leading to the dining room. She came back all excited. "Sure is a lot of people out there.''

Katy gave the child an indulgent smile, then resumed her stern demeanor. "All right, is everybody ready?" she called out, turning to the crew. "Y'all go on and get to it.''

Three men and two women, one of them Julie Lee, made their way down the ramp and into the dining room. Each was carefully balancing a tray loaded down with Miss Clementine's delicate crystal glasses. On her way out, Julie Lee turned to her mother and said, "Wish me luck, Mama."

Roxie blew the girl a kiss.

"Love you, baby."

Once the waiters and waitresses had left, Roxie turned to Katy. "Did you see my baby, Katy? She's just growing up so quick. She's a right good-looking girl, too. Ain't she?"

"She sure is," Katy agreed, remembering how much Roxie had despised the child at first. My, how time changes things, Katy thought.

The activity in the kitchen was frantic. It seemed like every fifteen minutes another waiter or waitress was coming back to get a tray refilled. "Lord, they is really lapping up that wine tonight," Roxie said as she poured out more liquor.

"Yes, indeed," Katy replied. "I guess I better ask Miss Clementine if she wants me to start serving the food before they all get too drunk to taste it."

A group of fiddlers had been hired to come out from Richmond to play, but the music could hardly be heard over the constant chatter and laughter of the crowd. Everyone seemed to be having a wonderful time.

Everything was just the way Miss Clementine had planned it. She wanted the party to be a tremendous success. She wanted anyone who had not been invited to know that they had missed the social event of the season.

Throughout dinner there were exclamations of delight at the roast duckling, the steamed black-eyed peas, the candied violet petals. Although she stayed out of sight, Katy beamed when she heard the compliments. One of her greatest pleasures in life was knowing that people enjoyed her cooking.

After dessert, a peach cobbler served piping hot, the guests drifted back into the ballroom and the fiddlers commenced playing again. Many of the men retired to the library for smoking and masculine conversation, while their wives sat along the perimeter of the ballroom dance floor where they waved their fans and exchanged gossip. One woman, however, had refused to follow custom. Whilomene, Andy Jr.'s wife, followed Andy Sr. into the library. She was as infamous in the household for her independent disposition as she was for her frequent fits of jealous rage over her husband's visits to the women's dormitory in the slave quarter or her long bouts with imaginary illnesses.

Young Andy was incensed but not surprised when he realized she'd tagged along with the men. He wanted to tell her to get out, but he knew that if he did, she would just make an embarrassing scene. Besides, his father thought Whilomene rather amusing.

To make matters worse, once everyone was settled in the room, Whilomene draped herself over her father-in-law's chair, and while the men talked, she played with the old man's hair.

Young Andy conveyed his displeasure to his wife with a hard stare, but she stared back at him defiantly.

"I'll kill her," he hissed under his breath.

Katy had warned Julie Lee even before she went into the library to take ashtrays and tobacco and to be on hand just in case any of the men needed more liquor. "You just blend yourself in like you is part of the furniture, child.

44

Don't draw no notice to yourself or you just might end up being real sorry.''

"All right, Auntie Katy," the girl replied. She was excited to have been chosen for such an important assignment, and she was determined to do well. So Julie Lee stood off to the side as the guests in the library talked, and as Katy had told her, she tried to remain inconspicuous. The conversation had turned to the topic of abolition.

Clem Hooper, owner of another large plantation not far from the Lorelei, said, "Can you imagine them so-called abolitionists, trying to say that we should free our niggas 'cause they're human just like us? Why, the whole goddamned country would crumble if we weren't allowed to keep our niggas. Who's gonna pick our cotton and our tobacco? And who in hell is going to clean up our houses and cook our dinners?"

Old Massa blew a puff of smoke from his cigar. "I'm sick about the entire situation. I don't know what the damned world is coming to. We got white folks acting like niggas, and niggas acting like white folk."

"That's right, Daddy. We got lots of low-down white trash that's even helping the niggas," Andy Jr. put in. "What about that John Brown? A nigga lover if ever I did see one. Got himself hanged for killing white folk up in Kansas. A white man, mind you, killing slave owners. And he ain't the worst. What about that rail-splitter, Mr. Lincoln? Why that man believes we Southerners are just going to sit around and let our niggas walk away on his say-so."

Julie Lee hovered around the edge of the group, absently dumping tobacco out of full ashtrays into her apron pocket. She was fascinated by their discussion.

The old master cleared his voice loudly. "Well. I tell

you boys one thing: ain't never the day going to come that Andy Johnson is going to set his niggas free. I'd rather kill the black sons-of-bitches before I'd do that."

Whilomene couldn't resist an opportunity to display her knowledge of the subject under discussion. "My daddy always used to say that even if the niggas were given their freedom, they'd come running right back to the plantation. What else can niggas do anyhow except what we tells them to. I—"

Thaddeus Jackson interrupted. "I don't know if that's exactly true. There are some niggas who act fairly human. Some of them have done pretty decent too. I've been up North and seen some of them so-called free niggas with my own eyes. A few of them are working and have their own businesses."

"Yes," Andy Sr. said, "but most of those niggas is half human. The ones that do anything usually got some white blood."

Julie Lee came by and mopped up a small puddle of water on one of the tables. The younger Andy noticed her and felt like she shouldn't be there, but he didn't want to say anything for fear of drawing attention to her. She was, after all, one of those half-human niggas about whom his father had just been speaking—in fact, Andy's half-human daughter.

Matthew Carney, a distinguished-looking, silver-haired planter put in, "All I know is that the abolitionists and their talk about setting the niggas free seem to be gaining some momentum." Carney leaned forward in his seat. "Look at that woman—oh, what the hell is her name? You know the one. They say she just spirits the niggas right off the plantation and takes them up North. Say she gets a lot of help too from them nigga-loving abolitionists."

"Well if I ever catched her spiriting any of my Lorelei niggas away," the elder Johnson muttered, "I'd kill the bitch right on the spot, and they wouldn't have to give me none of that reward that they got on her head."

The conversation droned on, and as it did, Julie Lee's interest turned to rapt attention. Although she and her mother and Hannibal had often talked about getting their freedom someday, never until listening to these white people talk did she realize that the possibility was so real. She didn't understand all the twists and turns in the conversation and the meanings of some of the big words escaped her, but she was able to deduce that the white folks sounded scared. Lord, freedom might be just up the road apiece, she thought, and that prospect took wing in her imagination. What she would do if she were free!

A dull thud brought her back to reality. She was as surprised as everyone else in the room by the unexpected sound. The conversation stopped and all the attention in the room riveted on her.

A heavy ashtray had dropped out of her hand and onto the floor, its contents scattered all over the rug. She mumbled an apology and quickly dropped to her knees to pick up the mess. She was afraid to look up, particularly in the old master's direction.

Her back stiffened when she heard his voice. "Girl, what you doing?" For the first time he was cognizant that she'd been in the room all the while. "You been listening to our conversation?"

She kept her head down. "No, massa, sir. Ain't been listening at all. Been cleaning these here ashtrays like I was supposed to." She could feel hot tears beginning to well up in her eyes.

"You been listening to our goddamned conversation,

47

haven't you? Don't lie, girl, or you'll get a whipping like you never had before.''

She stood up, protesting all the while. "No, sir. Ain't been listening to nothing. I swear I ain't.''

When Julie Lee's face came into full view, one of the men laughed out loud and said, "My God, Andy, if I didn't know that was just another nigga girl, I might be thinking that she's one of your grands. Sure does appear that somebody been playing in the quarter. Look like . . .''

The man would have gone on if Matt Carney hadn't tapped him on his knee. The man stopped laughing long enough to follow Carney's discreetly pointed finger in the direction of Whilomene. "Oh," he began to apologize, "excuse me, ma'am. I didn't mean no harm. I plumb forgot that you were here. I didn't . . .''

Young Andy's face flushed scarlet. His embarrassment, however, was no match for Whilomene's utter humiliation. Her eyes emitted angry sparks, and abruptly she bolted from the room. Obviously she too had noticed the resemblance, and now that mention of it had been made in public, she would be hell to live with.

An uneasy silence hovered over the library once Whilomene had fled. The heated conversation of just a few moments earlier had shut off, as if someone had suddenly choked all the air out of the room.

"Get out of here, Julie Lee,'' the old master bellowed at the frightened girl.

She ran out through the door and closed it behind her. She was terrified now, fully expecting to get the beating of her life the next day for being so clumsy.

Once she was safely back in the kitchen, she trembled

with fear. "What's the matter, child?" Katy asked, eyeing the girl with concern.

Julie Lee cried and threw her arms around Katy's waist. "Oh, Auntie Katy! I dropped an ashtray and Old Massa got mad at me. He yelled and told me to get out. What he gonna do to me? He's gonna beat me, ain't he?"

Katy ran her hands through the girl's hair to try to comfort her. She couldn't answer her question. She had no idea what the old master would do.

Chapter 5

A high-pitched scream tore through the house, shattering the morning quiet. All who heard the deafening sound froze in place and tried to determine from which room it had come.

A cold chill ran down Katy's back. She dropped the handful of carrots she'd been holding and raced toward the staircase that led to the second floor.

She'd been in the kitchen when Whilomene had sent for Roxie. Now she was certain something horrible had happened between the two women. By the time Katy had arrived, out of breath, at the top of the steps, a group of slaves was gathering about the open door.

"Get out of the way," Katy said as she pushed her way through and burst into the room. "Oh, my God!" she screamed. There was blood everywhere—on the bedspread, on the curtains, on the walls and dripping down from the heavy iron poker Whilomene was still holding in her hands.

Katy's eyes darted from the poker to Whilomene and finally to the prone figure stretched out on the floor. A pool of blood formed at the place where Roxie's head lay. Katy rushed over and turned her face up. She wanted to vomit at the sight. Roxie's face had been transformed into a hideous mask of blood and flayed flesh.

Someone had already summoned the old master and Andy Jr. back from the fields. Julie Lee had been working in the garden and she came running in as well. The old master pushed all the servants out of the way as he entered the room. He looked at Roxie lying still and then at Whilomene, who stood glaring at the fallen black woman, the poker still in her hand. "What in the goddamned hell is going on here?" he demanded.

Andy Jr. was right behind his father. Immediately, his eyes went to Roxie. "Oh, my God. Oh, my sweet Jesus." Something came over him. He shook Whilomene by her shoulders, which caused her to drop the poker, and then he slapped her with every ounce of his strength. "Are you crazy, woman? Have you lost your mind? This time you really did it, didn't you? Didn't you?"

Andy Sr. pulled his son off his daughter-in-law. "Calm down, Andy. Just calm down. Please."

Andy Jr. started to cry. "She really did it this time. Her and her damned stupid, petty jealousy."

The old master turned his attention to Whilomene now. His voice dripped with rage. "Why'd you do it?"

Whilomene suddenly broke away and fled to the bedroom next door where her children were. Whilomene yanked the children away from an old slave who held their hands and squeezed both of them in her arms.

Katy sat on the floor and rocked Roxie in her bosom. Tears streamed down her fat cheeks, and she kept repeating, "She ain't never hurt nobody. Poor child. Poor, poor child. What we gonna do? What we gonna do?"

"First thing we gonna do is get her up out of this room," Andy Sr. answered Katy. He turned to Big Foot

Ben, a huge slave who worked in the carpentry shop. "Ben you go on over to the Warwick place and get the doctor to come over here. Tell him I need him right away. Looks like one of my niggas been hurt real bad." Ben was out the door before the old master had even finished.

"Lyle, come on over here and help the woman up," the old master commanded. Lyle, one of the stable grooms, gently lifted Roxie from the floor and held her as if she were a baby. Blood oozed from her skull and onto the stairway carpeting.

Julie Lee ran behind Lyle, screaming all the while. "She done killed my mama! Miss Whilomene done killed my mama!"

Just then Hannibal came running in. "What happened? What happened?" Hannibal screamed. When Julie Lee saw her brother, her own screams grew even louder. "Hannibal, Miss Whilomene done killed Mama!"

"No, Julie Lee. Mama ain't dead. Can't be dead. No, Julie Lee, not our mama." He grabbed his sister's hand. Katy followed behind the hysterical, sobbing teenagers.

A small crowd gathered outside Roxie's cabin door. "Don't just stand there looking stupid!" Katy yelled. "One of you niggas go fetch me some water and some clean rags. I declare, sometimes you all act so ignorant."

Katy gently wiped the blood that had clotted on Roxie's forehead. The woman shuddered when the cold water touched her face, but she didn't open her eyes. "Say something, child. Please say something," Katy cooed. "What happened, Roxie? What you done to make Miss Whilomene so mad that she bash your head in like this?"

Katy lifted her head toward the cabin roof. "Oh, Lord Jesus, what has this girl ever done to deserve this?

She ain't been no bad nigga. She does everything just like she supposed to.''

Hannibal and Julie Lee were still sobbing hysterically in the corner and their crying only made Katy more nervous. "Hush up, y'all. Hush up, before you scare both your mama and me to death.''

"What happened, Roxie?" Katy repeated. The response she got was a feeble moan that came through Roxie's blackened and swollen lips. Both her eyes were bruised, and once the blood had been washed away, Katy saw the large open gash in Roxie's head.

She rocked Roxie again and prayed, "Lord, have mercy. Please, God, don't let this woman die. She ain't done no bit of harm to nobody. She's a good mama, Lord, and her little 'uns need her.''

Katy was still praying when she finally heard what she'd hoped for. "Where my babies?" the voice said so softly that it was barely audible. "Where my Hannibal and my Julie Lee? They all right?''

"They here," Katy said. She turned around and motioned for the two to come over to the pallet where their mother lay. "See, Roxie, they right here. Here's Julie Lee and Hannibal too.''

"Please don't let that woman hurt my babies. They ain't done her no harm. They . . .'' The words died in her chest and Roxie lapsed into unconsciousness. Her labored breathing, however, was some comfort, since they knew that she at least was still alive.

A short time later, Andy Jr. arrived at the cabin with Doc Warfield.

The doctor knew Roxie well. He'd helped deliver her two children. In fact, he knew almost all the blacks on the plantation, for he was often called upon to treat them when home remedies failed.

"Get out of the way! Get out of the way!" the young master screamed at all the slaves who'd gathered outside the cabin. "Ain't you niggas got work to do? I don't want nobody in this cabin except for Roxie and those children over there. The rest of you niggas get your asses back to work!"

Katy moved over to make room for the doctor. "You've done a good job so far as I can see," the doctor said, as he smeared a salve on Roxie's wound. "Got to get her cleaned up so I can determine the extent of the damage."

Warfield turned his attention to Andy Jr. "You say Whilomene hit her in the head with a poker?"

"Believe so, Doc."

The doctor worked on Roxie for more than an hour before he closed his bag and walked outside in the sunlight with the young master following close behind him. They headed in the direction of the big house.

"What you think, Doc?"

"I don't know if Roxie's going to make it, Andy. She done lost a lot of blood. The best I can tell you is let her rest a few days. You know niggas has a way of healing quicker than white folks. Don't rightly know why that is, but since Roxie is only half nigga, ain't no telling how long she may take to heal. May not heal at all. I'll stop over every day and check her progress. I left some medicine with Katy in case she should break out with a fever."

The doctor stopped in midstride and turned to Andy. "My God. What possibly could the poor woman have done to make your wife mad enough to beat her half to death?"

Andy wouldn't look into the old doctor's eyes. "I'm not sure, Doc, but I got some ideas."

Throughout the day other women came to the cabin to give Katy some relief, for despite the morning's tragedy, Katy had to go back up to the big house to prepare the meals for the family.

Roxie regained consciousness more than once, but only for a few moments each time. She always asked for her children. One time she screamed out for Harvey.

By that evening, although exhausted, Katy went back to Roxie's cabin. She would pass the night with her.

Before she left, Zeph, a young kitchen maid, gave her a report on what had occurred while Katy had been with Roxie that day. "Miss Whilomene never came downstairs. I heard Young Massa arguing with her. Heard him screaming at Miss Whilomene. 'What you hit that poor woman for? You just jealous about something that happened long before you ever came to the Lorelei. You didn't have no right to whip her like that for no cause.'

"Miss Whilomene was real mad too 'cause she told Young Massa, 'You acting like that nigga bitch is better than me. You know that Julie Lee's your daughter. Don't deny it. Everybody else knows it too. No wonder you always got so much business down in the quarter, and no wonder you've got the mama and the daughter working up here in the big house, flaunting your indiscretion in my face. What about your white children, Andy? What about them. Yes, I hit her. Tried to kill her, too. I don't like everybody laughing at me because your bastard daughter works right inside the big house.'

"And then Young Massa, he got madder and he told Miss Whilomene, 'I have never denied that Julie Lee was my child. She is. I've never denied that. You knew it.

55

You knew it almost from the time you came here. But you, Whilomene. If you weren't in that library where men were talking, you wouldn't have heard anything. That's what you get for not knowing a woman's place.

" 'Damned right Julie Lee is my child, and you know what? I got others too. So what? They still just niggas. Roxie was my wench for a long time, but I ain't been with her since you came up here from South Carolina. I was a single man then, so I was free to use the nigga wenches down in the quarter when I felt like it. But since you came . . .'

"And then Miss Whilomene she cut Young Massa off before he could finish. She say, 'You're lying Andy. I know you're lying. You think I've been sleeping all those nights when you slip out of our room? You've never stopped going down to the quarter. And Roxie ain't the only one either. Maybe you got Zeph too. She's one of them hot-assed niggas. I wouldn't even be surprised if you done had Katy.'

"It went on like that all day, Katy. I swear, I got tired of listening. They just kept saying the same things over and over again."

Miss Clementine was disgusted by everything that had happened that afternoon. She wondered how it would sound when the word got out and her friends started spreading the gossip about how her daughter-in-law had tried to kill her son's nigga wench. "People will never stop talking," she told her husband. "Oh, that woman. She's never going to stop doing things to embarrass this family."

The old lady knew that Julie Lee had been fathered by her son, but damnit, why couldn't Whilomene learn that there were some things for white women to be concerned about, and other things that they couldn't do anything about. When Andy Sr. was young, he caroused in the quarter too, and so did most of the other husbands who had slave women around, but it's a wife's lot to hide her jealousy. Whoring is just a fact of life on the plantation.

As far as Miss Clementine was concerned, Whilomene's actions that day was just another black mark against her. "Her family might have money," she told her husband, "but that girl acts like poor white trash. She'll never fit in, because she'll never understand what it is to know her place."

Chapter 6

The scent of death lay heavy on every heart at the Lorelei. Throughout the long, pitch-black, moonless night, the slaves kept vigil outside Roxie's cabin, coming and going, talking in small groups, singing a little, praying a little, weeping a lot.

For the first time in a long time, Cleola had few words to offer, and no smile on her face. She trod somberly through the crowd, wringing her hands and crying, "Lord, oh my sweet Jesus, keep your hands on her, Lord."

Inside, Roxie lay still on her pallet. Julie Lee and Hannibal took turns patting their mother's forehead with a damp cloth and rubbing her limp hands. Julie Lee traced the outside of the wide gash on the side of her mother's head. There was an awful bitterness in the girl, an anger so overwhelming that it frightened her. As she touched her mother's face, she kept thinking about the conversation she'd overheard in the library.

She whispered low to her brother, "I'm gonna escape, Hannibal. I'm gonna go away from this place. But before I leave I'm gonna make Miss Whilomene pay for what she done to Mama. I swear before Jesus she's gonna pay. I ain't sure how I'm gonna do it, but I tell you one thing: Miss Whilomene ain't gonna live to be no old lady.''

Hannibal took his sister's hands in his. "Ain't got no time to be worrying about Miss Whilomene now. We got to be thinking about Mama. We got to hope Mama get better. Mama always said that there was a God, but how come He let this happen to her. She believe in Him so much and what happen? God let Miss Whilomene hit Mama in the head.''

Though she was younger than him, for some reason Julie Lee felt older and wiser than her brother at that moment. "Mama ain't gonna get well, Hannibal, no matter how much we wishes it.''

He stared at his sister in horror as if he refused to admit that possibility. "Don't say that, Julie Lee. Don't say that Mama's gonna die. I don't want her to die. What we gonna do without Mama? I'm gonna be too scared if Mama ain't here.''

She took her pinkie finger and wiped a tear from his eye. "Hannibal, me and you got each other. That's what Mama always tell us.''

Katy had been sitting for hours only a few feet away from Roxie's pallet. She rocked in Roxie's chair—back and forth and back and forth. She was so tired, but she struggled to stay alert. She wanted to be ready if Roxie regained consciousness.

She could tell by Roxie's stillness and the peaceful look on her face that she was traveling. The old folks used to say that before people died they traveled between the living world and the dead one.

Katy looked over at the children and she felt a deep

sense of sorrow, not so much for Roxie, but for them. She believed that Roxie was already beyond pain and was only staying awhile because so many people were willing her to stay on. Hard enough being niggas and slaves, Katy thought, but even harder for the little children without no mama or daddy to protect them.

The dampness in the air caused Katy to draw her shawl tighter around her shoulders. "Hannibal, go outside and bring some wood in here. It's getting mighty cold and we don't want your mama getting the pneumonia on top of everything else."

"Yes ma'am," the boy said quickly. As he went out the door he bumped into Zeph, who was carrying a kettle from the big house. "I brung some of this soup from this afternoon. I figured that maybe y'all might be getting hungry about now. You ain't hardly ate nothing all day."

He smiled at her. "Thank you, Zeph. That's real nice. Go on inside. Julie Lee and Aunty Katy's in there."

Katy was glad to have Zeph come and sit awhile. "You sure been a blessing today, Zeph. I ain't exactly sure how I would have done without you. I know you must be plenty tired yourself. Trying to do most of my job and yours too."

She patted Katy's arm. "Ain't nothing. In times of trouble, we got to pull together. Roxie's like my own sister, she is."

Katy got up and pulled the cover up over Roxie's neck. She looked at her face. "Look at her, Zeph. She look just like a baby sleeping."

"She do, don't she. I suppose that's why Young Massa carrying on so. You and I both know he kind of sweet on Roxie, even though she just supposed to be a slave. Look at all the things he give her and do for her, and he never make her work too hard. He can tell Miss Whilomene that he ain't been out in the quarter no more, but you and me both know that's a lie. The man is acting like somebody in his family done up and died.''

Katy shook her head. "Ain't that the truth."

When Hannibal returned, Zeph stood up and smoothed out her skirt. She went over to the pallet, bent down and kissed Roxie on the cheek. Then she summoned Hannibal and Julie Lee to her and took them in her arms. "I got to be getting back but y'all be strong now. You know we all praying for you and your mama. Whatever happen, it's God's will."

Katy, Hannibal and Julie Lee walked Zeph to the door. "Night, Zeph. See you in the morning," Katy said.

Katy took three bowls down off the shelf and ladled the soup from the kettle. It had cooled off some, but it didn't matter because they were hungry. The room fell quiet except for the sounds of their spoons scraping against the sides of the wooden bowls.

"Hannibal, you and Julie Lee go on over on your pallet and try to get some sleep. I'm gonna sit here with your mama."

The boy stood up and suddenly put his arms tightly around Katy's neck. "Auntie Katy, Mama's gonna be all right, ain't she?"

She looked at him. "Baby, whichever way it goes, believe me, your mama is gonna be all right. Dying ain't always the worst thing, you know. We has to figure that sometimes God knows what's best."

He wasn't satisfied with that answer, but he didn't press for more. The boy and girl fell off to sleep in each other's arms, exhausted.

The heat from the fireplace caused Katy to fall asleep

61

too. The shadows from the fire's embers danced on her face, and after a while, her ever-present white scarf slipped out of place on her head to reveal her thin white hair. Few people had ever seen Katy without her scarf, and without it, it was obvious that she was getting very old.

Hannibal woke up during the night. After checking and finding his mother still unconscious, he went outside and stood by the door. Looking up at the stars, he cried bitterly, feeling so utterly, utterly helpless.

Back up at the big house, the light in Whilomene's room still burned brightly. She pushed her head down into the pillow, wanting desperately to drown out the tormented sobs and chants of the blacks down in the quarter. The sound was coming in, despite her having shut tight all the windows in her room. The singing and the moaning, she thought, would drive her crazy. For the first time in her life, the girl who had everything felt afraid. She was afraid of the blacks outside, afraid that they might burst into the house, drag her outside and kill her. She was afraid too of the whites inside the house, worried that this time maybe she had gone too far. Even her father-in-law, who had always been so quick to defend her, had not set foot in her room to offer any comfort or solace. He hadn't even come to inquire about how she felt or to ask her what had actually happened. She hadn't expected her husband to ask. She knew that he was angry enough to wring her neck with his bare hands.

It was all so strange, she thought, a reversal of what should have been. After all, Roxie wasn't anything but a slave. If it was true that niggas weren't human like white folks, then why was everybody carrying on so about her? Whilomene couldn't figure it out.

"She shouldn't have made me do it," she said to herself. "I didn't mean to hurt the nigga, but I can't let no wench talk back to me. I'm Mrs. Andrew Johnson, Jr. of the Lorelei plantation. My daddy is one of the richest men in South Carolina, but everybody is acting like I'm the nigga and Roxie's the white lady. Everybody acts like I'm the whore and she's the wife. Everybody is acting like my kids is the bastards instead of hers."

Nothing Whilomene said or thought gave her any comfort, for there was always that subtle conviction at the back of her mind that her husband cared more for Roxie than her.

"I wonder if Andy would carry on so if I was dying instead of his nigga bitch?"

She turned on her stomach, hating herself, hating everyone. She lay there for another half-hour, but sleep wouldn't come. Finally she got out of the bed and propelled herself to the roll-top desk in the corner. She fumbled around and found the pretty stationery that said Lorelei across the top. She wrote:

Dearest Daddy,

Something terrible has happened up here. I think I want to come home and bring the children for a while. Please come, Daddy, so I can tell you all about it. And Daddy, please come soon.

Love,
Willie

Chapter 7

Only one black woman refused to partake in the vigil: her name was Jeddah. She stayed inside her cabin, hunched over a bowl of a foul-smelling, smoky brew and recited ancient words that no one else could understand.

She threw her small, bony head back and laughed. Her voice sounded like a man's.

"Let the rest of them stand around praying to the white man's God. Me, I'll settle things in my own way and in my own time. Settle things the way they supposed to be settled. Ain't no matter what the man do to me. Me, I'm always going to be free. If it ain't my body, then my soul, so it don't matter what the white man do to me."

She was jet-black with a long, narrow face and piercing eyes that stared out angrily at the world. She had a loathing for all white things and white people. Jeddah, the woman from the spirit world.

The other slaves spoke of her in hushed awe. "Look at her hands. They all wrinkled up and black as she is, they got blue veins showing through. She look like some hundred-year-old woman, yet she ain't near to being old."

When Jeddah walked down the quarter's road in her

pigeon-toed, long-legged gait, no one dared step in her path. "She got magic," the slaves all said.

Jeddah didn't associate with the others much and when she did it was usually to admonish them about the foolishness of believing in the white man's God. "Why y'all go to listen when that old half-crippled white preacher come up here? What kind of religion be telling you to act like a child no matter how old you is? That you supposed to scratch your head and look down at the ground when some old pale-faced, blue-eyed white man be talking to you.

"Y'all need to tell me what kind of religion that is that say it's a sin to think about getting free 'cause you gonna get free on the other side after you die. White man have his heaven on earth, but you supposed to wait until after you die.

"We may be slaves, but that ain't because of no God that nobody can't see. We ain't free 'cause all of us ain't yet decided that we want to be."

Though they would argue often, Jeddah and Roxie had become close friends over the years—a fact that sometimes amazed Jeddah. "Most of these niggas is too afraid to be seen talking to me at all," she said to Roxie one day. "Why you talk to me anyhow?"

" 'Cause I ain't ascared of you, and I believe in my God as much as you believe in yours," came the unflinching reply.

Jeddah had arrived at the Lorelei by a circuitous route. She told Roxie the story one day when they were talking. She thought it rather amusing.

"Old Massa didn't want to buy me. I could tell. He didn't believe that I could heal. The peddler said, 'Let me show you what this nigga can do.' And Old Massa, he said, 'Speak, nigga,' and then I said, 'What I'm supposed to say?' And then Old Massa say to the peddler I was a rude, ugly old bitch. Say all his niggas knew how to act.

"And when the peddler said I cost nine hundred dollars, Old Massa got so mad he told the peddler, 'You expecting me to pay nine hundred dollars for this old broken-down nigga? No sir. I got a hundred slaves on this place and everyone of them is worth more than this one. 'Sides, she look like one of them pure African niggas, and I don't like them too much because some of them is dangerous. Got them funny ideas. I like my niggas already broke in and knowing what they got to do.'

"But for all that fussin', I knowed Old Massa was gonna buy me anyhow."

"Now, Jeddah, how you knowed Old Massa was gonna buy you?"

Jeddah shrugged away Roxie's disbelieving look. " 'Cause I knowed it, 'specially after I put my mo-jo on him."

Roxie threw her hands up. "Oh, Jeddah, what mo-jo you talking about?"

"Never you mind *what* mo-jo. I'm here, ain't I? After Old Massa say I'm a worthless, ugly old bitch. And he paid that peddler his nine hundred dollars, too."

Roxie wasn't sure that she should say what she wanted to say next, but she did anyway, even at the risk of making Jeddah angry with her. "What I don't understand is, why, if you got mo-jo, you still a slave. Why don't you just use your mo-jo and make yourself free?"

Jeddah rolled her eyes. " 'Cause I don't want to. Not yet I don't. I got my work to do."

"What kind of work you got to do?"

"Ain't telling nobody that, not even you, Roxie. If I tell everybody, then it ain't gonna be no secret, is it?"

The younger woman was thoughtful now. "I guess you right about that. Ain't never heard of no mo-jo that wasn't secret."

"See, that's why I like you, Roxie. You know when to stop getting into other people's business."

Secretly, Roxie did believe Jeddah had some kind of magic, or at least some control over Old Massa, for she'd seen him give Jeddah a whole cabin to herself, while most of the other slaves had to stay in the dormitory until they had children. Even then they would get a cabin only if Old Massa saw fit.

Roxie also recalled plenty of times when the old master permitted Jeddah to go off in the woods all by herself at night. He didn't seem to be worried at all that she might try to escape. Yes, indeed, maybe that old Jeddah did have some magic. But Roxie never asked the spirit woman to perform one of her spells as a favor. She wanted no part of it. If they were friends, it was in spite of Jeddah's magic—not because of it.

So on the night that Roxie lay dying, Jeddah wouldn't pray for her, as much as she cared about her. "Ain't never gonna pray for no nigga to live like this and be a slave. Roxie better off dead. Anyhow, my magic wouldn't work for her. She don't believe."

Chapter 8

Cleola brushed Roxie's hair until it shined. Today, the severe upswept style she ordinarily wore would not do. Instead, Cleola left it loose, let it drape over her shoulders so that it would frame her perfectly oval face. She oiled Roxie's face first and then put some powder on it to camouflage the black-and-blue bruises around the gash in her head.

Before the first streaks of daylight silvered the sky, Katy brought to Roxie's cabin the dress, all neatly pressed with an iron up at the big house, that Roxie would wear for this most special occasion. It was pink with a butterfly pattern and ten cloth-covered buttons down the back. It had a high neckline and frilly lace cuffs. Roxie loved that dress. It was the highlight of her meager wardrobe, though it was only a castoff of Miss Clementine's.

Outside the cabin door sat the plain wooden coffin that Big Foot Ben had lovingly fashioned with his own hands. The sounds of his tapping had not ceased all night long.

While all the preparations went on, Julie Lee and Hannibal sat off by themselves, on a rock near the barn.

The Africans

Hannibal cried bitterly and profusely, but Julie Lee was fresh out of tears. She didn't want to say anything or do anything but sit there and try to imagine, try to contemplate a future without her mother. And she wanted to feed the burning bitterness that welled up from deep inside her.

She turned to her brother. "I told you, Hannibal, that Mama was gonna die. I told you." She took a stick and drew meaningless patterns in the dirt. She kept thinking that one day she would get revenge for her mother's murder, even though she knew that her mother wouldn't have wanted her to feel that way.

"What we gonna do, Julie Lee?" Hannibal asked over and over, but she didn't answer him. She just sat looking at the patterns on the ground, thinking about her mother's death.

During the night Roxie had passed quietly away, and much to Katy's disappointment, she hadn't given any message or sign. That being the case, Katy tried to imagine what Roxie would have wanted her to do in her memory.

Katy knew that Roxie would want her to look after her children. She also knew that vengeance had not been part of Roxie's character, though her own heart cried out for just that.

When everything was finally ready, Katy wouldn't let anyone else carry Roxie's body out of the cabin. It felt light, as light as a baby, as Katy laid it in the box.

One by one the slaves filed passed the open coffin. Some of them bent down to kiss Roxie. It was a Saturday, and they all should have been at work, but Old Massa had decided to suspend all activities until after Roxie's burial. "If I don't let the niggas mourn proper, I might end up with some kind of rebellion on my hands," he told his son, "and God knows I don't want none of that. 'Sides,

69

it'll probably be good for them. Give them a chance to let their vinegar out.''

When it was Katy's turn to bid Roxie good-bye, her big bosom heaved and her body shook with grief, and she keened in a heartbroken voice, "She's in your hands now, God. Please take care of her like I tried to do."

Then she leaned down into the box, put her mouth close to Roxie's ear and whispered, "No more need to worry, child. You is finally free from all your griefs and cares. Before you know it, I'll be right up there with you, and then we can laugh and talk like we used to do.

"I gonna be missing you Roxie, every day, but I swear to my Lord Jesus that I'm gonna take care of what's yours. You ain't had much of nothing, so to speak, but God done blessed you with two fine children, and I'm gonna raise them as if they was my own.

"So rest easy, child. Rest in the arms of the Lord. Can't nobody hurt you no more."

She started to cry loudly again. Zeph came forward from the crowd and propelled Katy backward from the box.

Hannibal made his way up to the box. He was fighting tears with all his might. He kissed his mother's face over and over again. His tears dropped on her eyelid. "Bye-bye, Mama, bye-bye."

Julie Lee was the last one to look on her mother's face, and still she had no tears. Her hunger for revenge was yet greater than her grief. She kissed her mother and stepped back.

Big Foot Ben lifted the coffin lid, which he'd stood up on the cabin's outside wall, and with aid from a young apprentice named Turkey he lowered it over the top. The light of day would never again cross Roxie's face.

Four men, including Turkey and Ben, hoisted the box up on their shoulders and walked in the direction of the clearing on the other side of the hill where so many other Lorelei blacks had been buried. The diggers had already done their work. Roxie's grave was near the biggest tree. "It's cooler there," Katy had said, when she'd picked out the spot.

The mourners walked in twos behind the box. Julie Lee and Hannibal came first. Katy and Zeph were right behind them, and then came two old friends named Ginny May and Lizzie, and behind them marched all the others. Only Jeddah had stayed behind in her cabin.

Andy Sr. and Andy Jr. joined the procession before it reached the appointed spot. Once there, Andy Sr. mumbled a few words from the Bible, then turned around and walked back to the big house. Andy Jr., without a look at Katy or Julie Lee or Hannibal, turned and followed his father. He was walking so fast that he beat the old man back to the big house by several minutes.

When the box was finally lowered into the hole, Hannibal screamed and fell down on the ground. The rustling of the trees in the wind was the only sound to be heard other than the voices of two children crying.

Chapter 9

It was past midnight, but Julie Lee had been unable to doze off. She was exhausted from her day's work at the big house, but she just couldn't seem to turn off the thoughts that crowded her mind. She lay in the darkness and listened to the sounds of her own heartbeat.

She'd suffered many similar sleepless nights since her mother had been buried. Now, lying on the same pallet where Roxie had died, she believed she could feel her mother's presence. It was like a warm glow enveloping her, protecting her.

The sounds of Hannibal's stirring across the room directed her attention to him. She thought about how much she loved him, but the fact was that things had changed disturbingly between them in the weeks since their mother's death.

She and Hannibal used to talk together all the time, but they no longer did. They used to share their innermost thoughts and feelings, but now they didn't. They used to whisper about getting free, but now they didn't. They'd come to a terrible detour in the road. She wanted to fix things, make them right again, but the last time she'd brought the subject up, Hannibal had refused outright even to discuss the matter.

"I don't want to talk about it, Julie Lee," he'd said, slamming his fork down on his tin dinner plate.

"But Hannibal, we've got to talk. I want to know what's wrong."

He got up and had intended to leave the cabin, but she stopped him by standing at the door so he couldn't pass. She put her arm on his shoulder, but he pushed it off. "Julie Lee. Why you so hard-headed? Don't you understand when a man just wants to be left alone? I just want to do my job and keep from getting whipped or killed like Mama did. Don't want to talk about nothing, no John Brown, no abolitionists, no nothing."

She put her face right up to his. "But Hannibal, you used to—"

He stomped away, fell into their mother's old rocking chair and stared into the fire. "Julie Lee, please. Why can't you just leave me alone? I love you, you know that, but please, things just ain't the same."

Since Roxie's death, Hannibal, it seemed to his sister, had lost his passion. He just went from day to day, doing whatever he was told without complaint. He seemed like a man without hope.

The only pastime he enjoyed was working with the horses in the stables. Some nights he never even made it back to the cabin, and when she went to look for him, Julie Lee would find him out among the stalls, sound asleep on a pile of hay.

She began to feel lonely. She needed him now more than ever. She was afraid to discuss some things with anyone but Hannibal. She could discuss them with Katy, but she knew what Katy would say. She loved the old cook, but she also realized that Katy accepted slavery as her lot and did not aspire to be free. She wanted to talk about freedom and about the things she'd heard discussed in the library by the old master and his friends. Questions filled her up inside.

What could Hannibal be thinking? Julie Lee wondered in the dark. She sat up on her pallet, trying to think what the solution might be for her quandary.

Then it dawned on her that help might be as near as the cabin next door. She had considered it before, but had always dismissed the thought as too ridiculous. Actually, she was afraid. And her mother probably wouldn't have wanted her to seek Jeddah's help. Mama would have said, "Just pray, child. Just put it all in the hands of the Lord. Your brother's gonna come around." Mama said to put everything in the hands of the Lord. Now Julie Lee thought bitterly, it sure seemed like Mama's praying hadn't done her much good. In fact, it seemed like it hadn't done anything except send her to an early grave.

"I'm gonna do it," Julie Lee said softly to herself. She moved quietly and quickly in the dark, and found her shoes and a shift dress. She looked over at Hannibal to see if he'd heard her. He snored. She tiptoed to the cabin door, opened it and softly shut it behind her. She wasn't prepared for the chill outside. A gust of wind blew right through her thin garment.

She looked around at the other cabins. They were all dark. She began to walk quickly. Within a few seconds she was standing at the door of Jeddah's cabin, contemplating whether to knock. She knew that Jeddah was strange and was afraid of incurring her wrath.

She tapped on the door softly. There was no response. She thought about going back to her own cabin, but she was determined to talk to Jeddah. She rapped again, this time a little harder. "Miss Jeddah, it's me, Julie Lee." The wind whipped up the edges of her dress and chilled her naked behind. She shuddered and hopped up and down from one foot to the other. She sure is a hard sleeper, Julie Lee thought.

She heard movement inside and suddenly a voice that didn't sound friendly at all called out, "Who that at my door this time of night? I say, who that at my door?"

The girl swallowed hard. "It's me, Miss Jeddah. It's only me. Julie Lee. I need to talk to you real bad. I think you is the only person in this world that can fix my problem." The words rolled off her tongue much more quickly than she'd intended.

She waited for a response from the woman inside. In her head she counted the seconds and hoped that Jeddah would soon open the door. She was freezing and her teeth were chattering like a set of china dishes on a buckboard.

She could hear Jeddah padding her way toward the door. "Just a minute child, let me put something on."

Jeddah lifted up the latch across the doorway. She was the only one in the quarter who had a lock on her door. When the door finally opened, Julie Lee's nose was assaulted by a pungent odor so powerful that it made her want to cry—the same way she felt when she had to chop up onions for Katy.

Jeddah impatiently looked her up and down, eyeing her as if she were a stranger. "Well, don't just stand there, girl! It's cold out there. Come on inside. You ain't got old Jeddah out of the bed just to stand there and look stupid. Come on in."

Julie Lee felt afraid again, but followed the woman inside.

"What you wanting, girl?" she asked as she showed Julie Lee to a chair in front of the fireplace in which there was no fire.

"I come to talk to you about something. I been thinking on it for a while."

Jeddah pulled up a chair next to her. To her own surprise, Julie Lee quickly adjusted to the odor of the cabin. "What it is, Julie Lee, that done upset you so bad that you done finally come to Jeddah?"

Julie Lee started to talk, but couldn't. Instead, she began to cry with nervous fear.

Jeddah patted her hand to calm her. "Oh baby, don't cry. Everbody got to come to old Jeddah sometime. Most of them come just like you—in the middle of the night."

Jeddah never even bothered to light the candle. Instead the two of them just sat there in the dark. Julie Lee was grateful for the darkness.

"Miss Jeddah, I don't know what I'm gonna do. I just don't know what . . ."

Jeddah held up her hand to silence the girl. " 'Fore you start to talking, let me tell you, Julie Lee, that you ain't come here by accident and you ain't come all by yourself. I been wanting to talk to you ever since that woman killed your mama, but I just bided my time to give you a while to mourn. I knowed you'd be coming to me sooner or later."

Julie Lee was surprised by the woman's revelation.

"That's right, girl, you think old Jeddah ain't looking, but I done seen you lots of times up there by that tree where they buried your mama. I seen you talking to her."

Jeddah pulled her shawl around her shoulders and let her body relax. "I done seen your mama lots of times since she died, and even though she didn't never agree

76

with what I does, she was my friend. Fact is, your mama was my only friend on this plantation. She wasn't scared of me like all the others.''

Jeddah closed her eyes and waited for the girl to speak.

Julie Lee started off slowly. "Miss Jeddah, I wants to talk with you about the two biggest problems I got.''

"Tell me girl.''

"Well, first off, I want to know if you can do something about me and my brother Hannibal. I want to know if you got something that can make us close like we used to be. Seems like since Mama was killed, Hannibal and me done split some, and you know that our mama always raised us to be close like the fingers on a hand.''

Jeddah opened her eyes to look at her, but didn't interrupt.

"Since Mama's been gone, it look like Hannibal, he just ain't got no life in him. When I tries to talk to him most time, he just shut me up with mean words and hard looks.'' The girl dropped her head and cried.

Jeddah stood up and put her arms around her visitor. She patted the girl's back understandingly. "Get it all out, child, much as you can. I knows it hurts when you love somebody and it don't seem like they want to love you back. But you has to understand your brother Hannibal maybe ain't as strong as you is.''

Jeddah went back to her chair and continued. "Some people think that men is stronger than women, but they really ain't in a whole lot of ways. It's true that they stronger in their bodies, but when it comes to the mind, men just don't seem like they can take what we women takes.

"Don't get me wrong, Julie Lee child. I ain't saying

77

that life for no man, 'specially not no nigga man, is a party. Hell, slavery ain't no party for no niggas, but it's we women that get so much of the load. We the ones whats got to lay down, spread our legs and push out them babies every year. We the ones whats got to work in the fields when we be having our blood. We the ones that the white man come and take whenever he want.

"Honey, I done seen lots of nigga men in my time who act like they don't even mind being slaves, long as Massa let them be studdin' and funnin' with the women."

Jeddah grew reflective and Julie Lee wondered why her question hadn't been answered, so she asked it again.

"Miss Jeddah, what I'm gonna do about my brother Hannibal?"

"You ain't gonna do nothing about him. Some things Jeddah can't fix. You just got to give him time to clear up his head. Your brother is like a lot of men I knowed in my life. Men don't always cry like we does. They keeps it all balled up inside and sometimes the pain reaches up and chokes them. Hannibal, he missing your mama something awful. She didn't care nothing about being no slave, she tried to raise y'all like a regular family just like white folks got. He aching for your mama 'cause he miss your mama's love."

"But *I* love Hannibal. He knows I love him. I—"

Jeddah interrupted. "I knows you love him, and he knows you love him too, but baby girl, you got to understand that sister love ain't like mama love. He miss his mama 'cause she gave him hope, and now he feel like he ain't got no hope at all.

"No, Julie Lee, your brother don't need no medicine that I can give. But once he sees how strong you is, then he gonna be strong too. It ain't gonna be easy, and he

78

probably gonna be mean to you for some time, but don't pay that no mind. He just hurting and don't rightly know how to get it all out. Give your brother some time."

"After a time he'll be better?" Julie Lee asked anxiously.

Jeddah nodded.

"I hope so."

The two women fell silent after that for a long while. Finally Jeddah spoke again. "Now what was that other reason why you said you came to see old Jeddah?"

Julie Lee unconsciously fumbled with her dress. "About Miss Whilomene."

The old woman stood up and walked around the cabin. She looked out the window in the direction of the big house. "You don't have to tell me, child. I been thinking about her myself. I knows what you want, but I'm getting a little tired right now. What you want for Miss Whilomene gonna take a little longer, but I promise you, I'm gonna help you, and the medicine I'm gonna give you for Miss Whilomene, it's gonna work. Now you go on back to your cabin and let old Jeddah get her sleep."

To Julie Lee's surprise, her fears of the woman had melted, and as she stood up and prepared to leave, she kissed the old woman on the cheek.

When she stepped outside the cabin, the wind was kicking up more than it had been when she had gone in. She ran the short distance to her own cabin, quietly opened the door and slipped in. She lay down on her pallet and felt warm inside her soul. She turned her face toward the wall and went off to sleep, confident that everything was going to be all right.

Chapter 10

Hannibal was filling the trough with water when the young master walked up to him. He was so involved in his work that he didn't even hear the man approach.

"How you this morning, boy?"

Hannibal turned around, startled. "I'm just fine, massa, sir. Hope you is passing a good day too."

The young master stayed there and Hannibal figured he must want to talk. The boy took off his battered hat and looked up at the sky. "Seem like it's gonna be a fine day, don't it, massa, sir? Seems like maybe it's a good day for a fox hunting or riding in the woods. Sure would like to go on one of the fox hunts sometime. I would—"

Andy Jr. interrupted the boy's nervous rambling with a pat on the head, just like he patted the horses. "You know, boy, I think me and my daddy made a damned good decision to put you out here with Jasper and Lionel to work with the horses. Y'all get along right good together. Ain't no fighting and arguing like most niggas tend to."

Hannibal lowered his eyes. His smile was hidden. He looked up again when the young master began to talk some more. "'Course you still got a lot to learn, but you learn quick. Reminds me a lot of your mama. In some ways you're just like her. She was a quick learner. You been staying out of trouble, getting up real early and doing your work. That's what me and daddy like to see. Come on over here, boy, and sit with me a spell.''

Hannibal dutifully followed his master over to a long bench outside the stable. His mind raced, trying to imagine why the young master was talking to him so much that morning.

''Been thinking, Hannibal. Me and Daddy has been thinking about retiring old Jasper. He's gotten kind of hard of hearing, and that's dangerous when a man works with horses. Got to have good ears and keen sight. Got to know when the horses are coming up behind you.''

Hannibal was surprised when Andy Jr. reached up and thumped him playfully on the head. ''Now don't you getting no swelled head, but me and Daddy been thinking about getting the vet out here for a few days to teach you and Lionel a little bit about horse medicine. Don't expect him to make you all no horse doctors, but sometimes when me and Daddy are out riding all over the county, we need somebody here who would know what to do in an emergency. Horses are expensive these days, and when they get sick, they need quick attention.''

The young master's tone was more serious when he began to speak again. ''Listen, boy, I didn't just come up here to talk to you about the horses. Want to talk about something else too.''

Hannibal felt comfortable with the man now, so he said, ''What it is you want to talk to me about, massa?''

Even as he asked the question, Hannibal was trying to outthink the man, but he just couldn't imagine what they would have to discuss beyond the horses.

Andy Jr. hesitated, as if he wasn't sure what he wanted to say. He took off his hat and looked in the direction of the graveyard where Roxie was buried. "Been thinking a lot since your mama died, boy. Been feeling like maybe I owe something to you and Julie Lee."

Now Hannibal was really curious.

Andy Jr. reached down on the ground and picked up a long piece of straw. He stuck it between his teeth. "Been thinking, Hannibal, that you're big enough to know that your mama was a damned good woman. Miss her, I do. She was too good to die the way she did, but it wasn't nobody's fault, just a tragic accident—a misunderstanding. You understand what I mean, boy?"

"Yes, sir," Hannibal said, but he knew that his mother's death had not been any accident or tragic misunderstanding. The plain truth was that Miss Whilomene, the young master's wife, had just hit Roxie over the head and killed her.

"What you trying to say, I think, massa, is that ain't nobody's to blame for Mama's dying. Maybe Mama did something to make Miss Whilomene so mad that she just took that poker and hit her upside her head."

Andy Jr. looked at the boy's sad eyes. He didn't know why, but he felt guilty at that moment. "Oh, hell, Hannibal, that ain't exactly what I'm trying to say. What I mean is that all of us is caught up in this thing—you niggas and we white folks. Can't nobody change that. That's just the way it is. You see, boy, there's a difference between white folks and niggas. God made it that way. Don't know why because I'm not God, but it's just how things worked out."

Andy leaned up against the wall. Hannibal wasn't

sure whether he was actually talking to him or himself when the young master continued to speak. "See, y'all is human in most ways. Take your mama, for example. She was a fine woman, and maybe if she had been white—in fact, I know if she'd have been white—she would've been a fine asset to a man.

"Sometimes I used to try to talk to your mama when I'd come up to her cabin. You was just a little boy then. But your mama, sometimes she acted like she hated me. I guess you know that your mama was more than just a nigga to me. I used to try to tell her that it wasn't my fault that things were the way they were between the niggas and the whites. But I don't think she heard me much at all."

Hannibal reached down and pulled up a piece of straw too. He stuck it between his teeth. He was feeling more and more comfortable in his master's presence. It seemed to him that they were talking almost like equals, but he didn't want to break the spell of the moment by saying anything to interrupt, so he just listened while his master talked on.

"Fact is that we Southern whites and you niggas got a lot of things in common. I guess it's 'cause were all people of the land. Now, of course, you got some troublemakers from up North that don't agree with how we live and who want to change things. They just don't understand how we get along. But you understand, don't you, Hannibal?"

"I guess I does," Hannibal lied. He wasn't sure what his master was talking about or why he was saying what he was saying.

Andy picked up the conversation again. "I can imagine that it must be hard being a nigga. I wouldn't want to be one myself, but hell, ain't nobody up in the North can tell me that life up there is any better. At least here we can breathe and we can ride our horses and eat fresh food right off our own land. At least here niggas can get their own food out of the ground—they can raise vegetables if they want. People up North, niggas and the white folks too, is suffering. Life is harder up there, and everything is crowded and people is living right upside one another. It's just too much hustle and bustle up in the North. You understand what I mean, boy?''

"I guess I does understand a little bit, massa, but 'course I don't understand as much as you. Ain't never been up North to see for myself. Fact, I ain't never been off the Lorelei.''

Andy smiled now and rubbed Hannibal's head again. "And you don't want to go up North neither, boy. Got everything you would ever want right here on the Lorelei. 'Sides, you know that as long as me and my daddy is alive, we gonna take care of you and all our niggas.''

Hannibal was beginning to feel halfway friendly toward his master, but he was still not completely comfortable. He knew that the young master could be sitting there talking to him as if they were friends and then turn around and have him sent to the beating house to be whipped half to death. At the moment, however, he rather thought he liked him. He sure wasn't like some of the masters he'd heard about from slaves who'd lived on other plantations.

His master stood up and threw the straw he'd been chewing down to the ground. He rubbed his behind and stretched his back. Hannibal also stood up, respectfully.

"Somethin' else I want talk to you about, boy,'' the master said unexpectedly.

"What it is, massa, sir?" Hannibal said, his mind once again working to figure out why the young master was taking time to talk to him.

"Don't want you to go back to your cabin tonight. You can stay with the other boys, or you can sleep out here in the stables, but I don't want you back at the cabin."

Hannibal was very confused now. He wondered if after all his master was actually angry with him about something. "But why you don't want me to go to the cabin, massa? What I done?"

At that the young master laughed lightly. "Oh, Hannibal, you ain't done nothing. Didn't I tell you that you been doing real good? I don't want you to go back to the cabin because I've arranged for your sister to become a woman tonight."

Andy didn't need to say any more. Hannibal knew what he meant. He was curious about who the young master had picked to bed down with his sister, but was too afraid to ask right out. His master might get angry and think he was being uppity.

Suddenly, the unthinkable crossed Hannibal's mind. Surely the young master wasn't considering bedding down with Julie Lee himself. After all, he was her father, and people just didn't do things like that. The thought was unbearable and Hannibal wondered then if he should warn Julie Lee.

He waited for his master to tell him who would take Julie Lee's virginity, but the man didn't volunteer any more information. He began to walk away from the boy. He stopped after a moment, turned around and said, "Hannibal, don't you tell nobody what you and me talked about today, or you're gonna be really sorry.''

Hannibal lowered his gaze. ''Don't worry none, massa. I keeps everything to myself. Ain't even gonna tell Julie Lee.''

Chapter 11

Katy talked as she seasoned the meat for that night's supper. She never told anyone the secret of her spices, which she always mixed up herself and kept in small bottles on a long shelf that hung over the chopping board.

"How you feeling, child?"

"I guess I'm fine, Auntie," Julie Lee responded on her way through the pantry door to bring in some potatoes. "Me and Hannibal still ain't got too much to say, but I'm doing all right I guess."

Katy stopped sprinkling the seasoning. "Don't worry none about you and your brother. It's gonna be all right. I just know it is."

Julie Lee had been so caught up in her own problems that she had not really noticed how poorly Katy looked. She looked at her closely and began to worry. "How you feeling yourself, Auntie?"

"Child, I'm about fine as I can for a woman my age. But this morning Young Massa ask me to talk with *you* about something. Said he couldn't talk to you about it hisself."

The girl looked up. "I don't know what it could be.

What is it he want me to know that he can't tell me hisself." She felt insolent. "He's the massa, ain't he?"

Katy began slowly, almost as if she was trying to find courage herself to say what she had to say.

"Julie Lee, you know you getting to be a pretty big girl. You ain't no child no more. Been seeing your blood for a while now, ain't you?"

The girl was becoming impatient with the old woman's slow way of making a point. "You know I seen my blood, Auntie. Why you talking about that now?"

Katy pulled up a chair. "Stop peeling some and listen to me," she said in a voice that sounded like a command. Julie Lee stopped obediently.

"You know, child, most of the girls around here your age done already had a baby or two, and they done learned good about pleasuring with a man. You ain't had to do none of that 'cause Young Massa say he ain't just wanting any old boy to get a hold of you.

"But Young Massa, he say this morning that he think it's about time you learned something about pleasuring with a man. Say he done already picked out the one he think be best for to bed you down for your first time. Say he try to make it easy on you."

The girl's eyes flashed in anger. She jumped up from the table, causing all the potatoes to go rolling across the floor.

"What? Massa say he think I'm ready for pleasuring and that he done picked the man?" She began to cry. "I ain't wanting no man to pleasure with me, and I ain't wanting nobody climbing up on me and wanting to do what that Lightfoot man wanted to do. I don't ever want no pleasure in my life. I ain't gonna do it and nobody gonna make me do it neither. Not Massa, not nobody."

88

Katy didn't like what she had to do, but she got up anyway, pushed her chair out from under her and went over to where the girl was standing. She pushed her face right up into Julie Lee's.

"You hush up that hollering, girl, and you hush up now. What you want? You want Young Massa to hear you and come down in this kitchen and whip your butt? Now you get on in that chair and sit down and listen to what I has to say."

In frustration the girl sucked her breath in through her teeth. She knew that if she said anything more she might regret it. A whipping from Young Massa, she already knew, would not compare to what Katy would lay on her if she didn't obey her.

Katy put all her weight on the girl's shoulder and talked in a low, but menacing tone. "Now you listen to me, girl, and you listen good. If Massa say you is ready, then you ain't got nothing to say, no choice.

"Don't you even know that you ain't been having to do what lots of the girls your age have to do around here because Young Massa knows he your daddy. Now when your mama was alive she protected you, but your mama ain't here no more, and I done tried to protect you and your brother from everything I could. But Julie Lee, there's some things I can't protect you from. There is some things we got go along with just because we is niggas. The fact that Young Massa is your daddy don't mean that you can escape everything. Do you understand what I'm trying to say, child?"

Julie Lee was angry. She wished Katy would stop leaning on her shoulders. "But Auntie, you just don't seem to understand what I mean."

Katy wasn't as angry as she tried to sound. "Hush up, girl. I understand better than you think I does. You think that just because I'm old that I don't remember being a girl and having to pleasure lots of times. You ain't seen none of my children, has you? But I had children—about five or six, I think. You think I wanted to get them babies? That I felt like pleasuring with any old man my massa sent? No, I didn't like it neither, and I'll tell you how much. You know *why* you ain't seen none of my children?"

Katy hadn't intended Julie Lee to ask. "You ain't seen none of my children 'cause I suck the life out of every goddamned one when they was borned. Massa might could make me pleasure, but he couldn't make me let them babies live. He never knowed what I done. He just think that all my babies just up and died.

"But you, Julie Lee, you is born and half growed up, and you got to learn that we belong to Old Massa, and to Young Massa too when his daddy die. And you got to know that there's some things that niggas just have to put up with."

Julie Lee could feel Katy easing the pressure with which she'd pinned her down into the chair. She could even hear her voice changing, its tone softened some. Katy came around and faced Julie Lee. With her fat hands she cupped the young girl's face. "Child, I knows what you feeling. I told your mama before she died that I hoped what that Lightfoot man did to you wouldn't turn your head against pleasuring. Child, when you is pleasuring with a man you like, it ain't nearly so bad, after the first time. You know women get full of sap just like men does, and when they do, they need some pleasuring to get some release."

The Africans

Katy sat down now. "Julie Lee, ain't you seen some of the women around here when they gets to acting all evil? Well sometimes they be acting that way because they ain't had no pleasuring in a long time."

She patted the girl's hand with compassion. "Sometimes pleasuring is the only thing we niggas got to look forward to. Work hard almost all the time without no rest, and sometimes it's pleasuring that makes us feel good. Makes us feel like getting up in the morning, you know?"

Julie Lee felt safe in speaking now that Katy's anger had subsided some. She didn't quite believe all this talk about the joys of pleasuring. "So what his name, this boy you say Massa done picked for me? Do you know?" To her surprise she suddenly began to weep, and buried her head in Katy's shoulder. "I don't want no pleasure with no boy I don't like. If I got to pleasure, I want somebody like Hannibal's daddy, Harvey. Mama, she never stopped talking about Harvey, say she and Harvey they loved each other. If I got to pleasure, I want to pleasure like Mama with somebody I care about. I ain't seen no boys around this place that I even think I'd like to pleasure with."

Katy wrapped her arms around the girl. "Oh, baby. Don't cry. Sometimes we nigga women get lucky like your mama did and finds a man who we thinks we loves and likes to pleasure with. But I got to speak the truth. Most time it don't be that way."

The girl began to cry even more bitterly than before. She felt so helpless, so lost and confused. She wished her mother were alive, and that she were just a child again, so she wouldn't have to hear anything about pleasuring. She longed for the time when Hannibal was the only man in her life.

Between sobs, she asked again, "Auntie Katy, who this boy you said Massa done picked?"

"A boy named Dancer. He's one of them fancy types what got curly hair and funny-looking eyes like white people's. Say his mama was a half-breed. Everybody calls him Dancer 'cause everybody say the boy can move his legs like rubber when the music gets to going. I seen him, and he's no ugly boy like some of them that run around here with them lumpy heads."

Julie Lee couldn't help it, she had to laugh when Katy talked about some of the boys on the plantation. It was true, some of the boys did have heads that were all pushed down in the middle. One boy's head was so bad that everybody called him Saddlehead.

The girl's mind went directly to the image of the boy she knew as Dancer. He was about her own age. She told Katy, "I seen that dancing boy. I seen him looking at me one day, but I just turned my head and ain't looked at him at all. One time I even remember him trying to show off his dancing in front of me. But he ain't never tried to talk to me. Act like he's scared or simple or something."

"Then you knows the boy?" Katy said with relief.

"I knows him all right, but not good. Mostly, I hear the girls talking about him, saying how pretty he is and all. Say he can sing, too, even better than he can dance."

Feeling that she'd been able to penetrate Julie Lee's armor, Katy pressed on. "Massa say that if you and Dancer get on real good, maybe he let him work up here with us in the big house. Say that Dancer boy would make a good show for when company comes, and you knows Massa likes to make a show."

Julie Lee was becoming more interested. "How old you think that dancing boy is, Auntie?"

Katy looked thoughtful. "I ain't sure, but I know he can't be not too much older than you is. Anyhow, sometimes it's hard to guess the age of them fancy niggas. Some of them seem to hold their age pretty good. Seem to me like he gonna be real gentle with you, especially since you say he done already give you the eye."

Julie Lee flinched. She was still unhappy about having no say in the matter.

"Listen, child," Katy went on, "suppose Young Massa picked out one of them sorry-looking niggas and then you got knocked up and had a ugly little baby."

The idea of having a baby was distasteful to the girl. "Oh Lord, don't want no babies, I don't. Everybody say it hurt real bad. Oh Lord, what I'm going to do? First I got to pleasure and then I got to worry about getting a baby. I just think I'm going to die."

A twinkle appeared in Katy's eye. "You ain't gonna die, girl. Ain't neither thing gonna kill you—not pleasuring nor having no baby. Women is made for that."

Julie Lee dragged through the rest of the day. Katy and Zeph were all excited and they'd told her what to expect. "You better put a rag underneath you, Julie Lee," Zeph said expertly. "Some women bleeds the first time they pleasures with a man. I know I did. Ain't nothing to be scared of, just a little blood. And you tell that Dancer don't be pushing too fast. Just tell him to go real slow and easy like."

Zeph stole a little sweet powder from Miss Clementine's room and told Julie Lee, "Now you wash up good and you put some of this powder on you before that Dancer comes to your cabin. You want to be smelling good."

The day's work came to an end quickly. Katy had

literally pushed her out when she'd run out of excuses to keep hanging around.

It was dark outside when the knock came on her cabin door. "Who is it?" she called out nervously.

"It's Dancer," the voice from outside said.

She walked slowly to the door, hoping that if she waited long enough the dreaded visitor would go away. She listened for the sounds of his footsteps, but when none came, she realized that he hadn't budged.

She was surprised after finally opening the door that Dancer was much taller than she'd remembered. Everybody was right too, now that she was right up close to him. He *was* good looking.

Suddenly she realized that she was staring. It was with much embarrassment that she finally said, "Come on in."

She did what Katy had told her to do: she offered him a cup of coffee and a sweet roll. He drank and ate in silence, staring at her all the while from the opposite side of the table.

It was she who finally had to break the heavy silence. "I guess we both know why you come up here tonight, Dancer. I expect they told you just like they told me. But if you don't want to do it, it's all right with me. We can just pretend like we done it anyhow." She wondered why that thought hadn't occurred to her earlier.

He cleared his throat before speaking. "I ain't rightly sure what I'm supposed to say, and I'm hoping that you ain't gonna be mad or hating me just because Massa say I got to pleasure with you, 'cause I sure do like you a lot. I ain't wanting to pretend. I wants to pleasure with you, and make you happy. I swear, Julie Lee, I ain't aiming to hurt you none. I'll be real gentle."

His words softened her, and after another lengthy silence, she said, "Maybe it ain't gonna be so bad. And don't you worry. I ain't gonna hate you none. Like Auntie done told me, we just niggas and we got to do what Massa say. Ain't that right, Dancer?"

"I guess we does," was the hushed reply.

Chapter 12

Dancer was a gentle lover, so gentle, in fact, that Julie Lee wondered if there was something wrong with her because the first time they made love, she enjoyed it, and didn't have any pain and didn't bleed.

When Dancer moved inside her body, it was as if he was supposed to be there. When she told Katy about the easy and beautiful time she'd had, the older woman clucked with indulgent laughter. "You is lucky, girl, 'cause you done found a man what fits."

Katy had been right about one thing, though. Pleasuring a man sure could make a woman feel good after working hard all day, especially if the man she was pleasuring with was somebody she liked a little bit.

Julie Lee began to think of herself as a woman now, for she was doing almost everything that the other woman did, and like them, she sometimes talked about it and sought womanly advice.

Dancer was always nice to her, and when she didn't feel like pleasuring he didn't try to make her. And, she thought, thank God, Dancer had a little sense and some dreams worth dreaming. He knew how to play the game when in sight or earshot of white folks, but when they were alone at night in their cabin, Dancer talked about his dream of one day getting up and performing for crowds of people, not just for fun, but for money, money he could use to buy freedom for himself and Julie Lee.

"If I was to get free one day, Julie Lee, everybody would be coming from miles around to see me do my dancing. Dancing is why God put me here in the first place. Hell, look at me girl, I ain't no field nigga, ain't no house nigga either, I'm a nigga what's supposed to be free. I'm a dancer, and a good dancer too. Can't nobody round this place dance better than me. Ain't that right, Julie Lee?"

And she would respond like she often did. "You sure is right Dancer, you sure is the best. You is the best man and the best dancer that I ever did see." She would then add teasingly, " 'Course I ain't never been no place except for the Lorelei, so I ain't rightly sure if you is the best in the whole wide world."

Dancer looked hurt. "Shucks, Julie Lee, you know I'm the best. Why you always like to fun with me? You know I'm the best."

She would hug him. "Aw, Dancer, I'm just playing with you. One day you will be dancing and singing for all the people, and I'll be right there with the rest of them, clapping my hands and saying, 'Go on, dancing man!' "

As the weeks passed, Dancer became a regular fixture at Julie Lee's cabin. Everybody knew that she was his woman, and the young master ordered Hannibal to vacate the cabin, so Julie Lee and Dancer could have some privacy. Hannibal moved to the dormitory.

Because of Dancer's almost constant presence, Julie Lee didn't pine for Hannibal as she thought she would.

And to her surprise she was getting along better with her brother since she and Dancer had hooked up.

Dancer and Hannibal acted almost as if they were brothers, and often, after work, they would sit with Julie Lee around the table talking and laughing late into the night. It wasn't long before the three had become a family. Julie Lee enjoyed cooking for her two men, and supplemented their rations with as much food as she could safely steal from the big house without being noticed. Katy always helped by stuffing Julie Lee's sack with plenty of leftover meat, vegetables and bread.

With Dancer, Hannibal, Katy and Zeph all in her corner, Julie Lee believed she had the best of all worlds. She didn't really have many friends among the quarter girls her own age, mostly because they all said she didn't look any more like a black girl than the young master's wife, but Julie Lee didn't care. Life was fine. Then, suddenly it wasn't.

Outside the kitchen one morning Julie Lee was mashing up potatoes when a small boy named Junie, who was no more than eight or nine years old, ran up to the big house back door screaming wildly, "Julie Lee! Julie Lee! You better come quick!"

She stopped what she was doing. "What's the matter, boy? Stop that crying and tell me what's the matter."

The boy was breathing hard. "It's Dancer! Dancer and Jack. They fighting out in the barn, and they fighting about you. I come to get you 'cause I want you make them stop."

"Fighting about me? What I got to do with them boys?"

"Don't know exactly, but you gotta come quick. Jack

done said something that done make your Dancer plenty mad. Come on, Julie Lee. Make them stop fighting so they can be friends again.''

Julie Lee ran behind the boy. By the time she reached the fight a small crowd had gathered. She could hear Dancer screaming at the top of his lungs. ''I'm gonna kill you, nigga. I'm gonna kill you right now.''

Dancer was so angry that he didn't even notice when Julie Lee walked up. ''Dancer! Dancer! What for you and Jack is fighting?''

Dancer let go of Jack's arm, but not before he'd pushed him down on the ground, causing the other boy to bump his head on the side of the barn. For the first time since the fight started, Dancer turned his back on Jack. ''Ain't nothing, Julie Lee. You just get on back up to the big house. Ain't needing no woman to come out after me. I can take care of this nigga all by myself.''

Julie Lee screamed, but not in time. Jack had sneaked up behind Dancer, brandishing a pitchfork. By the time Dancer turned around, Jack had jammed the fork into his foot. Blood spurted out. Julie Lee's scream was no match for Dancer's. He fell down on the ground.

''Goddamned nigga done cut off my foot,'' he yelled. ''The nigga done cut off my foot.''

Now Jack was in charge. He stood over the wounded boy. ''Bet you ain't gonna be dancing no more, nigga. I done made sure of that.'' In that instant, Jack snatched the fork out of Dancer's foot and aimed it at his chest. Drops of his own blood fell on Dancer's shirt. But before Jack could strike out at his helpless target, a husky boy named Johnny Bee grabbed his arm and wrestled the fork away. ''What you wanna do, kill him?'' Johnny Bee screamed.

Beads of sweat poured down Jack's face. ''Yeah, I

wants to kill this nigga. This here nigga what all the girls think is so pretty. Wanna mess up that pretty face of his, and make sure he ain't dancing around here no more. Think he some big nigga just 'cause he's sleeping with that half-white nigga.''

Suddenly it was clear to Julie Lee what the fight had been about. She held Dancer's head in her lap and looked up at Jack. ''Why you saying them things about Dancer, Jack? We ain't never done nothing to you. Ain't never been mean to you. Why you want to hurt Dancer just 'cause he's my man?''

Jack's response was quick and cold. ''You and this Dancer nigga, I hates the both of you. I told this nigga, and now I'm telling you, y'all ain't nothing. I'm sick of this nigga always bragging and talking like he's better than the rest of us, just 'cause you looks like a white woman.''

The sight of the old master heading toward them caused the crowd to scatter. Left behind were Dancer, Julie Lee and Jack.

''What in the goddamned hell is going on here?'' the master screamed. When he looked down and saw the bloody stump that was Dancer's foot, the old man screamed even louder. ''Who done hurt my nigga? Somebody's ass gonna be hurting real bad when I find the one who done it.''

Later on that evening, Dancer lay on the pallet in Julie Lee's cabin. His foot had swollen up and turned blue. When he looked at it, old Doc Warfield said he was afraid that it might have to come off. He told the old master, ''You can save the foot and lose the nigga, or you can let me cut off the foot and have a crippled nigga. Least he'll be worth something.''

Oh God, Julie Lee thought, if they took off Dancer's foot, they might as well cut his heart out. That was all the boy lived for, his dancing.

By this time, Jack was locked up in the beating house. The old master had threatened to take care of him later. Jack was frightened for the first time. He knew, as well as everyone else, that fighting was a serious offense and this had been more than just an ordinary fight. He'd wounded Dancer, and badly. He knew that the old master wouldn't take kindly to that. He'd destroyed the master's property. He could have kicked himself for letting himself get so angry.

When the old master finally pushed open the door to the beating house, Jack jumped up quickly, noticing with alarm that he was accompanied by two of the biggest and strongest slaves on the plantation. Oh, my God, they gonna kill me, he thought.

Julie Lee was glad that Dancer had fallen asleep. Jack's screams could be heard all over the quarter. She felt responsible. And she was afraid to think of Dancer's reaction when he learned he would have to lose his foot.

She did something that she hadn't done in a long time: she got on her knees and prayed. She prayed for Dancer's foot to be saved, and she cursed her whiteness before God. Her whiteness had killed her mama, and now because of it, Dancer had almost been killed. She ached deep down in her soul.

Chapter 13

As the days wore on, Dancer's foot grew blacker and blacker. By week's end the gangrene had spread halfway up his leg. The foot and the leg gave off a terrible odor and caused the cabin to smell like rancid meat. Green pus oozed out of the holes in his foot from the pitchfork, and though Julie Lee worked feverishly to keep the leg from stinking by washing it and applying the salves and ointments the doctor had left, nothing did any good. She didn't have to be a doctor to know the leg would eventually have to come off—if Dancer could be saved at all. Even Jeddah, who had mixed up roots and herbs of her own and applied the lotion to his leg, knew that nothing could be done.

Sometimes Julie Lee covered her ears at night when Dancer screamed out in his sleep. She knew that he was reliving the horrible nightmare, that he could feel again the prongs of the pitchfork digging down into his foot.

And she felt it was all her fault. There was nothing Hannibal, Katy, Zephyr or even Dancer could say that could convince her otherwise. He was going to be a cripple, a one-legged man named Dancer. It was the cruelest kind of irony.

But Dancer never blamed her, and he loved her too much to let her blame herself. He told her, "Sometimes a man, even if he ain't nothing but a slave, gotta take care of somebody who talks about the one he loves. I ain't never told you flat out that I love you, but I does. I love you so damned much that I'd give my other foot for you if I could. I'd give my life for you, Julie Lee. My life, 'cause it wouldn't be worth nothing if I didn't have you.

"So what if I can't dance no more, long as you still want me to be your man, long as you still let me be your lover. Dancing ain't everything. I only used to think it was.

"Some nights I lay here in this bed and think about how it could have been worse. I may become a cripple, but I ain't gonna let nothing cripple me on the inside. I'm still able to see. I'm still able to take you in my arms. I'm still able to pleasure you and make you feel good. I'd be the happiest nigga in the world if you just let me love you and stay to be your man. Maybe massa will even let us really be married like man and a wife."

When Doc Warfield finally arrived several days later to perform the amputation, Julie Lee fled the cabin, pushing past Hannibal, Katy and the young master, who'd accompanied him. She stood outside the cabin door, weeping uncontrollably until she felt a hand press down on her shoulder. It was Jeddah. The look on the woman's face was so compassionate and understanding that without thinking, Julie Lee fell gratefully into her open arms.

"You ain't gonna do nothing just standing out here crying," Jeddah said. "You got to get hold of yourself and figure out what you gonna do now. Besides, your man ain't wanting you to see him suffer no more than you has to.''

Arm in arm the two women walked toward Jeddah's cabin. When Jeddah opened the door, Julie Lee's nose was once again assaulted by the sickening smell inside, though it wasn't nearly as bad as the stink from Dancer's foot in her own cabin.

When they were inside, Jeddah sat Julie Lee down on her pallet as she poured water from a pail she'd had sitting in the corner into a pot to make the coffee. While waiting for the water to come to a boil, Jeddah sat down beside the younger woman and began to massage her head, neck and back. Her hands moved expertly, and before long, unwillingly, Julie Lee felt herself beginning to relax. And as Jeddah rubbed, she talked. ''Ain't gonna tell you everything gonna be the same once that doctor finish putting the knife to your man's leg, 'cause that would be a lie. And I ain't gonna lie and tell you that a one-legged man is just the same as a whole man, because he ain't. But you and Dancer is young, and young folks can sometimes overcome what us old birds can't. Sometimes these things happen to shock people back into doing what they know they has to do.''

''What you mean, Miss Jeddah? You saying we ain't did what we was supposed to do?''

''I'm meaning, girl, that you and Dancer been so happy for these months that you seem like you done forgot all about taking care of that witch in the big house what killed your mother. Seem like you done clean forgot about all your talk about getting free. Sometimes you has to understand how white folks think. They know that most niggas ain't happy about being no slaves, and when they see you really starting to think hard about it, they give you things to keep you quiet. Now I ain't saying that Dancer ain't no good man. I just saying that Massa was smart enough to know that you ain't no dumb nigga, so he give you somebody to take your mind off maybe wanting to get free.''

The possible truth of Jeddah's words cut through her grief like a giant knife and that truth went even deeper than the knife the doctor would soon be using to amputate Dancer's leg. If it were true, then why hadn't she been smart enough to figure it all out for herself? Why was she sitting there, letting Jeddah tell her what she should have known all along?

''Don't get Jeddah wrong, girl. I ain't scolding you or nothing. I understand how it can be sometime. I ain't even mad 'cause you ain't hardly talked to me since that first time you come to my cabin.

''I guess all I'm trying to say to you, girl, is that if and when you gets ready to do what you know you has to do, don't forget about old Jeddah. I'm here, and I'm ready to help you. Somehow, Julie girl, I believes there is something special between you and me, like maybe you and me is sisters. Maybe there is something between us what ain't been showed yet. I done met hundreds of people in my time, niggas and white folks, but you and me, we got something, even though I ain't rightly sure exactly what it be.''

They'd been talking about three-quarters of an hour and were in the middle of their third cup of coffee when Dancer's scream split the air. Then it was cut off abruptly as if someone had stuffed a rag in his mouth. It startled Julie Lee so much that she dropped the coffee in her lap. The hot liquid quickly penetrated her thin shift and burned her legs. She made no move to get up. She just sat there, letting the coffee burn. She wanted to suffer, wished she could suffer the way Dancer must have been suffering at that moment.

The deed was finally done. Now there would be no more speculation about how things would be *if* Dancer became a cripple. Now he *was* a cripple. Time would tell the rest.

She continued to sit dumbly, unable to cry. A foul taste suddenly rose up in her throat and made its way toward the front of her mouth. When she felt she could no longer hold it back, she raced toward the cabin door. She made it outside just in time. Her stomach felt as if it were tied in a huge knot. She didn't even hear Jeddah come up behind her and was momentarily stunned when the woman hit her hard on the back. "Get it all up, girl. You gonna feel a whole lot better when you get it all out," Jeddah said.

When she finally could stand up, she felt dizzy and needed Jeddah's assistance to go back inside the cabin to sit down. "Lay down girl," Jeddah commanded. "You just lay there and let old Jeddah take care of it."

She watched as Jeddah took something out of a sack that had been lying on top of the fireplace. When she handed a piece to Julie Lee, she hesitated, trying to figure out exactly what it was. "Chew it, girl," Jeddah snapped with great annoyance in her voice. "I ain't gonna give you nothing to hurt you. It ain't nothing but bark for you to clean your mouth out."

As Julie Lee chewed, Jeddah talked. "How many times you done throwed up like that, girl?"

"Ain't rightly sure, but seem like I been doing it quite a bit lately. Ain't surprised none though, I been nearly out of my mind ever since Dancer and Jack had that

106

fight. I ain't been eating too good. Just been feeling mighty tired like. Even felt lightheaded a couple of times. Day before yesterday, I almost nearly fell down the steps at the big house, my head was so light. Only thing kept me from killing myself was that I was able to grab a hold of the rail. I swear since this thing done happen with Dancer I ain't been feeling too good at all.''

"How long you and Dancer been pleasuring now, Julie Lee?" the woman asked.

"Ain't rightly sure, but it's been quite a spell now, seems like maybe three or four months.''

"Three or four months of pleasuring. Hmm, what about your monthly bleeding? You been bleeding regular?''

"Now you mention it, I ain't had my bleeding this month, but it ain't nothing. I'm just upset. Besides, Katy say that sometime when a woman pleasures regular like that sometime her body change and the monthly bleeding come different for a while. Say I'm just really getting broken in.''

"Broken in or not, sound to me like you is in the family way. That's what it sound like to me.''

The idea took a while to settle in Julie Lee's mind. Pregnant. The thought hadn't even crossed her mind until that moment. A baby, she thought. What in the hell I'm gonna do with a baby now. She fell back on the pallet, mumbling to herself. "A baby. Lord, have mercy.''

When Julie Lee opened the door to the cabin, Katy, sitting in the rocker, started from a light sleep. "Where you been all evening, girl? I been worried about you.''

"Been over with Miss Jeddah just sitting and talking. I guess you knowed I couldn't stand to see what Doc

Warfield was gonna do to Dancer. How he be, Auntie?'' she
asked, looking at the still, sleeping figure on the pallet.

"He's gonna be all right, I guess. But you should
have seen him, Julie Lee. He took it like a natural man. I
was proud of him, and you should be too.

"Now that you here, I guess I'll get on over to the
big house and get some sleep. Gotta get some rest so I can
get my tired body up in the morning. It be all right if you
don't come over to help with the breakfast, I'll be able to
get along with Ginny May.''

Katy stood up to leave, but Julie Lee blocked her
path. "Gotta tell you something, Auntie. Only gonna take
a minute or two. Sit back down so I can tell you my
news.'' The look on Julie Lee's face was so grim that Katy
sat back down expecting the worst. "What is it, girl? Lord
child, what else has gone wrong on this sad day?''

"Ain't rightly sure if my news is good or bad. Just
ain't sure at all,'' Julie Lee said looking at Katy straight in
the eye. "Auntie, I think I'm gonna have a baby. Miss
Jeddah say I got all the signs.''

Katy jumped out of the rocker and swept Julie Lee
into her massive arms, almost lifting the younger woman
off her feet. "Child, don't you know that if you is pregnant that the Lord done move in his mighty and mysterious
way? The Lord, He giveth and He taketh away. The Lord
done took Dancer's leg, but look here, it seem like He
done give y'all a baby to make up for it. Girl, don't you
know that if you is gonna have a baby, you is blessed?
That's what the man need right now. Need something to
make him feel whole. Make him feel like he ain't less than
a man just 'cause he got only one leg.''

"I ain't thought about it that way. Ain't had much
time to think about it much at all.''

"Well girl, you think about it that way now. I gotta go back to the house." She chuckled as she went out the door. "Thank you, Lord," she murmured. "You done help these children."

When she was gone, Julie Lee took her place in the rocker. She sat there, looking at Dancer's face. He was handsome. Maybe this was the kind of love her mother had told her about. Maybe this was what it meant to be a woman. She rubbed her stomach, and in minutes had fallen off to sleep.

Chapter 14

Four women had come to the cabin to assist with the delivery, including Katy and Jeddah, but Jeddah was clearly the one in charge. She relished her responsibilities and barked out orders sharply. Katy, who was fully used to being in charge, followed Jeddah's orders now without argument or complaint. Julie Lee lay helplessly lashed to the table by her feet and hands, looking on while the women scurried about her.

Her hair was plastered to her head. Rivulets of hot, salty sweat streamed down her face and burned when a few of the droplets eased their way into the cuts she'd bitten into her bottom lip, as the lightning hot pains shot through her body.

How could pleasuring be so good, and birthing so bad? Julie Lee kept thinking. Right now, as another pain hit on her left side, Julie Lee had the feeling she wanted to die on the one hand, and on the other, to leap up from the table and to jump onto the chamber bucket sitting a few feet away.

Katy ignored her complaints that the ropes were too tight. "You just thinking they too tight 'cause you is hurting right now. I tied them ropes myself, and I ain't gonna do nothing to harm you, you knows that. Pretty soon, when this baby be born, you is gonna forget all about this pain and them ropes on your feet. You'll see. You gonna forget.''

For the first time in her life, Julie Lee did not believe Katy's words. She would never forget how much she was hurting just then. She would never forget and would never have any more babies, no matter what anybody said. She wouldn't. She'd kill herself first.

From her vantage point on the table top, all Julie Lee could see was the crown of Jeddah's head. The woman's face was buried between Julie Lee's legs and was further hidden from view by the white blanket Lottie had draped over her knees. But she could feel Jeddah's fingers poking and probing inside her, first one finger, then two and then three. She was glad she'd convinced the young master not to call Doc Warfield when her time came. She would have died if any man, black or white, saw her in this condition, with her legs all bucked open and her bottom all naked and sweaty. Not even Dancer had been able to see what was now on display, since Julie Lee had always made him put the lamp out before they started to make love.

Since they had been shooed out of the cabin by the women, Dancer and Hannibal had no choice but to stand outside, but they could clearly hear Julie Lee's sobs and sighs. Dancer was frightened, more frightened even than the night his leg had been amputated. He stood as rigid as the cane on which he leaned. Hannibal had given him the cane a few weeks after Doc Warfield had taken off the leg. Hannibal had spent two weeks working on it, and had taken the time and the effort to smooth out the rough wood and to carve into it an elaborate design of big-eyed birds from the cane's handle to its stem.

Both Julie Lee and Dancer were surprised and touched the night Hannibal appeared in the cabin doorway to present his gift. It was with a shy smile on his face that he'd advanced toward the pallet, holding the cane in his hands. Dancer's eyes filled with tears. Not only was the cane beautifully crafted, but it was the first time in his life that anyone had given him a present. Hannibal had to catch Dancer in his arms when the boy nearly fell after getting up from the pallet, to grab him and to show his gratitude.

Julie Lee yelled out in excruciating pain, and Dancer turned to Hannibal and said, "Damn, it sound like Julie Lee gonna die in there. Ain't never heard nobody scream like that. Lord, I sure hoping she don't die trying to have my baby. I figure she must be thinking right now that she ain't never wanting to sleep with me no more now that I caused her all this pain."

Hannibal was as nervous as Dancer, but he tried to calm his friend. "All the women go through that, Dancer. By the time it's all over, they is ready to have another baby. Julie Lee is just doing what women was put here to do."

Still, Dancer couldn't calm down; he didn't even want to stand still. He began to pace, steadying himself on the cane.

"You just wait, Hannibal," he said. "You just wait till your woman be having a baby, and then we'll see if you act like it ain't nothing. I bet you gonna be even more scareder than me."

"I bet I ain't," Hannibal said.

Inside, Julie Lee grunted like a pig when the pains came faster. It was almost time, Jeddah knew. "Push,

112

girl. Come on, push. Work with me, girl. Work with old
Jeddah. This baby is coming. Ain't nothing but a little
bitty thing. Don't you worry. Now push!''

It was far worse than Julie Lee had imagined it would
be. Her body felt as if it were splitting apart at the seams.
A sharp pain started in her head and shimmied down her
body to the tips of her toes. It was so sharp that it nearly
lifted her off the table. "Oh, my God!" she screamed.
"Oh, my God. I'm gonna die. I'm gonna die. Oh, Mama.
I want my mama. I'm gonna die. I'm gonna die.''

"You ain't gonna die, you ain't gonna die, Julie
Lee,'' Katy kept saying in her ear. "You gonna have this
baby, that's what you is gonna do. That's right, think
about your mama. She done this same thing when she had
you. I done done this before, and so has all of us. Your
mama, and me and Jeddah, all us here to help you have
your baby. You ain't gonna die, Julie Lee.''

She grunted and pushed down again, wanting now
more than anything to relieve the pressure, to get that baby
out and to stop the pain. She'd been lying on the table for
only a few hours, but it seemed like she'd been there for
days. Julie Lee kept her eyes so tightly shut that tiny tears
squeezed out from their sides.

Another push, another grunt, and Julie Lee knew that
the baby was almost down. At that same moment, Jeddah
began shouting. "Katy, Katy lookahere. It's coming, girl!
Look at all that hair. It's all black. Come on, Julie Lee,
keep pushing, baby girl, keep pushing. The head is nearly
out. All we gotta worry about now is them shoulders.''

Julie Lee was panting like a caged animal, taking
short, quick breaths as Jeddah had instructed her to do.
She knew the shoulders would be the hardest part, and she
only hoped that she wouldn't be torn up.

Jeddah's hands were working furiously, struggling to help the baby wiggle out. "Come on out, baby. Come on out," she cooed, as if by talking softly she could coax it.

By the time Jeddah had turned the baby upside down and slapped it on its bottom, and screamed for all to hear, including the boys outside, "It's a boy! A pretty baby boy," Julie Lee was drifting off to another place, away from the pain, away from the excitement and all the noise.

There, she saw her mother sitting in a chair, wearing the pink dress in which she'd been buried. Her hair was loose and hanging over her shoulders. Roxie looked down at the baby and smiled at her daughter. "Well done, Julie Lee," she said. "Well done, baby girl. He's a beautiful little boy, the most beautiful baby that I ever did see."

Roxie's image began to blur and Julie Lee cried out to her, "Don't go, Mama. Please don't leave me now. I need you so bad. Katy and Jeddah is good to me, but I need *you*, Mama."

"I don't want to leave you, baby, but I gotta go back. Gotta go on back to my place with the others. But whenever you need me child, you just call my name, and I'll come, even if I can't stay as long as you want me to. Mama loves you. Mama loves you and Hannibal and don't you ever forget that. Bye, my sweet baby child. Take care of that pretty, pretty baby. Take care." As quickly as she'd come, Roxie departed, and as she disappeared out of sight, Julie Lee could hear her saying, "Whenever you need me girl, just call my name. Just call my name . . ."

"Mama, Mama," Julie Lee was crying out when she felt Dancer's hand touch her cheek.

"Wake up, Julie Lee. Wake up. It was only a dream. Julie Lee, wake up."

It took her several minutes before she realized that

she'd been asleep. She thought at first that she was still tied to the table, but she was now on the pallet. She hadn't even remembered being moved or who had moved her. The pain was gone now, and as she ran her eyes down the rest of her body, she could tell even with the blanket over her that her stomach didn't feel so taut now. The baby must have been born already, she thought. And as if reading her thoughts, Dancer said softly, "Don't you want to see him, Julie Lee? Don't you want to see our little boy? You ain't asked about him yet."

"Little boy?" she replied feebly. "Seem like I near 'bout clean forgot. But how could I forget our little boy when I worked so hard to bring him here? Didn't I work hard, Dancer? Didn't I? Ain't you proud of me?

"How he look, Dancer? How he look? Where my baby? I want to see my baby." Suddenly a dark and foreboding thought crossed her mind, and Julie Lee was dimly frightened. "He all right, ain't he, Dancer?" she suddenly cried out, tugging at Dancer's sleeve. "Tell me now, is our baby all right?"

In moments, Jeddah was there beside the pallet, placing the blanketed infant in the crook of Julie Lee's arm. "Oh, he be fine, Julie Lee," she said. "He be the most beautiful baby that I ever did see."

Those words were so familiar, and Julie Lee laughed a little. She knew where she'd heard them before. "That's what Mama said when she seed him, Miss Jeddah. Mama said he was the prettiest baby that she ever did see." Jeddah looked at Dancer and winked. Katy, for perhaps the first time in her long life, had nothing to say.

When she'd found the most comfortable position, Julie Lee hesitated before peeling back the blanket, which had been draped over the baby's face. She looked, and thought, he looks a little sickly. Too white. She had to laugh when she examined his ears, though, and saw how they stuck out just like Dancer's. She giggled at the thought of how she often teased Dancer and now, here was their baby with those big ears.

Now Julie Lee pulled the coverlet all the way back off his head, and was delightfully surprised at the baby's little shock of jet-black curls. "He *is* a pretty baby, ain't he Dancer!" she beamed. "Oh, look at him squinching up his little face," she laughed as she wiggled her finger under his nose. "I guess he gonna be wanting something to eat. He gonna be balling in a minute, I can tell." Then she looked up anxiously at Dancer. "Sure hope he gonna get a little darker though, don't you?"

She was still looking over the baby in delight when Andy Jr. came into the cabin. He spoke to no one in the room, but headed straight toward the pallet. Standing over her now, Julie Lee thought he looked awfully tall. He had that nasty toothpick hanging out of his mouth like he usually did. She hated men who chewed on toothpicks. But the young master's face softened as he knelt down beside the pallet and whispered, "How you feeling, Julie Lee?"

"I's feeling just fine, massa, sir. Just fine. I guess you done come to see my little boy."

"I reckon I did," he answered with a nervous laugh. "Y'all created quite a bit of excitement around here today. Everybody buzzing about the new baby we got. Let me see him," he said. "Please?" he added.

When she pulled back the coverlet, the young master was startled by the feeling he had looking down on the face of the tiny child, his grandson.

"Oh," he said, trying to recover from the queer

feeling. "He's quite a handsome boy. No wonder Dancer is grinning from ear to ear. This is one fine baby boy. You should be proud, Julie Lee. I'm sure proud. We're all real proud of you. Daddy was too tired to come to see for himself, but he said for me to tell you that he would be here first thing in the morning before he goes off to the fields."

"That's nice, massa, sir. That's real nice of your daddy." Andy had the baby's fingers entwined in his fist when Julie Lee asked him to come closer so she could whisper something in his ear.

"I know, massa, it be your right to name all the children born round here, but I is asking, please, if you could let me pick my own name for my baby? Please, massa, sir, ain't meaning no disrespect, but I just wants to name him myself."

Andy smiled, thinking to himself that Julie Lee was so innocent, with all the things that had happened to her, she was still so very, very innocent. Surely, he couldn't deny such a request, especially for this baby. "Be all right with me if you choose the name," he finally said. "Now, what name you have in mind?"

She was delighted that the young master had granted her request. "Well, Dancer and me, we was talking before I had the baby, and we thought if he was to be a boy that we would like to name him from the Bible. He wanted him to have what Dancer said was a real name, not like his of Dancer, which ain't really no name. We thought and thought, and then came up with the name of John. We'd like to call him John."

"Well if that's what you like, Julie Lee, then that's what it will be. His name will be John Johnson. I'll mark it down on the record book, along with the date that he was born.''

Julie Lee smiled. ''Thank you so much, massa, sir. Thank you so kindly.''

And Dancer then added his own thanks: ''You is a kind and good man, the best massa in all of Virginia.''

Having run out of things to say, Andy strode out of the cabin. He hadn't yet rid himself of the curious feeling he had when first looking at the baby. Wasn't it a god-damned crazy world, he thought. Here it was, his first grand, a boy at that, and it was born a nigga.

Once the young master had left, everyone in the cabin began chattering at once, except Julie Lee, who whispered to little John, ''You ain't named for no John from the Bible. You is named John for a very brave man, and one day when I is free and you is all growed up, I is gonna tell everybody that your name is John Brown. You hear me baby boy? Your name is John Brown.''

Chapter 15

There was a great deal of excitement in the Lorelei slave quarter. Word on the grapevine was that by the time the sun set, the masters would be returning from Richmond with a coffle of new slaves. Starved for news from the outside, the quarter residents eagerly looked forward to meeting the new arrivals.

But the old master had his own reasons for wanting to buy slaves at that precise time, and none of them had to do with what the slaves wanted. His first reason was pure necessity. He had to get replacements for the slaves who'd died during the year and the others who'd just gotten too old to be useful. How many times had the big house servants heard the old man ranting about how much he hated old, *useless*, niggas.

But his main reason for wanting to buy now was rooted in the threat of war which hung heavy in the air. Although there were few farmers or planters around Henrico County who would openly challenge his business acumen or political understanding when it came to his views on war, the old master hadn't been getting the one hundred per cent agreement he'd come to expect.

They were all fools, Andy Sr. thought.

The week before they left for Richmond he'd told his son, "Hell, Andy, we gonna be able to get us some prime niggas dirt cheap. I know them breeders are as jumpy as a cat 'cause Abraham Lincoln, who even *I* have to admit is sympathetic to niggas, done gone and got hisself elected president.

"Now that Lincoln fella may be a lot of things, but I don't believe he's goddamn fool enough to think that we gonna just let our niggas walk off the plantation.

"And I don't believe that we gonna end up getting ourselves into no war about no niggas neither—I don't give a damn *what* all the politicians is saying. I believe to my soul that Mr. Lincoln gonna end up having to compromise before it's all said and done.

"Mark my words, boy, and listen to your daddy. We gonna end up keeping all our niggas and we gonna come out of this whole goddamned mess a lot richer than we was before. Just mark my words."

Although he listened, Andy Jr. had no faith in what his father said. As far as he was concerned, the abolitionists had gotten too bold, especially since the incident at Harpers Ferry. In the months following John Brown's escapade at the Harpers Ferry arsenal, Andy Jr. shared the fears of other plantation owners and farmers in the countryside. When out of his father's earshot, the young master often commiserated with the other men his own age. They all agreed war was inevitable.

Julie Lee was even more excited than the rest of the quarter residents about the arrival of the new blacks. She'd heard bits and snatches of conversations about what was going on throughout the South and the North with respect to freeing the slaves, but there were too many gaps in her knowledge. She hoped that some of the newcomers could fill her in.

When she expressed her concern to Hannibal and Dancer, however, both remained unimpressed.

Hannibal only said, "There you go again, Julie Lee, getting all excited about something you ain't hardly knowing nothing about.

"I just don't understand why you keep hanging on to every little word about us niggas getting free. What for you keep talking about it? You got a good man and a baby who you know ain't gonna be sold away, and you still hollering about getting free. You getting your food every day, you got clothes, you is warm and you sure ain't working that hard up in the big house, don't care how tired you say you be when you finish, so why you keep hollering about freedom?''

Dancer acted as if he were afraid to comment at all. He didn't want to antagonize Julie Lee and certainly didn't want to get in the middle of what had become a running disagreement.

Later he told her that he hated to come between her and her brother and then he cast more light on his reticence.

It was with tears in his eyes that Dancer said to her, "Julie Lee, you remember me telling you when they took my leg that I would be just about the same. Well, it ain't true. I ain't the same, I can't do too much. Don't you think if I had two good legs I would try to run away with you and this baby? But like I is, I wouldn't do much of nothing, 'cept slow you down.

"You know I want to be free, but I expect I just got to sit here and wait for somebody to make us free. Somehow, since you done had the baby, getting free don't seem quite so important, if you know what I mean. I got you,

121

little John and Hannibal, and like I said before, I be a simple man and don't need much else. I'd like to be free, but if I can't, then I just be satisfied to stay with you and this baby."

Julie Lee was both touched and disappointed by Dancer's little speech. She'd caught the glimpse of fear in his eyes. He probably figured that one day she would run away to freedom and leave him behind. And it was because of that fearful look that she decided never again to discuss getting free with either him or Hannibal. If she ever did run, Dancer and Hannibal wouldn't know until she was gone. That way if any punishment were meted out, she wanted them to be as ignorant of her whereabouts as possible.

Chapter 16

There were ten new slaves, seven men and three women, in the coffle that the old master and Andy Jr. brought back to the Lorelei. The men, walking single file, were chained together at the ankle and the wrist. The women rode in the back of the wagon with Candy, the slave trustee who always accompanied the old master on his buying trips, and who over the years had earned a well-deserved reputation as a man with a sharp eye for prime niggas.

Although Massa liked Candy and trusted him implicitly, most of the other blacks hated him because they considered him a spy. Whenever Candy came around, the other slaves stopped talking because they knew the old master would have the news before God could get the message. Candy knew he wasn't liked, but it didn't bother him. His special privileges made up for that.

Most of the new males brought in appeared to be in their late teens or early twenties, and though they didn't know it, some of the women standing along the road watching had already made secret plans to get their hands on the most attractive ones.

The three women in the wagon all appeared younger

than most of the men, and one who appeared to be about fifteen was so obviously pregnant that she looked as if she might have her baby any minute. Pregnant as she was, there was little doubt that she was considered a good buy—two for one, the breeders had advertised.

The girl, who had large, expressive eyes, which now looked very sad, was light enough in complexion to have been considered a fancy negress, but she fell short of that standard primarily because her hair was tight, nappy, as the slaves said, and fit around her skull like a tight-fitting cap of ringlets.

Julie Lee stood in the crowd that had gathered alongside the road to size up the newcomers. She silently tried to figure out who among them might bring her the best news, who among them might know something about John Brown and the war. That was what she was thinking when she caught the eye of a slave at the back of the line. He was tall and muscular, had curly hair, but was not particularly handsome. Despite the chains on his ankles, the man walked with a semblance of dignity and his face did not wear the resignation so obvious in the others. He held his head high and his back straight.

As was always the case, once unchained, the new arrivals were given a hot meal and were then ordered to go immediately to their beds in temporary domiciles. That first night, newcomers were always isolated from the others.

The next day, however, shortly after light streaked across the morning sky, all were brought together for their general orientation from Andy Jr. He told them what the rules and regulations were and what infractions of plantation law were punishable by severe whippings or death— among them trying to escape, impregnating a woman not selected by the old master or Master Andy, sassing back any white people and not doing one's job to the best of one's ability.

After the orientation, the newcomers reported to the seamstress's cabin, where they were given their basic clothes, which for the men included two shirts and one pair of pants, and for the women, two loose-fitting shifts. Depending on the condition of the shoes they were wearing, some of the new slaves were given a pair of ill-fitting brown brogans.

Following the issuance of their clothes, permanent sleeping assignments were given, and after that the slaves were escorted around the plantation, were shown the various buildings, and were told what work went on in each of them. Later on that night, Master Andy would come back to tell them what their specific work assignments would be.

She'd been kept so busy around the big house in the day and with John and Dancer at night, that Julie Lee still had not, after three days, gotten around to meeting any of the new slaves.

The next day, however, Julie Lee was on her way to the nursery with John when the man who'd caught her eye in the coffle line suddenly appeared in the middle of the quarter walkway. She was so surprised by the encounter that she found herself at a loss for words, despite having silently rehearsed what she would say when she got a chance to talk to the man.

"How you be this fine morning?" she said. She didn't want to be too forward, lest the man get the wrong idea and think that she was interested in more than conversation.

"I'm as well as can be expected," the man said, and then—something that had never before happened to her—

the man bowed graciously and added, "How are you, good woman?"

Where in the hell did he come from, Julie Lee thought to herself after his gesture. He sure looks like a nigga, but why he acting like a white man? No man had ever bowed to her. Sufficiently impressed nonetheless, Julie Lee recovered from her initial shock and was able to say, "My name be Julie Lee. What name they call you by?"

"My name is Antonio Bustelo de La Madrid, lately of Boston."

Telling her who he was and where he was from heightened his mysteriousness for Julie Lee. First, she thought, where in the hell did he get all them names from? She'd never heard of any slave with three names. Finally she said, "Ain't never heard of no *Boston* plantation."

"Oh my dear, I forgot. Boston is not a plantation. Boston is a city in the state of Massachusetts, where I lived for more than fifteen years and where I worked as a silversmith until a bunch of rowdies knocked me over my head one dark night, kidnapped me and sold me into slavery."

He was talking too fast and over her head. She would soon have to end the conversation, since both she and he had to get to work. However, she did want to know more and to hear more about this man with three names, so she said, "I'd be mighty pleased if you would bring your rations tonight and come to our cabin. I'd like to hear about this place you call Boston and I know Dancer and my brother Hannibal would like to talk to you too. Our cabin is right over there," she added pointing to the one.

"I would be delighted to come," the man said pleasantly, a bright smile across his face. "Until later then, I bid you good day."

As she walked away from him, Julie Lee's head was abuzz with wonder. She wondered how and why Master would buy a nigga like Antonio since he seemed to be a smart nigga and smart niggas, she'd always been told, were trouble. Well, there wasn't any sense in racking her brain at the moment. She would find out more that night.

When Dancer found out that Julie Lee had invited the stranger, he was so jealous that he was furious. "How come you go inviting some nigga you ain't knowing nothing about to come to our cabin? What you doing, girl? You looking for a new man what got *two* legs?" Dancer spit the words out in such an ugly tone that Julie Lee was shocked.

"Now Dancer, you know I ain't interested in no other nigga but you. If I was, you think I be telling the man to come to my cabin when I knows you gonna be here? Boy, you sound like you done lost your mind. I just invited the man so we could talk. We all needs to talk to somebody new sometime. Ain't you tired of just talking about the same old things over and over again?

"Anyway it's too late now, I done already told the man to come and he's coming, and the least you could do is be nice. You know how it is for new niggas. Don't know nobody, ain't hardly got nobody to talk to and such."

When Antonio knocked on the cabin door that night and Julie Lee went to answer it, Dancer sat on the pallet, staring silently at John who was awakened by the knock and had started screaming. Dancer wouldn't even shake the man's hand, pretending he was too busy with the baby.

"Come on and sit over here," Julie Lee said trying to be pleasant. "I'm gonna make us some hot tea. I done told my brother Hannibal that you was coming. He said he be here after a while.''

"Thank you so very much," Antonio replied. Then, shifting his attention to Dancer and the baby, he said, "What's the child's name?"

"This here be little John," Dancer answered suddenly. "This here me and Julie Lee's baby. Pretty soon now, Old Massa say me and Julie Lee can jump the broom and get married. Me and Julie Lee been together for a long while now, almost like we is really man and wife. Yeah, we just waiting for Old Massa to give the word for we to jump over the broom. Gonna be married any old day now."

Julie Lee was embarrassed by Dancer's emphatic explanation, but Antonio was mildly amused. He was used to that kind of response. Men, it seemed, had always believed him to be a scoundrel, as if he were interested in taking their women away. What was it about him that caused that kind of reaction? he wondered.

A short time later Hannibal pushed his way into the cabin, and much to Julie Lee's relief, was considerably more civil than Dancer, who still had not even come over to the table to drink his tea and to talk. When Antonio stood up and extended his hand to Hannibal, he took it and shook it and welcomed him to the Lorelei.

Seeing how well Hannibal got on with Antonio, it wasn't long before Dancer decided to drop his act and join the others at the table.

Antonio, a fine storyteller, held Julie Lee in rapt fascination as he unfolded the tale of how he'd come to be at the Lorelei. Hannibal too was clearly impressed, but Dancer decided to reserve his judgment.

"I guess you can tell by now that I'm not an ordinary

colored man," Antonio was saying, "and certainly I was
not cut out to be a slave. I'm the seventh son of the late
Count de La Madrid of Spain."

Hannibal interrupted, wanting to be sure that he fully
understood what was being said. "Hold on there, boy, you is
talking a might too fast for we niggas. I ain't never
knowed no nigga to have as many names as you got, and I
sure I ain't knowing about no place called Spain. Where
that is?"

"Oh, excuse me, I forgot that you would have no way
of knowing what I am talking about. Believe me, I have
yet to get used to this situation.

"Spain is in Europe. That is another *continent*, as
they call it. Just as we are all descendants of Africans, and
Africa is a continent. The language of the land of my birth
is Spanish, but alas I have lost the ability to speak Spanish
because I have had no one with whom to talk.

"My father was a count, meaning that he was a man
of royalty. I suppose that if your master was in Europe he
might too be a count, or a lord, or a duke.

"Although my mother was a woman without title, she
was very much like Julie Lee—black, but possessing the
whitest of skin. My father, dear man, recognized all his
children, including those had by mother.

"It was my father who brought me to this wretched
land when I was but a boy, but alas, he died, leaving me
all alone and without funds to return to my homeland. I'm
sure that my mother's heart was broken because she never
saw me again. Perhaps I shall one day return to Spain and to
my mother and to my brothers. I think that she would
surely die, if she is not dead already, if she knew my
terrible fate.

"After my father died, I was taken in by a kind white

family, and it was there in their home that I learned my trade. As I grew older, they helped me to establish my own business. They were wonderful people, but alas they have since died and so I am all alone in this world, having never married or fathered any children—at least none that I know of,'' Antonio added with a knowing grin.

When he finished his story, Julie Lee thought to herself that she'd never heard anyone, black or white, speak as well as he. Dancer was thinking to himself that the nigga was putting on airs. Hell, he thought, ain't none of us ever been nowhere. This nigga could tell us anything and we would have to believe him because we ain't got no way of checking up on him.

Despite his misgivings, however, Dancer said nothing. He didn't dare accuse the man flat out of being a liar and a showoff. To do so, he knew, would only start an argument with Julie Lee, and it seemed to him they'd been arguing much too much lately. No, he would just keep quiet and let Julie Lee enjoy herself.

Antonio was such a smart man, so obviously educated, that Julie Lee wondered how he could have hidden it from the whites. Antonio explained that he'd met many runaway slaves in Boston and that they'd told him many stories about slavery. He realized that once he'd been kidnapped and put into bondage, instant death awaited him if he let on who he was and how much he really knew.

"Now that I've told you so much about myself, I do hope that you will keep my secret," Antonio said, in a low voice. "I believe that you are good people who will not betray me. I do not plan to stay long in this place, but until I am ready to make my escape, I will do what I have to do to stay alive."

Because she knew how Hannibal and Dancer felt

about such things, Julie Lee had refrained that evening from asking Antonio many of the real questions she wanted to ask, all of which revolved around what was happening outside the Lorelei, the possibility of war and the people she had heard called abolitionists. No, she would save that talk for later when she and Antonio were alone. Perhaps, she thought, he was to be her salvation, her ticket to the freedom that each new day she desired more than anything. Maybe Antonio would help her, and maybe she could help him. God was good, she thought. God must have sent this man.

Chapter 17

When Miss Whilomene stumbled into the kitchen that afternoon, everyone stopped dead in his tracks, and when it appeared she was about to tumble over, Katy rushed to her side, grabbed her by her arms and eased her down into a chair.

Except for the dark rings beneath her eyes, Whilomene was as white as a sheet. She looked like she'd been drinking. She hadn't been feeling well for several weeks, and her appearances downstairs had become more and more infrequent. She took most of her meals in her room, and the only people who really saw her were Zephyr and Young Master Andy. Zephyr had told Katy and the rest that Whilomene didn't even get out of the bed most days and that sometimes even two or three days went by before she would ask to see the children.

"It's the saddest thing," Zephyr said. "Seem almost like them children ain't got no mother, 'cept me. She ain't even acting like she interested in them. She just stay in the room taking all them pills Doc Warfield give her. When I tries to ask her what's hurting and if I can help, she just use all them cuss words and tell me to get the hell out.

Seem to me like she ain't wanting no help. Seem like she just want to stay in that room and die. Maybe she going out of her head."

Doc Warfield had examined Whilomene two or three times and he told Andy Jr. that his wife seemed to be suffering from fatigue.

"Why don't you send her back to South Carolina to her daddy so she can take a good long rest. Zephyr can mind the children. I'm really worried about her, Andy, but I don't know if there's anything I can do. I've examined her, but I can't rightly seem to find out what's wrong.

"She keeps telling me she's having these headaches, and so I've been giving her some pills to ease the pain. But she says that the pills don't do any good, and that the headaches keep coming back. I know she's not pregnant again."

"I know that better than you," Andy said hotly. "I don't know what she got to be fatigued and tired about. She ain't done a goddamned thing around here. Half the time she won't even get off her behind to walk down the steps. Zephyr has the little ones all the time, and I'm the only one who spends any time with them in the evenings so they'll know someone loves them.

"Do you know that my son, my own goddamned son, asked me if his mama loved him and Melissa, since she never pays them any attention? What am I supposed to tell him? Your mother's got fatigue? Hell, I'm fatigued too. I'm working harder than the niggas, and she—she's so goddamned fragile she can't get out of bed. What the hell is a man supposed to do, Doc?"

"I can't answer that for you, son. All I know is that the woman is running down from something. I still think you should send her home to her daddy for a rest."

"I'd like to send her home to her daddy forever."

Now, as Whilomene sat in the kitchen chair, she appeared to be in a daze, only dimly aware of what was going on around her. She was mumbling incoherently.

Although she didn't like Whilomene much, at the moment Katy felt sorry for her and was worried about her health. She seemed so helpless. All the spit and fire was gone, and the red hair she prided herself on just hung limply like a wet mop.

"Miss Whilomene, what can old Katy do to help you, child?"

"Oh, Katy, I just feel real hot, like I'm burning inside. Can you give me a glass of cold water? I want something cool to drink."

"Yes, ma'am." Then turning to Ginny May, who'd been standing there with her mouth open, Katy commanded, "Ain't you heard what Miss Whilomene say? Bring her a glass of water and stop standing there with your mouth wide open before a fly go in."

Katy took one of the clean aprons from the pantry and began fanning Whilomene. As Ginny May handed her the water, she turned to Katy and said, "I think somebody better call the doctor. Miss Whilomene looking mighty poorly to me. Yes, indeed she looking mighty, mighty, poorly."

"If you thinks she needing a doctor then why you standing there? Get on out and find Young Massa Andy and tell him Miss Whilomene is real sick and that he need to call Doc Warfield right away."

Katy was still fanning Whilomene when Julie Lee burst into the kitchen. She'd just finished dusting all the upstairs furniture. When she saw Whilomene sitting in the chair she was surprised, but quickly regrouped.

"Miss Whilomene is feeling poorly," Katy said sympathetically. Julie Lee tried mightily to fix her face with a sympathetic look, but it was hard. This was the woman who had killed her mother for no reason. This was the woman who had bashed in her mother's head.

Despite what she had been thinking, Julie Lee feigned interest in the woman's condition. "Miss Whilomene feeling sickly," she said sweetly, so sweetly in fact that Katy became immediately suspicious.

Could Julie Lee have had something to do with Whilomene's sickness? Katy wondered. Is that why she didn't act surprised to see the woman's condition? Katy tried to push the idea out of her head. Julie Lee was raised as a Christian, and she would never do anything like that.

"Auntie Katy," Julie Lee said, interrupting Katy's thoughts. "Is there anything I can do to help?"

"No, child, ain't thinking there is much we can do, except try to keep Miss Whilomene cooled off till Doc Warfield get here."

It seemed like it had been a long time, but it was hardly a half-hour before Doc Warfield and Andy Jr. made their way into the kitchen. The young master was strangely calm, almost detached, as he looked at Whilomene sitting in the chair and babbling like a child.

"How long she been like this?" Doc Warfield asked Katy.

"Ain't rightly sure, but she been here for a little while. Came falling into the kitchen just after I put the lunch dishes away. Ain't sure how long she was sick upstairs in her room.

"We gived her some water and I been fanning her all over, just trying to keep her cool. She say she hot. Say she feel just like she burning all up inside. When I rubbed her

135

head, it feel like she got the fever. Lord have mercy, Doc Warfield, Miss Whilomene is real sick, real sick.''

"Thank you, Katy, you done good," Doc Warfield said, and then turning to Andy he said, "We got to get her upstairs to her room."

Obeying resentfully, Andy picked Whilomene up in his arms, and when he did her head fell back limply as if she were dead. When Julie Lee saw that, she said to herself, "I hope you die. I hope you die and I hope you suffer afore you die, like you made my mama suffer."

Before getting all the way out of the kitchen, Andy looked over his shoulder and signaled for Katy and Ginny May to come with him. He looked at Julie Lee too, and for a brief moment their eyes met, and to her, it felt like he understood.

When everyone cleared out of the kitchen, Julie Lee leapt off the floor, clicking her heels together. She was ecstatic. Jeddah had told her it would work.

"Just a little bit at the time," Jeddah had said when she handed Julie Lee the small sack of brown powder. "Just sprinkle a little bit of this in her food every day, and I tell you, Julie Lee, all your prayers gonna be answered. She ain't gonna know what hit her. Gonna feel like her head is busting open like a watermelon, and she gonna feel like she wanna die.

"Just remember, girl, you can't give her too much at one time. Don't want nobody, 'specially that nosy Doc Warfield to get no scent of what done happened to Miss Whilomene. Gotta give it to her slow and this way you draws out her suffering.''

Lord, Julie Lee thought, wait until I tell Jeddah what done happen today! She got the magic! She got magic so good even old Doc Warfield can't figure it out. Yes, indeed, Miss Whilomene ain't gonna have no more good days in this life, and I'm sure hoping that when she get to the next one, mama be standing at the gate to greet her.

Chapter 18

Whilomene was dead before the week was out. The plantation was plunged into official mourning. It had taken hours
just to drape the heavy black cloths along the big house
columns. Visitors poured in from all over the county to
express their sympathy, and telegrams arrived by the stack,
including one from the governor of Virginia.

Most of the visitors were accompanied by their best-
looking house slaves whose arms were laden down with
flowers and food. There were cakes, dozens of them, pies,
mountains of fried chicken and so many vegetables that
even Katy couldn't name them all. It seemed that once
word of Whilomene's death had crisscrossed the county
every cook in Henrico had been lashed to her stove. The old
master estimated that on the day of the funeral three
hundred people would be there.

It was two days before Whilomene's family arrived
from South Carolina in a large delegation. They'd come
partly by wagon and partly by train.

Whilomene's four sisters and her mother all had the
same flaming red hair, just like Whilomene's. The family
entourage included a few uncles, cousins and aunts and

several children as well, much to Miss Clementine's dismay, since she did not believe in children attending funerals. Still, Miss Clementine was pleased that the Lorelei was large enough to accommodate them all. They would never go back to South Carolina talking about how badly they'd been treated in Virginia, she thought.

When the day of the funeral finally arrived, the old master suspended all work on the plantation, and several of the slaves used the opportunity to rest, while many more followed discreetly behind the white folks as they headed for the cemetery where all the Johnsons had been buried since coming to America. The only two blacks mixed in among the whites up front were Katy and Zephyr, Katy to assist Miss Clementine and Zephyr who had Whilomene's two children, one on either side.

Julie Lee stayed in her cabin with Dancer and John.

"Sure is sad, ain't it, Julie Lee?" Dancer said. "Miss Whilomene sure was young to die. Seem like it's different when older people passes on. Seem more like they supposed to go. They done lived already and just gotta get out the way to make space for more people. But a young woman like that—sure is sad."

"My mama was young when she died. You ain't forgot, has you, that it was Miss Whilomene that killed my mama. Sorry, Dancer, I just can't feel no sadness in me. Least her children still got their daddy. When she killed my mama, me and Hannibal ain't had nobody 'cept for Katy. Fact is, Miss Whilomene was evil, and she cussed all the time and drank liquor right along with the men. Ain't even thinking Massa Andy gonna be too sad. Heard him say lots of time that he was tired of her anyway. That's why he be sneaking around in the quarter so much at night."

139

Even as she was slowly poisoning Whilomene, Julie Lee had felt no guilt. And now that the woman was dead, she was not sorry. Even the Bible said an eye for an eye and a tooth for a tooth. Whoever it was who said that vengeance wasn't sweet had just not been telling the truth because Julie Lee felt better than she had felt for a long, long time.

Julie allowed herself a small, private smile. She felt no remorse. Now that Miss Whilomene was out of the way, she could get on with the next thing she had to do, and that was to break out of this cage called the Lorelei.

Chapter 19

Blackeyed Susie, the fat black cat that lived in the big house, was so close at Julie Lee's heels that she tripped over it and the old feline shrieked like a baby. The cry ripped through the air with such volume that she felt sure everybody would be awakened by it.

At that moment all she could think of was what would happen to her if she were discovered now, dressed up in Miss Whilomene's favorite yellow dress.

"Scat cat, goddamn you! Scat," she hissed frantically in an effort to shoo the bewildered animal away.

Her blood raced as the cat meowed in response. The hairs on the back of her neck and on her arms stood straight up. Her eyes darted in all directions. She listened closely, trying to figure out if Susie's cry had awakened anyone, particularly Dancer or little John, whom she'd left sleeping soundly inside the cabin.

She trembled and unconsciously fingered the talisman swinging by a string from around her neck. Jeddah had given her the charm a few weeks earlier with a promise that it would protect her from bad spirits.

Other than Antonio, her coconspirator, only Jeddah

knew that Julie Lee had finally decided to take her leave of the Lorelei. Since Jeddah didn't know the exact night she had planned for her escape, however, the woman was now sleeping peacefully in her cabin unaware that Julie Lee was on the first leg of her flight toward freedom.

When she felt certain that Susie's cry had awakened no one, she pushed on. She pressed her body close up against the back wall of the cabin. Susie, sensing that she wasn't wanted, made no effort to follow, but sat at a respectable distance.

The cat's green eyes glowed in the dark. Maybe the cat was an omen, she thought, a bad omen. Everyone always said that black cats were bad luck. On the other hand, she'd never seen this particular cat bring misfortune to anyone. No matter. She was determined to go.

She sprinted between the open spaces separating one cabin from another. Occasionally she would pause to look over her shoulder. There was no one behind her.

In the dark, everything seemed to be alive—creeping, crawling or screeching out. Every shadow loomed big and ominous, and phantoms lurked everywhere, waiting to reach out and grab her.

Her destination was the stables. There she would rendezvous with Antonio, who was supposed to have two horses and one of the carriages ready for their departure.

When she came to the end of the slave quarter buildings, she broke into a furious dash across the wide open field to the stables.

But as she ran, an awful thought flashed through her mind. Suppose, just suppose Hannibal, as he often did, had decided to sleep in the stables this night rather than in the dormitory with the rest of the boys.

Oh, God, she thought silently, her brother would

probably try to persuade her to stay. He would start off by reminding her of all her responsibilities—to Dancer, little John and to him. He would call her selfish and crazy.

As the night wind blew sharply around the edges of her face and up the long dress, she tried to push thoughts of Hannibal out of her mind. She didn't want to see his disapproving frown, his accusatory eyes.

Hannibal would never understand that she was leaving not out of selfishness, but out of love for him, Dancer and little John. She wanted for all of them what she wanted for herself—*freedom*. The simple freedom of coming and going as they pleased. She had never had that freedom, and she hungered for it as for nothing else.

Running into Hannibal was a risk she had to take. He probably wasn't there and even if he was, she couldn't believe that her brother would betray her to the master.

She'd run so fast that her throat hurt by the time she reached her destination. Water ran from her eyes and she put her head down toward the ground trying to catch her breath. She pushed open the stable door cautiously and peeked inside. There was no sign of Antonio.

Where the hell is the nigga? she thought disgustedly. Don't tell me the nigga done backed out on me. Don't tell me that after all that big brave talk that the nigga done got scared!

Her heart stopped when a hand came down on her shoulder, then reached around and clamped down over her mouth, stifling the fearful scream she was about to let out.

"Shh," a voice said. "It's only me."

Her bones stopped rattling long enough for her to realize that the hand and the voice belonged to Antonio.

"What the hell you trying to do, nigga? Scare me to death?" she said hotly when she turned around.

143

"No, Julie Lee, I wasn't trying to scare you. I was trying to save your life and mine. If you had screamed when I came up behind you, then you could have given us away."

He was right and she knew it. "So where you was anyway?"

Antonio swung around in front of her and grabbed her by both shoulders. "Girl, have you ever tried sneaking out of a cabin over eight people? I had a hard time. One of them was gritting his teeth and snoring like a bull. I kept thinking he was going to wake up and start screaming."

She'd heard enough. "All right, all right. So you had a hard time, but you is here now, so I guess we best be getting on out of this place before somebody wakes up. We done already lost too much time and I want to get some road behind us before daybreak."

Antonio had already walked away from her. He was peering into the darkened stalls trying to decide which horses to take. He stopped what he was doing long enough to ask matter-of-factly, "Did you get the money?"

It was a ridiculous question and she intended to let him know just how ridiculous she thought it was. She put her hands on her hips, sashayed up to where he was standing, pointed her finger at his face and finally said in a hoarse and angry whisper, "Did I get the money? Sure I got the money. You think I is stupid or something? You think I'm just a dumb, ignorant nigga just 'cause I been a slave all my life and you been free all of yours?

"I done had the money since early this morning, for your information, Mr. Smart Ass Nigga. Snuck them dollars out of that old box Old Massa keep hiding up in the attic. I seen him go up there lots of times and hide his money. He got so much money in that old box, I bet he ain't rightly sure how much he got.''

Antonio was almost afraid to proceed with the line of questioning, but he pushed on. He had to be certain, because if there wasn't enough money, it wasn't even worth taking the risk. "How much did you get?"

Julie Lee backed off a few feet. "I took what you told me to take, Antonio," she snarled. "I took three hundred dollars. Ain't that what you say we might be needing to get us to Philadelphia and to pay off any of them old white trash that might gets suspicious?"

"I could've taked all the money if I wanted to, but I didn't. Ain't wanting Old Massa to think I'm one of them stealing niggas, 'cause you know that's what they always say about us. Say niggas steal. Say niggas stink. Say niggas be lazy. Say niggas is stupid. Say nigga. Say nigga. That's all they say. They always saying something bad about niggas.''

Julie Lee pursed her lips and continued proudly, "I ain't no stealing nigga. Fact is, when I gets free and gets me my own money, I is gonna pay Old Massa back every last dollar I took."

Antonio was so amazed by her reasoning that he stopped what he was doing and said, "Pay him back? Pay him back for what? You don't owe that man anything. Don't you know that all that money he has in the box he has because of you and all the other slaves on this place? Don't you realize what being a slave means? It means that you are not bound by their laws because they don't apply to you. It means that you are not bound by their morality because they have none. If they did, you wouldn't be a slave."

She knew that her face was turning red and she

145

burned with rage. "So what you saying? You saying again that I'm stupid? Listen, I ain't exactly sure by what you meaning with all them words, but it sound to me like you is trying to say I'm stupid. Well you listen, nigga," she seethed, "if you think I'm so damned stupid then maybe we just ought to drop this whole idea right now. Seem to me like I'm getting to like you less and less!"

Antonio was embarrassed and sorry. If anything, he admired her. She was courageous and intelligent. He was deeply moved by her willingness to die rather than to go on being a slave. Ah yes, he thought, Julie Lee was an extraordinary young woman, and as she became older she would become even more so.

"Julie Lee, I never meant to insult your intelligence. Please believe me. I was only trying to get you to think more realistically. You want to do good when everything around you is bad. I only want you to see that this is hell, truly it is. Just wait until we get to Philadelphia and you see other people, niggas as they call them down here, walking free, talking free, being free. Maybe then you'll have a better understanding of the hell under which you, your mama and grandmama have survived.

"No, Julie Lee," he said softly, cupping her chin in his hands, "I don't think you're dumb. I think you're a great woman and one day the world will know who you are, and I will be so proud to say I knew you."

They were both crying now, and without even realizing it they fell into each other's arms, as much out of fear as for comfort.

Straightening herself up, she said, "Come on, Antonio. We ain't got no time to be standing here jabbering. Let's get on out of here before I start crying again."

In a few more minutes Antonio had the horses hitched

up to the carriage. He kept patting the animals, hoping to keep them calm and quiet. He motioned to her to open the stable doors.

She pushed them ajar cautiously so she could look outside. The moon was full and it lit up the countryside. She motioned him forward.

Antonio eased the horses and carriage toward the door. Before stepping outside he whispered, "Good luck, Julie Lee. It's now or never."

And then he said abruptly, "Now you climb on up inside the carriage. I'm gonna walk alongside the horses until we get to the open road. They might make too much noise if I try to drive them."

She followed his instructions without comment. She'd never been up in a carriage before. She nearly fell trying to climb up the steps because her foot got caught in the hem of Whilomene's dress. "Lord," she said to herself, "how do white folks wear all these clothes? I'm just gonna have to learn."

Inside the carriage the smell of rich leather tickled her nose. As she slid over the seat, she sunk down into the deeply padded satin cushions. She gently touched the heavy brocaded curtain at the carriage window, then pushed it back slightly and peered outside from her high perch. The bright light of the moon came in. She imagined that the moon had a face and its smile was so wide that it spread from one side to the other. That's a good sign, she thought. That's a good sign.

Leaning her head back, Julie Lee smilingly said to herself, "So this is what it's like." She retied the loosened strings of her bonnet. Then she playfully flicked her hair back over her shoulders the way she'd seen the white women do and she turned her nose upward.

147

"Why, sure," she whispered sweetly with a toothy grin and in the tone she'd heard Whilomene assume many times, "I'm Miss Annabelle Brownless of North Carolina. Just traveling to Philadelphia with my nigga here, Cleophus."

She took out a small hankie and pressed it to her eyes. "Going up to Philadelphia to see my dear sweet sister Luciebelle. She's so sickly, that poor girl, my mama and daddy about to *die*. They told me to go on up and see about the child. Do you think that me and my nigga Cleophus will be safe traveling along the roads with so much talk about war and all?"

And then assuming the role of one of the white men they might encounter on the road, she deepened her voice and said, "Why sure, ma'am. You and your nigga is gonna be safe. Ain't nobody would hurt a poor, helpless woman like you."

Then she switched back to being Miss Annabelle Brownless. "Oh, thank you so much, gentlemen. I was so afraid with just me and Cleophus here. I would be in such a tither if something should happen."

She fell back into the seat laughing, momentarily forgetting that she hadn't even gotten off Lorelei land yet.

Outside, Antonio led the horses slowly, keeping his eyes peeled in the direction of the big house. He prayed, wished and prayed some more that no lights be lit. They edged toward the road ever so slowly.

Chapter 20

Young Massa Andy stormed out onto the porch, muttering curses under his breath. The sound of his boots coming down on the porch's wooden slats were dull thumps. His face was crimson, his nostrils flared, and thick veins throbbed in his temples. His eyes were squinted to angry little slits and the corners of his mouth were turned down into a snarl. He paced the length of the porch several times, all the while beating the palm of his left hand with the thick end of a leather switch.

The field slaves were working as usual when the gong sounded. First one ring. Then two. Then three. Then nothing. Then one ring again. Then two rings. Then three. That was their signal to stop all work and head back to the quarter. The old timers had heard the early morning gong before, and they knew what it meant. Their eyes locked, their hearts raced, and their stomachs churned with fear.

The old timers walked slowly and silently. The younger ones and the newcomers chatted innocently as they walked, aware that something was happening, but not sure what. None of the old timers bothered to tell them. No need. They would find out soon enough.

As the field slaves were trickling into the quarter, Katy and the rest of the house staff were rounding the back corner of the big house. They too were heading in the direction of the quarter. There was cold fear in their hearts, but no words were on their lips.

As she walked, Katy felt as if she were going to bury the dead. Somehow she'd known instinctively when Julie Lee failed to show up for work that morning that something was amiss. She hadn't even bothered to send anybody down to her cabin to see if the girl had overslept. Katy could now only think to herself, Lord, have mercy, my sweet Julie Lee. What you gone and done? You always been so quick, so wise for a young'un and yet there is just things you can't never understand until you get some years behind you. My sweet Julie Lee, what you gone and done?

The young master was going through the quarter like a madman, pounding and kicking open cabin doors and ordering any and all occupants, who were primarily the elderly and the ill, to get outside.

Mammy Grace nearly dropped the baby she'd been nursing when Andy Jr. rammed his way into the nursery, nearly knocking the door off its hinges. He was shouting at the top of his voice and cursing so much that several of the sleeping babies woke up in a fright and immediately began to squall.

"Leave them goddamned nigga bastards where they be and get your black asses outside!" he ranted. The three women moved quickly, trying hard to stay out of the young master's line of reach as they scampered out the door. Their minds were ringing with the question: What's going on?

The young master struck a frightening pose. The silver handle of his side arm gleamed brightly in the morning sun. He held his whip in such a manner that it was clear he was prepared to strike anybody who got in his way.

The field hands were streaming into the quarter now, and the sound of their voices rose in a cacophonous din, which did not cease until the young master cracked his whip through the air and bellowed, "Shut up, goddamnit! Shut up, all you black bastards. You shut your goddamned mouths. I'll tear the flesh off the ass of any nigga that makes a sound!" Suddenly and quickly everyone became silent but one young boy who apparently had no feeling for the gravity of the situation. That boy gave out a shrill and quick scream that died in his throat when the tip of the whip came down on the side of his face without warning. Like a seam unraveling, a gash in his face opened up. Bright red blood gushed out and in seconds red drops were staining the boy's dingy white shirt. The child was so frightened that he was unable to move even a hand to try to stop the bleeding. Huge, wet tears welled up in his eyes, but he stood there rooted in place, terrorized. The other slaves, not wanting to feel the dreaded taste of the lash themselves, made no move to assist the boy. A few of the men and women muttered under their breath, but that's all they did.

The young master kept walking around in a circle so that he could see everywhere at once. He hit the whip against his high leather boots as he bellowed, "All right, I want you niggas to split up. I want the men over here, the boys over there, and all you women and children on this side of me. Line your asses up single file."

The crowd moved swiftly. The lines they finally formed nearly stretched from one end of the quarter to the other. The people near the ends jostled some, fully expecting that those standing in that position would get whatever was coming, worst and first.

Dancer and Hannibal were standing together about midway in their line. Dancer wasn't fearful of the young master, but his heart pounded like a hammer on an anvil. His body ached and he could hardly breathe. His mind was racing. Jealousy was gnawing his soul to pieces.

Julie Lee had gone off and left him and little John. Even worse, she had gone off with that fast-talking nigga, Antonio, who said he wasn't really a slave. He knew Julie Lee had believed the nigga. He should have put a stop to her talking to him. Now the fast-talking nigga had taken his woman. He closed and opened his fist, thinking about what he would do to Antonio if he ever saw him again, and even worse what he would do to Julie Lee. He would squeeze the breath out of her body like somebody squeezing the juice out of a grape. He would yank every hair from her head by the root. He would take an axe and chop her up into little bitty pieces and then throw them in the fire to roast. How could she do such a terrible thing to him and little John?

Hannibal, not feeling betrayed, felt fear, real fear for what would happen to his sister. She'd run away with Antonio, but not because they were lovers. Hannibal knew that Julie Lee loved Dancer and their baby. But Julie Lee also loved the idea of being free.

But why didn't she tell anyone she was going to leave? Did his sister, his very own flesh and blood, actually believe that he would have betrayed her? Argued with her, yes. Tried to change her mind about going, yes. But betray her? No.

Hannibal was afraid for her now. He was afraid that the master would squeeze the breath out of her body like somebody squeezing the juice out of a grape. He was afraid the master would yank every hair out of her head by the root, or take an axe and chop her into little bitty pieces and then throw them in the fire to roast. How could she leave herself open to that fate? he thought.

It was chilly outside. All the blacks were trembling, partially from the cold, but mostly from fear. The old people were suffering the most. They were followed in their misery by all the slaves who had inside jobs and who had been ordered to get outside so quickly that they never had a chance to throw on something to keep warm.

The young master didn't care about their discomfort. In fact, he wanted them to suffer. What a goddamned motley crew, he thought, walking up and down the lines. Simple-minded fools! he muttered to himself, watching their fruitless efforts to get warm—hopping from one foot to the other, patting their chests and beating their arms together.

He stopped at several different slaves and looked at them square in the eyes—daring them, hoping that they would try to avoid his by glancing up or down. He was waiting for one of them to say one wrong word or make one wrong gesture. He would take their damned heads off with his pistol. He wanted to kill something. He felt power surging through his body, and now that he had his slaves assembled, he wanted to crush them, to pick their eyes out and feed them to the barn owls.

He kept thinking to himself, you can't do a goddamned thing for niggas. You feed them, you clothe them, you try to be fair, you don't work them too hard, you don't beat them too often, and still the nappy-headed sons of bitches would betray you the first chance they got. Stinky niggas, he thought. Things around the Lorelei were going to change after this! If the black bastards wanted to run, he'd give them something to run from. He'd cut the rations in half and would whip ass for any infraction, large or small. So this was the way they wanted it? This was the way they would get it!

Antonio, the hell with him, Andy Jr. thought. He was a new nigga and not all that expensive—but Julie Lee, hers was the greatest sin. He had been kind to her. He had done favors for her. He had done everything he could to try to make up for her mother's unfortunate death. He'd never beaten her, never worked her hard. He'd tried to protect her from being raped, and still the bitch got up and ran.

Katy had known Young Master Andy all his life, but she had never, never seen the man in the state that he was in that morning. Never had she seen the look that now filled the whites of his eyes. Those eyes were cold like dead fish. And in the damp air his face had turned a pale white, as if it had been drained of all the blood. All Katy could think of was how frightening and how frightened he looked. That's what she was thinking, when she suddenly heard him shout out her name.

"Katy! Katy get your black ass front and center!"

The big round woman rocked on the balls of her feet as she waddled toward him, feeling the pressure of those hundreds of wide eyes boring through her.

"Hannibal and Dancer, get over here!" Then he called Zephyr, Ginny May and all the rest of the big house staff. Ten blacks stood around him in a semicircle, looking from one to the other, wondering what he had in mind for them. Zephyr was so frightened that she began crying. Without a word, the young master took out his pistol and aimed it at the center of her face. "Cry a little more, I'll blow your goddamned miserable head off, bitch!'' Zephyr continued to sniffle, but her crying had stopped as suddenly as it had started.

All the large, wide eyes were riveted on the people in the center of the quarter's dusty road. The old master came up and walked over to join his son unnoticed by the crowd. The old man would say nothing, do nothing. This was for Andy Jr. to handle. This was his business, and if he was ever going to run the Lorelei, he might just as well learn now as later what it would take to keep his niggas in line.

With his whip hanging at his side and his hand fingering the pistol he'd put back into its holster, Andy Jr. addressed the slaves surrounding him. ''Now, which one of you niggas gonna tell me about what happened last night? Which one of you niggas gonna tell me what happened to Julie Lee and that goddamned scoundrel, Antonio?''

If Andy thought he wanted an answer, he would never know how much the slaves themselves wanted an answer— and quickly. They didn't want to be punished for something they didn't know anything about. Jeddah knew something, but she wasn't a part of the inner circle the young master had called together, and she was glad she wasn't, because she told herself, I'd spit in that white man's face.

''Well, I'm waiting for a goddamned answer!'' Young Master announced as he strode about looking into those frightened faces. ''What about you, Dancer? You was sleeping with the bitch. You got a baby for the bitch, what do you know?''

Dancer's voice was barely a whisper. ''Don't know nothing, sir. All I know is I waked up this morning and Julie Lee was gone. Don't know nothing. You think I'd

155

want my Julie Lee to leave me and little John? No sir, I would never want that.'' Dancer lowered his head and looked at the small pebbles in the dirt.

"And you, Hannibal! What do you know?'' Young Master said, suddenly swinging around, so suddenly in fact that Hannibal was unprepared to say anything. "She's your goddamned sister! She must have told you something before she took her ass on out of here in the middle of the night!''

"Ain't knowing nothing, sir. Ain't know nothing. First I knew Julie Lee was gone was when Dancer come running to the dorm this morning, hollering and screaming that she done left him and little John. You know if I even thought Julie Lee was gonna run that I would talk her out of it. She ain't told me nothing about her leaving.''

"How about you, Katy? You fancy yourself queen of the niggas. You supposed to know so goddamned much about everything. What you know about all this?''

Nervously fingering the scarf on her head, pulling it down to cover the edges of her hair, Katy said, "I don't know where Julie Lee done gone, massa sir, but I knows she a good girl. I think she just got all mixed up with that fast-talking Antonio. What I thinks is that he done put in in her head to leave.''

The young master was frustrated and was getting angrier by the second. "I didn't ask you what you thought. I asked you what you knew. So what I hear you saying is that you don't know nothing.''

He went around to them all, and every one in the inner circle said the same thing. They knew nothing.

"I see how all you sons of bitches stick together,'' the young master accused. "Hang down them big lips of yours and get to blubbering and acting dumb. But ain't none of y'all worth a damn. Just a bunch of ungrateful niggas! Do you know what happens to niggas like you on other plantations? Do you know? Well, I tell you what. Since y'all don't seem to know nothing, I'm gonna let you stand out here in the cold some more, maybe some of y'all's brains will get to functioning.''

With those words the crowd outside the circle began to grumble. They were angry, and feeling quite ugly, not toward Young Master, but toward their counterparts in the inner circle who they believed were lying.

All it took was one person to start it off before there were dozens of different voices, shouting and hooting.

''Tell Massa what he want to know.''

''We is freezing to death out here. Tell him!''

''Why we all has to suffer just 'cause of you house niggas?''

''We ain't done nothing. We don't know nothing. And still we got to stand here out in this cold!''

''Go on and tell Massa what he want to know!''

And so the whole crowd stood. An hour went by and then another and still they stood. They were so tired that they stopped mumbling and grumbling. Only their eyes looked mad.

The young master hadn't sat down either, but his father was perched on a stool he'd taken out of one of the cabins. It was his anger that gave the young master continued energy. He knew he had to do something. He had to take some action if he wanted the slaves to take him seriously.

With only one leg to stand on, Dancer was suffering terribly. The blood circulation in his good leg had slowed so that it felt numb. He nearly fell off his cane onto the ground when Andy Jr. broke the silence and said to him,

"Go into the nursery. Get little John and bring him out here."

"What for you want little John, massa sir? You ain't gonna hurt him. Is you, massa?" Dancer's eyes were filled with fear. Hannibal wanted to ask the same question, but he felt it best at the moment to keep his mouth shut.

"Get that baby nigga before I shoot off your other leg," Young Master said coldly.

Dancer hobbled over to the nursery, his brain scrambling furiously trying to determine why Young Master Andy wanted little John. In their haste to get out of the nursery, the women had left the door wide open. It was freezing inside. Dancer moved quickly from one pallet to the other, looking for little John among the babies, all of whom seemed to be crying. He found his son down at the end. Just like all the others, little John's mouth was open and he was screaming at the top of his little lungs. Dancer picked him up. Little John's skin was wet and clammy. His bottom was pissy and smelly. Taking the blanket in which the baby had been wrapped, Dancer pressed the infant tightly to his chest. He kissed little John's face trying to get the baby to quiet down. As he left the nursery, Dancer mercifully closed the door behind him, and looking down at the baby in the crook of his arm, kept saying, "Why he wanting you, little John? You ain't done nothing to nobody. You is all I got in the world. Your mama done gone off and left us. What he want with you? He can't take you from me. Please God, don't let him hurt my little boy."

Dancer arrived back and was hardly standing there a minute before the young master commanded that he and all the slaves nearest to them, about fifty in all, follow him down to the river. The rest he ordered to get back to their duties.

In all this time, the old master had said almost nothing. He remained watching, silent but alert.

Everyone's brain was afire now, with nervous thoughts about what the young master had in store for them. For some, whatever he intended to do, it was time already. They were plenty tired of just standing there and looking into each other's faces.

When the delegation reached the bank of the river, Young Master said, "Dancer, bring me that baby."

With more urgency and even greater fear, Dancer asked, trying to sound respectful, "Please, massa sir, what you gonna do to little John? He ain't done nothing. He can't help what his mama do. You want to take it out on somebody, massa sir, take it out on me. Whip my behind. Do anything you want to me, but please, massa sir, please don't hurt little John. Please . . ."

A whip cracked the air and the lash fell across his head. "Shut up, nigga, and give me that baby. I'll do any goddamned thing I want to do and ain't required to give you or no other darky around here no explanation."

The tears blinded Dancer's eyes as he handed over little John. In the exchange, the baby's blanket slid to the ground. The naked infant cried out pitifully as the cold air hit his body. The scream was choked off, however, when Young Master suddenly turned the infant upside down and held him by the heels of his feet.

Dancer could stand it no more. He charged forward, oblivious to whatever Young Master would do to him now. He was almost up on top of the man when the shot rang out. Young Master was holding the baby with one hand, and had taken his gun out with the other. The force of the bullet pushed Dancer back several feet. Bright red blood began to form a pool in the middle of his chest. He fell to the ground, but was able to crawl so that he was only inches from the young master's high leather boots when his eyes saw the toe of the boot come up at him and an instant later, the kick stopped his advance. Dancer was writhing on the ground, and the young master buried his foot in the black's bleeding chest. Dancer's eyes rolled around in his head, his hands stretched out and all five fingers opened like a fan and stayed stiff. He twitched only one more time. After that Dancer was still.

Removing his foot from Dancer's chest, the young master snarled at the assembly. "All right! Any more of you niggas want to try to rush me? Step right up and try me. Come on," he said, daring them, while at the same time swinging the baby, whose body had begun to turn blue.

Katy didn't know what had given her the strength or the courage, but she leapt forward, throwing herself at Young Master's feet. She was just a few inches away from Dancer, who lay there with his eyes wide open.

"Please, massa sir," Katy begged, crying all the while. "Please, massa. I knowed you since you was a baby yourself. Don't do this. You is a man who believes in God. Please, massa, don't hurt nobody else. Please, massa, don't hurt the little baby. Look at it. It's turning blue. Please."

When he looked at the woman's fat, black face, he felt overcome with hatred for her, and all who looked like her. He kicked her with the same boot he'd just removed from Dancer's chest. He acted as if she were an insect, trying to crawl up his leg. But Katy crawled back up to him again. This time grabbing him at the knee, she pleaded, "Please, massa sir, please."

Then Katy turned to the old master. "Please, massa sir. This ain't like you. This ain't what kind of man you and the Johnsons is. Don't let him do no more." But the old man just looked at her in silence. She could feel that he wanted to do something to help, but he did not. Not even he had the courage to take on his own son just then.

With a sudden, desperate cry, Katy flung herself toward the child and seized the swinging body in her arms. Caught off guard by her impetuous action, Andy stared at her in amazement as the baby was torn from his arms. But he hesitated for only an instant.

"Dirty nigger bitch!" he shrieked. The boot flew upward, catching Katy in the chin, and she was flung against the ground, blood pouring from her nose and mouth. But still she held the baby close in her arms, protecting the child as she lurched backward. Panting with anguish, she writhed and turned, cradling the child in the curve of her body as the blows of the young master pummeled her back and shoulders, each kick sending her into a new frenzy of pain.

"Andy!"

The old master's voice seemed to shock the younger man, freezing him in midstride. Andy looked around bewildered to see who had called his name. For an instant, his eyes met those of his father.

"Andy, that's enough now, son. We lost three niggers already. Can't afford more. And who knows, that baby child might grow into somethin'."

Andy backed away and spat, guarded resentment in his face. But he appeared exhausted by his exertions, and his father's words had no obvious effect.

"Sell 'em, I say," he retorted. "They ain't worth the ground that holds their weight." Then he looked at the assembled slaves and waved his gun. "All right! Break it up! Break it up! I think you niggas done seen enough. I want all y'all to get back to work except for you," he said, pointing to three boys about fifteen or sixteen years old. "I want you three to bury this here dead nigga." He indicated Dancer by again kicking his prone, lifeless body.

The crowd dispersed. The people felt numb. The more religious among them prayed.

The young master said nothing when he noticed that Hannibal hadn't moved with the others. The boy fell down on his knees and took Dancer's head into his lap. His wet tears cascaded down onto his dead friend's face. Taking one hand, he tenderly closed Dancer's eyes. He knew that he would carry that picture with him for the rest of his life.

Rocking back and forth, Hannibal keened, "Oh, my God, Dancer, I just stood there while he killed you and tormented little John. Oh, my God, I just stood there, like a dumb-assed, stupid nigga and let him kill you. Oh Dancer, Dancer." His low sobs soon turned to a wail.

Katy stumbled to her feet, the baby clutched in her arms. She was crying too, tears mingling with the blood on her face. Hannibal looked up at her.

"Katy, I was scared. I was so scared, just too scared to die, too scared to try to help Dancer and little John. I know God ain't never gonna forgive me for letting him die like that.

"Oh God, I hope Julie Lee gets far, far away. I hope that I can see her just one more time so's I can tell her that she was right. I want to see her so I can let her know that I know now why she wanted so bad to get free. What are we, Katy? What are we? We ain't nothing. We ain't

162

nothing but dumb, stupid, scared niggas, and me, I is the worst of all.''

As Katy clasped her arms more tightly around Julie Lee's child, she whispered in Hannibal's ear, ''I know, I know. I know Julie Lee gonna be all right. You is gonna see her again and then you can tell her what happened. It's gonna be okay, Hannibal. There is a God in heaven and He will judge what done happened here today. I know child. I know.''

For years afterward, the Lorelei slaves would whisper the story of Katy—how she had faced the master's gun to rescue that baby from his arms. They looked at her with a kind of wonder, regarding her as a woman who had walked into the jaws of death and by some miracle emerged whole again. And they watched her care for that child, showing a kind of solicitude that seemed to express the hope they all shared.

But Katy soon realized that something was wrong with the child. All through that summer and late into the fall, while the picking and harvesting continued—during those long days when they waited for some word, some sign from Julie Lee—the child seemed to languish and fade. He refused his food and his cries became fainter.

In the evenings, Hannibal sat beside Katy and watched her croon, rocking the child and singing, offering her prayers and her comfort to make him lie easy and eat again. There was nothing Hannibal could do but watch. And it was he who first saw the inevitable signs, even when Katy was blind, refusing to admit what soon became visible to all.

The child was dying.

There seemed to be no cause, no reason. They tried

the medicines with him and the nursing mothers on the plantation left their own babies to spend long hours with John, trying to make him suck as they rocked him in their arms. But their ministrations were futile. To each of them, Katy would turn with wide eyes, mutely asking what she had done wrong, what else she could do. Until, at the end, there was nothing for her to do but look at John's still body and cry silent tears of frustration and anguish.

Julie Lee's baby was buried in November, on a Sunday morning. The Lorelei slaves sang hymns and filed silently past the coffin. There were prayers and then the others gathered around Katy.

But there was no comforting her. Even Hannibal could not meet the look in her eyes after Julie Lee's baby was buried.

Chapter 21

Julie Lee felt tired and hungry. In their haste to get away from the plantation, she'd forgotten to pack any food for the trip. Now that her stomach was growling and contracting, Julie Lee realized how serious her oversight had been.

Of course, it didn't help matters any that Antonio had stopped along the road twice and had come back to report that he was uncertain of which direction they should take to get to Richmond, the first stop on the way to Philadelphia. He said he believed that they had lost some time going in circles. The expression on his face was almost silly when he told her, "You must remember, Julie Lee, when I was brought to the Lorelei, we traveled in the daylight and on the main roads. And I'm a stranger to these parts."

She was too exhausted to argue. The jarring, bouncing motions of the carriage as it moved along the bumpy back roads, combined with hunger and the deep-seated fear of getting caught, which had kept edging into her consciousness, had made it all but impossible for Julie Lee to drop off to sleep for more than a few minutes at a time. Even when she had been able to nod, she was haunted by a vision of Dancer, his eyes flashing hurt and anger at having awakened and found her gone. Inevitably he would come to the wrong conclusion; that she had forsaken him and little John for the love of another man.

After hours of being jostled around like a potato sack, the carriage didn't seem quite as fine and elegant as it had when she'd first stepped into it. Now the smell of the rich leather seats was making her nauseated. Every bone and muscle in her body ached. No matter how many times she shifted around in an effort to get more comfortable, it seemed as if her blood had stopped circulating, particularly in her behind, which now had a tingling sensation.

Perhaps running away wasn't such a good idea. Maybe they should have waited a little longer. Perhaps she should have been more certain that Antonio knew where he was going. Maybe she should have told Dancer of her plan and about how she intended to come back to get him and little John. Perhaps she should just have been patient and waited for the abolitionists to come and deliver her from slavery.

Perhaps. Maybe. The questions swirled in her mind. But, she concluded, she couldn't go back now, even if she wanted to. She would have to take her chances outside even if going ahead meant death. At least she could speculate about what was ahead. There was no doubt that she would die if she were to return to the Lorelei now.

As she sat deep in thought, the carriage came to a halt. Her unnamed fears rushed forward. She could feel her hands starting to shake and her face turning red. She couldn't move. She just sat there, waiting for one of the paddy rollers to yank the door open and drag her out onto the road. They had been caught. On, my God, she kept thinking. Oh, my God, what we gonna do now?

She waited a few minutes, but when the door never opened, she cautiously and fearfully peeked out the window to see what was going on. There was Antonio, standing in the middle of the road, chatting casually with two other black men. She couldn't hear what they were saying to one another, but decided to take the risk of finding out.

She stuck her head all the way out the window and demanded in her best Whilomene imitation, "Cleophus, what you stopping here for, boy? What in Hades is going on, I want to know."

Picking up her cue, Antonio walked away from the men and came up beside the window. Almost sticking his face right into hers, and in what she thought was a most disgustingly servile tone and manner said, "Ain't nothing going on, and ain't nothing wrong, ma'am. I just finding out from these boys how far we got to go before we gets to Richmond. I done told them how we is rushing to Philadelphee to see your poor, sick sister and about how it look like me and my dumb self done got us a little lost in the dark."

Then, with a grin that extended from one side of his face to the other and which revealed all his pretty, straight white teeth, Antonio bowed and added, "Don't you worry none, ma'am. Ain't I always been your best boy?"

Upon seeing what they believed had been a white woman, the two men took off their hats and bid her a good morning. Well, she thought, at least these two niggas had believed her masquerade. The important thing, though, was whether she would convince all the white folks they might meet between there and Philadelphia.

As she slid back into her seat, Julie Lee let an audible sigh of relief escape from her mouth, which had gone dry only moments earlier. Even the sweat which had started pouring out from under her arms had ceased to run.

After a few more minutes, Antonio was back in the driver's seat and they were off again. She let him get a respectable distance from the men before tapping on the carriage wall indicating that she wanted him to stop.

"Man, ain't you even gonna tell me what them men said? No, nigga, you just gonna keep on driving like a smart ass and leave me sitting here wondering where we is. I swear to God, when we gets through this one, if we gets through this one, I ain't never wanting to see your ugly face again. You hear me? Never again!"

Antonio was amused, and showed it. She wanted to slap his stupid-looking face when he transformed into Cleophus again. "Now, ma'am, you ain't knowing where Richmond is nohow, so why you need to know where we is right now? Trust me, Miss Annabelle, ma'am, I is gonna get you to Richmond and on to Philadelphee faster than you can wink your eye. Them mens back there, they say we is right outside the city a few miles. Just trust me, ma'am."

Antonio had already started shuffling back toward the carriage, but not before she could spit out angrily, "I hope to hell we is near Richmond, nigga, 'cause I'm gonna kill you myself if we ain't. I'm so tired and hungry right now, I could eat damn near anything. I want to wash my face and just lay my body down somewhere. I know I must be the dustiest-looking white woman around with all the dust that done blew up in my face since we been riding."

His response was quick. "No, ma'am, you looking real fine to me, just as white as we when we left the plantation. I think you is looking just fine."

The man was an incurable ass, Julie Lee thought.

How could he act so playful when there was still so much danger? Here she was afraid of getting caught, afraid of getting hanged and he was playing stupid games. "Can't wait to get shed of this nigga," she said aloud to herself.

Once the carriage was in motion again and moving at a regular, steady pace, Julie Lee, for the first time since the start of the trip, sank into a deep sleep. This time there were no dreams, no haunting images, only blessed darkness and even more blessed peace. Her mind was blank.

She had no idea how long they'd been riding when she was awakened by strange new sounds—the sounds of the city. She had never been to the city before. She pushed back the curtain and feasted her eyes on more humanity than she'd ever seen in one place. There was activity and people—people everywhere—men, women and children, running here and there, and all appearing to be in a rush. So this was what it was like—the city.

Chapter 22

Antonio was following closely behind her, and with the edge of the bags he was carrying he literally shoved her into the doorway of the hotel, the Grand Richmond Palace. When asked, a stranger recommended it as the finest place in Richmond to stay.

Her knees were knocking and her heart was pumping fast. Her eyes widened at what she saw in front of her. She had thought the Lorelei big house had to be just about the prettiest place in the world, but that was because she'd never seen anything else. The beauty of the Palace took her breath away. The wood-paneled walls were shining like polished silver, and there were chandeliers, dozens of them, that would just put Miss Clementine's to shame. The rugs on the floor were colorful and had intricate patterns and designs. She'd never seen any so pretty before. Standing discreetly off to the side, Julie Lee couldn't help but notice, were jet-black men dressed in bright red suits with tight-fitting pants and big gold buttons. She didn't know what their jobs were, but she guessed that they must be important. She wondered if they were slaves or free.

She was thinking about it when she again felt Antonio nudging the bag into the back of her leg trying to get her to move forward and out of the doorway. "Julie Lee," he whispered frantically, "don't just stand here gawking. Go on up to the desk and do what I told you to do, and for God's sake, stop staring at everything like you've never seen anything before."

When she walked up to the front desk, the clerk was deeply engrossed in a newspaper. As soon as he became aware of her presence, however, he snapped to attention like a marionette manipulated by some unseen hand. "Yes, ma'am," he said. "How can I help you?"

A few hours later, sitting in the main dining room waiting to be served, the initial awe had worn off, and Julie Lee had time to contemplate the enormity of the feats she and Antonio had accomplished in a few short hours. It had been a day of many firsts and it was not over yet. She was already exhausted by the masquerade, but Antonio told her they still had a long way to go before reaching Philadelphia, before she could completely relax and go back to being Julie Lee.

"Lord, Antonio," she'd said earlier, "I'm so tired of smiling and grinning and batting my eyes. Damn if these white folks ain't got a lot of put-ons."

She'd had to learn so much so quickly. She followed Antonio's instructions to the letter—so well, in fact, that he laughingly told her that she hadn't done half bad for a backward country girl.

Antonio knew the ways of white people probably even better than they knew themselves. He'd been forced to learn the ways of white people just to survive, since even up North Negroes had their assigned places, and most white folks were hardly interested in letting them move too far away from those positions.

"Yes ma'am, Miss Julie Lee, ma'am," Antonio had said mockingly in the Southern drawl he'd heard so much of late and had grown to hate. "We niggas gotta learn the ways of white folks, 'cause it's a white world. We ain't in no Africa here. Just a lot of white folks, and we niggas here to serve them."

She was taken off guard when Antonio's tone became deadly serious and went on in his normal voice. "I'm not a person to give anybody much advice, especially a woman like you, Julie Lee, but as long as you live, whether slave or free, don't ever go to sleep on white folks, or you just might find yourself dead.

"Don't get me wrong, there are good white folks. I was raised by white folks, and they were good people, maybe the best I'll ever meet in this life, but believe me, Julie Lee, there was never a time that I didn't remember that I was black and they were white. Sometimes they'd be talking about something, and when I'd walk into the room, they would just stop. I can't tell you how many times I knew inside that they were talking about me.

"But like I said, there are good white folks and bad ones. Unfortunately, most of us never get much opportunity to know which is which, and that, young lady, can be fatal. You never know what side of the mask they're peeking out from at any time."

When he stopped talking, the muscles in his face sagged and relaxed, and in just moments it seemed as if he'd never touched on a subject that was obviously so meaningful and painful to him.

Here they were two travelers on the same road dependent on each other for their very survival, and they were just beginning to know each other. She wondered how he could play-act so carefree a fellow when there was obviously so much on his mind. She had always thought that, having been free, he hadn't known much pain. Didn't being free *mean* no pain?

She looked into his eyes and she said softly, "I'll always remember what you said, Antonio, and I'll never forget where I learnt it from neither."

Since they'd arrived in Richmond, Julie Lee was so grateful that her mother had taught her to read and write a little. In fact, Julie Lee believed the most difficult task she had had thus far was signing the hotel guest book, but some of her nervousness dissolved when she scanned its contents after the clerk had pushed it toward her. My God, she thought, these people writes even worser than me. But following their leads, she scribbled Annabelle Brownless across the ledger, just as she and Antonio had practiced. Even as she was writing, she knew no one would be able to make out what it said.

"So that's how white folks do it?" she said to Antonio afterward. "They just puts down some chicken scratch and call that letters. They just spreads that scratch all over the paper and say they signing they name."

She wished that she could eat with Antonio since they had so much to talk about, but such was not the case. Slaves were not permitted to eat in the hotel's main dining room, and the same was true for any free Negroes who might be around. As he headed off in the direction of the long, low building attached to the hotel where the servants and slaves had to eat and sleep, Antonio quickly squeezed her hand, as if to give her encouragement.

But they would be together soon because Julie Lee, as Antonio had instructed, requested an attached room for

Antonio furnished with a pallet. Such a request, according to Antonio, would not be thought unusual since many whites when traveling preferred to have their servants nearby should they need anything.

The desk clerk readily complied with the request and promised Julie Lee that he would have a pallet sent up for Antonio well before bedtime. Even though it was a rather mundane and routine request, Julie Lee couldn't help but notice the rather lewd smirk on the pimply-faced clerk when she requested the accommodations. Of course, he said nothing. Such affairs were common, but illegal.

At dinner she requested a table in a rather dark corner of the dining room. Julie Lee had served enough big house dinners to know which implements to use for which foods. She wanted to make every effort to be careful, and she certainly didn't want to be out in the open and take the risk of being recognized by some of the old master's friends who just might happen upon the Palace that day.

From her vantage point, she could see the other diners. Her attention was quickly drawn to a trio of well-dressed women sitting at a table not far from hers. Whatever they were talking about must have been wildly amusing since the women cackled so loud that other diners looked up in annoyance.

Off to her left, Julie Lee saw someone peeking from behind a curtain. The man was wearing a big, white chef's hat. Julie Lee had never seen anyone who looked like that. He was small in stature, but his eyes were slanted, almost as if they were closed. He didn't look white and he didn't look black either. My God, she thought, what kind of man is that? They sure do got all kind of people up here in the city!

She finished her meal, but she'd been too nervous to

enjoy it, and besides, the meat wasn't cooked rare the way she liked. She was about to order a cup of tea when a striking, blond-haired man came and stood in front of the table.

"Excuse me, ma'am," the man said pleasantly, "I don't mean to be forward or to interrupt your meal, but is it possible that I have seen you before?"

Lord, she thought, please don't let him see my hands trembling! Still, she said nothing, hoping that the man would be discouraged from pursuing the conversation. He persisted.

"Oh, pardon me, ma'am," he started up again. "I haven't yet introduced myself. I am Jay Langston of the Langston plantation in Natchez. I thought perhaps that I had seen you before down my way."

She'd never even heard of Natchez and certainly had no idea of where it was, nor how far it was from Richmond. It could have been a mile away, or a hundred miles, she just didn't know.

She realized, however, that the man had no intention of giving up and that it might be best if she said something to get him moving along. "No sir, I can't say that I've been there," she said. Without realizing it, Julie Lee pressed a finger to her neck, feeling through her dress the talisman Jeddah had given her for luck. If you is really good magic, Julie Lee thought, do your stuff right now and get this man away from me.

Her heart dropped when the man, without any invitation, pulled out one of the three empty chairs at the table and sat down. Now that he was at eye level, Julie Lee was more than convinced that she had never seen him before. That, at least, was a relief.

"I'm not usually this forward," he explained pleasantly, "but I swear I've seen you in my neck of the woods. Maybe you've got a double. I'm trying to—"

She cut him off in midsentence and tried to sound as rude as Whilomene had when she no longer wanted to be bothered. "Sir, I've told you, I've never seen you before."

Much to her amazement and chagrin, Langston pressed on. "But I could swear—pardon me, ma'am, but what did you say your name was?"

"I didn't," she replied, certain that her face had turned red.

While waiting to see what his response would be, she scanned Langston's face and stature. He wasn't a bad-looking man. He had the smooth, flawless skin, the pampered look of many of the young men who'd come to visit Andy Jr. at the Lorelei from time to time. And she could tell by the fine clothes he wore and the fine fabric that they were made from that he was a man of some wealth. She guessed him to be a few years older than herself, maybe in his midtwenties.

As they sat in uncomfortable silence, she realized that his knee was brushing up against hers beneath the table. She moved back instinctively. "Please, sir," she said in a tone which begged him to excuse himself.

Still Langston refused to be deterred. "I'm here on business for my daddy. Been out here for three weeks now. A man sure does get lonesome so far away from home. It seems quite impossible that a woman as beautiful as yourself would be traveling alone in these very desperate times with the threat of war hanging in the air."

There was something in the tone of his voice that suggested he wasn't going to be shaken off until he was good and ready.

The waiter had no idea how much Julie Lee welcomed his intrusion when he sauntered over to ask if she wanted coffee. He also asked Langston if he wanted to order anything. But before he could answer she announced suddenly, "Excuse me, Mr. Langston, but I've got to go back to my room and fetch my servant. Good evening."

As she rose to leave, Langston pulled her chair out for her. His eyes caught hers, and he stared unabashedly. Did he know? Did he suspect that she was traveling incognito? Even worse, had he seen through her pretense and realized that she wasn't really white? Whatever he thought, she was determined to exit as quickly as possible.

She could still feel his eyes burning into her back as she walked quickly across the dining room. She was moving so fast that she brushed up against several diners as she swept past. She was afraid that Langston might follow her. He didn't. Once out of the room, she went to the front desk and asked the clerk if he would be kind enough to call Antonio from the servant's quarters. Rather than going himself, the clerk punched down on a silver bell sitting on the edge of the desk. At the sound, one of the red-coated black men she'd seen earlier rushed toward the desk.

She was still standing there in the lobby waiting for Antonio when Langston came out of the dining room. Fearing that he would come toward her, she turned her head away quickly, but not quickly enough. From the corner of her eye, she caught sight of Langston tipping his hat in her direction as he strolled out the front door.

The feeling was more than relief when she finally saw Antonio's familiar grin coming through the side doorway. She said nothing to him, but indicated with a nod of her head for Antonio to follow her up to the room. Once inside, she collapsed on the bed, still trembling, as she related to Antonio what had happened to her downstairs.

When he realized how truly frightened she had been
by the experience, Antonio tried to soothe her and spoke in
soft tones. "Don't worry, Julie Lee. The man was simply
doing what men do sometimes when they've been traveling a long while and haven't had the pleasure of a woman's company. After all, you're a good-looking woman."

Before she knew what was happening Antonio had
seized her by the arms and had pulled her off the bed. He
was propelling her toward the large mirror that hung over
the dresser.

She did not rebel as he undid the laces of her bonnet,
lifted it off her head and took the pins out of her hair.
When he was done, he took her chin and forced her to
look straight ahead into the mirror. "Look here, Julie Lee.
What do you see?"

Though she stared at the image staring back at him,
she still didn't understand what he meant. Oh, she knew
she wasn't ugly, but that was only because she'd never
worked too hard and bore none of the early aging signs of
most slaves.

Antonio went on, "Of course men are going to try to
talk to you, Julie Lee. What happened to you downstairs is
going to happen at least a thousand more times before you
die. Face it, woman, you're pretty. No, I take that back,
you're beautiful. You're beautiful as hell and you're smart
too. There aren't too many women, black or white, that are
both beautiful and smart. Why, think about all that you've
learned and done in no time. Now how many women
could do that?

"If you really were white, you'd probably have the
world at your feet. Men would be fawning and falling all
over you, and not that poor white trash either, but rich
men. What's so damn sad about it all is that they've made

178

you a nigga for so long, you don't even know what you look like."

Before long Antonio was massaging the nape of her neck. His fingers were gentle and felt good. She could feel her tension melting away, like creamery butter. She allowed him to go on for several more minutes before it dawned on her where this was all leading. She caught him off guard when she wheeled around, looked right into his face, and said angrily, "Is you crazy, nigga? Here we is running for our damned lives. These white folks could kill us for what we doing, and you here thinking about pestering me. I likes to pester as much as anybody, and when I gets free that's what I'm going to do, but when I do, it'll be with Dancer. Dancer is my man, and don't you forget it for as long as you live. Don't play with me, man. I wants to get free and that's all."

Not really surprised by her outburst, Antonio backed off but looked at her sheepishly and said, "I'm only a man, Julie Lee, only a man."

Chapter 23

Julie Lee found sleep difficult to come by that night. The ghosts were walking and talking. First, there was Dancer. She could have sworn that he sat right down on the bed and talked with her. Little John's image kept fading in and out, but she could hear him crying clear as a bell. Finally, Roxie came, but only for a moment. There was concern on Roxie's face. She didn't have very much to say, but she asked one question: "Do you know what you doing, child?"

By the time daylight began streaming in through the thin lace curtains at the window, she couldn't remember if she'd even tried to answer her dead mother's question. Did she know what she doing? No, not really, she thought, but it didn't make any difference anyhow. She couldn't go back. Surely by now the old master had spread the word that two of his niggas had run. Surely by now the young master, her own father, was leading a group of his friends through the woods trying to find her and Antonio, swearing with every step that he would kill them if he caught them. The penalty for trying to escape, she knew, was not negotiable. How many, many times had she heard the old master say that running niggas were dangerous niggas since they only served to give others ideas about doing the same. "Can't do nothing with a runaway but kill him," was the motto he lived by.

As she sat there, she wondered what it was that always made her feel different than most of the other slaves about their condition. What was it that always made her feel like she could take on the whole damned world and win? Why couldn't she just enjoy her status as one of the privileged house slaves. She didn't work too hard, and certainly hadn't suffered too many beatings. Why couldn't she just have sat back and waited for freedom to come? After all, hadn't she heard the white folks say that there might be a war? A war over the niggas, they said.

As always, she answered her own questions. She was not like everybody else—never had been, for that matter—and it wasn't just because her skin was white. She just knew that God hadn't intended for one group of people to own another, for one to buy and sell the other at will, to beat them and maim them, to kill them, to make them have babies every nine months. No, there was just something wrong about that. She understood enough of the Bible to know that it was wrong, plain and simple.

Her thinking was interrupted by Antonio's stirrings in the next room. He hadn't gotten much sleep either, having spent most of the night running to her bedside trying to comfort her whenever she cried out in her sleep. She had no recollection of Antonio coming on one occasion and gently stroking her hair when she had called out for Dancer. She had even reached up and stroked his face.

Now he stumbled into the room, disheveled. He'd slept with all his clothes on, not wanting her to get suspicious about his motives.

181

"Julie Lee, girl, I think we best get moving. Time for us to put some more road between us and the Lorelei."

She agreed.

They were starting to map out their plan for the day when a knock came at the door. It startled them both. "Ask who it is," Antonio whispered hurriedly. She obeyed without question.

The voice from outside the door sounded like a black. "It's just me, the water boy, ma'am. I come to bring your water so you can get a good washin'."

Before she could answer, Antonio said, "Tell him to leave it outside the door." And when they heard a pail touch the floor, they knew the boy had complied. They listened for his footsteps as he moved on down the hall.

They washed and dressed quickly, and before an hour had passed were safely out of the hotel and back on the open road again. As Richmond's skyline began to fade in the horizon, they both relaxed a bit.

The ride was going along smoothly and Antonio had gotten directions as far as some place called Coatesville. The man giving the directions said it was just on the other side of the Maryland border. If they rode hard, the man had said, they could be in Maryland before nightfall.

Julie Lee had fallen asleep when the carriage suddenly lurched forward and stopped. Automatically she stuck her head out of the window to see what was going on. Antonio had already jumped down. His face was long and disgusted as he looked at one of the carriage wheels. Apparently they'd ridden over a big rock and now the wheel's rim was bent in several places. Antonio stood there looking at it, wondering what in the world they were going to do now. He walked several feet away from the carriage, looking for something he could use to smooth out the wheel so they could get going again. He'd just found a heavy rock that he thought would do the job when a group of riders came up fast. They were all white.

Oh, my God, he thought, we've been caught. And just as he had heard many people say when they thought they were going to die, his own life passed in front of him, from childhood right up to the moment.

He was standing with the stone in his hand when one of the men pulled his horse up so close to him that he thought he would be knocked over.

"What you doing, boy?" the man snarled.

He looked particularly mean, Antonio thought. His clothes were filthy with road dust and he had a heavy beard. When he opened his mouth his teeth were yellowed from chewing snuff.

Despite the man's appearance, Antonio figured it best to say something and to say it quickly, lest he inadvertently arouse the man's suspicions.

"I'se just trying to find something to fix the wheel for my lady's carriage," Antonio stammered out with due deference.

"Your lady?" the man snarled again.

Without another word, Antonio pointed in the direction of the carriage. Though she hadn't gotten out yet, Julie Lee could hear what they were saying. Springing into action, she stepped down from the carriage daintily, and she put upon her face the most distressed look she could conjure.

"Good day, ma'am," the men said almost in unison when she approached them.

She smiled sweetly and in her honeyed voice poured out her unhappy tale about making her way to visit her sick and dying sister in Philadelphia. Even as she was telling the story, she could feel the eyes of one of the men penetrating through her dress. It was a most uncomfortable feeling, and suddenly she thought it was possible that the men might try to rape her and kill Antonio.

She was quite relieved, however, when the one who was doing all the talking spoke up again. "Sure am sorry to hear about your problems, ma'am."

Her heart was beating so fast she thought it would pop right out of her dress. And poor Antonio. She could almost hear his knees knocking in fear.

The man ordered two of his companions to help get the wheel straightened out. "Wouldn't want to have a pretty little lady like you in trouble out here and all alone with nothing but a nigga to protect you."

Taking off the wheel, straightening it out and putting it back on took the better part of an hour, and during most of that time the man who'd addressed them chatted with Julie Lee. Every once in a while Antonio would look up nervously, hoping that Julie Lee would bear up under the pressure and not say anything that might give them away. He could barely focus his attention on what he was doing, he was just so scared. A wrong word and that would be that. It was obvious by now that the men weren't looking for them.

Just as the others had finished with the wheel, the man admonished Julie Lee to be careful. "You better watch out little lady," he said. "There's a lot of runaway niggas round these parts, trying to get up North. They'd be real hot for a pretty white woman, if you don't mind my being so blunt."

She thought to herself, I think I'd rather take my

chance with any nigga than with that man you got with you.

"Thank you so much for your kindness, sir," she replied. After he helped her back up into the carriage and Antonio had taken his place in the driver's seat, Julie Lee had expected the strangers to leave, but they didn't.

They offered to ride along with them for a few miles just to give her some added protection. Despite all her pleas that they would be fine, the man insisted.

Julie Lee and Antonio were relieved when after about five miles the men begged off, saying they had business to attend to that was off in another direction.

Before he rode off, however, the man came up beside the carriage and said to Julie Lee, who had stuck her head out the window, "Remember what I told you, little lady. You better be real careful. I got a daughter myself about your age, and I know I wouldn't have allowed her to come this far practically by herself. But since you done come this far, all I got to say is, you take care. You hear?"

Then he galloped up front and yelled to Antonio, "Take care your mistress, boy, and don't you let nothing happen to her."

"Yes sir, sir," Antonio said back quickly.

The men were still in sight when Antonio whirled his whip over his head, admonishing the horses to move faster. The sweat poured down and burned his eyes. He'd never been so scared in all his life.

They rode for another hour before Antonio stopped the carriage again. This time there was no emergency, but he knew he had to get the horses some water and let them rest a bit. So far, they'd performed valiantly, and he thanked God for that. "Something has got to go right on this trip," he grumbled to himself.

From the way the horses greedily lapped up the water in the small stream once Antonio had released them from their harnesses, it was obvious that he had stopped none too soon.

While the animals drank, Julie Lee and Antonio sat down on a grassy spot beneath a tree. By now they were looking pretty filthy and dusty themselves. Julie Lee couldn't decide whether she was more tired or more hungry.

"I'm about to fall out, Antonio. It's so hot inside that carriage and them leather seats done started to stinking."

Antonio was sympathetic. "I know all this is hard on you, Julie Lee. It's hard on me too. But if you want to be free, you must understand that you have to suffer some. Even after you're free, there will still be suffering. Freedom is good, but it is not without its drawbacks."

She allowed herself to rest her head on his chest. "Oh, Antonio, I miss my people something terrible, and we ain't hardly been gone more than a minute. I wonder what Dancer, little John, Katy, Zeph and Hannibal is doing right now. Sure do hope Old Massa ain't took it out on them 'cause me and you done run away. I sure hope too that they ain't thinking that they ain't never gonna see me no more 'cause I'm going back someday and when I does, I'm taking them right on up to freedom too. I want Katy to get a chance to see freedom one time before she close her eyes, and I want Dancer to get his chance to sing, to sing free. You know what I mean?"

Antonio smiled at her and nodded his head.

They both stood up and were brushing off their clothes when a little mutt ran up to them. Though he was barking furiously, he appeared to be more afraid of them than they were of him.

She was wondering where the animal had come from

186

when her eyes came to rest on three little blond-haired boys who stood staring tentatively several feet away. The oldest, she figured, was no more than nine or ten. The dog ran toward the boys when they called out his name, "Charlie! Charlie!" He jumped right up into the arms of the boy who appeared to be the youngest of the trio.

From where he was standing, and without moving any closer, the oldest-looking boy demanded, "What you doing on our land?"

She looked at the children and decided to respond warmly, despite the boy's coldness.

"We're sorry. We didn't know we was on anybody's land. We just stopped because our horses wanted some water to drink. They were really thirsty. You know how it is when horses get thirsty."

The boys continued staring silently at them. Their little eyes were full of questions. They stood there a few more moments, then, almost as if on cue, they all turned and ran away with the little dog following close behind them.

Curious as to where they'd come from and where they were going, Julie Lee walked up to the top of the rise on which they'd been standing. From that vantage point she could see a farmhouse nearby. Sitting there all by itself, it looked pitiful and rather lonely, she thought.

There was longing in her eyes when she turned around and faced Antonio. He dreaded what she might be thinking.

"Maybe we could go up there and get something to eat," she said finally, pointing in the direction of the farm.

He walked to where she was standing and looked at the house. "I don't think that's such a good idea, Julie Lee. We still have a long way to go. We can't afford the luxury of an easy pace. Have you forgotten? We're escaped slaves, and the penalty is death."

She ignored his logic. "Aw, come on, Antonio," she insisted, this time pulling his hands. "You're such a fraidy cat. I'm willing to take the chance. Those boys seemed nice enough. Sure they were scared, but they didn't seem to be so bad."

"Julie Lee," he said with an edge of exasperation in his voice. "Those boys have a mother and a father, and maybe several other relatives up there in that house. We have no idea what kind of people they are."

But she kept begging, knowing that before long she would wear him down and he would relent. "Come on, Antonio," she said sweetly, stretching out the vowels in his name. "Come on. Maybe the people is nice."

Finally he caved in as she knew he would and soon they were both walking toward the farmhouse, with the horses and the carriage behind them.

As they came closer to the place, Julie Lee was struck by its trim neatness, particularly the vegetable patch off to the right of the front porch. And there were nice, fluffy curtains at the windows.

She was trying to imagine what the boys' family was like when the little dog, Charlie, ran up to them again. Close behind him were the three boys, only this time, they didn't seem so cautious, and in fact, appeared rather friendly and open.

Before long the front door of the house opened, and through its portal came a woman, very much pregnant, who was pointing directly at them with a long-barreled shotgun. "Stop right there," the woman called out. "And you children, get on over here behind me." In an instant, the boys were peeking from behind the woman's skirts.

Deciding to take a chance, Julie Lee advanced a few steps forward, careful to put a wide, open smile on her face, just so the woman would know that they didn't mean her or her family any harm.

"Please, ma'am," she offered pleasantly, "me and my boy here aren't looking to hurt you and yours. We're just tired and hungry after riding all this way. We thought that maybe you could give us a bite to eat, and then we'd be on our way."

The woman searched Julie Lee's face to assure herself that this stranger was trustworthy. Moments later, the shotgun was lying in a corner by the fireplace and Julie Lee was sitting at the table before a plate of hot food. She didn't even know what it was, but whatever it was, it would cure the hunger that was causing her stomach to do a jig.

Meanwhile, Antonio was eating too, but he was outside on the porch. The boys had gathered around him and were asking all kinds of questions. They were most interested, however, in his accent. They'd just never heard anybody talk the way he did. They weren't sure whether to be impressed or to laugh at him, he sounded so silly.

In an effort to keep the conversation from drifting too far into her and Antonio's business, Julie Lee asked the woman, who said her name was Catherine Lucas, how many months pregnant she was.

"Oh, I guess I'm going to be having this baby anytime now. That's what the midwife said. This one'll be my seventh."

After more than an hour of conversation Julie Lee had learned much about the woman and her family. She and her husband and the children lived off their land and they didn't have company very often except when her family

189

came up to visit a few times a year. Her family lived on the eastern shore of Maryland.

The poor woman seemed so desperate for conversation that Julie Lee couldn't find it in her heart to simply eat and run. She kept ignoring Antonio's impatient glances as he looked in on them through the open doorway.

"I ain't had no female company in a coon's age," Catherine said pathetically. "Only woman I get to see regular is the midwife, and she's pretty old. Just me and Jake and the boys. I sure do hope I have a girl this time. Maybe when she grows up some, me and her can sit down and talk woman talk. All I hear round this place is crops and horses and land.

"It's a lonely life for a woman, but I guess I can't complain. Jake is a hard worker. He takes care of me and the boys just fine, and I ain't never had a hungry day since me and Jake got married. That's a whole lot different than when I was growing up. With so many people to feed as there were in my family seems like there was never quite enough food to go around. I guess that's why I married Jake so young and all. He was the first good man to come around and he promised my daddy that he would take care of me. And he's done right by me so far."

The woman talked on and on, and soon Julie Lee realized that it really wasn't necessary to say too much about herself. The woman enjoyed talking about her family.

She wondered how Catherine felt about slavery. There appeared to be no slaves on the place. She decided to pursue the subject delicately, as they were sipping hot cups of coffee.

"No indeed," Catherine said, "me and Jake ain't got much use for niggas round here. Anyway slaves cost money, and when you get them you've got to clothe and feed them, and we just trying to feed ourselves.

"Anyhow, Jake always says he don't put too much stock in slavery. He says one day the South is gonna be sorry for putting all its concern on a bunch of niggas. Says he believes one day the niggas is gonna get tired and up and rebel, and then there's gonna be bloodshed. To his way of thinking, the niggas ain't got much to lose, but the white folks do.

"We don't go to church too often 'cause it's just too far away, but Jake is a man what believes in the Bible, and he said slavery just ain't right. It's a mean, mean thing, that slavery. They got a lot of nigga slaves up where I come from, though of course, my family never could afford them. But my brother was working up on one of them big plantations himself, helping out the overseer. He used to come home and tell us horrible stories about what they did to the niggas. It was kind of pitiful, I mean after all niggas is black, but they is people. God made them just like he made us. You know what I mean?"

Julie Lee shook her head in agreement, pleased with Catherine's position.

"And what about you?" Catherine suddenly said abruptly, so abruptly, in fact, that Julie Lee's only response was, "What about what?"

"I mean, how do you feel about this slavery thing? I guess you believe in it, seeing as you got a nigga traveling with you to take care of you and all."

"Oh no, ma'am," Julie Lee said, forgetting that she didn't have to call Catherine ma'am.

"I mean, yes, Cleophus is my servant, but he's not really like a slave. Fact is, me and him grew up together, almost. He's more like my friend than anything else. My

191

mama and daddy only had me and my sister, and she's a lot older than me and been gone from home for a long, long time. In a way, Cleophus was sort of like the son they never had. His mama worked for my mama for years. When I was a little girl, it seemed like I didn't rightly know who my mama was 'cause Cleophus' mama nursed me just like she did her own children. Fact is, Cleophus is the only nigga my daddy would even trust me to come up and see about my sister with.''

When she finished, Julie Lee was silently proud of the story she'd concocted on the spur of the moment. She could tell from the look on Catherine's face that the woman had believed every word of it. Yes indeed, she thought, this pretending stuff is getting pretty damned easy.

The two women continued talking and after another hour or so, the front door to the house swung open dramatically. There, filling up the doorway with a massive body, was the biggest man Julie Lee had ever seen. Jake. God, but he has some big feet and hands, Julie Lee thought.

Jake Lucas was as pleasant as his wife. He was friendly and surprisingly unsuspicious about coming home and finding two absolute strangers in his home.

Before long all the children had come inside, including three older boys. The youngsters dragged Antonio behind them. They were sitting around talking as if they'd all known each other for years. What a warm and friendly home, Julie Lee kept thinking to herself. She'd never seen white folks like these in her life, but she was pleasantly surprised to know that such people did exist. She almost felt like telling them the truth about herself, but she didn't, trying hard to keep in mind what Antonio had said repeatedly: "Never go to sleep on white folks, Julie Lee."

Suddenly Julie Lee looked out the window and noticed that the light was completely gone. Jake and Catherine insisted that they stay the night.

"I guess y'all is gonna have to stay anyway, 'cause you sure ain't gonna get too far with that wheel bent up the way it is. I took a good look at it before I came in and I ain't sure how y'all even got this far. That wheel needs to be fixed by the smitty, seems to me."

Considering the seriousness of her trip, Jake suggested an alternative. Both Julie Lee and Antonio could have kicked themselves for not thinking of it themselves.

"Why don't y'all just take the train on into Philadelphia," he said. " 'Course Cleophus here can't ride up front with you in the white folk's car, but they got places for the niggas too. We'll keep the carriage for you, and I'll get it fixed soon as I go into town. You can pick it up on your way back."

Now why hadn't they thought of that? They certainly had enough money to take the train, and it wasn't exactly the smartest thing in the world to be riding around in the old master's carriage. For two people desperate to get toward freedom, they sure weren't thinking too good.

It was settled then and there. After lunch the next day Jake would drive them into town where they could get a train at about three o'clock. Since the train was only a local, however, Jake said that they would have to ride as far as Baltimore and there change to a train that would take them straight into Philadelphia.

Catherine put the older boys out of their room so Julie Lee could have a little privacy. Poor Catherine, she was so excited and so glad for the company.

Antonio slept on the floor again, but not because he was a nigga or a servant. There was just no other place to sleep.

When they both finally dropped off, it was the first sound, restful sleep either of them had had since leaving the Lorelei. And as she drifted off into the deep black hole of darkness and rest, Julie Lee once again fingered the good luck charm around her neck and said softly, ''Thank you, God. Thank you.'' She had no dreams that night.

Chapter 24

Catherine had prepared a large lunch, and everybody, including Antonio, sat down at the long wooden table to eat. Even Jake came back from the fields to join them, something he rarely did, as he preferred to take his food with him when he left in the mornings.

Julie Lee had not yet ceased to be amazed by these white people, for she'd never known folks like the Lucases where she came from. How she would miss them when it came time to leave, and what little chance there would be that she'd ever see them again.

Earlier that morning, Jake announced, much to Catherine's surprise and delight, that the trip to the railroad station would be a family outing. Everyone would go. He seemed so shy, and so much smaller, when he playfully put his huge arm around Catherine's neck and said, "Little lady, you ain't been out in a while, and I think Miss Brownless here done give me a reason to give you a treat. After we get them on the train, you and me and the young 'uns, why, we gonna go and do ourselves a little shopping. Everybody could use a new pair of shoes, and I got a little money saved up." Then, with a twinkle in his eye, Jake added dramatically, ''And we gonna get a fine and pretty blanket for the new baby. Maybe we'll even get a pink one, since I know how much you want a little girl.''

Catherine's smile was as bright as sunshine. And Julie Lee, touched by the little scene, smiled just as brightly.

After the last sweet roll had been eaten and the dishes cleared away, it was time to leave. Jake had hitched up the wagon and by the time he pulled it up in front of the house, the boys and Antonio were already inside. One of the older ones jumped down to help his mother and Julie Lee to the front seat they would share with his father.

There was a lot of laughter during the ride, and Julie Lee almost forgot that she and Antonio were running. Catherine displayed a more than fair voice when she broke into a song. Pretty soon the boys had joined in, and once she'd gotten down the words, Julie Lee sang too.

The town, as it turned out, was little more than one main street, which had on one side a general store, a feed and grain shop and a blacksmith's shack. On the other side there was a bar, a little café, and much to Julie Lee's surprise, a run-down hotel. The train depot was at the end of the dusty street, and as the wagon moved toward it, several passers-by waved. Catherine smiled gaily and waved back.

Bouncing along pleasantly in the wagon, Julie Lee was seized by a sudden panic: she had no idea how to go about buying a train ticket. What was she going to do? She looked helplessly at Antonio, but he kept a passive expression. Her mind raced, trying to figure out how she would get through this charade.

It was Jake who came to her rescue. He had no idea how glad she was when he said, ''You just stay here and talk to Catherine awhile. I'm gonna find out if the train is on time and how much it'll cost for you and Cleophus to ride to Baltimore. I expect it shouldn't be too much, though.''

"Won't you just go ahead and get the tickets, then?'' Julie Lee asked sweetly, pressing a handful of uncounted bills into his hands, which she hoped would cover the passage for two.

Within moments, Jake was back. The train would come through in twenty minutes. Not only did he hand Julie Lee the tickets, but he also returned most of the bills she'd given him. She took the tickets, but refused the money. "Oh no, Jake,'' she insisted, "I don't want any money back.''

Now it was Jake's turn to protest. "I can't take your money. You just don't know what your little stopover meant to me and my family. I ain't seen Catherine so happy since her sisters came down a few months back. Ain't that right, honey?'' he said, seeking Catherine's agreement.

Julie Lee could see that Jake was embarrassed and uncomfortable, but she wanted him to take the money gracefully. "All right,'' she finally said, looking to Antonio for approval. "So you won't take the money for yourself. How about if you take it and use it to buy something for that new baby? That way you'll have something to remind you of me and Cleophus here. We sure would be mighty proud of that, wouldn't we?''

Antonio shook his head in agreement. What else could he do? he thought, all the while worried that they would still need money to get through the rest of the trip.

It took a little more convincing, but Jake finally broke down and took the bills. Much to Julie Lee's surprise, he leaned over and pecked her on the cheek. She swore she could feel a tiny teardrop slide down his face. Unconsciously, Julie Lee looked in Catherine's direction. She was just standing and smiling in approval.

Before long, the train was pulling into the station, and when the whistle blew unexpectedly, Julie Lee nearly jumped out of her skin in fright. She laughed nervously at herself, then casually but deliberately stepped back several feet from the track to give the train room—plenty of room. She didn't like the looks of the contraption.

Jake had already warned her that Cleophus wouldn't be allowed to ride with her in the white folks' car, but would instead have to ride with the freight and the baggage, so Antonio shuffled down to the end of the loading platform. Then a red-faced conductor took a gold watch and chain from his pocket, checked the time and sang out, "All aboard!" Jake still had Julie Lee's suitcase in his hand as he helped her up the small iron steps to the car. Besides Antonio, she was the only passenger getting on.

She had no idea what she would find once she got inside the train, and she was disappointed when it turned out to be nothing fancy. Most of the seats had worn upholstery, and the windows were so dingy that she could barely see out. Fortunately, Julie Lee was able to find a double seat unoccupied. With her bare hand, she cleared a small space in the window and looked out at Jake and Catherine and the children. They were all standing in a line, waving vigorously. She waved back. She would never forget them, the first white people she'd ever seen who had treated her like a real human being. She wondered, though, if they would have been so hospitable had they known that she was as much a black as Antonio. It was a question for which she would never have an answer.

Chapter 25

She was amazed at how fast the train was moving. The countryside went whizzing by so quickly that her eyes could hardly adjust, and her stomach began to grow queasy. Then she was overcome with a sudden surge of panic, and she gripped the arms of her seat so tightly that her knuckles turned red where the blood had rushed to the pressure point.

Noticing her uncomfortable predicament, the conductor, a fat, jolly-faced man, stopped near her seat and said in a friendly tone, "Just try to relax, little lady. We ain't never lost a passenger yet."

She blushed with embarrassment, but the conductor's good-natured smile did seem to relax her. Then, tearing off the bottom half of her ticket, he moved on toward the back of the car.

She moved forward slightly, trying to judge from the backs of heads how many passengers were in the car. It was then that she noticed a woman, sitting in the seat in front of her, rocking a young baby in her arms. When the woman shifted position, the baby's tiny head popped up over the top of the seat and Julie Lee could see it clearly.

He appeared just a bit younger than little John. His tiny eyes were wide open, and he was dribbling down the side of his face, the way little John always did. And when he cooed, she thought, he even sounded a little like John. She couldn't suppress the smile that spread across her face.

She found herself wishing she could feel the familiar tug of John's tiny arms encircling her neck, his gurgling in her ear and wet kisses, his little head bumping up against her face.

It had been nearly three days and she had thought of little John and Dancer constantly. She missed the pressure of Dancer's body closing down on hers in the dark when everything was quiet outside. The natural smell of his body, the way his hair flattened out as he sweated during their lovemaking.

Wet, salty tears slid down her face, and she felt rather relieved after her brief cry. She pressed her face against the glass. Her body sagged as if a ten-ton weight had been dropped in her lap.

Oh, how she hoped she had done the right thing, leaving her man, her baby, to find freedom.

Three cars back, sandwiched in between luggage and parcels and boxes of all kinds, Antonio stretched his body out to its full length. Looking down through the slats, he could see the gleaming tracks racing by. He raised his head and looked at all the boxes the train had collected on the numerous local stops it had made. He even took a few moments to read some of the destination tags.

Quickly becoming bored with the exercise, he turned his thoughts to other things. That baggage car certainly wasn't the most comfortable place he'd ever been, but compared to the plantation, this was paradise.

The rocking motions of the train began to make him feel drowsy. He thought about Baltimore, the first destination on this leg of their journey. Baltimore was still the South, but he would feel more comfortable there because they would be unlikely to bump into any of Master Andy's friends.

After Baltimore, they would have to get through Delaware, another slave-holding state, and then it was on to Philadelphia. He warmed at the thought. Everything he'd ever read about the city of brotherly love suggested that it was one place where even Negroes could find some measure of freedom—and prosperity if they had the wherewithal to do it. With that happy thought, he dozed off into a sound sleep.

After several brief stops in little towns, one uglier than the next, the conductor walked through the car, calling out in an animated voice, "Fifteen minutes to *Bal*timore!"

Julie Lee sat up in her seat. She was weary and bone-tired. The train swerved a bit as it rounded a bend and began making its way into the city.

He was in the next car, but Julie Lee could hear from where she was sitting when the conductor again bellowed, "*BAL*timore. *BAL*timore. Last stop."

Baltimore, she thought. It was only a word. She had no idea what kind of place it was or what kind of people lived there. She didn't even know exactly where it was, except that it was north of Richmond and far away from the Lorelei.

Before long, the train passed under a dark underpass. It scared her and she couldn't help thinking what would happen if that little rise fell down on top of the train.

201

Even before the train came to a complete stop at the station the other passengers were standing in the aisles, but she didn't dare. She was afraid that she would fall down.

Soon the passengers had herded up toward the front of the car where she was sitting, and more than once, their bags brushed up against her head. She wondered why they were rushing since nobody could get off until the train stopped anyway.

She waited until all the other passengers had exited the car before pinning her hat back on. When it came her turn to get off, she momentarily panicked, not sure what to do next. She was relieved to see the smiling conductor when he appeared at the door through which the other passengers had left the car. He held out his hand to her and helped her down the three metal steps to the station platform.

As her foot touched the ground, the conductor, once again with sparkling eyes said, "Hope you enjoyed your first train ride, little lady. Come see us again."

"Thank you," she said moving away toward the station house. "Bye, now."

The platform was alive with people coming and going. Her eyes scanned the throng frantically searching for Antonio. Where was he? she thought as she stood there, clutching tightly onto the small bag she'd been carrying ever since they left the Lorelei. After all it had been through, the brocaded fabric bag looked a might dusty and its sides were bent since she did not have enough clothes in it to fill it up.

When Antonio finally emerged from the crowd, a big smile spread across his face. God, he sure looks a mess, Julie Lee thought. But haggard or not, Antonio looked mighty good to her in this crowd of strangers. She smiled back at him and before she knew it he was right up beside her, taking the bag out of her hands, and whispering instructions in her ear.

Following the flow of the crowd she made her way to the station master and asked about getting tickets to Philadelphia.

"Sorry, ma'am, but the tracks are all washed out up ahead, and there won't be nothing going out of here tonight. I expect that you and your boy," he said motioning toward Antonio who was standing nearby, "gonna have to find yourself some place to stay the night. Maybe you'll be able to get something out tomorrow, but ain't no way of telling now."

She was devastated by the news. In frustration and disgust she turned away from the man.

She wanted to cry. "I don't wanna stay in no Baltimore. I just wanna get to Philadelphia," she said under her breath to Antonio.

"Lord, Antonio, we don't know anything about Baltimore, and now we gotta find ourselves some place to sleep and get ourselves something to eat. Lord, we been riding so long, and now we ain't even going nowhere. If I would have known this, we could've stayed with Jake and Catherine for another day or so."

"Don't cry, Julie Lee. We're all right. Just think how well we've been living. What do you think most runaways have to contend with? I assure you they do *not* stay in hotels and travel first-class. They have to travel by night, through the woods, on foot, in all kinds of weather. You ought to be ashamed of yourself, crying like that."

"But I ain't ashamed, I'm scared. Don't know nothing about no Baltimore, and I don't know too much about no other niggas escaping, since ain't nary one never came back and told me how they got away."

"Take my word for it, Julie Lee, we're doing much better than most. And besides, I don't think we'll have to stay here more than a day. They'll get the tracks fixed, and then we'll leave first thing."

They walked out into the street, with Antonio following behind her at a respectable distance.

"We'll look around to see if we can find ourselves something to eat and some place to stay the night, or maybe *you* can find us some place to stay," he said. Baltimore was north of Richmond, but it wasn't *that* far up from the South. "I don't imagine we'd be permitted to dine together in this city any more than we would have in Richmond."

It was growing dark as they wandered through the streets. Suddenly a carriage went speeding by and splashed water up from a dirty, stagnant puddle in the street onto Julie Lee's dress.

Now she really wanted to cry. "Oh, my God, Antonio, look at me. Lord, I'm getting sorrier by the minute that I ever ran away from the Lorelei. This city life is too much for me. I wish we'd never gotten on that train. What I know about a train? What I know about Baltimore? What I know about anything?" She began sobbing uncontrollably.

He was rapidly becoming impatient with her. She had to pull herself together. This game they were playing was dangerous enough as it was.

He almost snapped at her, but he caught himself. How could he get mad at her? After all, she was out of her element, far away from the Lorelei and far away from anything she had ever known or imagined.

Just then a white man walked by, and from the look he gave them, it was clear that he suspected they were up to no good.

Antonio tried to think of something quickly. They had to get a move on, for they couldn't walk the streets all night.

"Julie Lee, why don't you go on back in the station while I look around and see what I can find."

By the time she'd agreed and reluctantly gone back inside, the crowd had thinned considerably.

She sat on a long wooden bench not far from the door. She was hungry and scared, so scared that she sat rooted to the spot, afraid to say anything to anyone. She began to suffer from powerful pangs of hunger in the pit of her stomach. The time seemed to drag. After an hour or so, she realized that Antonio had been gone an awfully long time. She didn't want to panic again. No, she did not want to draw any unnecessary attention to herself, so she sat a little longer.

Suppose something has happened to him? she worried. What was she going to do? Where was she going to go? She would be lost without him. "Oh God," she muttered under her breath, "don't let Antonio be lost."

After a while, she figured she had to do something. The station was getting emptier and emptier and still there was no sign of him. There was nothing else to do. She would have to go outside to try to find him.

When she went out of the station, she looked in both directions, perplexed and frightened. She decided to walk to the left. She hadn't gotten far from the station when she realized she was not in what would be considered a safe neighborhood.

She continued to walk. By now the sky was completely dark and the street seemed eerie, and all the more frightening because she was alone.

She tried to stay close to the low buildings, but in a

while a trio of men turned a corner together. They were drunk.

She attempted to move out of their path, but the men quickly spread in a line in front of her. In order to get past, she would have to push her way through. In a mighty effort to be calm, she said, with no little bit of arrogance, "Excuse me, gentlemen."

One of the three laughed out loud. "Why, I ain't been called a gentleman in years."

"Fool, you ain't never been called a gentleman in all your life," one of the others replied.

She tried to ignore them, but when she attempted to get past, they encircled her. One of the men tipped his hat in mock courtesy. He then stuck out his tongue and wiped it around the edges of his lips. It was a suggestive and nasty gesture. She knew she was in trouble.

"Please, sir," she trembled, "please let me by."

"Naw, ma'am, don't think I can do that," one of the men said, and he began advancing toward her. In seconds, two of them were dragging her toward a dark alley between two buildings. She screamed, but there was no one around to hear her.

She tried to struggle out of the men's grip on her arms, even as they drew her deeper into the shadows. Suddenly a huge fist slammed down into the very center of her face. The blood rushed to her head, and when she looked down, bright red drops were running down her dress. Her scream was cut short by the hand that clamped down over her mouth with such force that she nearly lost her breath.

They were pulling her to the ground, and she could hear them laughing.

"I seen her first, so I should have her first," one voice said.

"Naw," said the other, "I'm going first."

The third man, apparently disgusted with his two friends, said, "Listen, y'all stop all that goddamned arguing about who gonna go first. Take your turns and I'll keep watch out here on the street. When y'all two is finished, then I'm gonna get me some."

When the man removed his hand from her mouth, she realized that screaming out again was useless. She tried another approach. Maybe it would work. In the kindest voice she could summon up, she said, "Please don't hurt me, please. I ain't done nothing to y'all. Please."

"Naw, you ain't done nothing yet, but you gonna," one of the men sneered.

It was so dark that she couldn't see, but she could hear her dress coming apart as the two men ripped it from her body. When her breasts fell out, one of the men squealed with delight.

"Gawd damn, Wendell, the girl got titties, real big titties. I likes them big-tittied women, I does."

Soon the hands were all over her chest and other hands were trying to force her legs apart. She lay there on the hard ground, afraid to move, afraid to scream, afraid to talk—just afraid.

Her face was wet from sweating, and from the men slobbering on her. She felt sick.

Then she was nearly naked. One man pinned her arms to the ground while the other anxiously pulled out his private parts.

She turned her face away, not wanting to watch what was coming next, but she couldn't turn her body away. The sudden intrusion of his lance sent a wave of pain through her. The man was large and rough and he hurt her. He didn't care. He continued forcing it in, higher and higher. At the same time, he started sucking on her neck and, even to her disgust, tried to say some endearing words as he continued to force himself on her. The more she attempted to twist and turn away to keep him from hurting her so badly, the more the man seemed to enjoy it. When he started to pant like a wild dog, she knew the end was near. There was an explosion of hot liquid inside of her. The sticky stuff oozed down the sides of her thighs. He wanted to lie there on top of her a few more minutes, just to catch his breath and to savor her, but his eager friend pulled him off her and jumped down in his place.

They ignored her cry. Her back was stiff and sore from being on the hard ground. She was so wet from the first intruder that by the time the second had mounted her, his organ slid right in. It was small, mercifully, she thought.

She turned her head back again and faced the man eye to eye. He was riding her like a bronco and kept jerking his body and quivering. He laughed and muttered, ''Move bitch, move,'' slapping the sides of her thighs. He was the meanest of the three, but at least he was quick. It didn't take him long at all to finish.

She had never felt so helpless in her life. She was exhausted and revolted. She had thought she was running to freedom, and instead, here she was a slave again, and not to fine white people, but to low-down dirty white trash. And she realized that it didn't matter that she had white skin, she was being treated just like a nigga anyway.

By the time the men had switched places again and the third man, who'd been guarding the alley, came to take his little bit, it didn't matter to her anymore. What else could they do to her? What else? Only then did it cross her mind that they might kill her. After all, she had served their purpose. Now she grew terrified and desperate.

The third man seemed to be in no hurry. Rather than quickly thrusting himself in, he stretched her open with one hand and took two fingers of the other and poked them around inside her. There was no pain now. It was too wet and soggy. Nasty, she thought. No matter how much she washed and for how long, she could never wash this nastiness away. She would never forget the stink of that alley and the greasy white hands pawing and pulling at her.

He was a foul-mouthed, vile man. He cursed her as he did his work. He continued poking, deeper and deeper. Her lips had dried up, and she could feel a sticky film starting to cake on her thighs. How could anyone want a woman after two others had already been there? she thought. But obviously it didn't bother these men. They wanted only to take.

Maybe, she kept thinking, when this one is finished, they'll just leave me alone. The two men were laughing, but once again she reminded herself that they just might kill her. She decided she really didn't have much to lose. So, the next time the man put his face close down next to hers to curse in her ear, as he had been doing all along, she pulled one hand free and raked her fingernails across his face. She wanted to leave marks. If she was going to die, she was going to make him remember her until they threw the dirt over his miserable body.

"You fucking bitch!" he winced. He began beating her. "Goddamn you!" he seethed as he punched her in the face and chest. She could feel her eyes swelling up and welts begin to rise all over her body. And then she felt nothing more.

She had no idea how long she'd lain in the alley. By the time she regained consciousness, she felt as if she had been taken apart limb by limb. She ached everywhere, from the top of her head to the tips of her toes.

Somehow, she managed to start crawling toward the edge of the alley. A few times she looked over her shoulder, wondering if the men were still there, watching her and just waiting to pounce on her again. The ground scraped her skin as she crawled. Her body was on fire.

It must have taken a half-hour for her to crawl out of the alley and into the street. Her strength had gone. She turned her face just in time to see a foot almost come right down on it.

"Oh, my God," the owner of the foot gasped.

The man standing above her knelt by her and turned her over on her back. Then he lifted her head, balancing it on his thighs.

"Who did this to you? Who did this?" he kept asking. Her lips had ballooned out to two or three times their normal size and she could not answer. She couldn't even whisper. And then all went black, and she heard nothing.

Chapter 26

Antonio was frantic. He looked everywhere, but Julie Lee was nowhere in sight. She wasn't in the station or anywhere around it. He knew he'd been gone for a long time, but he had told her to wait. Goddamned woman, wait till I get my hands on her. I'll break her neck! he told himself.

He'd found a place where they could eat and a little ramshackle boardinghouse in a colored neighborhood where they could stay the night out of harm's way. But she was gone. Where? Where could she be?

Why couldn't she listen to me and just stay put? he complained to himself. Why?

After walking around for more than an hour and not seeing any sign of her, he had no choice but to seek assistance. There had been another black man standing around the station. He would ask him if he had seen a white woman in a yellow dress. He asked, but the fellow shook his head. Once Antonio felt satisfied that the man had nothing to do with Julie Lee's mysterious disappearance, he decided to ask the man for his help in finding the lady.

The man, who said his name was Buster, listened sympathetically as Antonio told how he and his mistress had only arrived in Baltimore and how she had disappeared while he went to try to find them something to eat and a place to stay for the night.

But when Antonio insisted that he had to find the woman, Buster quickly lost sympathy and began to berate him. "Nigga, why you carrying on so about a white woman who owns you? You ought to be glad, nigga. Hell, man, you can just walk right on to freedom and never look back. This is your blessing."

"But you don't understand," Antonio pleaded.

"No, nigga, I guess I don't. I done known some crazy niggas in my time. Fact, there ain't many niggas crazier than me. But I know I wouldn't be crying for no white woman what owns me. Boy, this is your chance to be free, maybe the only one you'll ever get. You better grab it."

Buster was friendly enough, but Antonio remained wary about entrusting him with their secret. He just maintained that his mistress was a good woman and deserved his help.

Buster was a free Negro. He'd bought his freedom several years earlier from a plantation on Maryland's eastern shore. He'd worked in Baltimore as a day laborer after being hired out by his master. It took another three years, but he'd finally been able to get enough money to buy his wife and their three children. Now they were all in Baltimore, and two more children had been born free, he said.

Buster showed Antonio to the hospital, but refused to go in with him. "That a white man's hospital," he said.

He waited outside for the ten minutes it took Antonio to find out that no woman fitting Julie Lee's description had been brought in.

After walking around for half the night, Buster was

finally able to persuade Antonio to give up for the time being, but he promised that he would help him look again the next day. "Come on home with me," he said, putting his heavy arm around Antonio's neck.

To Antonio's mind, Buster's wife, Margina, turned out to be a saint. The two men had hardly walked in the door before she had two plates of hot food in front of them. So much had happened in the last several hours that Antonio had forgotten he was hungry, but now he wolfed the food down ravenously.

With five children in the house, there was no bed in which he could stretch out and sleep, and Antonio wouldn't permit Margina and Buster to move the children out of their beds. Instead he sank down into a heavy, comfortable chair in the living room, but though he wanted it badly, sleep would not come.

His mind throbbed with questions and admonitions to himself for being so stupid as to leave Julie Lee in the station all by herself. Now something terrible might have happened to her. Maybe she was dead! If she was, he would feel just as responsible as if he'd killed her with his own hands. Continually slapping the top of his head with his hand, he muttered, "Why didn't I take you with me, Julie Lee? Why didn't I? Why did I leave you? Forgive me, Julie Lee, if you're still alive to be able to grant forgiveness." His eyes were blinded by tears, and though he was hardly religious, maybe God would hear his prayers this night. "Dear God, don't let any harm come to that sweet woman. God preserve her."

Chapter 27

Julie Lee tried to sit up, but fell back weakly into the plump pillows behind her head. She ached all over. Even her fingernails seemed to be tingling with pain. At first she was afraid even to look at her bruised and battered body.

In all the days she'd been a slave, she'd never been beaten, only thumped upside her head a few times when she slacked in some of her duties. But a *real* beating, never. As she lay there she vowed silently that if anyone ever so much as threatened her again, she would send him home to Jesus. Man or woman, it would make no difference.

The afternoon sun, pouring through the several windows in the room, hurt her eyes, so she closed them again. They were puffy from the blows she'd sustained the night before. She tried to imagine what she must have looked like. Her mind was becoming more alert, but her body simply would not follow directions. She had to give into the pain and just try to lie still.

"Antonio, Antonio. Where are you?" she murmured. She hardly recognized her own voice. When she pressed her fingers against her swollen face and jaw bone, she realized why she sounded strange.

She lay there awake for some time, but with her eyes still closed. After a while she felt the presence of someone else in the room, but even then she did not bother to try to open her eyes. Only when she felt the presence come closer did her eyelids fly open.

The bright sun created a haze around the figure standing at the foot of the bed, but she could tell that it was a man, a white man. Afraid that she was in danger again, she pushed herself down beneath the covers and waited there for the presence to say or do something.

"Don't be afraid, please," she heard a kind voice say. She did not, however, come out from her dark place. She waited awhile, and when the person said nothing more, she spoke from beneath the covers. "Who are you? Where am I, and where's Antonio? I want Antonio." She began crying and babbling childishly. "*I want Antonio!*" She beat her fists on the mattress and stopped only because it caused her to hurt even more.

"Please calm down and come out from under there. No one is going to hurt you," the voice said, slightly annoyed. "I assure you that you are in no danger, and I further assure you that I do not know this Antonio of whom you speak. As to where you are and how you came to be here, I will tell you, but not until you come out from under there and talk to me face to face."

She did not move. She was both frightened and embarrassed. The voice didn't speak, but she knew that the presence was still there, waiting. It was hot. The air was close. Soon she had no choice but to come out. When she finally did, the man was standing there, right beside the bed near her face. She eyed him carefully. He did not appear threatening.

"I promise I won't hurt you," the man said again. "I

215

found you last night crawling out of an alley. It appears that something horrible happened to you. I picked you up and brought you home. I suppose you don't remember the doctor attending to you last night.''

''No, I don't. But I remember what happened earlier.''

''What *did* happen?''

She fell silent. Her pain wasn't the business of a stranger.

''I had the doctor come in to look you over. He said that you had been beaten pretty badly and asked that I call him again when you woke up this morning. He said that I should let you rest. You were crying out a great deal during the night, but Maria and I took care of you. You'll be fine in a few days, I'm sure.''

She could feel herself relaxing, despite the spasms of pain cutting across her body, and the throbbing ache in her head.

The man now pulled a long cord near the side of the bed. Within moments, a pretty woman with dark hair appeared in the doorway. The moment the woman saw that Julie Lee was awake, a large smile spread across her bright, friendly face.

''Maria, our guest has awakened. Would you be kind enough to send Alejandro for the doctor?''

''Yes, Mr. Duvalier, sir,'' came the pleasant response. ''Alejandro, he will go quickly.'' Then turning her attention to the woman in the bed, Maria said, ''Maybe madam would like something to eat. I've made some hot soup.''

Julie Lee's voice was small and grateful. ''Yes, I think I could stand something to eat. I haven't eaten since yesterday.''

The man interrupted. ''Perhaps we would all be a little more comfortable if we introduced ourselves. My name is Pierre Duvalier and this is my home. We call it LeChateau. And this," he said, gesturing toward the still-smiling woman, "is Maria. My Maria. I don't know what I would do without her.

"It was she who took care of you so well last night. She did everything the good doctor told her to do. But, I'm sure you don't remember too much of that, you were hysterical much of the time. Isn't that right, Maria?"

As she moved toward the bed, Maria nodded her head in agreement. "*Si.* You were crying so much, and you ask over and over again for the señor you call Antonio. I am so happy that today you are feeling a little better. But no more talk right now. I will get your food, and I will send Alejandro for the doctor. Excuse me, please."

Julie Lee had never heard an accent like Maria's, and it fascinated her. She wondered where the woman had learned to talk so oddly.

Maria had vacated the room, backing out all the way, all the while with a smile on her face.

"But now that you know who we are and where you are, how about you?" Pierre said. "Who are you?"

What *was* her name, she thought rapidly. That is, which name should she use, Julie Lee or Annabelle? At first she thought she should tell them her real name, but common sense quickly prevailed, and she stammered out, "Annabelle. My name is Annabelle Brownless."

"Well, what happened to you, Miss Brownless? Or is it Mrs.? How did you happen to be in *that* part of town at night? Do you know how many criminals gather around the train station after dark?"

She explained that she was a stranger to Baltimore and that Antonio was her servant.

217

They talked a little while longer, just general talk of trivial things, but she was uncomfortable with so *much* small conversation, afraid that she might give herself away. Without Antonio nearby to advise her, she feared she would miss some cue, make some social blunder that would undo her.

She fell back to sleep several times that day after the doctor had examined her. He recommended several more days' rest. She was forced to tell him the story of what had happened, since he claimed the only way he could treat her adequately was to know exactly what had gone on.

Pierre disappeared for the entire afternoon, explaining that he had business to tend to. He would be back in time for dinner, he said.

Maria was good company She was sweet and made pleasant conversation when Julie Lee was up to it.

Maria told her she was from Mexico and had been working for Pierre for a little more than a year. She met him when she had been working as a maid in a brothel. "I couldn't stand it no more," she explained. "Cleaning up behind those people, and washing with my own hands those filthy sheets."

Maria talked quickly, but soon Julie Lee adjusted to her accent and was able to catch most of what she said.

To Maria, Pierre was a god. He had even given her money to send for her sons back in Mexico. "That man, he is so good, a saint. He heard me cry for my babies, and he said, 'Maria here is the money. Every mother should be with her children.' That man is so good. He never treat me bad, and he never treat me like a slave, you know what I mean?"

Julie Lee smiled. She knew very well what she meant, much better than Maria realized.

Every mother should be with her children, Julie Lee thought. Yes, as she should be with little John. Her mind flew back to the Lorelei. She wondered what Dancer and little John were doing just then.

Chapter 28

Julie Lee had been at LeChateau for nearly a week and still had seen nothing of the house beyond the room in which she had been sleeping and taking her meals. Only in the past two days had she begun to notice that many of the more serious black-and-blue bruises had started to disappear. She was still in pain. The doctor had said the beating she had sustained had been severe. He warned her that there would be dizzy spells and frequent headaches. "But," he had added cheerily, "don't look so glum. Thank God you're alive. Those scoundrels could have killed you."

The same questions circled endlessly in her head whenever she was awake. She wondered what had happened to Antonio, whether he was all right, whether he was even alive. She thought about all her friends back at the plantation. She tried to remember what duties people were doing at different times in the day. Right about now, she guessed, a warm grin creeping across her face, little John was probably screaming his little head off and driving Nanny crazy in the nursery, and Dancer was probably out in the stables with Hannibal. Katy, no doubt, was cooking something good, and Zephyr was probably somewhere in the house, muttering about how Miss Whilomene's children were about to drive her out of her mind. She laughed at the bittersweet thoughts, and she wondered sadly if everyone had forgotten about her already, even though it had been only a short while.

So far Pierre had demanded nothing of her, nor had he tried, as she had expected, to pry into her background. The closest he came to that was when he asked if she wanted him to contact any of her relatives to let them know where she was and that she would be all right. "No need to do that," she had said quickly. "I'll be feeling better in a few days, the doctor said. Then I'll just be getting on."

She hadn't told Pierre the tale about her sick sister in Philadelphia. In fact, she hadn't told him anything. After that conversation, Pierre never mentioned the subject again and she was glad. She hardly felt up to filling in the details and keeping her story straight.

Maria was much the same as her boss. She never asked Julie Lee questions about herself, only made innocent inquiries about how she felt and whether she wanted or needed anything. Although she talked a lot, Maria's conversation was generally about her sons or Pierre.

Julie Lee was always amazed at how Maria seemed to appear whenever she was wanted without being summoned and she was especially grateful for that. She had no intention of pulling the cord that hung beside her bed. It reminded her too much of the plantation. She could not bring herself to treat Maria the way she herself had so long been treated.

It was still early. Maria had not yet come to take away the breakfast dishes. Julie Lee sat up in bed, staring at nothing in particular, when the gentle tap she now recognized as Pierre's sounded at the door. She invited him in.

As he came closer to the bed, she realized that he must be on his way to work. He was dressed smartly. His curly black hair was oiled so heavily that it gleamed. Also, much to her dislike, he smelled sweet. She didn't like it when men sweetened themselves. She thought it was all right if women wore perfume but it bothered her if a man wore cologne. Dancer had always smelled natural and she loved the odor when she pressed up close to him.

"I just came in to let you know that I'll be gone for most of the day," Pierre said, as he sat down on the chair near the bed. "I've got some business on the other side of town, and afterward, I'm going to an exhibition with a friend."

She had no idea what an exhibition was and wondered if Pierre was really going to one of the bawdy houses. She said nothing, however, allowing him to talk on.

"I've already told Maria that I won't be home for dinner, but she'll make something good for you. She likes you very much, you know."

"I like her too," Julie Lee said. "She's a very dear woman. You're lucky to have her here with you."

Like most of their conversations, she knew that this one would not last very long. She wondered why Pierre always seemed anxious to get away from her. Only once had they talked for any length of time. She could tell, however, that he liked her by the way he looked at her. That's what she found so strange. Well, it didn't matter, she told herself. She wouldn't be there long anyway.

He was on his way out the door when he turned abruptly and came back toward the bed. "Oh, I almost forgot," he said. "I thought you'd be interested in reading the newspaper. It's a day old, but now that you're feeling a little better, I should think you'd want to know what's going on in the world outside this room.

"The biggest news, I guess, is that South Carolina finally made good on its threats and seceded from the Union. I do believe there's going to be a war soon.

"With President Buchanan on his way out and Abraham Lincoln and the Republicans on their way in, I know many of the slave holders think the end is near. Something has got to give.

"Well," he continued nonchalantly, unaware of how many questions he'd raised in her mind, "I had better get going. I'll stop in to see you tonight when I get back. If you're asleep then I'll see you in the morning."

When Pierre finally departed, she eagerly spread the newspaper out in front of her. It looked very much like the ones that had come to the Lorelei. After several minutes, she pushed the paper off to the side in frustration. She could read, but not well enough to make out all the big words contained in the stories crowded on the page. She tried sounding them out, the way her mother had taught her and Hannibal to do when they were children, but she quickly realized that being able to sound out a word had little or nothing to do with understanding what it meant. After pulling the paper back toward her and trying once again, she decided that one of the first things she would do when she got the chance was to learn to read better.

Chapter 29

Pierre had gotten used to her being there. He enjoyed stopping by her room in the mornings before leaving for work and at night when he returned home.

Now that nearly all her bruises had healed and she was able to walk around without pain, he realized that she was even better looking than he had at first believed. She had an exotic quality, but he couldn't quite put his finger on what it was that seemed to make her different.

Her body was a woman's, but he realized rather quickly that she was hardly a sophisticate. Perhaps that was her attraction for him. There was a fresh sort of naiveté about her, a childlike innocence. Yet he suspected that beneath that demure exterior was a hot-blooded, strong-willed woman waiting to get out. Yes, he thought, she could probably make a man bend to her every wish. God, how he would love to find out. If she would just give him some opening, some sign that she thought of him as more than just a kind benefactor. He desperately wanted to know her better, but he was afraid to approach her. There were plenty of women who were interested in him—after all, was he not a man of the world?—and most of them were wealthy and influential, from the very best society. Still, he wanted her.

It was a Sunday, a beautiful December afternoon, an almost perfect winter day, when she dashed his hopes before he ever expressed them to her. The last vestiges of a brief snowfall the night before were melting as the warm sun found its place in the sky. He and Julie Lee were sitting in the dining room. They had just finished a hearty breakfast, a special one that Maria had prepared to celebrate, she said, Annabelle's recovery.

Julie Lee was peering over a cup of coffee that she held delicately between her unpainted fingers. She was lovely in the morning, he thought, as he sat at the other end of the long table. Even without makeup she looked as beautiful as if she were going to a grand ball.

"Pierre," she said finally putting down her cup, "I suppose you know that it is time for me to go."

They were the very words he had not wanted to hear. He wished he could stuff his ears and pretend that they had not been spoken. Regaining his composure, he said, "I know you must go, my dear. I have felt it for the last two or three days, your restlessness and how you seem to be somewhere else when I'm talking to you. Yet, I don't want you to go. I don't want you to leave me here all alone."

He got up from his chair, walked around the long table to where she was sitting, slipped his arms around her shoulders and touched his chin to the crown of her head. He was surprised when she flinched. "If you must leave," he continued, "if you must go away, won't you even promise me that you'll come back soon? I'd ask you no questions about where you'd been or what you'd done.

Just tell me that you'll come back, and I shall wait a lifetime if I have to."

"I don't make promises to anyone," she said, gently slipping out from under him. "I can't because I don't know exactly what I'm going to do or where I'm going to end up." She tried to be gentle, to be kind.

She stared straight ahead, uncomfortable because she feared what was coming next. Although she and Dancer had been lovers, she had never heard a man talk to her like Pierre did. Things with her and Dancer had always been so simple, so basic, so uncomplicated. They loved each other, so they pleasured. They loved each other, so they made a baby. That's the way it was. Simple. Nothing like this.

Pierre pulled up another chair beside hers. His voice seemed to be coming from some faraway place. "Annabelle, don't you understand? I don't want you to leave me. You have, in so short a time, brought so much joy into my life. You've given me a reason to be glad to come into this house, which was for me so long an empty, miserable symbol of my dead wife and my marriage.

"You've been my joy, my delight. Annabelle, you can't go. Don't you know that I've fallen in love with you, desperately, helplessly in love? All I want to do is make you happy. I know that you don't know me well, and I hardly know you at all, but I'm sure that I can make you happier than any other man could. And you would make me so happy. It's something I just know."

She knew the moment had come. The moment for honesty, and if he dreaded this time, she did even more. He'd saved her life. He'd been kind to her, but she didn't love him. Never would, never could. She didn't need love. She needed freedom. But she couldn't tell him that. It was going to be difficult and hurtful, she knew, but she had no choice.

"Pierre, you've been my friend and so has Maria, and Lord knows I'll be thanking you for it each and every day of my life. You took me in. You called the doctor. You did everything you could do for a stranger, but I *must* go. There is some business I must take care of. Serious business, so serious that I can't discuss it with you or anyone.

"I like you, Pierre, but I don't love you. I love one man, and he is far away now. He doesn't even know where I am. I know he's worried about me. I'll go back to him one day. He's my man, my only man."

She pushed the chair back from the table and stood up. Because he remained seated, she towered over him. When he turned his face upward to look into hers, she saw the tears filling the corners of his eyes. She wanted to turn away. She wasn't used to seeing grown men cry. She felt sad and ashamed, but there was nothing she could do.

Trembling, he took her hand into his and held it there. His voice rose to a loud plea, "Don't you know that I adore you, that I worship you—"

She cut him off in midsentence. "Stop it. Stop it, Pierre," she snapped. It came out harshly, and more cruelly than she had intended. "I don't want to hurt your feelings. Don't make me. But I have to go away and there just isn't anything you can say that will make me change my mind."

Julie Lee paused a moment and regained her composure. She didn't want to upset him any more than was absolutely necessary. He'd helped her immensely, and besides, she would need his help getting out of Baltimore.

Pierre looked at her for a long moment and finally

said softly, so softly that she hardly heard him, "So, when do you want to go?"

"Soon," was her response. "Tomorrow if I can. But you know I don't have any money. I don't even have any clothes. Those men, they took everything I had."

Obviously she desired that he not only let her go, but that he finance her leaving. She had nerve, he thought bitterly.

"So what do you think you will need for this trip, this great mission of yours," he replied, his voice edged with sarcasm. "You need money? You need clothes?" He sighed in capitulation. "Tell me what you need. I'll buy you anything you want. I'll help you go, if that is what you really want."

Monday came quickly, too quickly for him, but not quickly enough for her. Their confrontation of the day before had only made her more eager to get out. She felt smothered, sidetracked from what she had come for.

Pierre had awakened early. In fact, he'd hardly gotten any sleep at all. He washed and dressed quickly and soon found himself outside her bedroom door, tapping there, he thought angrily, like a servant in his own home. That's what she did to him. She'd made him her slave! And yet he kept tapping, knowing that by the time she opened the door and he looked at her, the anger would be washed away. Maybe he would repent and try to convince her once again to stay. No, he thought, enough is enough.

"Come in," she answered formally. When he went in, she was already dressed. She wore a simple cotton frock that Maria had lent her from her own wardrobe.

"Are you ready?" he asked, trying to avoid her eyes, and feeling shame at his behavior of the previous day.

228

''I'm ready,'' she said, with finality.

It was cold when they stepped outside the house. She pulled the coat Maria had lent her tightly across her body, but it did no good. She shivered, but he made no move to put his arm around her.

Chapter 30

It was even chillier inside the train. She pushed her hands deeper into the white fur muff Pierre had bought her to go along with the long black walking coat and ankle-high, lace-up boots. This time there was no magic for her as the iron horse hummed along the rails. She had been through it all before. Even the scenery was stale.

She thought about Pierre, and how he stood silently beside her at the train station in Baltimore waiting for her to board. He didn't speak. He didn't have to. His eyes said it all, spoke rivers about his sense of loss at her departure.

She sighed. He knew nothing about her and she could tell him nothing. But she could not remain in Baltimore and marry him. He didn't understand. How could he? He was white. She was black. He was free. She was trying to get free. He had been his own master all his life. She had been a slave all of hers.

The ride north was long and tiresome, and this time she rode without the comfort of knowing that Antonio was only a few cars back, waiting to guide her over the rough spots. How she had depended on him, his knowledge, his encouragement! She was afraid, but she knew that wherever he was, he would expect nothing less from her than that she push on to the end of the journey they had started out on together.

As she sat there thinking, she felt a strange presence in the empty seat next to her. She had the oddest feeling that somebody was there. Perhaps, she thought, it was her mother. Maybe Mama had decided to come along for the ride. Maybe she had come along to look out for her baby girl. Unconsciously, she reached out for the talisman Jeddah had given her. She drew back, however, remembering that when they had raped her, the men had ripped the amulet from her neck. Her good luck charm was lost. Maybe it was still in that stinking alley.

She jolted awake from an unplanned sleep as she felt the train beginning to slow down. Lord, she thought, as she opened her eyes, she must have been asleep for hours. When she looked out the window, she caught her first glimpse of Philadelphia. Sitting there on the incoming train, it didn't look much different than Baltimore. Another city, another place full of unexpected dangers and opportunities.

She stepped out onto the crowded platform. As she had done before, she waited for all the passengers to leave the car. There seemed to be people everywhere. Friends and relatives greeted the arrivals, hugging and kissing, so that Julie Lee could barely find a clear path to the station proper. As she looked about her, she wished there were somebody to run up and kiss her and welcome her to Philadelphia. She longed to see Antonio's easy smile breaking through the crowd. She longed to feel him lifting her off her feet, triumphantly exclaiming. ''Julie Lee, we did it! We're free!'' But there was no Antonio. Nobody to embrace her or even to smile in her direction.

She wove her way into the station. Once inside, she headed directly for the first unoccupied bench that came into view. She put her bag on her lap, tapping it gently with her fingers, trying to give herself time to decide what she should do next.

She'd been sitting there for some time when she noticed a woman, a very tall, thin woman, elegantly dressed with a walking coat similar to Julie Lee's, but grey rather than black. The woman's face bore a sign of recognition at first, and then gave way to a broad smile, which remained there until she was almost on top of Julie Lee. The wide smile died right where it was. "Oh, pardon me," the woman said. "I thought you were someone else. I'm so embarrassed. I'm supposed to be meeting my cousin Adelaide, but frankly I haven't seen her in so long that I'm not really sure anymore if I know exactly what she looks like." And then she added, obviously in jest, "You wouldn't happen to be Adelaide, would you?"

"No, ma'am," Julie Lee responded automatically, silently kicking herself for reverting to slave jargon. Julie Lee had hoped the woman would say more, but she didn't. She simply moved off in the opposite direction, craning her neck, hoping to spot Adelaide.

Julie Lee continued sitting on the bench, looking at nothing in particular, until her eyes met with those of a wiry black man, who was passing by, pushing a wooden cart. Piled high atop the cart were several pieces of luggage.

She smiled at him, but he put his head down and turned away. She thought she had smiled in a friendly enough fashion, and was put off momentarily, but then she chided herself. She should have understood. The man obviously thought she was white, and he didn't want any trouble. She knew that if a black man wanted trouble, all he had to do was look too long at a white woman, any white woman.

When the man passed by again, the cart was empty. She got up and blocked his path. He had no choice but to look right into her face, although he tried at first to move around her. "Please," she said finally. "Please, I'm a stranger here and I need some help." She moved closer to him. He jumped back, looking around him to see if anyone had seen them.

"Listen ma'am, I ain't wanting no trouble. If you needs some help, you better go on over to the booth over there and talk with the man inside. Don't want no trouble."

Lord have mercy, she thought, is this how the niggas act up here in Philadelphia? Ain't they supposed to be free? The man was acting like the niggas down on the plantation. Suddenly, she was unsure whether coming to this place had been the right thing to do.

"Listen," she said. "I don't want any trouble either. I just want some help, and I believe you can help me. Now just stand still and let me talk to you for a moment."

At that he relented and gave her the directions she asked for, and within fifteen minutes she was standing outside the gate of what she knew had to be the Quaker meeting house. The Quakers, Antonio had once told her, were kind-hearted folks, even though they were white.

The meeting house, in stark contrast to the buildings around it, was painted a simple, clean white. It was long and low with several small windows along its sides. Three small wooden steps led up to a door that was covered by a wooden awning. Painted on the awning in black was the word Welcome. In front of the house was a garden, though no flowers were in bloom at the time.

She stood outside the gate deep in thought when she

was startled by a group of noisy schoolboys, apparently on their way home. They nearly knocked her to the ground. One of the boys had dropped his books. He picked them up quickly, looked up into her face and said, "Oh, 'scuse me, ma'am." She smiled at the child who was already halfway up the street, rejoining his friends who hadn't bothered to stop.

Summoning up her courage, she pushed open the unlocked gate and was on her way up to the front door when a man came from around the back of the house. He was carrying a huge kettle that gave off the rich-smelling aroma of a hearty soup. He was tall, gaunt, rail-thin. She couldn't tell how old he was. He stood straight and walked with a vigorous gait and yet his face bore a weathered look. He was dressed in black pants and wore a white shirt and a black string tie around his neck. Atop his head was perched a wide-brimmed, flat black hat. She'd never seen anyone dressed so.

"How goes the day with thee," the man said in a way that made it seem that he had known her before. He put the kettle on the ground and advanced closer to her. He looked at her inquiringly, but waited courteously for her to begin the conversation.

"I'm looking for the Quakers," she said finally able to begin.

"If that is who thee are looking for, thee have surely found the right place," he said. He spoke like the Bible read, just as Antonio said the Quakers did. Truly, she thought, she must have arrived among people who were good and honorable.

Without any further questioning, Levi Collins escorted her into the back of the house. As the building was on the outside, the huge room was stark. There was nothing in it beyond the furniture that was necessary and some books sitting neatly on shelves built into the walls. There was a fireplace, two long tables, and wooden benches running alongside them. There were other benches pushed up against the wall.

Levi invited her to sit and asked if she would like anything to eat. The heat from the fire had warmed her enough so that she removed the muff from around her neck by lifting the strings over her head. She opened the buttons of her coat, and was only halfway out of it before Levi had come up beside her and helped her with it. He hung both her coat and muff from a nail sticking out of the wall.

For a long while she sat silently. She felt she had finally found a place to rest. Levi waited respectfully. For the first time since she had left the Lorelei, she felt completely safe. She believed that she could tell the truth to the Quakers and that now all the lies could stop. She was relieved.

When she finally spoke with Levi, she learned that no one lived in the meeting house and that he was merely its caretaker. Sometime soon, he said, others would arrive for that evening's meeting. Then he begged her forgiveness and left her alone, for he had to finish up his chores.

She sat thinking. After a while, she got up from the bench and moved closer to the fire. She stared into the bright red flames that danced over the logs. Once again, she felt that strange presence near her—the same presence she had felt in the train. She turned around quickly to see if Levi was nearby, but he was not. Then she could have sworn that she heard somebody say, "Well done, daughter. Well done." So it *was* her mother. Mama had said she would be nearby always, and now there she was in Philadelphia. The feeling was comforting, warmer even than the fire. "Mama," she whispered low, "Mama, I know you is with me, Mama, and I'm glad. I just hope that I'm doing the right thing. I been so scared, Mama, and so much done happened since I left home. I misses my baby something awful. You know how much I love my boy. I hope you been watching out after him and Dancer, and Hannibal too."

The sudden sound of footsteps startled her. She turned quickly, just in time to see another man, even taller than Levi, advancing toward her. Her face was still tingling from the heat of the fire and she knew that her cheeks had turned red.

"I bid thee a good day, stranger," the man said. The smile on his face was genuinely friendly. She smiled back.

The man introduced himself as Josephus Pennington. He was one of the leaders of the Quaker flock. He had come to Philadelphia only a few months earlier to assist the group and to teach in its school, which he said, had black students as well as white. Though she had no way of knowing it then, Josephus Pennington would play an important role in the next phase of her life, and he would become one of her dearest and closest friends until the day he died.

Chapter 31

The next few weeks went quickly. Julie Lee was taken in by a kind Quaker family by the name of Tucker. When Josephus introduced her and asked if they would give her a place to stay, there was never any hesitation. The Tuckers, Wilmot and Levia and their five children, three girls and two boys, ranging in age from three years to fifteen, were wonderful. She immediately fell in love with the children, and they in turn seemed to be in love with her as she went with them to school every morning.

She had never learned so much so quickly, and no one laughed at her when she sat in the back of the room working right along with the children. In the evenings, they all did their homework together.

Her desire for knowledge was so great that there was hardly a night that she didn't fall asleep with a newspaper or book in her hand. She had awakened many a morning to find the paper crumpled up beside her where it had apparently slipped during the night.

By now Josephus had introduced her to nearly everyone in the flock, and she had gotten used to the way they talked. It was in fact Josephus who, after she had been there three weeks, encouraged her to tell the flock her story.

At the special meeting at which she was scheduled to talk, there wasn't one empty seat in the meeting house. Even the children made no noise as she unfurled her life story for them. During the question and answer period that followed, she tried to unravel some of the more mysterious details of the institutions of slavery that the Quakers found it difficult to understand.

She was amazed by her own performance. Never would she have thought that she could have stood up before a room full of people to talk about herself so easily. And as they crowded around her after the meeting, there were actually sympathetic looks in their eyes.

One Friday a few weeks later, excitement ran high in Philadelphia's Quaker community, for that night there was to be a special meeting to which a very special guest speaker had been invited. That speaker was a black woman, an ex-slave who was called by the name of Joshua. She had a heavy price on her head and had built her reputation around her many daring escapades back into the deep South to free her people. She was called Joshua because many compared her to the Old Testament hero Joshua, and just like the walls of Jericho, slavery had to come tumbling down.

When the hour of seven arrived, the room quieted down. From the back, Julie Lee could hear soft talking and the sound of feet. "She's here. She's here," she heard one woman say to another. "Praise be. She's here."

Before long, a tiny, cinnamon-colored woman shuffled into the room. She was dwarfed by the two tall men who walked on either side of her. One of the men was

Josephus, and the smile on his face was the widest Julie Lee had ever seen since meeting him. Behind the three of them came other people, among them two other black women and a black man. Joshua was much older than Julie Lee had expected, and certainly a lot smaller. Based on the things she'd been told, she expected a young, spry woman. Instead, Joshua was tiny and looked to be maybe a little bit older than Julie Lee's mother would have been were she still alive. In fact, Joshua didn't even appear to be in the best of health.

As she arrived at the podium, a few people at first, and then everybody, rose to their feet to honor her presence. The loud applause continued for several minutes and did not end until Joshua spread out her hands and bade them sit down.

Joshua's smile was as radiant as the sun. Her hands were animated as she spoke, tiny hands that had seen many hard days of work.

During the hour or so that Joshua talked, there wasn't a sound from the rest of the room, not even a baby cried, and the young children, usually restless after such a long time, sat perfectly still. It was a mystical, almost religious event, Julie Lee thought. Sometimes when Joshua's voice waned, Josephus appeared on the spot, bringing her a glass of water.

Julie Lee was enraptured during the speech. Joshua's descriptions were so vivid that Julie Lee wept softly at times. Even though she'd endured slavery herself, she hadn't thought about it as deeply as she did when Joshua described its horrors. Images of her mother, Dancer, little John, Hannibal, Katy, Jeddah and all the rest passed through her mind. She wished that they could be there with her to see, to hear. Soon her sobs were floating high in the air, and many in the audience turned in her direction. She felt no embarrassment or shame. She finally wept openly, causing even Joshua to stop for a moment to gaze in her direction. The crying brought her some measure of relief. She had put her head down to her chest, when she felt the arm of the woman next to her around her neck. It too felt comforting.

When the impassioned presentation was over, many from the crowd swarmed around Joshua. It seemed that some simply wanted to touch her, to be near her. There were few dry eyes among the adults. The talking, which soon became a din, stopped again abruptly when Josephus announced that a collection would be taken after dinner. The money would be used, he said, to help Joshua's crusade.

Julie Lee hadn't moved from her seat. She just sat there, staring at her hands, nearly oblivious to all the noise around her. She looked up and managed to catch Josephus' eye, and with her hand signaled for him to come to her.

"Josephus, please, can you ask Miss Joshua if I could talk with her before she goes? I must talk with her, even if it's just for a few minutes. Please ask her, Josephus."

"Why, of course, Julie Lee. I'll ask her. In fact, I rather thought thee might like to speak with her in private since thee and she have so much in common. Perhaps she is tired and she will speak to thee in the morning before she leaves. I understand she has a few other stops to make while she is here speaking and raising money in Pennsylvania. But, be assured, dear Julie Lee, that I will ask."

She touched his arm gently. "Thank you, Josephus. Thank you."

*　　*　　*

240

It was nearly midnight. Before Josephus left the meeting hall, he threw a few more logs on the fire so that the two women would be comfortable while they talked. He assured Joshua that all those in her party would be made comfortable in the homes of the families who had volunteered to give them places to sleep. As he closed the door on his way out, Josephus looked at Julie Lee, and gave her a knowing wink.

Joshua had had a very long and tiring day, but she had insisted on talking with Julie Lee that night rather than in the morning. She was never too tired to talk to a kindred soul. She knew how it was for those who were newly free. They needed to talk, but more than that, they needed to talk with people who really understood. White people, the ones who helped, just couldn't understand the way ex-slaves understood one another. She had needed to talk when she had escaped, a long, long time ago from the Maryland plantation on which she'd been raised.

Julie Lee knew Joshua was bone tired, but she couldn't help herself. She just wanted to spend a few minutes with the woman.

Joshua listened silently as Julie Lee spilled out her story. She never interrupted, never asked for clarification, just let her talk on and on. She'd heard such stories before, but never so often that they bored her. It was such stories that gave her the strength to keep going back into the South time and time again to bring others out of slavery.

She'd known mulattos like Julie Lee in her time, and though she was sometimes disgusted with them because they were usually the hardest to convince to leave, she always found people among these "privileged" slaves who were more than willing to escape, to sacrifice the good food and hand-me-down clothes from the master's house.

As she went through the story of her life, including the way her mother had died, Julie Lee wept again and again. Joshua wept too. They embraced and Julie Lee found herself pressing her head to Joshua's breast, just like she had when she was a little girl. Julie Lee had not cried so much since leaving the Lorelei.

"Cry, baby. Cry," Joshua kept repeating in her hoarse voice. "You just cry and keep on acrying, long as you like. God knows you got every right to cry. Up here in a strange place without your people. Chile, I know how it be when you leaves ever'body you loves behind. I had to leave my own when I decided it was time to go. My *own* people, my family, my flesh and blood, was too damned scared to leave. But chile, when freedom calls your name, you got to be ready. It's like when the Lord calls you, and it's your time to die. He don't care what you got to do tomorrow, when He calls your name, you got to go right then and there.

"When I first took leave of Maryland, I was sort of just like you is now. I was young and I was scared, and I was crying just about all the time. But girl, freedom had called my name. And my massa had done beat me just about enough that I was soon ready to go.

"That's why even now when I goes to bring people out, they got to be ready. I leaves all them scared peoples behind, 'cause it's them that will get everybody kilt. Some of the people who came along with me up on into Canada wanted to turn around, but I wouldn't let them. I tells 'em that if'n they starts with me, they's got to finish the trip. If'n we let peoples turn around, then sometimes they goes right back and gives everybody away.

242

"This underground railroad, now, it got black folk and white folk workin' for it. These people be helping all the time and they be doing so for no money and be putting themselves right in the path of death. Now we can't afford to let nobody go back and give these good people away. Besides, if'n they gets caught 'cause of some scared runaway what can't keep his mouth shut, then other peoples be too scared to help. This railroad is a big ole thing, and we got peoples working with us from Canada clean on down into the deeper South, like Georgia and all them places, where they be treating slaves something awful.

"Some of our people done already went to jail. Sometimes they kills the runaways outright, but they hates the whites even more than us. Calls 'em nigga-lovers and such. People like these Quakers, they ain't liked much because everybody knows that Quakers be helping niggas get free."

Julie Lee listened as Joshua talked. Occasionally, she would ask a few questions, but the more Joshua talked, the stronger Julie Lee felt and the more convinced she was that she had done the right thing. Joshua convinced her now that she had to go back home soon. She only wished that when she did she would be as brave as Joshua. No wonder they had given her that name.

Soon daylight filtered in through the windows, and yet Julie Lee was nowhere near tired. Joshua had told her what she needed to do in preparation for her return journey south, when Julie Lee would try to save her family. Joshua even suggested that she plan her trip so that she would arrive at the plantation on a Saturday. "This way," Joshua explained, "by the time the massa find out some of his niggas done gone, he have to wait till Monday to put an ad in the paper saying he looking for some escaped niggas.

By that time, you can be far enough away so you won't have to worry none.''

She felt that she'd already intruded upon Joshua enough, but Julie Lee couldn't help but ask a favor from her, a big favor. She was elated when Joshua said, ''Chile, I was thinking you'd never ask. Sure, I'll go on back with you. Bring your people out right on along with some other folks I was expectin' to bring out of Henrico County on my next trip there. 'Course, you had no ways of knowing it, but we got lots of railroad people round where you come from who be glad to help. Now, all we got to do is wait a few more weeks. I can't read and write myself, so I got to get somebody to send a message to our peoples down there, so that they will know when we coming and how many peoples we thinks we gonna take. You know, sometimes we can't always tell just how many we gonna have, but two or three more don't make too much a difference.''

And so, the plan was hatched. They would set out for the Lorelei by the end of the month.

Chapter 32

It rained off and on for the better part of the week. Julie Lee hadn't gotten much sleep since the rainstorm began. She spent her nights lying in bed and listening to the steady rhythm of the rain as it poured down on the roof above her head. It was impossible to drown out the sounds.

For three days the sun had fled from the sky. It was the worst storm in Philadelphia's history. With the sky remaining black night and day, it was difficult to distinguish the time. All the schools in the city, including the Quaker school, were closed. Nearly all the stores and shops were closed. God help those families who did not have sufficient provisions in their cupboards or enough wood for their fires. The storm struck so suddenly that even emergency aid, where available, was hard to come by. It was dismal and gloomy, and the weather matched Julie Lee's mood.

Philadelphia's normally bustling thoroughfares had emptied, and only a few brave souls dared venture out onto the streets. The storm's heaviest toll had been reserved for Philadelphia's poorest families. Because most of the streets in those neighborhoods were little more than dirt roads, muddy water swirled angrily in the deep eddies that had formed, and what had been walkways were transformed into running streams.

Behind closed doors, the storm was taking yet another toll. Families—husbands, wives and children—were at each other's throats. They had been cooped up for too long with little to do to escape the boredom. Mothers could not send their children to school or outside to play, and drinking men could not slip down to the local watering hole for a nip. If the storm did not let up soon, mayhem surely was going to break out all over town.

The Tuckers and their guest, Julie Lee, were more fortunate than many of their neighbors. Their house sat atop a hill and so far had been spared the flooding that plagued those homes lower down.

Julie Lee sat staring out the kitchen window, watching the water cascade down the panes. She was in one of her quiet moods. The Tuckers respected her silence and did not try to intrude upon her thoughts. She thought about many things sitting there looking out the window, about her mother, about Dancer, Hannibal, little John and all the folks back on the plantation. She prayed that the storm would soon stop and for the ground to dry sufficiently for her to keep her important date with Joshua.

She'd been gone for three months. Surely God had to understand, she kept thinking, that she had to return before she was forgotten, before she became little more than a memory to her family. She had to get back before Dancer found himself another woman to love, and before little John started calling some other woman Mama.

Surely, she thought, God had to know how much she wanted to take her son into her arms, kiss his little head, tousle his hair and rock him to sleep at night. God had to know that she wanted and needed her man beside her. God must know something about family.

She was so engrossed in thought that she didn't hear the door open and close. But when she turned there was Josephus, standing in the middle of the room, soaked from head to toe. Water was swirling in the brim of his hat, and his boots were wet and caked with mud high up at the knee. Wasn't it just like him to be out in the storm, she thought. She brought him a towel, heated up a cup of tea for him, and they sat down to talk. It was Julie Lee who started the conversation.

"You know that I'm going with Joshua on her next trip. She promised me that she was going to help me get my people free. I don't know if we're going to make it, and I don't even know if I'm going to see y'all again any time soon. I just want you to know how much I appreciate all that you, the Tuckers and everybody else here, done for me since I come up to Philadelphia. Lord knows y'all lifted me from a dark, dark place. I didn't know what I was coming to. I only knew that I had to get out. You understand what I'm meaning to say, brother?"

He knew well what she was trying to say, and felt almost embarrassed by her sentiment. As far as he was concerned, they hadn't done anything special. They had only done what was right.

When he looked up at her, there was inquisitiveness in his eyes and in his voice. "But why is thee telling me these things this night? Surely, thee is not planning to leave in the morning."

She laughed, an easy, relieved laugh. "No, brother, I don't think I'm leaving here in the morning, but I got to be ready when Joshua say it's time to go, and I'm praying that all this rain don't keep her from getting back soon."

Now, it was Josephus who was confident. "If Joshua said she will be coming, then she will. Have faith, child. A little rain won't stop her."

As usual he was gentle and compassionate as he spoke with her, and she could feel some tenseness leaving her body. When she began to talk again, her voice sounded different—strangely husky and heavy. "You know, Josephus, I guess I just wanted to talk to you. I know I don't have to thank y'all. You know how much I appreciate what you done. But I get to feeling scared sometimes, more scared than I ever been before. Way up here without any of my people, I get to feeling alone, and sometimes I ache all up inside just to see my baby, but I'm so scared.

"You see, before I only dreamed about what freedom was like, but since I been up here in Philadelphia, I know what freedom is, and I know what I'd be losing if I fail. And I ain't talking just about losing my life, 'cause my life ain't worth nothing if I was to be a slave again."

Josephus frowned at her remarks, but she continued. "Now, I know that to your way of thinking that killing myself just ain't God's way, but I don't think God can judge us niggas the same way He judges other folks. God made niggas kind of special, the way I think, and I know that God makes some special provisions for us what done been slaves. Ain't nothing worse than being a nigga and a slave, ain't nothing, *nothing* worse than that, and God knows it."

She was eloquent, Josephus thought, without even knowing it. He took her hand and held it in his. "Have faith, child," he repeated. "There is nothing that is going to stop thee. Joshua is a woman of faith, outstanding, unshakable faith. She has seen a lot in her time, and yet she still has faith. If thee ask her, I'm sure she will tell thee that it is her faith that has brought her safely out of the South countless times. She has often said that it is God and the North Star that guide her. Thee must believe that it is God who brought thee this far and that He will be with thee as long as it is thy time to walk upon this earth.''

He knew he was sermonizing, but what he was saying was inspirational to him, even as he talked. He was only trying to make her feel stronger in her faith.

Josephus had studied Julie Lee long enough to respect her as a woman of fierce determination. As he looked at her, he realized how easy it would have been for her to pass as a white woman forever, never to look back, and, he thought, she was the epitome of what made color distinctions so ridiculous. Here she was as white as any white person, but inside the blackest of blacks, a fugitive slave. She was to be admired and respected. Her years were tender, but her heart had acquired the scars and the wisdom of many, many years.

''You're right, brother,'' she said to him, ''just like you always seems to be. It's going to be all right. Maybe it's just this weather that's making me feel so bad.''

She rose from her seat and moved back toward the window. She watched the water pouring down and said as much to herself as to Josephus, ''You know when I was a little bitty girl, I was always afraid when it would rain too hard and drown me. I used to get so scared on those dark, rainy nights. Sometimes I climbed right up next to my mama. And Lord, if it thundered and lightnined, I would be shaking like a leaf. Then Mama would hold me tight and stop me from shaking so bad. I'm all grown up now, but it ain't changed, I still gets scared when it rains. I remember crawling up underneath Mama, but now I ain't got no mama and I guess I'm just scared.''

She suddenly realized she was rambling. When she turned from the window and looked at him, she was ashamed at keeping him so long. He looked tired. Still, she knew he would stay until he knew she had said all she had to say.

"Brother, I really don't think I has nothing much else to talk about right now. Just wanted to hear you say something to take some of this scaredness away. Don't worry, brother, when Joshua comes this girl is gonna be ready. Yes indeedy, I'm gonna be ready."

She broke into a wide smile and so did he. She took both his hands in hers, and held them for a long moment. "Me and Miss Joshua, we gonna tear down them Jericho walls, just like it say in the Bible. Ain't that right?"

He looked genuinely happier. "That's the way I like to hear thee talk, Julie Lee. That's the spirit that's going to take thee back into Virginia and back out again. Keep that faith, child, and the walls will surely come tumbling down."

She helped him into his coat and handed him his hat. After he had gone out the door, she watched his back for as long as she could. He did not rush, but took careful steps. She reflected on their conversation and smiled to herself. Even the steady patter of the rain wouldn't stop her from sleeping this night. Holy night, precious night. She was certain that God would stop the rain.

"God's surely gonna fix everything," she muttered to herself as she blew out the lamp and walked toward her room.

Chapter 33

The covered wagon with the deep false bottom in which they were to make at least part of their dangerous trek sat outside the door. The rain stopped four days before Joshua had arrived. The roads were passable, although still wet. It would slow them down a little, but according to Joshua, not enough to cause a cancellation of the trip.

When she looked out the window at the rickety old vehicle, Julie Lee wondered if it would be able to survive the journey. It sure looked mighty old and beat up to her. Even the horses looked ancient and tired. But she consoled herself with the thought that if Joshua said that wagon would ride, then it *would ride*, straight on up to heaven's gate, if it had to.

Everything they needed for the first part of the trip was packed neatly in a wooden box in the corner of Josephus' house. Inside the wagon were several changes of clothes. Joshua was known as a master of disguises. She had to be. There was a heavy price on her head—dead or alive—in all of the slave-holding states.

She was a woman feared by some, and respected by others. Now, as Julie Lee sat looking at Joshua, she thought it odd that anyone could be so frightened by such a tiny wisp of a woman. Why, Joshua was as gentle and kind as a little baby. Rarely even raised her voice. Didn't look like she could harm a fly. She could have been anybody's grandmother or old auntie.

Joshua couldn't read or write, but she had enough common sense for three people. That was why everyone who worked with her listened when she talked. She carefully planned the details of all of her trips. Said she worked that way because God would give her the sign and her job was only to make it understandable to those who didn't know. She was relied upon for her confidence, expertise and experience. There was no better conductor, male or female, black or white, on the underground railroad than she.

In preparation for this mission, Joshua's agents had already sent coded messages to all the conductors along the way. That's why, Joshua explained, it was not only important but mandatory that they leave on time and try at least to keep up with the schedule. Of course, there were always those unforeseen problems, but everyone understood when they were told approximately when and on what date they could "expect delivery."

The messages usually were signed, "Love, Caroline," or "Love, Virginia" or "Love, Louisa," meaning Louisiana. The names signified the states out of which the fugitive slaves were to be brought. In instances where a state name did not accommodate itself to a signature, the author would always mention the state somewhere in the text.

But timing was most important, Joshua explained in her own labored way. Julie Lee was terribly impressed by the intricacies of the planning. Lord, she thought, she'd never be able to do anything like that, and she *could* read and write. It wasn't easy being no conductor on the underground. That Joshua must be some kind of brave, smart woman. So God didn't give all the good sense to the white people.

Their first stop on the way down, Joshua said, would be at an old farmhouse out in the woods in some part of Delaware that Joshua wasn't even sure had a name. It didn't matter though, because she knew the area like the back of her hand. The railroad had many friends and supporters there, most of whom Joshua had cultivated and trained herself. They were black and white and rich and poor. Each knew his responsibilities, and so far, not one had ever let her down.

They talked as they were eating. Josephus and Julie Lee listened intently as Joshua reviewed the plan. Josephus' wife, Lillian, had prepared a hearty meal. She'd been worried for her husband before, but never quite as worried as this. His sudden decision to go along on this trip had alarmed her. She knew that nothing would stop him once his mind was made up. He was a man who did more than just talk about his religion, he practiced it as well. He was a man of action. She knew that when she married him, and now, concerned as she was as she watched him hunched over his elbows studying the crudely drawn maps spread out in the middle of the table, Lillian glowed with pride.

Maybe Josephus had made his mind up to go weeks ago, but he had never mentioned it to Lillian until the previous night when they were lying in bed after the children were asleep. She knew, as she looked at the deep lines stretching across his forehead and the determination in his jaw, that she could do nothing less than to wish him Godspeed and safe home.

According to the plan, to which Lillian listened in silence, Josephus and Julie Lee were to pretend to be father and daughter. Just to round out the little make-believe family, a white infant had been volunteered to be Julie Lee's baby. Now, Joshua reasoned, who could question a widowed man, traveling with his young daughter, his one and only child, and his grandchild, to deliver them to the husband who hadn't seen them since before the baby had been born.

Joshua and Dough Boy, her assistant on this trip, would ride inside the wagon as long as it was reasonably safe. They would be presented as family servants, a grandmother and grandson.

When they were in dangerous territory, or in counties where Joshua might be recognized, the old woman would be hidden beneath a false bottom in the wagon and covered over with a heavy blanket.

After they had talked it all out for more than an hour, Joshua said, "Now if'n y'all has any questions, better ask 'em now, 'cause we can't take no chances once we get down there. Now Dough Boy, he knows most of the way, so when I'm down under he can help, but y'all got to be the eyes and the ears when I can't. If'n somebody should stop us, y'all got to be able to explain something mighty darn quick.

"So if'n you needin' me and Dough Boy to go over anything again, then that's what we'll do. We'll go over the whole thing again. I ain't minding."

When there were no questions, Joshua folded up the maps and everyone prepared for bed. They would need a good night's sleep for the next day's task.

*   *   *

When they were finally settled in bed for the night, Julie Lee listened to a cricket outside chirp its sweet melody. Here she was, lying next to a great lady, a woman who until a few weeks ago she had never even heard of, but who now offered her what she had been wanting ever since leaving the Lorelei.

The older woman stirred slightly, then her snores settled into a rhythmic pattern to which Julie Lee easily adjusted. Lying there with her eyes wide open and staring up at the ceiling, Julie Lee swore she could feel fire coming from the woman's body. That fire gave her strength, and some of her fearful feelings melted away.

She closed her eyes, but before drifting off to sleep, offered up her own little prayer. She said it softly. "Lord, just give me the strength to let me do like Joshua told me to do, and Lord, make it so we can go in and come out all right. You know that I get tired sometime, and maybe, Lord, you gets tired of me, little old Julie Lee, always asking for something, but I know you understand. We niggas need some extra attention now and then 'cause you made it hard for us down here on the ground. We's going in the morning, Lord. Watch over us and bring us back safe and sound."

Chapter 34

The first part of their journey, within Pennsylvania, was uneventful, and despite the seriousness of their mission, took on an almost picniclike air. The weather was good, if a bit nippy for Julie Lee's liking.

The longer they rode, the better acquainted the four travelers became. The baby was well-behaved and had slept through most of the trip thus far. The group swapped stories and anecdotes about their childhoods, and as the stories unfolded themselves, so did the speakers' personalities.

Julie Lee, Joshua and Dough Boy sang a few old spirituals. Dough Boy had a pretty, tenor voice, and Julie Lee told him so. "Boy, you could make money with that voice of yours. People would come from everywhere just to hear somebody sing as sweet as you.

"Just wait till you meet up with my Dancer. He can sing too, though he can't dance no more 'cause he only got one leg now." Her eyes sparkled when she talked about Dancer.

Dough Boy blushed when Julie Lee told him about his sweet voice, but admitted that singing was something he just loved to do. Once, he said, when he was a little younger, a white woman friend of his mother's had wanted to give him professional lessons. "But Mama said, 'No, my boy ain't gonna be no sissy. He got work to do. When he gets old enough, if he wants to sing he can take them professional lessons. In the meantime, he can do his singing in church.' "

Julie Lee laughed. It sounded practical to her.

They rode on at a leisurely pace. That was the way Joshua had planned it. "You be moving too fast, and you brings attention to yourself. We ain't wantin' no attention."

It was still daylight when Joshua fell off to sleep in the back of the wagon. Just in case of emergency, she pushed her body down into the false bottom and drew the blanket over her. Prior to taking leave of them, however, she said, "Since I is the oldest one in this here crowd, I is entitled to act like the old lady that I is.

"Got to get myself some shuteye, 'cause when night come, then I got to be a wise, old black-faced owl. I keeps my eyes wide open, turns my head all around, and sees everything and everywhere at the same time."

It was dark by the time they reached the Delaware farmhouse where they would spend the night.

Just as Joshua and Dough Boy had promised, the farmhouse was filled with provisions. It was a bit more ragged than Julie Lee had expected, for it hadn't been occupied for several years. Inside was everything the travelers would need: clothes, food and sleeping pallets. Much to Julie Lee's surprise, there was even fresh milk for the baby.

They would take turns sleeping, Joshua announced. One person would stand lookout while the others would get their rest. Josephus would keep the first watch, then Julie Lee, and finally Dough Boy and Joshua.

The first streaks of daylight had hardly begun to make their way across the sky before Joshua was up and ordering them all to get up too. Julie Lee's whole arm was wet, and she realized that the baby needed changing. She pulled out a clean rag to replace the baby's soiled one, and as she did, she imagined he was little John, all soft and cuddly. While she was changing the baby, Josephus and Dough Boy were out front, loading additional provisions into the wagon.

Once again, they were out on the open road. They stopped two more times before finally crossing into Virginia. At the state border Julie Lee began to cry. Hers was a feeling of anxiety and fear. Joshua tried to comfort her.

"I knows how it be, child," the older woman said. "I cried myself the first time I went on back into Maryland. Just cry, child. Cry yoarself a river if you want, 'cause ain't gonna be much time for no cryin' later on. You gonna need all your strength. So cry, child. But don't foiget to pray."

Chapter 35

They were only a few miles inside Virginia when they stopped once again. They would leave the baby and the wagon at the home of one of the regular railroad conductors. After a short rest and a good meal, they started out on foot.

"Now, girl," Joshua said to Julie Lee, "you gonna find out what runnin' is really all about. So far it been easy, but now comes the hard part. You thinkin' you up to it?"

" 'Course I'm up to it," she snapped, hurt at the implication that she might not stay with it until the bitter end. After all, it wasn't as if they were going in to fetch a group of strangers. They were going in after her family—Dancer, little John and Hannibal. This was a day she had dreamed about ever since leaving Virginia.

Everyone changed clothes. Julie Lee slipped into a pair of moccasins and slid on a pair of men's pants. They were a little big, but she pulled a belt tightly around them and they stayed hitched up. She would be able to move better, dressed like a man, Joshua explained.

"Now," the old woman commanded Julie Lee, "tie up that hair and put it underneath this here hat."

As they headed off in the direction of a dense wood, Joshua took the lead. The underbrush was thick and tangled, and everybody stumbled more than once.

The air was fresh and sweet as it always was in springtime in Virginia. The trees had already filled out, and the bushes, which had been scrawny only weeks earlier, were now fat and plump.

Julie Lee sucked in the air through her mouth, sniffed it through her nose. Perhaps it was her imagination, but she could swear that that air was the sweetest and the freshest she'd breathed in months.

They kept close behind Joshua, and so when she stopped short, everyone behind nearly fell atop her. Joshua paid them no mind. She was too busy listening for sounds in the darkness. She was that big old black owl. She cupped her hands over her ears and opened her eyes wide. Then, just as she said she would, she began turning her head in every direction.

They were moving a little bit fast for Julie Lee. She was tired, and the lump in her throat seemed to have grown larger. The hairs on the back of her neck were moist and itchy.

Josephus had said little as they walked. He didn't complain, but the pain he felt was evident in his face, which was now a scarlet red. The veins in his temples were throbbing.

Amazingly, old Joshua's feet held steady. There was even dignity in the long strides she took. She climbed over fallen logs better than her younger companions. When she got stuck in some underbrush, she simply untangled the mess and went on moving, never complaining, never even cursing under her breath as Dough Boy was wont to do.

They kept walking for what seemed like an eternity.

Finally, mercifully, Joshua signaled that they could rest. They were beside a stream, so at least they could soak their feet. And thank God for that, Julie Lee thought. Her feet felt like they were on fire.

The night creatures were filling the darkness with their cries, and more than once those nocturnal calls made Julie Lee's teeth stand on edge.

After a rest that hardly seemed sufficient, Joshua once again was on her feet. "All right, children," she ordered. "Time to get to movin' again. We ain't on no picnic, you know."

As they walked, Julie Lee became worried about Josephus. His face was strained with exhaustion and he looked so haggard. She had to do something.

She caught up to Joshua, who was marching several feet ahead and she begged the woman to stop, not for her own sake, but for that of Josephus. Joshua turned around, took one good look at the man, and agreed.

They made camp a short time later. In moments, Joshua's charges fell to the ground. Julie Lee was breathing hard, but once she'd caught her breath, she eased out of her shoes and before long was massaging her feet and toes. It felt so good. And the better it felt, the more she rubbed.

She sat back against a tree with her eyes closed and quickly drifted off to sleep.

She was dreaming when the sound of Joshua's voice woke her up again. At her command, Josephus tried to spring to his feet, but he couldn't. He fell back to the ground. He was still sweating, despite the long rest they'd had. He just couldn't go any farther. "I guess I'm not as young as I used to be," he apologized. "Even if I could keep going, I would only slow the rest of thee down."

Joshua realized that he was right. They would all be better off if he remained behind. "We'll come back and get you on the way back," she told him. "But don't you go nowhwere. You stay right here."

Josephus' face broke into a grateful, albeit weak smile.

"Anyways," Joshua added, "we ain't needin' you so much for this part of the trip. We needs you when we is on our way back. And if'n they finds a white man sleeping in the woods, it won't raise much suspicion. You can tell 'em most any old kind of story, and they'll believe you. Don't forget though, you can't talk none of that Quaker talk, 'cause if'n you does, they might get to thinkin' that you is working on the railroad. They knows a lot of Quakers like you be helpin' us."

She was a wise soul, Josephus thought. He apologized again, disappointed that he couldn't continue the trip, but accepting his fate.

Before leaving, Julie Lee put her arms around his neck and whispered in his ear, "Don't worry none, brother. We gonna be back 'fore you knows it. Ain't nothing gonna happen to you or us. You gonna pray for us?"

"Don't worry, little girl. I'll be praying as hard as I can. God's blessings be with thee. It is all up to God now."

As the miles fell behind them, Julie Lee began to notice familiar details about the landscape. Lord have mercy, they had set foot on Lorelei land. She knew every creek and stream, and even some of the trees, which she and Hannibal had marked when they were children.

It was an eerie feeling, being back there. She was tired, but the very idea of being so near had renewed her energy and enthusiasm. Now it was her turn to be in the lead. Joshua fell back and let her go to it.

Soon they came upon the small hill that descended to the roadway leading to the big house, and there, off to the side, was the quarter.

"We got to get down from here on," Joshua said, exerting her authority once again. Julie Lee knew the land, but Joshua was the expert on getting in and out safely.

"Never can tell who be walkin' after dark," she said. "Sometimes people can't sleep at night so they start to walkin'. Can't remember how many times I coulda got catched 'cause of some fool that couldn't sleep. We got to stay low. Done come too far now to mess up."

She received no argument. The three began crawling down the hill toward the quarter. All the lights inside the big house were out, so the only illumination about the place was from the lamp the old master kept lit at night on the porch.

Julie Lee was tingling with excitement, and without thinking, she stood up as they neared the quarter, preparing to run toward it. She might have run too had it not been for the abruptness with which Dough Boy pulled her back down to the ground.

"Is you crazy, girl?" he spit harshly. "I knows you is all excited about being so close, but this ain't the time to go actin' the fool. Carelessness can get you killed. Act sensible, girl."

She knew Dough Boy was right. She could feel Joshua's eyes scolding her, but the woman said nothing.

The backside of the quarter was shrouded in blackness. The three interlopers crawled on their stomachs. Julie Lee's face was so dirty that she looked as dark as Joshua and Dough Boy.

Suddenly the sound of a door opening caused them to freeze where they were. A man stepped out into the darkness, away from the cabin that had been occupied by an old fellow named Meno. Perhaps it was the darkness, but this man seemed unfamiliar to Julie Lee. Maybe Meno had died.

Once the man was safely out of sight, the trio continued crawling closer to the quarter. When they got to it, they stood and pressed their bodies as close as they could against the cabin walls.

Shortly, they were right beneath the window of the cabin that Julie Lee and Dancer had shared. Julie Lee held up her hand, signaling for Joshua and Dough Boy to stop. Cautiously, she slid up the wall and peered into the window. Some embers from the fireplace were still aglow, giving off just enough light that she could make out the room.

She was surprised to see that her mother's chair was not in its usual place. Her eyes darted quickly, searching for something familiar, but she found nothing. Maybe Dancer had gotten so angry with her for leaving without telling him that he'd thrown out everything that reminded him of her.

She slid back down to the ground, wondering what to do next. Here she was right at the door of the cabin she had lived in all her life, yet there was nothing of hers in it. Even the little rocker Hannibal had made for little John wasn't in its place beside the pallet.

"Well, child, does we go in or don't we?" Joshua asked anxiously.

Julie Lee took off her hat and scratched her head. "Ain't rightly sure what we should do. That's me and

Dancer's cabin all right, but ain't nothing in there that belongs to us. I just don't understand.''

"Don't go gettin' yourself upset yet," Joshua said. "Must be some way to explain why your stuff ain't in there. Maybe your massa changed the cabin after you left. Maybe he give it to somebody else. Do it look like somebody live in it?''

"Somebody living in there, but I don't know who.''

Julie Lee said nothing more, but immediately began crawling. Joshua and Dough Boy followed as she headed for Jeddah's cabin. Surely Jeddah would know where Dancer and little John had gone.

She knew she'd come to the right place even before she got close to it. That smell of roots and herbs swept into her nose.

She was still lying on the ground when she tapped at the cabin door. She tapped urgently, but there was no response from inside. Jeddah just had to be in there. Julie Lee finally pushed open the door and crawled inside. Joshua and Dough Boy did not follow, but waited for her to tell them when to come in.

Though the cabin was dark, she knew where Jeddah's sleeping pallet was and headed toward it. The woman's soft moans in her sleep filled the cabin. Her hand was dangling off the pallet and touching the floor. Julie Lee didn't want to startle the sleeping figure so she gently rubbed the woman's hand. Jeddah had always liked that. She liked to have her long fingers massaged.

Julie Lee spoke softly. "Jeddah. Jeddah, it's me, Julie Lee. I come back to get y'all, Jeddah.'' Now she began to shake the woman. "Wake up, Jeddah. It's me.''

She didn't open her eyes, but Julie Lee knew she was

265

awake when she felt the pressure of the woman grasping her hand.

"That you, Julie Lee, baby? That you?" Now her eyes opened. "My sweet child done come back. Yes, she did."

Jeddah did not appear to be surprised. She seemed to have been expecting Julie Lee to come to her cabin in the middle of the night. She roused herself quickly, and welcomed Joshua and Dough Boy warmly, as if she'd known them for years. "Child, I dreamed nearly every night that you would come back one day," Jeddah said, addressing herself not to Julie Lee, but to the two strangers. "Anybody that done bring this baby back for my old eyes to see, got to be a friend. I sure did hope to see the child again. She's like my own, you know."

She inspected the girl back and front. Julie Lee had picked up a few pounds, but it was her all right. She was healthy looking, even with her face so dirty. Jeddah pulled back Julie Lee's hair.

"Lord knows you is lighter than your mama, but you sure do look just like her now. I know she would be poppin' the buttons on her dress if she could see her baby now. You ain't been gone long, but it sure seem like you done growed up a lot." Jeddah was chuckling now, as if at some secret joke between her and Julie Lee's dead mother. "Yes indeed, this child is growing up just fine."

It wasn't like Jeddah to be talking so fast. They'd been in the cabin for nearly fifteen minutes and so far Jeddah hadn't said one word about Dancer and little John. In fact, though the words kept tumbling from the woman's mouth, she wasn't saying much of anything. She kept rambling on until Julie Lee stopped her. The girl's tone of voice was sharp.

"Jeddah," she said, taking the woman by her arms, "you been talking all this time, but how come you ain't said nothing 'bout Dancer and my baby? How come?"

Jeddah fell silent. She looked past Julie Lee and straight into Joshua's eyes, which were full of their own questions. A fleeting look of sadness ran across her face, and then Julie Lee began to fear the worst. Jeddah fell back into a chair. The candle she'd lit was burning brightly and she was unable to avoid Julie Lee's questioning gaze.

The silence was heavy. Jeddah began her story slowly at first, but soon the words were coming more quickly.

"Child, your baby and your man is dead, been dead for a while."

Julie Lee was too stunned to cry. She wanted to know every detail. "What happened?" she demanded.

"Young massa, he killed Dancer, and little John, well he just had the life knocked out of him, losin' his mama and daddy and all."

Julie Lee's hands swept up to her face as she tried holding back the tears and the rush of anger. "Go on. What happened?"

Jeddah rubbed her hands together, unable to look directly at the girl. She began to mumble. "Young Massa, he was awfully mad when he found out that you done run away. He said Dancer knowed where you was gone. Made everybody come out their cabins and out the big house. Had a gun on all us niggas. It was awful. It was one awful day round this place. Everybody was scared.

"Things round here ain't been the same since you left. Young massa done got mean and onery. Even his daddy is scared to say anything to him.

"You know we ain't never had too much beatin' around here before, but child since you been gone, niggas

267

been gettin' beat all the time. 'Course Young Massa don't mess with me. He scared of me just like his daddy is. They scared of my medicine. Afraid I'm gonna put some mojo on them. I would too, if he put his hand on me. But the rest of the niggas, they ain't got no protection. Julie Lee, that man would slap a nigga down quick as look at him.''

Joshua was shaking her head. ''Uh huh. Nothing ain't never gonna change. Lord, have mercy,'' she proclaimed, looking toward the roof of the cabin. ''Lord, have mercy.''

Jeddah picked up where she'd left off. ''A few days ago, Young Massa even hired some old white trash to boss the field workers. Said they was gonna look after us niggas since it seemed that no matter how good we be treated, we just can't be trusted.

''Massa done sold some niggas too. 'Member that Big Foot Ben? Well, child, he sold him first. Sold him off to one of them old white-trash nigga peddlers that be coming round here all the time looking to buy cheap so they can sell the niggas more farther down south.

''Sold some other niggas too, mostly men though. Said the women was more valuable for breeding. Zeph said she heard Young Massa say that he was going to sell off all the niggas that might give him trouble. Sell the niggas they seemed likely to run off. Sell the niggas that has to be beat too much.

''It's been real bad round this place, child.''

Julie Lee trembled with a rage that rattled her bones and set her blood afire. It was her fault that all of this had happened. Not only were Dancer and little John dead, but now people were beat unmercifully and sold. As she had sworn herself to vengeance for her mother's murder, she now vowed silently that she would get her revenge for these outrages as well.

"Tell me what he done to Dancer and little John, Jeddah. How he kill them? What he done?"

Jeddah was reluctant, but Julie Lee was becoming impatient.

"I want to know what he done," she demanded in a hoarse whisper. "Tell me, woman."

"Ain't important, Julie Lee. Ain't important what he done—they just as dead."

Julie Lee crossed the room and stood directly in front of Jeddah. Sparks flashed from her eyes. "I said I want to know what he done to Dancer and little John."

Jeddah looked helplessly at Joshua. It was a tense moment. Joshua said nothing. It was none of her business and all of Julie Lee's. The girl had a right to know.

"He was dangling the baby upside down and when Dancer tried to stop him, Young Massa just shot Dancer down cold. Then Katy run up and she got little John away from Young Massa, but it was too late. That poor baby wasn't never the same after that day—always tired, never eating, just crying all the time—and a couple months later he just quit altogether. Just went to sleep one night and never did wake up again."

Julie Lee's knees buckled. She would have fallen had it not been for Dough Boy rushing to her side and catching her. He helped her down onto the pallet.

"He killed my baby, just as sure as if he'd shot him too." She looked down at her hands. The blue veins were throbbing. A volatile rage roared within her. She wanted to run up to the big house, swinging an axe and killing everything white in sight. Didn't matter if she got caught or not.

She fell back onto the pallet and opened her mouth to scream, as well she might have, if Jeddah hadn't stopped her. Jeddah covered over her mouth and Dough Boy pinned her to the pallet by both arms. She tried to wiggle free but couldn't. Still, fury had made her strong and Dough Boy had a hard time keeping her quiet. He held her until he felt her rage subside and saw her face grow calmer.

The next voice she heard was Joshua's. It was soothing and soft. "Julie Lee, stop it, child. Stop now. You got to calm down. Cry if you wanna, but you can't scream. Girl, you got to be a woman now. You got to be a woman and think carefully about what your next move is gonna be. White folks think all the time, and niggas got to think too. You got to think, plan out what you want to do."

Joshua released her hand from the girl's mouth and she signaled for Dough Boy to let her arms go. Julie Lee didn't move. The three others made a semicircle around the pallet.

Then she started to cry, softly at first, and then more powerfully until her body was racked with sobs.

"It's my fault," she berated herself. "It's my fault they dead. They all dead 'cause of me. 'Cause *I* wanted to be free. 'Cause *I* decided to run. They dead 'cause of me."

Jeddah knelt down beside the pallet and took Julie Lee's hand into her own. "Naw, baby. Ain't nobody dead 'cause of you. They dead 'cause that's the way it is. They dead 'cause Massa own them and that mean he can do what he want.

"Child, don't you know that peoples has to follow their star sometime? You had to follow yours. Some of the niggas round here try to say you was wrong to go, but you wasn't. They tried to say you didn't care nothing about

270

Dancer and your baby, but I knowed that wasn't true, and the proof is right here. You come back for them. No child, when white folks kill us niggas it ain't never our fault. They just kill us 'cause they can do it, and nobody won't do nothing about it. What you gotta do now is save your strength. We need you to make sure nothin' like this don't ever happen no more. We need you to help all of us see the light.''

Jeddah fell silent, but Joshua picked up the conversation. ''Where is Julie Lee's brother, Hannibal? We maybe can't do nothing about her man and the baby, but we can sure take her brother back with us. Can't we, Dough Boy?''

Dough Boy nodded affirmatively.

''Where them overseers be sleeping?'' Joshua asked cautiously.

''Well, most of them goes home at night. Only one stays on the place. He's the meanest of them. He stay in a little house out back of the quarter. I'm surprised you didn't see it when y'all come up. Massa had it built real fast. That's where that white trash stay. He got a wife and some children and they all staying in the cabin. It ain't no better than one of these nigga shacks.''

Joshua was thinking quickly now. ''He ain't doing such a good a job, 'cause we was able to get in here and nobody seen us.''

Julie Lee stopped crying. She asked Jeddah if she would bring Hannibal to the cabin. Of course, the woman was willing to accommodate. While she was gone to fetch the boy, Dough Boy massaged Julie Lee's neck and back. It felt nice, so nice. She began to relax and her heart-wrenching cries were replaced by sniffles. She was still sitting on the pallet when the door to the cabin opened.

271

Hannibal was following closely at Jeddah's heel. Accompanying them was a small boy whom Julie Lee did not recognize. Hannibal bolted from behind Jeddah, leaving the boy standing in the doorway with his mouth open.

Julie Lee stood up and Hannibal swept her off her feet and held her high in his arms.

"Julie Lee! I don't believe my own eyes. You come back! Lord, how I missed you."

He kissed her again and again and she clutched him to her.

He finally put her down, but he kept holding on to her. "Your face is dirty, but you lookin' good. I been praying for you every day since you gone. Some people say you was probably dead, but I ain't never thought that. I had a feeling you was coming back."

He continued babbling and it was several minutes before both of them realized that he had not been introduced to the others in the room.

"These my friends," Julie Lee said, pointing in the direction of Joshua and Dough Boy.

"This here's Joshua. You see this lady? She's a great woman. Real famous too. She a conductor on the underground railroad, they call it, and she brung me here. She goes all over helping people to get free. Everybody scared of her 'cause she be freeing niggas all the time. Just stealing them from right underneath the white man's nose. Ain't that right, Miss Joshua?

"And this boy here, this Dough Boy. He helps Joshua. He work on the railroad too. But you knowed I was coming back, didn't you, Hannibal?"

"Yeah, I knew it," he said, cuffing her playfully under her chin. "I knew it all the time."

The young boy said nothing, but stood peeking from

272

behind Jeddah's skirt. She introduced him, and as she did, pushed him forward into the middle of the room.

"This here is Lytell. He's a good boy. Been almost like a son to me," Jeddah said proudly. "He ain't got no mama or daddy. Massa bought him from a peddler who said he come from some plantation down south where the owners died and they was selling some of the niggas real cheap. Been here about a month or more." She rubbed his head, like she would a puppy dog's. "This child, he just come to me, and we been together ever since 'cept at night when he stay over in the dormitory with Hannibal and the rest of the boys."

Hannibal turned his attention from the others in the room to his sister. He wondered if Jeddah had already told her about Dancer and little John. He hoped she had because he didn't want to be the one to have to break the news. He touched her face.

"I know, Hannibal. I know. Jeddah told me about Dancer and little John." She stared vacantly. "They dead, Hannibal. I know they both dead."

Without any coaxing Hannibal tried to explain. "I was so scared, Julie Lee. I was scared just like all the other niggas when Young Massa started acting crazy that day after you left."

He dropped his face into his hands, once again feeling the fear and shame and guilt. Then he put his head on her shoulder and cried as he talked into her ear.

"I love you, Julie Lee, and Lord knows I loved Dancer and little John, but there wasn't nothing I could do. I couldn't believe Massa done it like he did. Just like the man ain't had no heart at all. First I was mad for you leaving, and then I was mad 'cause I was yellow. If it wasn't for Jeddah and Katy I might've lost my mind.'

His sister patted him gently. "I know, Hannibal. I know."

"But you don't understand, Julie Lee. You don't understand. I let Massa kill them and I was too scared to move. Katy, she tried. She run forward to help, and Massa kicked her down. But she kept on trying anyway. But me, I just stood there, too scared to do anything."

"I know, Hannibal. It's all right. I come back to take Dancer and little John, but they dead now. They dead," she repeated, making it sink in, hardening herself to the truth. "Now, Hannibal, we got to go forward. That's what we got to do. Come on, go back with me. If I can't have my man and my baby, at least I can have my brother."

He pulled away from her. "I want to go, Julie Lee, but I can't. I can't leave the Lorelei just yet. Everything I know is here. I ain't got no love for Massa, but I ain't like you. Sometimes I think that God should've made you the boy and me the girl. You braver than I is—always have seemed to be, even when Mama died."

He looked deep into her eyes, praying for a flicker of understanding. He stood up. "See, Julie Lee, I got me a baby coming soon. I found out after you left. You remember Cleopatra? No? Well, me and her was fooling around and Cleo done got knocked up. I can't leave her here all by herself. She done already had trouble with Massa. He beat her once 'cause he told her that he wasn't ready for her to be messing around. He was mad 'cause he wanted some other boy to pleasure her. But it was too late. Cleo done already got knocked up with my baby. I can't leave her now. She say she love me, and I think I love her. Ain't rightly sure, but I can't go without finding out."

"Cleo can come with us. Ain't that right? You can

274

bring Cleo and then when she have the baby it be born free.''

Time was so short and it was rapidly running out. She looked hard at Hannibal. She knew him well enough to know that he was unconvinced.

''I just can't go, Julie Lee. I can't go with you.''

She heard his words cut through her own determination that he *would* go. She heard what he said, and then knew suddenly that she had to accept. Hannibal would not go. She kissed him on his forehead. ''Maybe one day, Hannibal. Maybe one day when freedom come, we'll be together. The day is coming soon. I know it is 'cause that what's all the papers say up in Philadelphia. There's gonna be a war, Hannibal, and a lot of people gonna get killed and hurt, but we gonna be free.

''Do me something, Hannibal. When the freedom day come, I want you to be ready. You hear me? When that day come, you be ready for it.''

He smiled at her, grateful for her understanding.

''You ain't no coward, Hannibal. I know you ain't, and I don't care how much you say it, I know different. Different people does different things, and you doing what you has to do.''

In the little time left Hannibal told Julie Lee about Katy. Katy was very ill. She'd been off her feet for weeks. She wanted to go back to work, but the old master wouldn't allow it. Young Master Andy wanted to send her back out to the quarter to live out her time, but his father would have none of it. Katy was an old and trusted servant.

Jeddah picked up the story from Hannibal. ''Zeph say Katy ain't nothing but skin and bones. Say she ain't been eating hardly nothing. Just laying up there in that bed like she waiting to die. I was gonna make some medicine to help her heal, but Katy said she ain't wanted no medicine. She just want to be left alone.''

Julie Lee could hardly believe what she was hearing. Not Katy. She was one of the strongest women Julie Lee had ever seen. Poor Katy. Maybe she was just tired. Maybe she did deserve to be allowed to lie still and to die if she wanted to. God knows she'd seen enough grief in her lifetime.

Julie Lee wanted to see her, but was too afraid to ask Joshua to wait any longer. She turned to look at the older woman and saw in her eyes an annoyed impatience. Julie Lee couldn't blame her. After all, her life was in jeopardy too, not to mention Dough Boy's.

Jeddah had not actually been invited to join them, but it was obvious that she planned to go. All the while the talking was going on, she'd been throwing things into a big sack. She didn't have much in the way of clothes, but she sure had plenty of little bottles and tiny sacks of her medicine. She wrapped the bottles in rags, not only to keep them from breaking, but to keep them from making noise.

The time had come to take leave. Hannibal embraced his sister once again. "We'll be seeing each other another time," he promised. He kissed Jeddah and shook Lytell's hand. The little boy was going too.

Julie Lee watched sadly as Hannibal left the cabin. "I love you," she said softly as he made his way back toward the dormitory.

Joshua looked at Jeddah and said, "Well, we ain't got all we come for, but least we ain't come this far for naught. Bringing even one soul out is all right with me." Jeddah smiled. The two of them would be good friends.

Jeddah blew out the candle, which had nearly burned down. She took one more look around the cabin and followed the others out the door.

They had made it. They had cleared the hill, but when they stopped to catch their breath, Julie Lee made an announcement.

"Can't go without seeing Katy. Just can't. Joshua, I'm gonna go back for a minute. Y'all go on ahead, and I'll catch up."

At first Joshua tried to talk her out of it, but soon relented. Julie Lee was adamant.

"All right, Julie Lee. You go. You go back, but you're on your own. You taking a big risk, but it's your hide. We gonna wait for you back at that place by the stream, but I tell you now, daughter, we ain't gonna wait too long. You hear me?"

Julie Lee promised that she would meet them. "I won't get caught, Joshua. I promise. You just take care of Jeddah and little Lytell. I'll meet up with you, and then we'll go on back and get Josephus."

Jeddah kissed her on the cheek before she turned around and went back in the direction of the quarter. Julie Lee didn't hear her, but Jeddah told the others, "I ain't worried none about Julie Lee. She gonna be all right."

Julie Lee had no difficulty getting into the house, and she quietly tiptoed past the floor where the family slept and on up to the third level where Katy's room was.

The door to the room was half open. The smell of sickness and liniment permeated the air. The moonlight pouring in through the high window of the room silhouetted the figure on the bed. It was Katy all right. The white scarf was in its usual place, tied tightly around her head.

277

Julie Lee gently closed the door and headed straight for the bed. Dried sweat was caked around Katy's temples. She touched the woman's hand. It was bone-thin and frail. Katy's once-fat cheeks were slack, and her jawbone jutted out.

"Katy? Katy, it's me, Julie Lee. I come to see you, darling. I come all the way back to see you. Won't you say something to me?"

The woman's mouth moved and her eyelashes fluttered, but her eyes did not open. Julie Lee pressed her face tightly against her chest, listening for a heartbeat. It was there, but it was very faint. She whispered again more urgently. "Katy, it's me."

Taking Katy's hand into her own, Julie Lee closed her eyes and leaned near the woman's ear. "I love you, Katy. I love you. I come back just to see you. They said you was sick. I couldn't go without seeing you one more time."

Once again the woman tried to move her lips. They were dry and chapped, so chapped that when Julie Lee brushed up against them, a tiny line of blood opened on her face.

Katy's mouth was opening and closing, but no matter how close she got, Julie Lee could not make out what she was trying to say.

Time was running out for Julie Lee. She had to go. She was about to put Katy's hand back at rest on her chest, when she felt the woman apply pressure to her hand. It was feeble and weak, but it was pressure nonetheless.

Now she knew for sure that Katy was aware of her.

She waited a few more minutes hoping against hope that Katy would try to say something, but she didn't. The feeble pressure disappeared. She put her head to the wom-

278

an's chest again. This time she could hear no heartbeat. Nothing.

Katy was dead. Her Katy. Sweet, sweet Katy was gone. She'd already gone on to join all the other people Julie Lee had loved. How could God have made her homecoming so tragic?

She placed both Katy's hands on her stomach and rearranged the scarf on her head. That done, she tiptoed out of the room.

Chapter 36

The Civil War was raging. The days found Julie Lee restless and short-tempered. She'd scolded poor Lytell any number of times for nothing in particular. In between trying to fill her in on all that had happened after she had left the Lorelei, Jeddah spent her time trying to calm the girl down.

Jeddah was always careful to avoid talking much about Dancer and little John. She couldn't stand to see the dark cloud that glazed over Julie Lee's eyes at the very mention of their names. So far, the girl had been bearing her shock well, but Jeddah could tell they were on her mind, and it was what had happened to Dancer and little John that in no small measure contributed to Julie Lee's eagerness to strike a blow for the Union cause.

Since arriving back in Philadelphia, Julie Lee had sucked up every morsel of information she could get about the war. She hung around in places where women generally were not found. She went through every newspaper she could get her hands on with a fine-tooth comb.

As the days passed, the headlines in the papers became more gloomy and the situation worsened as the Northern and Southern positions hardened.

Most of the Southern slave-holding states had already seceded from the Union. They had adopted their own constitution, and had even elected their own president, Jefferson Davis of Mississippi, a month to the day before Abraham Lincoln took office as President of the United States.

The rebels had formed an army of no slight capabilities to defend the Confederate cause. They were attacking and winning battles and even taking over Federal military installations throughout the South. Confederate Brigadier General Pierre Beauregard had bombarded and taken Fort Sumter down in South Carolina. The Rebs had even taken the Federal arsenal at Harpers Ferry in West Virginia.

President Lincoln was continually putting out calls for more volunteers for the Federal army. It was rumored he would soon institute a draft.

As the situation worsened, those who believed the North's superiority in weaponry, experience and finances would make it a short war were silenced. The so-called "bad boys" of the South were not easily beaten.

Julie Lee had read about how her home state, Virginia, had finally relented and joined the Confederacy on April 17, 1861. She wondered what it meant for the people she had left behind at the Lorelei.

She could barely stand being so inactive. She wanted desperately to do something to aid the Union cause, but what could she do? Part of the answer came the very next day when she was shopping in a produce market for her employer, a nice woman who paid her a decent fee to cook and keep her house clean. She was leaning over into one of the stalls, talking to the female merchant about how much prices had gone up because of the war, when she overheard two men standing nearby discussing the war.

"I'd say the Johnny Rebs is the stubbornest bunch of

mules I've ever seen . . ." one man said to the other disgustedly. "I thought for sure we'd have this mess cleared up by now. Hell, it doesn't make any sense to me that people have to keep dying. Let them keep their slaves. It's just not worth it."

The other man said, "I hear that some of those rich slavers are acting like there isn't any war down there. Some of them are still having big fancy balls. Can you imagine that? A war is going on and the South is still having tea parties. I'll tell you what I think . . ."

Suddenly, the men noticed Julie Lee was listening to what they had to say, and they abruptly stopped talking. As they walked on, both turned back at least twice to look at her.

All the way back to work, she thought about what they'd said: "A war is going on and the South is still having tea parties." Since her return to Philadelphia, Julie Lee had made many friends, many of them outside the Quaker community. Of course, some knew that she was a Negro, but most did not, and she didn't bother to tell them any different. She'd met and talked with quite a few Union officers and soldiers. Their response to her eager questions and apparent avid interest was generally the same. They thought it amusing that she, only a woman, a young woman at that, would have such a deep interest in the war. After all, war was men's business. Women's business was babies, clothes and other such domestic matters.

Now that a germ of an idea was sprouting in her head, she thought of one man who could help her, one man in whom she could have complete confidence, who had the wherewithal to get her into the war effort in some meaningful way.

Claude McIver. Everybody called him Ivy. He was a

book dealer and had lived in several Northern cities. He had friends up and down the eastern seaboard. In addition to his books, Claude also peddled newspapers and no little amount of political information. There was hardly a book or a newspaper in his shop that he hadn't read.

A rotund, middle-aged man, there were those who always teased McIver about his striking resemblance to Benjamin Franklin. Nearly every Philadelphia politician, and even many of those who served in Washington, found their way to McIver's with great regularity. Julie Lee had heard that any number of important political decisions had gotten their start in McIver's back room.

Ivy was deeply supportive of the Union cause. He believed slavery to be an abomination and he had raised thousands of dollars for the war. Whenever there was some rally designed to encourage volunteerism, McIver was at its helm. Some nights the man went from door to door encouraging mothers to send their sons off to what he described as "the noble cause."

Yes, Julie Lee thought, she would go to McIver. If anyone could give her some idea of what she could do to help the war effort he could.

The very next day she sought her employer's permission to take off an hour early. She went directly to McIver's, and as usual, he was surrounded by his cronies, talking about the war.

When she came into the store all the men rose respectfully. Those who wore hats tipped them in her direction. They stood standing until McIver bade them sit down. "My God, you all act like you've never seen a pretty woman before. What can I do for you today, young lady?" he inquired, walking around from behind the counter.

"I need to talk with you in private, Mr. McIver. Can we go in the back room?"

"Why, yes," he stammered, looking at the interested expressions of his friends.

"Charlie, take over for me behind the counter."

The back room was not unlike what Julie Lee had expected. There were unopened cartons of books, old newspapers and order pads all over the place. There were several chairs, and in the middle of the room stood a long, wooden table. So that was the famous table, the table behind which great political deals had been made. Oh, if that table could talk, she thought.

She sniffed at the musty air in the room and McIver hastened to open two of the room's four windows.

He closed the door and offered her a seat in a huge wooden chair with wheels on it. It was of a quite different design than the table and in fact, all the chairs were mixed and matched, though a few looked rather expensive, if old.

McIver pulled up a chair for himself and faced her, adjusting his glasses on the bridge of his nose. He peered at her through watery blue eyes and waited for her to say something.

"Mr. McIver, I need your help."

"Well, what exactly can I do for you, young lady? After all, you're one of my best customers. Do you really read all those papers you pick up every week?"

"I sure do. I want to know everything that's going on."

He smiled approvingly. "So what can I do?"

"I'm not rightly sure," she said, becoming suddenly and mysteriously flustered. "You see, Mr. McIver, I want to do something to help the war effort. I mean I really

284

want to do something that's going to make some difference. Do you know what I mean?''

"I'm not sure that I do know what you mean exactly, but I know there are a lot of people who feel the way you do." He looked thoughtfully at her. "Every day the casualties are mounting and every day it seems as if the Rebs are getting more and more adamant. It doesn't look like they're going to give up anything without a lot of bloodshed. Of course, I don't always agree with Mr. Lincoln, but I don't know what else the man can do."

McIver was a political animal, and he was not above seeking help for the cause wherever he could get it. He took women's interests in war and politics seriously, unlike colleagues who pooh-poohed their involvement. Finally, he said, "I believe they could always use a few more nurses at the front. There are always so many men wounded."

McIver took a handkerchief out of his pocket and began rubbing his glasses. They clouded up when he blew onto them. This finished, he once again turned his attention to the woman sitting before him.

"I don't want to be a nurse, Mr. McIver. I don't know anything about nursing. Surely there is something else I can do. I want to be a soldier or something like that. I want to fight if I can."

McIver patted one of her hands. "My dear girl, the army certainly needs a lot of things, but I don't think they're ready for women to be donning uniforms and fighting on the field.

"Me, now, I'm for anyone fighting for the cause if that's what they want to do. But I'm afraid, my dear, that my ideas are considered quite radical. No, ma'am, we've got to think of something else that you might do." He tapped his brow with one of his fingers. Ideas flitted through his head like fireflies, but none of them struck him as being just the right thing for this brave young woman.

She interrupted his thinking. "Mr. McIver, I have an idea. Why can't I be a Union spy?" The idea intrigued her so much that she stood up and walked around the back of her chair, talking as much to herself as to him.

She grabbed him by his hands enthusiastically as the idea took shape. "Why, Mr. McIver, I could get Reb information and pass it right on back to the Union generals."

"It is truly a romantic idea, young lady, but I'm not sure that you really know what spying is all about. It's extremely dangerous. Besides, I don't know one officer who would be willing to risk your life in that way."

"Mr. McIver, you don't know the half of my life. I ain't afraid of nothing."

"That's not the point, my dear. You may have all the faith in the world, but unfortunately those who are in charge of this war may not see matters your way."

"But Mr. McIver," she proclaimed, "this is everybody's war—men, women and children. We all got a stake in its outcome. How could they turn down someone who is willing, ready and able?"

McIver broke in again. "My dear, in times of war people do not always do what makes the most sense. Take yourself as an example. I'd wager you think spying is all romantic adventure."

She shushed him. "Now Mr. McIver, you're beginning to sound like those other men. A woman's place and all that. My place is wherever I'm needed. I want to fight, don't you understand? I want to make a contribution. I've got a lot at stake in this war."

McIver was curious about what might have given rise

to her passionate interest in the war, but he didn't press her.

"My mind's made up, Mr. McIver. I want to be a spy. All I want to know is if you will help me find the right people so that I can sign on. See, I heard some men talking about how so many people in the South are still having parties and balls just like there isn't a war going on. Well, don't you see, Mr. McIver? *I* could get into those parties, talk to some of them Reb boys and find out information. I could get dressed up and pretend to be one of them Southern ladies. You know, all sweet and syrupy-like. I know all about how to be like them ladies."

He could see it, but he couldn't imagine all the details of how she would pull it off. His heart was saying yes she could, but his logical mind was saying no, no, no.

Finally, he asked, "Please tell me, my dear, just how would you get invited to these fancy parties and balls? Those Southern families have deep roots, and they all know each other pretty damned well."

She wanted to reassure him. "Now, Mr. McIver, why couldn't I just be somebody's long-lost cousin or something?"

"I suppose you could," he said, but his tone remained doubtful.

There was nothing he could say to dampen her enthusiasm. After another twenty minutes of talking, McIver was as convinced as she was that she could in fact be a Union spy.

She kissed him on his forehead playfully. "Mr. McIver, have we got a deal? Will you get me to meet the right people? I want to get started right away. Don't want to waste no time."

"But my girl, don't you think we need to talk more?"

She was ready to fly out the door. "Ain't got no time to talk no more. Got to go home and tell my family what I'm aiming to do."

She was literally running out the door, leaving McIver standing there scratching his head, trying to figure out exactly who he could put her in touch with so that she could become a spy. She was so excited that she hadn't even noticed when all the men in front stood up to bid her good day.

By the time she got home, the excitement had gotten the best of her. Over dinner, Julie Lee spilled out her plan to Jeddah. The older woman's face was noncommittal at first, but soon she broke into a big smile. Even little Lytell began to grin, though he wasn't sure exactly why.

Over her third cup of coffee, Jeddah finally said, "Lord, child, I believe you gonna do it."

Chapter 37

It took him a few weeks to work out all the details, but McIver was as good as his word. In fact, better than his word as far as Julie Lee was concerned. They'd spent many an evening in conversation since he'd agreed to help her get started in her new career.

The two had become fast friends, and as she learned even more about politics and war, they became political allies. McIver liked her spunk, her inquisitiveness, and her willingness to persist in an argument without allowing it to degenerate into a shouting match. She was as clear-headed as most men as far as McIver was concerned. In fact, her ability to reason never ceased to amaze him and would have astounded him further had he known that she'd had no real schooling except for the brief time she'd attended classes with the Quaker children.

When the time arrived, she was told to report to General O'Neal Patterson in Washington D.C. Patterson was the head of all Union Intelligence and had made quite a reputation for himself as being a military man to the bone, and a shaker and mover.

Jeddah and Lytell were up early the morning Julie

Lee was to leave. Josephus, with his wife and his children, had come by the night before to wish her well. Josephus, who abhorred war, refrained from lecturing Julie Lee on what to do. He knew well enough by now that she was a woman of conviction and that she would do whatever she believed was best.

She made the trip to Washington by train. McIver had put a hundred and fifty dollars in her hand to pay for her ticket and for any other incidentals she might need.

She arrived at General Patterson's office a half-hour before their scheduled appointment. A young officer ushered her into an anteroom, and he offered her tea while she waited, but she declined. She was too nervous. She hadn't even had breakfast and her stomach was doing a jig inside. She looked down at her hands. They were shaking. To occupy herself she tried with one hand to keep the other still. But she couldn't calm down.

She looked around the room. It was very official looking, despite the couch and large plants. A flag hung from the wall in one corner, and at the end of a highly polished table, there was a gigantic portrait of Abraham Lincoln. It was, she thought, bigger than any portrait she'd ever seen at the Lorelei.

She looked closely at the picture. He was a rather fatherly and kindly-looking gentleman, though not particularly handsome. Most of what she'd heard about the President from McIver and the others had been good, but she still wanted to reserve judgment about the man. His motives had been questioned more than once by her abolitionist friends.

She was still deep in thought when she heard the sound of footsteps entering the room. This time another, even younger officer entered. He announced curtly, "The general will see you now."

The officer escorted her to the door of the general's office, and when the door finally opened, she was struck by the general's inspiring presence. General Patterson was a tall, stern-looking man. He had a long, gaunt face—something like Lincoln's, she thought, but his manner did not prepare her for the unexpected friendliness in his greeting.

When she told him why she'd come, however, Patterson said nothing. She went on to tell him everything about her early life on the plantation, the death of her mother, the escape, the rape in Baltimore, about how she'd been cared for by the Quakers in Philadelphia, about how she'd gone back to the Lorelei only to find that nearly her entire family had been wiped out. She couldn't help crying when she talked about Dancer and little John.

Through her tears, she watched him closely, wondering how her story was going over, but there was nothing she could see. No sympathy, no pity, no expression at all that she could see.

Suddenly, he spun his chair around toward the window, leaving her staring at his back. He stayed that way for several minutes. She didn't know what to think. Perhaps he would turn back around and order her out of his office.

When he did turn back to her, she saw that look in his eyes, the look to which she'd long become accustomed whenever strangers found out that she was a black woman. His eyes were searching fiercely. Up and down they went. She knew he was trying to see if there was anything about her that gave the telltale signs of mixed blood, but she certainly looked white to him. He seemed truly amazed.

Finally, he said to her, "That's quite an astounding tale. But let me make this suggestion."

She leaned closer to the desk, as if he were going to share some fantastic secret. "Yes?" she prompted.

"I strongly suggest that you keep the story of your parentage to yourself. I have my reasons, and perhaps after you're around a little longer, you will understand. Suffice it to say for now that there are those who will fight this war to the death, but who are not necessarily committed to freeing the slaves. I'm not sure what you've been told, but please believe me, there are many, many people on the Union side who do not in their hearts believe anything about Negroes except that they are inferior. They are fighting in this war only for the principle that the Union must be preserved."

Suddenly he broke into a smile, a gesture she had hardly expected. "Anyhow," he continued, "at this moment it is unimportant that you are a colored woman."

She wondered on which side of the fence *he* stood. She dared not ask, however, fearing that she would alienate him. He was the key to her getting what she wanted. Who cared anyhow? She had already lived with the hatred many Northern whites fostered in their hearts for people of her kind. How many times had she heard whites talking disparagingly in her presence about "them."

Patterson picked up the conversation. Yes, he told her, her proposal was an interesting one. But he would reserve judgment for a while. First he wanted to see how she performed in spy school.

The next two weeks were hectic. Up early in the morning and back to bed late at night. Patterson had sent her to the very secret Union Intelligence school where she met others who, like herself, wanted to be spies for the Union.

As the days went by, she became quite impressed with how much information she'd absorbed and the ease with which she was able to digest so much of it. She was the only woman in the school, but that didn't bother her. Some of the men tried to tease her, but that stopped soon after they realized that she was just as serious as they were about the task at hand. She was unaware that Patterson was regularly checking up on her progress. And she was certainly unaware that Patterson had ordered some instructors to push her even harder than the others.

At the end of her course of training, she found herself back in front of the general. He asked how she had liked the training, whether she believed it was necessary, and what were the most important things she thought she had learned. Then he said, "School is now over, young lady, and from now on, it's going to be the real thing. Real guns. Real blood. Real war.

"Tell me now if you're still certain that this is exactly what you want to do." Before she could answer, he added, "You can back out now, we'll put you on the train to Philadelphia, and you can forget everything you learned down here. The only warning that I will give you is that the revelation of any secret information which has been shared with you can result in your death, for that, my dear, would be treason."

She looked at him, hoping that her expression could measure up to the seriousness of his own. "No sir, I'm not backing out, now or ever. I came here to learn how to do a job, and that's what I'm going to do."

As Patterson listened, he realized that his respect for her had grown tenfold. He rose from his chair, came around the desk, sat on its edge and extended his hand to her, which she promptly took and pumped with as much gusto as she could muster.

"Someone will be around to your hotel in the morning. He'll give you your orders. Good day."

She was halfway out the door when she decided to turn around. "God willing, General Patterson, we'll meet again," she said.

Chapter 38

Julie Lee had been in the employ of the War Department for nearly six months. In all that time she'd stayed at her assigned post in Virginia. She kept in touch with events back home via correspondence smuggled to her from McIver and Josephus.

With the aid of white Southern friends of the Union cause, she had settled in with a prominent Virginia family, the Shirleys. Her cover was that she was a cousin of Lucinda Shirley and had come to stay with them because her own family had nearly been wiped out during fierce fighting between Union and Confederate troops deep down in the state, close to the North Carolina border. Her father had supposedly been killed by his own servants when he refused to free them. A pitiful tale indeed, and whenever she told it, Julie Lee elicited from her listeners great sympathy and understanding.

On the surface, the Shirleys were supporters and generous benefactors of the Confederate cause, but in fact, Sam Shirley had pledged his loyalties to the Union. He had come under the influence of Abraham Lincoln, whom he had met prior to Lincoln's ascendancy to national office. Though Shirley had once held many slaves himself, Lincoln made cogent arguments for their gradual emancipation.

Under the guise of raising money for the war effort, many families in Virginia gave grand balls, and the Shirleys were among them. Actually, most sponsors of the parties, nearly always certain to attract a fair number of high level Confederate officers, gave the balls in an effort to relieve some of the gloom that had settled over their lives since the war had begun. Like many Northerners, there were those in the South who had not expected the war to drag on as long as it did.

With so many men off fighting, many plantations had been left solely in the hands of women, who with the aid of faithful slaves, kept things going on the home front. There were few families who hadn't felt the tragedy of war through personal experience. Funerals for the South's battle heroes had become commonplace.

Julie Lee often wondered why she had thus far not run into anyone she knew. After all, the Shirleys' plantation was less than fifty miles from the Lorelei. Though tempted, she never tried to go back. She did keep her ears open for any news about the place, though. She wondered whether Hannibal had joined the growing number of slaves who had simply walked away from the plantations now that most of the masters were gone. Many of them, she'd read, had sought refuge behind the Union lines and had even offered their services as soldiers for the Union. She was disappointed at what she viewed as Lincoln's vacillation in permitting Negroes to be full-fledged Union soldiers. She kept her opinions to herself, however, and spent many a frustrating night and day listening to opposing views without defending her own.

The Africans

The Shirleys were hosting a ball in response to an urgent plea from Confederate President Jefferson Davis calling on white Southerners of conscience and means to raise vast amounts of money in support of the war effort. The money was needed, Jefferson said through his emissaries, to buy medical supplies, food and provisions for the troops. And there had nearly been riots among some Confederate troops who demanded to be paid in cash rather than platitudes.

Invitations to the Shirleys' ball that night were precious among the civilians, but the only invitation a soldier needed was to be in uniform. Some officers used parties such as this as a carrot to placate disgruntled junior officers and enlisted men. An invitation to the party was dangled in front of many soldiers as their reward for greater valor on the battlefield.

For their part, the soldiers looked forward to the evenings of pleasure. Many had been away from home for months, and during that time had had little or no contact with the opposite sex. For many, even the opportunity to drink in the beauty of women, to hear them laugh and giggle and see their smiling faces was worth anything a commanding officer could offer.

Of course, the young women, whose lovers had gone off to war, were equally desperate for some male attention, so the parties and balls served several important purposes and they were enthusiastically encouraged by Confederate officials.

By the time eight o'clock rolled around, the entrance to the Shirleys' home was filled with carriages of all kinds. Many of the women, though elaborately attired, wore gowns that they had worn before, for the war had caused shortages of textiles. On close inspection it was even easy to see that many of the dresses and waistcoats had been mended for the occasion.

Julie Lee wore a yellow gown with a neckline plunging so low that even Lucinda commented, "Why, my dear, even for the job you are here to do, don't you think that dress is a little too daring?"

Julie Lee threw back her head and laughed. She teased Lucinda about being so conservative. She fluttered her eyelashes and practiced on Lucinda what she would do later when the guests arrived. "Why, my dear Lucinda, how could you ever say such a thing? I declare, I think this gown is just about the prettiest thing that I ever did see."

Julie Lee waited until she was sure a crowd had gathered in the ballroom before making her entrance. All eyes looked up in her direction when she appeared at the top of the stairs. Coyly, she pretended not to notice the stir she'd created. She lowered her face into a dainty fan she held to ward off the imaginary heat.

She floated onto the ballroom floor taking a position near one of the windows, from where she could notice and be noticed. Deliberately, she laughed a little louder than the other women, even though the jokes were hardly amusing.

On more than one occasion that evening, she sensed particular attention from some of the officers in attendance. She danced with a Lieutenant James Dorsey several times. Dorsey was a veteran of the Fort Sumter affair, the very battle that had ultimately plunged the nation into the war.

Before the evening was over, Julie Lee predicted to herself, Dorsey would invite her to walk out onto the verandah with him for a moonlight stroll. That's the way it always went.

Dorsey was not a bad-looking man, she had thought at first, but then she noticed his teeth were crooked and stained from chewing tobacco. His breath nearly knocked her over, but she kept smiling. Bad breath was hardly a reason for her to miss out on any important war information which he might possess.

The party became so crowded by the middle of the evening that there was barely room to move. Many couples had already disappeared out into the night. She was still dancing with Dorsey when she saw *him*. She turned her face quickly, not wanting him to notice her. A sick feeling welled up within her. Her head began to ache.

"Would you mind terribly, Mr. Dorsey, if I sit the rest of this one out?" she asked sweetly as her face grew flushed. Dorsey escorted her off the floor and kept asking if she wanted something cold to drink.

"No, no," she protested. "I only need to sit down for a moment." Fortunately, she was near an open window. The air felt good. The rage and anger that had lain dormant within her for so many months sprang to life in an instant.

There he was, smiling and talking, holding a goblet in his hand. Andy Johnson in Confederate uniform. There he was alive, talking and grinning, while Dancer was cold in his grave and her baby was gone forever. Her father. How she hated him. He had killed everything she loved.

She had thought about this day so many times, wondered what she would do if she ever laid eyes on him again. And now, here he was. She needed time to think. She left the room and hurried up the stairs to her bedroom.

Sitting down in a chair, she looked into the mirror and traced the outline of her face. She pushed the chair back and leaned closer. How much resemblance did she bear to the man downstairs?

She didn't know where they came from, but soon the tears rushed forward. "Mama, I ain't called you in a long time, but I need you now. You said you'd come whenever I needed you." She waited. Then she heard it. It was a soft sound, like the patter of baby feet crossing the carpet. She felt it. A hand, then two hands on her shoulders. Roxie was there as sure as Julie Lee was.

"Mama, talk to me. Tell me what to do."

But Roxie did not speak to her daughter. Julie Lee leaned back in the chair to let herself be engulfed in the spirit she knew was present. Suddenly Lucinda burst into the room.

"Are you all right, dear? I missed you downstairs. That Mr. Dorsey's been asking about you. He said you weren't feeling well."

Angry at Lucinda's interruption, Julie Lee pushed her hair back off her face and blotted her eyes.

"Oh, Lucinda, I'm fine. It was just getting too hot down there. I thought I'd come up here to rest for a few minutes."

Lucinda came over and put her hands on her shoulders. "But, you look like you've been crying."

"No, I'm fine. I'm just fine. I was just a little hot, that's all."

Lucinda was becoming annoying now and she tried to restrain herself from lashing out at the woman.

"Do you think we need to call in the doctor?"

"Lucinda," she said with a stern tone, "I said I'm fine. Please. I just need a few moments to pull myself together. I'll be all right. Go back to the party. I'll be down in a few minutes."

The worried expression remained on Lucinda's face, but she took Julie Lee's rebuff in stride. "All right, dear, I'll see you downstairs," she said, as she closed the door behind her.

Lucinda's intrusion had driven Roxie away. Julie Lee sat for several more minutes, waiting to feel her mother's spirit come back into the room. It didn't. But before long what she needed to do was clear to her, as if she had always known. She went to her traveling case, ripped open the lining and removed something that gleamed in the lamplight. She hid it up her sleeve.

She freshened her makeup, combed her hair and went back down into the ballroom. It was still terribly crowded and even hotter than it had been when she'd left the room. She saw Dorsey head in her direction, but she moved quickly in another. She would get to him later.

She eased herself into a group of gabbing women, and she kept her back to the crowd, wanting neither Dorsey nor Andy Johnson to see her. After a few minutes of conversation, most of which she had not heard, she pulled one of the women from the group off by herself.

"Would you do me a favor, honey?"

The girl was anxious to please. "Of course. What can I do for you?"

As Julie Lee whispered into the girl's ear, the young thing began to giggle.

"You see, my dear, I've had my eye on a certain man all night, and I'd rather not appear too forward, but I would like to get a chance to talk with him alone outside in the garden. Well, would you? Would you ask him to meet me out there? You know, near the pond."

"Why sure, I'll ask him," the girl said, relishing her role. "Which one?"

Julie Lee scanned the crowd searching for him, and found him. "You see that man over there? The dark-haired one with the sword hanging down at his side."

The girl went to complete her mission, and Julie Lee rushed out a side door and made her way in the dark to the pond. She passed other couples on the way, but it was obvious that most were too engaged in their kissing and hugging even to notice.

She waited patiently in the dark. It was getting chilly, but still she felt hot. After ten or fifteen minutes she saw a figure coming toward her. It was him. Quickly, she turned her back so he wouldn't recognize her.

Her back was still turned when she heard him say, "Are you the young lady who sent for me?"

"Indeed I am," she reponded, still not turning around.

"Well, I'm not accustomed to being summoned, and I'm certainly not accustomed to talking to someone's back."

Abruptly, she turned to face him, and when she did, even in the dark, she saw the shock on his face. He had recognized her instantly, but it made no difference. He didn't see the long, slender Federal-issue army knife she pulled from her sleeve. After that brief moment of recognition, he never saw anything again.

Julie Lee was still in bed the next afternoon when Lucinda burst into her room, babbling hysterically about a soldier who had been found dead in the garden.

She feigned interest and listened. "What happened to him?" she asked.

"It appears that the man had been stabbed several times. Sam said that it seemed the man never even got a chance to draw his own weapon." Lucinda was flustered. "God, I hope word of this doesn't spread. Do you know what it could mean? The soldiers will be afraid to come here, and then how will we get our information?''

"What can you do about it?" Julie Lee asked, pushing herself down deeper beneath the coverlet.

"Well, I told Sam that we had no choice but to bury him in secret. We hid the body in a barn for now. Later some of the boys will take it off the property and bury him out in the woods.''

"I think that's a good idea," Julie Lee agreed sleepily, hoping that Lucinda would get the message and leave.

"Well, Julie Lee, what do you think could have happened to him? I mean what do you think?"

"Lucinda. I don't think anything right now. Listen. We're in the middle of a war. Anything could happen. Right now I'm thinking about going back to sleep.''

"You're right, dear. I know you weren't feeling well. I'm sorry I woke you.''

She started to leave and then said, "But, Julie Lee, you were out walking in the garden last night. Didn't you see anything?''

"I didn't see a thing."

Lucinda closed the door, but not before giving her a peculiar look. Julie Lee wondered if Lucinda knew. She lay there for several more minutes before getting up and going over to the mirror. Even before she looked she felt a smile crossing her face. Soon she was laughing hysterically.

"Good-bye, Mr. Andy Johnson," she said sarcastically to the mirror. "So long, Daddy!"

Lucinda heard her laughing through the door. She didn't go back in, but stood there wondering.

Chapter 39

Two weeks had passed since the incident, and still there was no official inquiry into the disappearance of Captain Andy Johnson, Jr. But one afternoon, just as Sam, Lucinda and Julie Lee were sitting down to lunch on the back patio, the sounds of horses' hooves interrupted them. Not expecting any visitors, Sam put down his napkin and started toward the front of the house. He was met halfway by the butler. Behind him were two Confederate officers. They held their hats in their hands, and the expressions on their faces were grave.

The three knew at once why the men had come. Hoping that no one would notice the blood rushing to her face, Julie Lee pretended to wipe her mouth with a napkin, even though they had not yet eaten anything.

The two officers didn't come all the way out onto the patio, but stood talking quietly with Sam. They nodded politely in the direction of the women, but offered no other greeting. Julie Lee and Lucinda nodded back and turned to face each other again. Their eyes met and each knew that the other was straining to hear what the men were saying.

The Africans

The officers had introduced themselves as Captain Clydie and Corporal Romeo.

"We're real sorry about interrupting your meal," Clydie said in an apologetic tone, "but we've come on official business. We're investigating the disappearance of one of our officers, Captain Andrew Johnson, Jr.

"Perhaps you know him since he's a local boy. He and his daddy own the Lorelei plantation over in Henrico County."

Sam acted as if he were trying to place the name. "Can't say that I've heard of your Captain Johnson. I think I've heard mention of the Lorelei though."

Romeo picked up where Clydie had left off. "We have information that one of the last places Captain Johnson was seen alive was right here during that big hoopla y'all gave a few weeks ago."

"It certainly was a party," Sam agreed. "One of the best in quite some time, if I do say so myself. We raised a couple of thousand dollars to support you fighting boys."

"*Was* Captain Johnson at your party?" Clydie asked suspiciously.

"My dear captain," Sam said, a wide smile spreading on his face, "it's obvious that you've never been to one of our parties or you would know that we rarely entertain less than one hundred people. And since our doors are always open to fighting men, more than half of the hundred were in uniform. It's quite possible that your Captain Johnson was here. I would not have known him in the crowd."

Rocking on the balls of his feet, Clydie looked embarrassed. "Excuse me, Mr. Shirley, but we'd be truly grateful if you'd allow us to ask your wife if she remembers him."

305

Sam's brain was shifting quickly now. He knew how nervous Lucinda could be under pressure, but felt that if he denied the men's request, it would cast even more suspicion on them.

"Not only can you talk with my wife," he finally said, "but you can talk with Julie Lee too. She's my wife's cousin, and she was here for the party."

Sam escorted the two men over to the table, and after brief introductions, offered them lunch. They refused, but both agreed they would be appreciative of something cold to drink. The butler, who had been standing nearby when only the men were talking, sauntered off in the direction of the kitchen.

Sam opened the conversation. "These two gentlemen have come all the way out here to ask a few questions about one of our guests at our last ball. What did you say his name was again?"

Romeo answered. "Captain Andrew Johnson, Jr."

Sam spoke slowly and deliberately, almost as if Julie Lee and Lucinda were idiots. "It appears that Captain Johnson was last seen at our party, and since he has not been seen since, the army has launched an inquiry. How am I doing so far, gentlemen?"

"You're doing just fine, Mr. Shirley," Clydie said, abruptly cutting him off. "It's been two weeks now and we ain't heard hide nor hair from Captain Johnson. Now for the first few days, we didn't worry none 'cause we thought he might have had a little too much to drink and was just sleeping it off at one of the plantations between here and his command post. But he'd have to have been pretty drunk to be gone this long."

Clydie leaned over and said in a lowered voice, "I don't need to tell you that we've had our share of desert-

ers, mostly young boys though, much younger than Johnson. They just get scared and whenever they get a chance,
they hightail it on back to their mamas and daddies.

"But Johnson didn't do that neither. And his daddy
said he would start his own war if we didn't find out what
happened to his boy."

Julie Lee waited before speaking, hoping that her tone
would convey sufficient interest in the subject at hand. "I
hope you gentlemen haven't come all this way for nothing.
I guess you know that there were so many people at Sam
and Lucinda's party that it was hard to know who all was
there. Tell me, what does this Captain Johnson look like?"

She had hardly finished asking before Clydie stood
up. He removed a dog-eared picture from a leather-bound
portfolio he'd been carrying under his arm.

He handed the picture to Sam first and said, "The
picture is a little old, but according to Johnson's daddy,
it's his likeness. Said his son hadn't changed that much."

Sam looked at the picture for several minutes. Afterward he shook his head no. "Can't say that I remember
that face. It's just like Julie Lee says. There were so many
people that night, and I just can't recall one looking like
this."

Sam passed the picture to Lucinda. She scanned it
quickly and promptly agreed with her husband. "I guess I'm
no better than Sam on this one." She avoided looking
Clydie and Romeo in the eye. "Sorry I can't be of any
help to you gentlemen."

Julie Lee and Lucinda's eyes locked as Lucinda handed
the picture over to her. Immediately a wave of memories
washed over her. Those eyes looking out at her. The man
was dead, and still he was watching.

Her face betrayed nothing of her discomfiture, and

she put the picture down in the middle of the table. She looked right into Clydie's eyes and declared, "I'm afraid I can't help you, gentlemen. I don't remember seeing this man either."

By this time, the butler had returned with water for their guests. After asking everyone to take yet another look at the picture, the two men drank up and prepared to leave.

"We've a couple more stops to make this afternoon," Clydie said. "Want to apologize again for interrupting your lunch."

"Oh, no bother," Sam assured them as he stood up along with the two officers. "No bother at all. Always willing to do whatever we can to help the cause."

Julie Lee and Lucinda shook their heads in agreement with Sam. Both smiled pleasantly. Julie Lee noticed that Lucinda was nervously tapping the table. When Lucinda caught her eye, she stopped immediately and put her hands down into her lap.

Sam escorted the two men out and watched them until they were all the way up the road. When he returned to the table, he could see that Lucinda was about to collapse from the pressure. Her eyes were watery and her hands were trembling. But not Julie Lee. She was as calm as could be.

After lunch, Julie Lee retired to her room. She lay there on the bed thinking that it was time for her to take leave of the Shirley plantation. She'd been thinking about doing it anyway, but the unexpected visit that afternoon had served to convince her that it was indeed time for her to clear out. If those officers kept snooping around it was possible they could run across the silly little girl she'd asked to tell Captain Johnson to meet her outside in the garden.

She waited until after breakfast the next morning to announce her decision. At first Sam and Lucinda said nothing, but finally he said, "If you've got to go, you've got to go." But Lucinda gave her a look that accused Julie Lee of deserting the ship just before it was about to sink.

Julie Lee would go back to Philadelphia, but would stop in Washington first. She wanted to talk to General Patterson and tell him that her spying days were over for a while. She would have to do something else to help the Union cause.

Chapter 40

It felt good to be back in Philadelphia among people who knew and cared about her. The tribulation of being a Union spy in the enemy camp had taken its toll, and Jeddah seized upon it as an excuse to pamper her just like she was a child.

Jeddah insisted on doing all the cooking and cleaning those first few days, and she brewed up a mild-tasting concoction which she ordered the girl to drink twice a day. "It'll clear up your system and help you get back to yourself quicker," she had said no less than a dozen times.

Lytell was glad to have her back too. Sometimes when she was resting but still awake, the boy would come and ask her all kinds of questions about what she'd been doing.

Julie Lee was amazed at how much the boy had grown in the time she'd been gone. "Boy, you're almost as tall as me!"

Lytell wanted to be grown-up so badly. Even though he was only ten, he wanted to be the man in the house. He said he wanted to take care of Jeddah and Julie Lee and protect them from the bad people, as he called them.

As she'd been instructed to do, Jeddah was sending Lytell to the Quaker school, and now the boy was reading and writing well enough to make out many of the words in the newspapers. Of course, Josephus' youngest son, Benjamin, had to take some of the credit since he often spent time in the evenings with Jeddah and Lytell.

One afternoon, when Lytell was at school and Jeddah had gone to her house-cleaning job, Julie Lee took time to browse through one of Lytell's school books. She was concentrating on the history of ancient Greece, when a knock came at the door.

She was not prepared for the sight on the other side of the door. A black man stood there, dressed in a uniform of the Union army. She didn't know why she should be surprised, since there were by then many blacks in the army, but the sight of him somehow unnerved her.

The man spoke first. "Oh, excuse me, ma'am, but I must have the wrong house. I was looking for a little black boy. His name is Lytell, and I thought this was the house he told me he lived in with his old auntie and big sister."

"You haven't made a mistake," she replied pleasantly, all the while thinking that he was some kind of fine-looking man. Now Dancer been good-looking, but in a boyish sort of way. This was a man, she thought, tall and smooth black with big, pretty white teeth. She felt embarrassed by what she was thinking.

The man was shifting around nervously. "Well, I just dropped by to see the boy. He's a good boy, and me and him have been getting on real friendly. I'm here in Philadelphia on my leave from the fighting. Gonna be here for the better part of a month."

With that he handed over a small wrapped package. She wondered what it was.

"I brung this for the boy. He said he liked to read and so I picked him up a little book. The man in the store said it was a children's book."

"Well, who should I tell him brought it?"

"Just tell him Jack Bratcher, ma'am. He'll know."

She pushed the door open wider. "Well listen, Lytell's coming in from school soon. Why don't you come in and sit a spell and wait for him. You're not in a hurry, are you?"

"No, ma'am, I ain't. But I think I best be getting a move on. Gonna go over to the restaurant and get myself something to eat. Some of the other fellas from my company is in town too, and we usually eat together."

She could sense his hesitancy. It took her several minutes to realize why he seemed so reluctant to come in. Oh, my God, she thought, he's scared. He thinks I'm white, and he doesn't want to be caught up in this house alone with me.

Rather than embarrass him by letting on that she knew why he was worried about coming in and waiting, she said, trying to sound as colored as possible, "Come on in, man, and sit a while. I ain't gonna bite you."

Relief came to both of them when Jeddah came from around the side of the house. Her arms were loaded down with groceries—some she had no doubt purchased, but most of which she had taken from the white woman's house where she worked. Jeddah never exactly called it stealing, just borrowing.

Jack reached out quickly to take the bags from Jeddah. He brushed past Julie Lee to set the bags down on the table.

"Why, thank you, kindly," Jeddah said, following the man into the house. She looked at Julie Lee with a twinkle in her eye, and Julie Lee knew what she was thinking.

Jack stayed for dinner that night. Lytell was in his own paradise. He liked listening to grown ups' conversation, and in the euphoria of having company, neither Jeddah nor Julie Lee was paying much attention to the fact that the boy was up well past his bedtime.

When Julie Lee finally went to bed that night she couldn't take her mind off Jack Bratcher. Lord, have mercy. The man sure did stir up some feelings in her that had been asleep for a long time.

Chapter 41

After that first day, Jack Bratcher became a regular at Julie Lee's house. Sometimes he received permission to bring along two or three of his army buddies. When they came, the men would bring groceries and special things they wanted Julie Lee and Jeddah to cook. They wanted food like they'd had at home and simply couldn't get through army channels.

They had some high old times, as Jeddah loved to say. Everybody swapped stories about their homes and about the war. Lytell was having a ball because of all the company in the house.

Jack and his buddies all came from different states, but mostly from the South. One of the boys, Lawrence Neal, was a free Negro from New York City on his way south to join the Union forces. Most of the time, everybody called Neal Shimmy Hips, a nickname he earned because of the way he moved the middle part of his body when he danced.

Shimmy Hips was one of the funniest men Julie Lee had ever met, and she told him so. He kept her in stitches with his jokes, and sometimes when he told whoppers, as he was prone to do, the other boys would tease him and tell him to "shut up that lying and sit his butt down."

Everyone enjoyed those nights, but they all knew that these times weren't going to last forever. There was still a war going on.

So far, Jack and Julie Lee had not been intimate, although Jack had stolen a kiss or two, usually when he and his friends were filing out and heading back to the colored boardinghouse where black soldiers on leave often stayed. Jack wanted her, Julie Lee knew that, and she wanted him too—wanted him so bad that she could almost taste it. But so far they hadn't been able to get to anything serious, because they were almost always around other people.

The night before Jack was leaving the opportunity came by way of Jeddah. She'd always said that her mama hadn't birthed no fool, and Jeddah knew that Jack and Julie Lee needed to be alone. In fact, she encouraged it.

When Jack came that evening, Jeddah announced abruptly that she and Lytell were going over to visit Josephus and his family. "Don't have to wait up for us, Julie Lee. Me and Lytell gonna be gone till late."

Julie Lee laughed to herself at Jeddah's less than subtle hint.

Before leaving, Lytell threw his arms around Jack's neck and made him promise that he would come back to see them.

Jack pointed his finger in the boy's face. "Now, Lytell, how many times I have to tell you that I'm going to come back to see you, Jeddah and Julie Lee? When have I ever told you anything that I didn't keep my word on?"

Lytell was happy with that. He skipped out the door behind Jeddah happy as a lark.

Once they were gone, Julie Lee turned down the lamp. She thought it amusing at how stiff and nervous Jack seemed.

Jack stretched his big arms across the table and put his hands into Julie Lee's. "I guess you know, girl, that I got you in my blood. You just climbed on up inside of me, and now you running through my veins. I don't know what I'm gonna do not being able to see you regular like I been seeing you.

"Now you know I ain't one of them fancy talking niggas, just an old country boy, and I guess you know that right now I ain't got much to offer. But it won't always be that way. I'm a strong man, and I'll work my fingers to the bone to make you happy every day. I'll be a good daddy to Lytell, and I'll look after Jeddah like she's my own mama, and you, you Julie Lee, girl, I'll love you long as there's breath in my body."

He was trembling now and his face turned deadly serious. "I'm coming back to get you, Julie Lee, and when I do, I want you to be my wife. I want you to be my woman, to have my babies and let me take care of you. Will you be my wife, Julie Lee?"

She wondered why he thought he had to ask at all. She loved him right down to his toes. She pulled her hands out of his, walked around the table, put her head on his shoulder and whispered in his ear.

"I love you, Jack Bratcher. I love you as much as any woman can love any man. I'll be glad to be your woman, your wife and the mother of your babies. I'll wait for you, Jack, till I'm old and grey, if I have to."

She closed her eyes as he ran his hands all over her body, and it felt good. Lord God, it felt good, she thought. She returned his favors, wanting him to like it so much

316

that he wouldn't be able to think of any other woman when he was away from her. She put everything she knew into what she was doing. When she was with Dancer she'd been a girl, but now she was a woman and knew what it took to make a man holler. And Jack in turn just carried her away.

From that day on, she pledged silently to herself, no other man would go where Jack had been. Lord. Lord. Lord, thank you, Jesus! she kept murmuring in his ear. The more she talked, the harder he rode.

They had washed up and fixed the covers back on the bed by the time Jeddah came back. The knowing look on the woman's face said she knew what had gone on and she was pleased.

Poor Lytell was fast asleep. He had tried to keep his eyes open because he wanted to see Jack one more time, but he couldn't.

"Girl, I had to half carry this little nigga all the way from Josephus' house, and this boy is some kind of heavy," Jeddah complained good-naturedly.

After putting the child to bed, the three adults talked quietly, not wishing to awaken him. Finally, the time came for Jack to leave, but before he did he addressed himself to Jeddah.

"Miss Jeddah, I want you to take care of this woman, my woman, whilst I'm gone, 'cause when I come back, I'm gonna make her my wife. Then we gonna have ourselves a whole passel of children, and we gonna live happy ever after just like in the storybooks. Ain't we, baby?"

"Ain't we, now," Julie Lee said with a smile so wide that it seemed to light up the room.

Chapter 42

Jack had been gone more than a month before Julie Lee realized that she hadn't had her period. If it was coming, it sure was late, she told Jeddah one evening. Had she gotten pregnant? Lord, Jack would have conniptions if he found out. There would be no way the army was going to keep him from coming home to see about her.

She knew she really was pregnant when she fainted one afternoon while drawing water from the well behind the house. Fortunately, Jeddah was home and heard the bucket when it hit the ground. She rushed to Julie Lee's rescue. After putting the girl to bed, Jeddah brewed a pot of tea and insisted that Julie Lee drink it hot. It was bitter tasting stuff, as were many of Jeddah's homemade concoctions.

A few hours later, Julie Lee broke out in a fever that was hotter than a wood-burning stove. The cramps were sharp and close together, so bad in fact that she screamed out, which brought Jeddah running. A big clump of blood came oozing from her private parts. Jeddah pulled back the sheet, and upon seeing the bloody mess, fled the room. She returned moments later with a pail of water and towels.

"Girl, it look to me like you done miscarried," Jeddah said, as she gently swabbed the blood.

Jack was off fighting somewhere, and here she was losing his baby. He would have wanted that baby. She did too. She decided, however, not to tell him about it when next she wrote. Maybe she would tell him when he came home, but there was no need to worry him now.

Several weeks after losing the baby, Julie Lee threw herself into abolitionist work. Philadelphia was teeming with antislavery activists, and none were more ardent than Julie Lee. Their numbers swelled when they invited prominent speakers, but when they couldn't get any of those big names, they relied on the locals, including Julie Lee. She spoke at several meetings, and once her talk was so passionate that parts of it were picked up in the newspaper along with a picture of her.

She cut the article out and sent it to Jack with her next letter. She knew he would be proud.

She coaxed McIver into the abolitionist cause. At first he was reluctant to go public, fearing that his business would suffer—and it did, but only a little. Before long, McIver was raising money, not only for the war effort, but for the antislavery movement as well.

One of the highlights during that year for Julie Lee was the formation of an all-female panel put together by the local abolitionists. Though many of the movement's most ardent and persuasive speakers were white, the female panel was made up entirely of black women, and one of them was none other than Joshua.

Sitting in that audience, Julie Lee found herself clapping longer and louder than anyone else when one of the panelists made a point she heartily endorsed. She'd brought

319

Jeddah along and could tell by her face that she was enjoying the talks too.

Finally, the time arrived for Joshua to speak. They had saved her for last. She was the oldest panel member and the best known. Word had it that she had gone back into the South, risking life and limb, no less than nineteen times and had personally helped no fewer than three hundred slaves escape to the North. She was indeed one of the Underground Railroad's most distinguished conductors.

Her age had apparently begun to take its toll. Her voice was not as strong as it once had been, and the people standing in the back surged forward in an effort to hear her. But Joshua had not lost any of her dynamism.

There was enthusiastic applause throughout Joshua's speech, and when she came near the end, she made an unusual request. She asked that every black person in the room stand up. Julie Lee helped Jeddah to her feet.

"I'm wanting to talk now to all my blood relatives—all my people—my beautiful black people. I know that we come like all the colors of the rainbow, and I know that we come in shades from the blackest of black to the whitest of white, and I know that our hair goes from the nappiest of the nappy to the straightest of the straight.

"It ain't none of our fault that we look like the colors of God's rainbow. Now some of you don't like to be called black—think there's something wrong with that. Some of you wants to be called colored, and I guess that's all right too. Some of y'all wants to be called Negroes and still some more of you wants to be called Africans.

"Well, children, it seems to me that we a little bit of all them things—African, black, colored Negroes."

The applause was deafening. Even white members of the audience had joined in the clapping. Joshua waited for the noise to die down before continuing. She wanted to be sure that everyone heard exactly what she had to say. "Now children, we can be African, black, colored, or Negroes, but what we can't be is niggas. I said what we can't be is *niggas*. Listen to me, children, and listen good. I done studied up on it, and I come to know that nigga is a slavery word. But we near 'bout to get all ourselves free and so we ain't gonna let ourselves be called—or call none of our other brothers and sisters—nigga.

"I knows we probably always gonna come across some African, black, colored Negro who's gonna act like a nigga and so we might be tempted to call him nigga. But I say before you tonight, children, before you say the word, before you think the word, understand that a nigga is a slave.

"Children, we got to erase the nigga from our talk, and we got to erase the nigga from our thought. Even when we funnin' we got to stop calling people niggas. 'Cause you know something, children? Ain't nothing funny about no nigga. A nigga is dangerous. A nigga will get you killed, and a nigga will be a slave no matter what.

"Reach out now and touch each other's hands, children, and promise old Joshua this night that you won't say nigga no more, and that you won't allow other peoples, whether they is black or white, to use the word nigga in your presence.

"Stand up and know that the nigga is dead and dying, and we got to kill the nigga in all ourselves. When you get to feeling, talking, thinking or acting like a nigga, pray to the great God above to help you. Ask God to take it off your mind and out of your heart."

When Joshua finished, pandemonium broke out in the meeting hall. All over the room, African, black, colored

Negroes were embracing one another. It was beautiful, Julie Lee thought. It was unity. She had never seen anything like it.

Joshua sat down humbly at the height of the applause. On her face was a victorious and jubilant smile.

Julie Lee noticed a peculiar look on Jeddah's face. She had seen that look before. It was Jeddah's gesture of resistance.

"What's wrong, Jeddah? What's the matter with you?"

Jeddah talked low. She didn't want the others around them to hear what she had to say. "Listen, child, maybe I'm just too old, but I ain't gonna promise nobody that I ain't gonna say nigga no more. Now maybe I'm just one of them tired niggas that's behind the times, but I tell you one thing, I ain't never been no slave, even when I was in slavery, and even if somebody called me nigga. Slavery is in your head and it ain't got nothing to do with a word. I understand the point, but nigga ain't nothing but a word to me, and when I die I don't care if you write on my marker, 'Here lies one tired old-assed nigga.' "

"Oh now, Jeddah, you shouldn't be talking like that. You can stop saying the word. At least you can try, anyway."

But Jeddah was as stubborn as an old plow mule. Julie Lee knew that, and so she wasn't surprised when the old woman patted her hand and said, "I ain't making no promise, Julie Lee. I ain't."

Chapter 43

1862 was viewed by many Negroes as a turning point in the quest for full emancipation.

In 1862 the air was rife with rumors and the newspapers were filled with speculative articles that the President would soon draft and release a proclamation that would set the Negro free.

Although viewed by some moderates as a friend of the Negro, Julie Lee and other abolitionist leaders saw Lincoln only as a great vacillator. They were upset and angered by what they described as his accommodationist proposals to appease slave holders and Southerners in general.

They were particularly irate that the President would seriously consider paying some slave holders up to three hundred dollars a head for the Negro chattel so that the Negro might be emancipated gradually.

"How dare he suggest paying somebody for something they shouldn't even have the right to own in the first place?" Julie Lee demanded at one abolitionist meeting to great applause.

And though the President had apparently won support

from some Negroes, Julie Lee was horrified that Lincoln was considering solving the nation's so-called ''Negro problem'' by colonizing the blacks in some other part of the world—South or Central America, the Caribbean or Africa. If they wanted to go, fine, but what about those blacks who wanted to stay in the United States? After all, hadn't they helped build the country with their own sweat and blood? Julie Lee demanded of those who came to her seeking her endorsement for the proposal.

In April 1862, Lincoln declared that slaves in the District of Columbia, the heart of the Union government, be freed. Once again, the President offered to pay the slave holders. In June of that year the President signed a bill abolishing slavery in the territories, primarily in the West, where statehood had not yet been granted.

By the summer of 1862, the rumors were more furious that emancipation was near, but though Lincoln's cabinet debated a draft of the emancipation proclamation in July, the majority of the Negro slaves still were not set free.

In the same month, Julie Lee was horrified to read in the newspapers about a race riot in New York that was dubbed the Draft Riot of New York City. Whites, fearful of losing their jobs to the black man and upset that they would be drafted to fight in the war while the Negro took their places in the factories, roamed the streets of the big city murdering and even lynching blacks from the lampposts in the street. It was horrible, Julie Lee thought, and she blamed Lincoln for it. Had he taken action, she maintained, things might never have gone that far.

By the time fall arrived, it appeared once again that total emancipation was at hand. On September 22, Lincoln threatened the rebellious Southerners that he would order all slaves in their territories freed as of January 1, 1863.

All during that year, Jack's letters kept coming, sometimes several weeks after they'd been written. And when she wrote him back, Julie Lee spared him many of her innermost feelings about Lincoln and the status of the Negro. She was concerned that the letters might fall into the wrong hands and that Jack might be punished because of what she'd written. More than that, however, she didn't want to cause him any unnecessary distress. He had enough to worry about on the battlefront.

Ultimately, in December of that year, the war ended abruptly for Jack. He was badly wounded in the chest; one lung had been punctured.

Once well enough, Jack was sent home to his family. The family consisted of Julie Lee, Jeddah and Lytell. They nursed his wounds and his bruised ego. He told Julie Lee that there were many times when the white Union soldiers called him a nigga just like the slave master and poor white trash had when he'd been a slave. He said he hadn't actually seen very much combat because Negro soldiers were often relegated to menial tasks, like cleaning the outhouses. He didn't really see serious action, Jack said, until shortly before he was wounded and sent home.

She cried when she realized how hard it must have been for him. She cried about how desperately he and the others wanted to fight but were not permitted to, giving rise to false notions that blacks were sitting back on their butts while white boys were fighting for their freedom— that blacks were sitting back, too lazy or too scared to meet the enemy. How many times had she heard people say that?

Jack had been home less than three weeks when he

restated his intentions to Julie Lee one evening when they were in the house alone.

"Julie Lee, I want to marry you. I want to marry you now, before this week is out. Don't want to wait no more, and don't want to worry no more that you might say one day, 'Ole Jack ain't the man I want, and so maybe I'll up and marry me somebody else. Ole Jack can't offer me nothing, so I'll marry another man.' "

On December 15, 1862, Julie Lee Johnson became Mrs. Jack Bratcher. They were married in the Zion African Methodist Episcopal Church, and only a few people were present since Jack had demanded that everything be done as quickly as possible. "Maybe one day later on, Julie Lee girl, we can marry all over again like the white folks do, have a big hoop-de-doo and such, but for now, baby, this is all we need. You my woman, and I'm your man, till the day one of us dies."

They were no sooner married than Jack started to talk about getting well enough to take a job. "I want to work so we can find ourselves a bigger place to live. It ain't good to be always putting Jeddah and Lytell out of the room at night so me and you can be alone together."

She agreed, but added, "You don't have to do it all by your lonesome. I'm working and we can afford to find ourselves another place. Fact is, I'd like to retire Jeddah. She still trying to work, but she's so old Jack, and old people like Jeddah that seen so much need some time to rest. Not like in slavery where a body just works until they dead."

In that same month, on December 31, Jeddah, Jack, Julie Lee and Lytell put on their finest clothes to attend a thanksgiving watch and prayer service for the emancipation of the slaves.

And on January 1, 1863 it happened. Lincoln declared that all the slaves, except those in states or parts of states not in rebellion against the Union, be freed.

Though the President's order was sweeping and though it was cause for joy, everybody knew that all the slaves were not free, that many, many thousands would never even hear about the Emancipation Proclamation until months later.

But the emancipation did not stop the war. Julie Lee was beside herself in the spring of 1864 when she got her hands on a newspaper report stating that Negro Union troops, nearly two thousand of them, were the first Union soldiers to wrest control of the James River in Virginia from the Confederate army.

"Lord, have mercy, Jack!" she shouted, lifting her head up from the paper. "Lookahere! The James River, that's where me and Jeddah come from. The Lorelei is right on the James. I used to play there when I was a girl with my brother Hannibal, and I used to walk down there at night."

She sat down quietly for a minute, wondering whether, with the battle being so close to the Lorelei, her brother might have been killed. She hadn't heard from Hannibal since the night of her visit, and though she had many friends and connections, she hadn't been able to find out what had become of him. In that respect, she had much in common with other ex-slaves in Philadelphia, who had also lost track of loved ones.

For the rest of the war, Julie Lee read everything she could find about the achievements of the Negro troops. How many battles they won, and which among them had won medals for bravery. Sometimes when she rambled on she had to catch herself, noticing the pained expression in

Jack's eyes when she talked about the Negro victories. Jack wanted to be there, she knew, but she counseled him, "God knows best, Jack, and it was God's will that you come back to look after me and Jeddah and Lytell. Seem like life ain't fair sometimes, I know."

One day in April 1865, Julie Lee was stirring a big pot of beans when she heard whooping and hollering outside. She nearly tipped the pot over, trying to get out the door to see what all the noise was about.

She had hardly stepped off the porch before a young boy ran by hollering, "The war is over! The war is over! Lee surrendered."

In minutes, it seemed, Jack came tearing around the corner of the house. He lifted her off her feet. "Baby, it's over! Thank God Almighty, the war is finally over. Them goddamned Rebs done run up the white flag. We beat them baby. We beat them. So put up them pots, girl, 'cause we gonna do some celebrating tonight."

She was enthusiastic, but chided him for handling her so roughly. He looked hurt when he allowed her to slide back down out of his grip. "What's the matter, Julie Lee? Ain't you happy that the war is over? That's all you been talking about. What's the matter?"

She turned and went back into the house without saying anything. He followed her inside, wondering what could be the matter with her.

She moved toward him and lifted his chin, which was pointed down at the floor. "Jack, ain't nothing the matter. I didn't want you to handle me so rough 'cause I didn't want you to hurt the baby."

He stopped still. The tears began to fill his eyes. He took her in his arms. "What you saying, woman? What you trying to tell me? You ain't telling me that we gonna have ourselves a baby?'' She nodded her head, and he grinned the widest grin she had ever seen and folded her in his arms.

Jeddah was watching it all. She knew all about the baby. In fact, she was the one who'd told Julie Lee to go to the doctor.

They all smiled at each other and finally Jeddah said, ''Yes indeed, we gonna have ourselves a big party tonight. Got lots of blessings to celebrate, yes we does.''

Jack and Julie Lee embraced the old woman warmly and then she eased herself down into a rocking chair. The three of them were still wiping away happy tears when Lytell came in.

''I came to tell you that—''

''Come here, child,'' Jeddah said, pulling the young boy onto her lap. ''We already know the news. You ain't nothing but a boy, but you done tasted slavery some. Well, from now on you ain't got to hold your head down no more. You can hold your head high and be free and go to school and learn and maybe be a famous man one day. You gonna be somebody special one day, make us proud, ain't you, Lytell?''

There was so much love in that house that night that it filled up every space. Much later, after all the grown people had gone to bed, Lytell got on his knees, looked up at the full moon and prayed.

''Thank you, God. Thank you for sending me a family, people who love me. I'm gonna make them proud, ain't I, God? Ain't I'm gonna be somebody special one day?''

PART II

Chapter 44

Shimmy Hips and Lena were among the crowd that had gathered on the pier to meet the ship bringing relatives and friends to New York City from various Southern ports. Most of those who had gathered were Negroes, since boat had become a primary and inexpensive mode for ex-slaves and their children to escape the South and seek the better life the North supposedly offered.

Shimmy put his arms tightly around Lena's waist, watching the ship slowly steam toward them.

"I can't wait for you to meet Jack and Julie Lee, baby. You gonna love them two. Why, when I was in the war, Jack was like a brother to me, and Julie Lee and her Aunt Jeddah, they treated me like I was family. You gonna love them. I know you will."

She smiled at her husband. "I know I will too, honey. If you love them, I know they're going to be all right with me."

He patted her gently, thinking how much he adored the woman. He couldn't imagine how it would have been had he married anyone else.

Lena was a country girl, sweet as she could be. Knew

how to make a man feel good about himself. Knew how to keep quiet when things were going wrong, and knew how to cheer him up in the darkest days. She was all woman, he had always said to his envious friends whose wives were lazy, or sneaked around with other men as soon as their backs were turned.

Down in the hold of the boat, as they were pulling and tugging to get their bags out from under all the others in the huge pile, Jack and Julie Lee were talking about Shimmy.

"You think Shimmy's as funny as he used to be, Julie Lee?"

"Now, Jack, does a hen lay eggs? That's one crazy Negro, but I love him anyhow. I can't imagine nothing that could cause that man to change. Not even New York City."

He put the bags he was lifting down in a heap and pulled her toward him. "Yes, New York City, baby, where a black man can make a dollar. This is the start of a new life for us and the children."

"Yes, it is Jack. A new life. A better chance for the children to get an education and make something of themselves."

They had come up on deck as the boat rounded a bend and headed toward its assigned slip. The weather was miserable. It was drizzling rain and the fog was so thick that no one could even see the skyline.

They had wanted to come by train, but Jack decided on the boat after figuring out how much it would cost to transport them all on the rails. After all, he said, and Julie Lee agreed, they didn't want to spend all their savings before they even got to the city. Jack might not, after all, find a job the day after they got into town.

Jack's friend, another war buddy, had worked down on the docks in Richmond for a ship company, and he'd told his boss that Jack was a relative. That was how they'd gotten a discount and were able to bring everybody North for only thirty dollars.

That was a bargain, Jack said, since traveling with them were their three children, George, Roxie Kate and Jack Jr., as well as Lytell and one of Hannibal's younger sons, Dexter.

In fact, Jack hadn't even had to put out the whole thirty dollars himself. Lytell paid his own fare and Hannibal contributed toward Dexter's fare. Whatever Hannibal could give was a sacrifice since he and Cleo had seven other children and were struggling to make ends meet. The only reason Hannibal finally agreed to let Dexter go was because the boy was still too young to go out and get a job to contribute to the family coffers.

Julie Lee had been so happy to find out that her brother was still alive after the war, and they had spent a few years with him, his wife and children. Once she'd been able to return to Virginia safely, one of her first orders of business had been to find Hannibal. As it turned out, Hannibal had never been more than twenty-five miles from the plantation throughout the war. For a while after the war, in fact, he had even stayed on at the Lorelei as a paid worker to look after livestock. But, he said, the plantation had deteriorated. The old master was not the same with his only son gone. The old man had stopped trying. And Miss Clementine, old and sick herself, simply could not run the plantation anymore. Then Union troops had destroyed much of the property when they came through. Some, Hannibal said, had even looted the big house, taking out many of the Johnsons' most prized possessions. But that had all been ten years ago.

Julie Lee was huddled now in Jack's arms in the hold of the ship. "Jack, did you notice little Lutiemae's face when she found out Dexter was coming to New York with us and she wasn't?"

"Yeah, I did, but honey we couldn't take everybody, and you know your brother. He wouldn't leave Virginia if they threatened to lynch him!"

"That's the truth. Hannibal loves Virginia, and now that that man's got himself halfway established in Richmond, he ain't about to give it all up for the unknown. But that Lutiemae, she just looked so pitiful. Poor little thing. She and Dexter, being so close in age, they always played together and everything."

He patted her shoulder comfortingly. "I don't think we need to worry too much about that child. You know how little ones are. They're upset one day and forgetting the next. Pretty soon she'll be playing with her other friends, and she won't miss Dexter hardly none at all."

"I'm not so sure children get over things so fast, Jack." She was thoughtful now. "No, I don't think they do. Sometimes I think children is smarter than we grown people make them out to be. There were lots of times, when I was a little girl, when grown folks said and did things they thought I didn't understand. But I understood. Maybe I understood too much."

It was his turn again to comfort her. "Now, Julie Lee, we getting ready to start a new life. You got to put some of them old hurts behind you."

"I'm all right, Jack. I guess I just think too much sometimes."

He kissed her forehead. "I love you, lady, and when you get to feeling sad, think about this big old black, ugly man that loves you."

"You ain't hardly ugly, Jack. You know I don't like no ugly men. And I love you too." Yes, she thought, she loved him, and she thanked the Lord for this chance to start a new life. Julie Lee's only regret was that Jeddah wasn't there to share it with her, but at least the old woman had died peacefully. She had just lain down one day and her tired heart had stopped beating. She was still warm when Julie Lee had found her. Jeddah had even folded her hands in front of herself.

The doctor decided that she had simply died of old age. "She lived a long life, even if it wasn't a happy one," he said, trying to comfort Julie Lee and Lytell in their grief. "But now she's resting, gone up to heaven to join the saintly at the right hand of God."

Lytell didn't mean to be rude because he knew the doctor was trying to be helpful, but he couldn't keep himself from saying, "I know you didn't know Jeddah, Doc, because if you did, you'd know that Jeddah didn't believe in no heaven in the sky. She always used to say that white folks tell slaves about heaven after they die while they be just enjoying their heaven down here on earth."

"At any rate, young man," the doctor went on, "wherever she is, it's probably a damned sight better than living as a slave."

Julie Lee nodded her head in agreement. "You got that right, Doctor. You sure got that right."

As they came up on deck, the fog and drizzle half blocked their vision. Jack strained his eyes, trying desperately to see if he could spot Shimmy in the throng.

When the gangplank finally dropped, all of the children on the ship scurried down it like little rats. Julie Lee joined the chorus of other women who were screaming at the top of their lungs for them to stop before they got lost.

After the youngsters had been collected and everybody accounted for, Jack instructed them all to wait over on the side of the dock while he looked for Shimmy.

Shimmy saw Jack before Jack saw him. Threading his way through the crowd and leading Lena by the hand, Shimmy came up behind Jack, tapped him on his shoulder and bellowed, "How ya doing, nigga? Welcome to New York City."

"Boy, you near 'bout scared me to death!" Jack cried out, whirling around.

The two men gave each other bear hugs and pulled at each other's cheeks as Lena stood by silently.

"Goddamn, I'm glad to see you, Jack Bratcher! Let me look at you, man." He patted his friend's stomach. "Boy, I think you done picked up a few pounds, ain't you?"

Jack pushed him away. "You better leave me alone, nigga, 'fore I whip your ass like I used to."

Shimmy pushed up in his friend's face. "When you ever whip me? You'se a lying nigga and your teeth don't shine."

The two were talking and teasing as if there were no other people around. Finally Shimmy said, "Goddamn, man, you done almost made me forget to introduce my lady." He pushed Lena forward into Jack's open hands. "This is my sweet Lena. Ain't she pretty just like I said?"

Lena was indeed lovely, Jack thought. She was Julie Lee's exact opposite. Where Julie Lee was white, Lena was black, smooth, creamy black. Where Julie Lee's hair

338

was straight, Lena's was much shorter and rather tightly curled and enhanced her big, pretty brown eyes.

When Julie Lee met her a few minutes later, she became instantly jealous. She knew that Jack loved her—he told her so practically ten times a day—but she often wondered whether he would have been happier married to a woman who looked more like him, who could give him pretty chocolate-brown babies with curly black hair instead of cinnamon-colored ones, with sandy brown and blond tresses. Sometimes she even wondered—though she often tried to push it out of her mind—whether her white skin reminded Jack of all the suffering he had endured at the white man's hand as a slave back in South Carolina.

If he felt any of those things, Jack never said so. Of course, that didn't stop her from thinking. Everybody had their devils, she supposed. But if there was anyone Julie Lee had no need to be jealous of, it was Lena. That woman obviously could not see any other man but Shimmy, and just like he'd always told Jack, Lena did nearly everything and anything to make him happy.

Though Lena and Shimmy could have used the money and the twins were big enough now not to need so much looking after, Shimmy insisted that she not work. "Don't want my pretty baby cleaning up some white woman's house and don't want her washing some white man's dirty drawers."

No indeed, Shimmy wanted Lena home to be there when his children got home from school, wanted her there to keep his clothes cleaned and pressed, his meals cooked and his bed warm at night.

And Lena didn't seem to mind. When they were sitting out on the stoop one warm night after they'd become close friends, she told Julie Lee, "My mama always

told me that the best way to get along with a man was to
learn how to steer the boat without sitting up in the captain's seat. Said I could steer it just as well from the back.
Shimmy's like most men. He always thinks he's in charge,
but I'm not hardly no fool. I know how to get him to do
exactly what I want.''

Julie Lee laughed when Lena told her that. ''Well,
girl, I guess it's too late for me and Jack to change our
ways. We always been more like partners in our marriage.
We don't do anything big unless we sit down and work it
out together. Just like now. We wouldn't be in New York
City if Jack and I didn't both agree that we should come
here and try to make it.''

''I guess that's what you call equality,'' Lena said,
stretching her arms over her head.

''I guess that's what they call it. Anyhow, it's the
only way I know.''

Chapter 45

Julie Lee tried hard to hide her disappointment, but Jack recognized the expression on her face when they arrived at the building in which Shimmy had found them a partially furnished apartment.

The outside of the building was so sooty and grimy that she could barely make out the numbers 594 over the dark green doorway. The children seemed disappointed too, especially Roxie Kate. All Lytell could think about was the close proximity of the railroad tracks, which didn't even have a fence to block them off from people walking or children playing. He had a bad feeling about those tracks, especially knowing how adventurous the children were.

If she thought she was disappointed, Julie Lee's heart took a dive and her head fell into her chest when she started to go inside the building and Shimmy suddenly said, "No, not in there. Y'all's place is down here."

He pointed to a deep set of steps leading down from the street into a hole. Oh Lord, don't tell me we done come all this way to New York City to live in a tunnel! she thought with alarm.

It was damp and wet in the alleyway leading to the door of the basement apartment Shimmy had secured for them. They had to hug the sides of the walls to avoid the big puddles of water that had formed in the alley as a result of the rain. And to Julie Lee's absolute disgust, the alleyway stank from all the tenants in the building putting their garbage out in the courtyard right at the end of the alley.

Shimmy seemed not to notice the long faces of the newcomers. He went right on talking. "The rent is real cheap here. I got it for a steal. The people who used to be the building superintendents moved out and as soon as they did, I told the landlord when he came to collect the rents—he owns nearly all the buildings on this block and rents mostly to colored—that y'all was coming and that I needed this apartment. He said I could have it, but that I'd have to pay him something to hold on to it. You know, vacant apartments is kind of hard for colored folks to find, especially with rents that they can afford."

Jack kept walking without replying to Shimmy's comments. All the while Julie Lee kept thinking to herself, do people really pay rent for places like this? Why, this is worse than the shacks back on the plantation.

The overwhelming silence behind him—even the children were quiet—was apparently Shimmy's first clue that they were not ecstatic about their new home. That was why he left so quickly when they reached the front door.

When they finally saw the inside of the apartment, Julie Lee thought she would fall down on the floor and cry. The place didn't even have any windows, and the only natural light came in through the apartment's front door, which had four glass panes—and one of them had been broken out. In place of the glass, someone had kindly installed a piece of cardboard.

The children all huddled around her. She kept thinking that no amount of paint and no cleaning was going to make that apartment a home.

Shimmy had been right about one thing, however. The apartment, which had three tiny bedrooms, running railroad style, did have some furniture in it, if you could call it furniture. The mattresses on the beds felt as if somebody had put marbles in them, they were so lumpy, and she could tell that there were bedbugs.

Lord have mercy, she thought, how we supposed to breathe in here? It was then that she noticed, high up on the walls of each of the rooms, vents with handles on them. She tried one out, and a shutterlike contraption opened up with a creak. The vents were almost as big as small windows, and once she had opened one, she realized that some light did come in as well as some fresh air.

Lytell had begun to say something, but just then a fat, healthy looking water bug scurried across the floor. He crushed it with his foot. In fact, he stomped on it as if it were a field rat.

Lytell looked up and said to no one in particular, "I guess I'm just a country boy at heart, but I don't think I'm aiming to live like this for too long. Got to get me a job."

Jack was embarrassed and angry with Shimmy. "It ain't like him to lie or nothing. Maybe this is what Shimmy and colored folks up here call living pretty good."

Lytell said, "Naw, Jack, it ain't like Shimmy to lie, but in this case, I think your man done stretched the truth more than a little bit."

Jack looked over anxiously at Julie Lee. She hadn't said much of anything after she'd put the children to bed.

She just kept looking around the apartment, those big tears sitting in the corners of her eyes.

"Cheer up, baby," Jack said, as the three adults sat around the rickety table on the mismatched chairs. "We ain't gonna be in this place too long. Shimmy's taking me to work in the morning with him. Said he was sure he could get his boss to take me on. Just wait till I get my first few pay days, and then we gonna move. Don't worry, Julie Lee, and you neither, Lytell. We gonna be out of this hole before the month is out. Just wait till I start working and be able to find my way around this big old city."

They both looked at him, but said nothing. All three were thinking the same thing. If this was Shimmy's idea of good living in New York, then what in the world could he possibly consider a good job? The thought was almost too frightening to contemplate.

Upstairs in their third-floor apartment, Shimmy and Lena had gone to bed. "Did they like the place, baby?" she said, cuddling up next to him.

"I'm not sure, but after all it sometime takes naturally country folks a while to get used to how we live up here."

Chapter 46

They had been in New York a month and a half, and Jack still had not found any steady work. He was able to earn a few dollars as a day laborer at various construction sites around the city, but even that sporadic work had been hard to come by. Jack's competition was keen, and he was often only one of dozens of men, mostly black, milling around the construction sites, waiting for a foreman to come through the crowd to select two or three strong arms for the day.

His first real prospect came unexpectedly one evening when, after having worked two days straight on one job, an Italian foreman named Rocco Petrone complimented his hard work and promised that if anything permanent opened up, Jack would be his first choice to fill the job.

He took the offer in the spirit in which it was made, but felt deep down inside that Petrone would catch hell if he tried to hire him before he hired any whites, who were also looking for permanent employment.

Shimmy had tried to help and had kept his promise to introduce Jack to his boss in the hope that there might be a job where he worked. Everybody, the blacks and the whites, called Ira by his first name. He was a Russian Jew who owned, with two other partners, a busy tailoring establishment in a dingy factory building off Mott Street.

Shimmy occasionally did tailoring, but mostly he worked as a deliverer, transporting finished work to fancy addresses uptown, where most of Ira's best customers lived.

Ira liked Jack immediately, but he had to say, "I'm sorry, but I don't have anything for you right now." He peered over the top of his thick glasses. Jack felt uncomfortable under the man's steady gaze, feeling that he was being sized up. He didn't like that. He'd been under the scrutiny of enough white men during slavery.

Ira went on talking as he felt obligated to give Jack more of an explanation. "I don't even know how long I'm going to be able to keep Shimmy. Times are hard right now in my business and money is tight."

They were sitting in Ira's office, which was actually nothing more than a corner of the large room sectioned off with partitions.

"My wife, Goldie, she's going to have another baby soon," Ira said pointing in the direction of a plain-looking woman in a photograph on the edge of his desk.

Ira looked at the picture too, and his mood turned thoughtful and reflective. "Goldie and me, we came to America from Russia twenty years ago. We were nothing but scared kids. In fact, your predicament reminds me a lot of ours back then. Neither one of us could speak English, so for us it might have been even harder than for you."

Ira looked up toward the ceiling. At first, Jack followed his eyes, then realized that Ira wasn't looking at anything in particular. "Oh, it was so hard those first few months, but thank God the Jewish people help one another. Those that had come over before, they helped Goldie and me to get settled, and they helped me to get my first job in a tailor shop. Goldie and me, we both took English lessons.''

Although he wasn't really interested at first, Jack's curiosity was piqued by Ira's story. He didn't know much about Jews, and in fact, had never even come across one until he came to New York.

''At first Goldie worked too, but I didn't like her leaving our two little ones running around the streets with latchkeys around their necks. The streets are no good for children without supervision. A lady who lived over us, she promised to watch out for our boys, but you know how people are. They get busy doing other things, and they don't always keep their promises. She was a good lady. She really was.''

Jack wondered why it seemed that Ira was trying to convince him about the sincerity of the woman. He thought about his own children, how even right then they might be running around in the street, as Ira called it, because Julie Lee was at work, and he was out looking for work.

''You know, Jack,'' Ira went on in a friendly tone, ''sometimes it seems that we Jews and you coloreds have a lot in common. One day my son was beaten up badly by the neighborhood bully. Of course, Goldie and I were both at work, but the other children who saw the fight said it happened because my son happened to be a Jew—a stinking Jew were the exact words they used. Now we weren't slaves like the coloreds, but there are people who despise Jews as much as they despise your people, and there are those who make fun of us and call us names. Such terrible names, like you never heard.''

347

Ira's gestures became animated and he looked pained as he continued. "When they beat up my boy, we decided that Goldie wouldn't work anymore. It's hard for us who are different, very hard. I wish you luck, Jack. I really do. I only say you shouldn't give up, and don't let the bullies get you down."

Ira rose from his chair behind the desk and Jack stood up too. He escorted Jack to the edge of the screen, and patted him on the back as if they were old friends. Jack thanked Ira for his time and descended the two flights down to the street.

When he got outside, there were crowds of people bustling around. He figured that many of them were probably just like him, looking for a job. As he walked, Jack thought about what Ira had said. He thought to himself that if Ira could make it, then he should be able to do make it too. And he would.

The weeks went by, and Jack still could not find work. One night after the children had gone to bed, he turned to Julie Lee. His eyes were filled with tears. "I wonder what the boys think about me now. They were always so big on talking about their father, and the strong man I was. Now here I am, the man in the family, and I'm not bringing home anything. I feel like a junkyard dog. Both you and Lytell, y'all working and making money, and me I'm just hanging around like a knot on a god-damned log. The boys must think I'm a failure. I know they do."

He was so sad, so pitiful, and she knew that he meant every word he was saying. She kissed him on his cheek and stroked his massive chest.

"That ain't true, Jack. The kids don't think no such thing about you. They know how it is, because I tell them. I tell them how hard it is sometimes for a colored man to make it out here in the world. You done fought in the war and you done everything that respectable white men do, but Jack, you and I both know that sometimes the colored people just don't get that much of a chance."

He sat up on his elbow and looked down into her face. "I know what you saying, baby, I know. I'm just trying so hard, and it seems like nothing is working out. Maybe we should have stayed in Virginia. What in the hell do we know about New York and about how these people are? Look at Shimmy. All those years he's been a free Negro, and even though we never talked about it, I thought he was doing much better, living much better. Here he is, a delivery man. It just seems like God sure gives us Negroes a damned hard way to go."

"Why don't you go to sleep, Jack? Don't upset yourself so. Tomorrow you'll go out looking again, and the day after that if you don't find anything. But I don't want to go back home. I don't want to go back because all these other Negroes have made it up in New York City, and we're going to make it too. You'll see, Jack. You'll see."

She fell asleep in his arms that night after they'd made love. Jack held on to her so tight she thought he'd take her breath away. She let him hold her, wishing she could take his pain away.

Julie Lee loved her job, not because she enjoyed taking care of somebody else's children instead of her own, but because she loved going up to Harlem every day. It was so clean up there, and the air was fresh, not like where they lived. Everybody was so well dressed in Harlem, and when she walked down the street, even strangers would tip their hats and say good day.

Her boss, Amanda Clover, was a bit of a snob. Her husband made a good living as a doctor, and he showered Amanda with beautiful things. He had even permitted her to hire a nursemaid, even though it was obvious that caring for two little children was not the difficult job Amanda made it out to be. Sometimes Julie Lee thought how much Amanda reminded her of Whilomene—as lazy and cunning as they come. She was a woman who knew how to get her way.

Because Julie Lee had children to feed and an out-of-work man at home, Amanda decided to be generous with her salary. At least she gave her what she believed to be generous, seven and a half dollars a week, plus lunch.

Fortunately, Julie Lee and the children, Melanie and Michael, got along well. They were bright and inquisitive, and quite well mannered most of the time. They often asked about Julie Lee's children and said they'd like to meet them one day.

Nearly every morning Julie Lee took the children to the park or on walking tours around Harlem. The tours were more for her benefit than for theirs. She wanted to get to know more about this strange and beautiful place. Sometimes she imagined what it would be like to live there, in one of the big, airy apartments she'd heard about. To her, Harlem was somehow different than Philadelphia and Richmond. Something about those streets were alive to her. More than anything, she wanted to live uptown one day, to get away from her hot apartment, the stink of the garbage outside her door and the railroad tracks. She wanted to escape the dirt, the noise, the prostitutes. She never discussed those dreams with Jack, not wanting to depress him more about his situation, but she quite detested the place where they lived.

The children went to the colored school, where the teachers, mostly blacks and a few whites, were very involved in the growing movement to bring literacy to former slaves.

At night Julie Lee would go over their lessons with them. Poor little George, he was always the slowest when it came to academics. He was a great athlete, but a terrible reader and speller. It hurt her to see him throw down his pencil in frustration when he couldn't understand something, and even though she didn't always know how to do the lessons herself, she worked hard with George.

Jack Jr. and Roxie Kate would laugh at George, and when they did, Julie Lee would slap their legs. But Jack Jr. was the worst. He teased his brother unmercifully. The baby of the family, Jack Jr. was smart as a whip, and most of the time he only had to be shown something once and he would get it right away.

So Julie Lee always felt especially protective of George because he, unlike the other two, always tried hard and always tried to please his elders. Whenever there was work to do around the house, George volunteered. He was a beautiful and sensitive child. Secretly, he was his mother's favorite, but she tried never to show partiality between her children.

Knowing that the children needed religious training as well as formal education, they hadn't been in New York City long before Julie Lee found a nice little storefront church for the family to attend. Jack went that first time, but refused to go afterward, claiming that he didn't like the preacher. But he told Lytell one day when Julie Lee wasn't around, "I just don't like that jackleg nigga. I think he got his eye on Julie Lee. If I ever even hear that that fool done said something out of the way to Julie Lee, I'll take his butt apart."

Lytell listened sympathetically. "Well, Jack, I tell you what. If I was in your place, and I was worried about my woman, I'd go to church just to keep my eye on that jackleg. The man ain't crazy you know—I ain't never seen a crazy preacher yet. He ain't gonna mess with Julie Lee with no big, black fella like you around."

"Naw," Jack said, "I ain't going. Julie Lee can take care of herself. Besides, I don't even like the sound of his voice. I can't stand even looking at him."

Lytell sipped at a cool glass of water. "Well, if you that upset about it, why don't you tell Julie Lee she can't go no more."

"Man, now I know you is crazy. You know damned well if you tell Julie Lee to stay, she'll go. She's not the kind of woman you'd say something like that to. Anyway, I don't want her to know that I'm jealous of that slippery nigga."

They laughed. Of course it had been a ridiculous idea to try to tell Julie Lee what to do.

Lytell had been lucky. He'd found work only a few days after they'd arrived in the city, a job close to home so he could walk easily.

His job was cooking in a down-home restaurant run by a woman that everybody called Pig Foot Sally. Sally came from Virginia just like they did, and because of that, Lytell had been given special consideration. Everybody tried to look out for their "homies."

Sally had come to New York ten years earlier, and she'd naturally fallen back on what she knew how to do best: cook. She had three children to raise and no man to help her.

After a few years of working for other people, Sally had saved up almost enough money to open her own restaurant. She knew from the start what it would be called, Pig Foot Sally's, for pigs' feet were her specialty. She went to her first boss to try to borrow some money to make up what she needed. Rather than lending, however, the wealthy white woman said she would put in the money and be Sally's silent partner. That way, she said, she could use her contacts to get Sally more business. Anxious to get out on her own, Sally had agreed to the deal.

"And that's how it all started," she told Lytell. "Boy, you'd be surprised at all the fancy white folks coming down in this neighborhood just to get some of my good old cooking. Well, as time went on, I decided that I didn't need no partner no more, so I had to figure out how I was going to ease my partner out. After all, I was doing all the slave work, and all she was doing was coming around every few weeks to collect her share, which was fifty per cent of everything I made."

Sally leaned on the table, laughing to herself as she talked to Lytell. "Well, child, you knows that white folks always like to think they're in charge. I just started acting real pitiful and told Miss Lucy Lamprey, that was her name, how I was getting so tired, that I was thinking about closing up the restaurant and going back and getting myself a job. I said I was just working too hard, and wasn't getting enough out of the deal.

"I played on her conscience. You know, made her

feel guilty about taking my money when she already had so much of her own. Pretty soon I had that old bat crying her eyes out. Had her believing she was taking the food out the mouths and the shoes off the feet of my children. And that's how I ended my partnership! She felt so bad that she didn't even ask me to pay back the money she she gave me at first. Well, ever since then I been on my own, and damned happy about it. 'Course, now all the excitement done wore off, and I don't get so many white people, but who needs them, everybody around here is from down home almost, and most of them live in rooming houses where they can't cook or nothing, so where they gonna eat? Where they gonna get collard greens like I cook them? And where they gonna get corn bread and apple fritters? And them good old red beans and rice?''

Lytell liked Sally. She was self-educated and as smart as an old fox. But Sally didn't make money just because her food was good. She made money because she was good to people when they were down and out, and when they got on their feet, they never forgot her.

She'd hired Lytell to work with his brains, even though she did teach him something about cooking. He was bright and good with numbers and he was able to help her keep her records and make sure that she didn't get cheated by the various wholesalers with whom she did business during the course of her work. And of course, Sally admitted, it never hurt to have a man around.

Lytell's salary was five dollars a week, though Sally said she would give him a few extra dollars if business was real good. It wasn't a great salary, but it was better than nothing. Besides, Lytell said, with all the food Sally gave him to take home at night, how could he complain?

So between Lytell's job and Julie Lee's job, they were doing all right, even with Jack still out of work.

One night, Lytell, Julie Lee, Shimmy and Lena were sitting around the table talking. It was getting late and Julie Lee wondered where Jack was. When another hour had passed, Julie Lee was getting ready to announce that she was going out to try to find Jack. "Where is that man?"

All four of them jumped up at the same time when they heard him coming down the alley, screaming at the top of his lungs. A cold chill ran down Julie Lee's spine. Her first thought was that Jack had been hurt.

The four of them nearly got stuck in the doorway, they were all trying so hard to get out at the same time.

It was dark in the alley, but even before he made it through to the courtyard, Julie Lee could see that Jack was drunk. He was bumping into both sides of the wall. They moved toward him cautiously, but retreated a bit when Jack screamed out again. "Wake up, everybody! Wake up, goddamnit!"

He threw his hat into the air, and as it came down into his hands, he seemed to be suddenly conscious of their presence. His words were slurred. "Guess what, y'all? Guess what?" he screamed even louder. "I done found me a job! Steady work! Oooooh weeee! Done found me steady work! Ain't got to beg no more, and guess what Julie Lee? You my wife, ain't you? You loves me, don't you? Well, guess what? We gonna move the hell out of this damned place soon as I can make us enough money."

Jack reeled forward, but Lytell caught him before he hit the ground. The children had gathered in the doorway, wondering what was going on. They'd never seen their father drunk. Lytell and Shimmy put Jack to bed. He was asleep almost before his head hit the pillow. They would have to wait until the next day to find out what kind of work Jack had gotten.

Through the open vents that night practically everybody in the building could hear the joyous laughter coming from the apartment in the basement at the end of the alley.

Chapter 47

Jack had been more than astounded when Rocco Petrone kept his promise. In fact, Rocco had gone out of his way to make good on it.

It was a Saturday. Julie Lee and Lytell were at work and all the children had gone off earlier that morning on a day trip with Lena. Jack was lying on the bed, scanning a newspaper when the rap came on the door. "Just a minute," he called out, searching for his robe in the dark room. The rap came again. "All right, I'm coming. I'm coming."

He nearly fell back inside at the sight of Rocco standing there. Jack felt suddenly embarrassed at having the man see where he lived. Julie Lee kept the house immaculate, but Lord, what someone had to go through to get there—the smelly alleyway and the garbage piled up only a few feet away from the entrance to their apartment.

"So how you doing, Jack?" Rocco said, extending his hand.

Jack was shocked as he stammered out a reply. "How you doing, Rocco?"

"Well, I'm fine, but are you going to invite me in or not?"

"Aw, man, I'm sorry, come on in."

Rocco hadn't even sat down before he asked Jack for two glasses. He'd brought along a couple of bottles of beer.

As he brought over the glasses, Jack said, "Man, how you find me?"

Rocco didn't answer until Jack had joined him at the table. He poured the beer carefully, tipping the glass. "I hate a beer with a big head," Rocco said. "Don't you?"

"But what you doing here, Rocco?" Jack asked anxiously, sloshing the beer around in his glass.

"Hey, Jack. Don't get nervous. I didn't have a hard time finding you. A good man is never hard to find. You got a good reputation out there you know. I mean almost every construction foreman in town knows you, and they all think you're a good worker. They like your style. They say you're different than a lot of the other colored guys."

Jack was becoming uneasy now. He'd heard that line before and didn't like it. It was always used by white folks to pit colored folks against one another.

"Hey listen, Rocco, I try to do a good job, but I'm no different than most. Give somebody a chance, and they work hard. There are a lot of good men out there."

The expression on Rocco's face changed. He realized that perhaps he'd said the wrong thing. "Hey Jack, I'm sorry. I didn't mean no harm. I only meant that you were a good man. How can I say that much about the coloreds? I only know what I read."

"Yeah," Jack said, leaning toward Rocco, "and what you read usually isn't good. But if you stick with me, you might even get to know that we colored folk, most of us, ain't no different than you whites—especially you immigrants. We're all trying to prove ourselves, aren't we?"

Rocco laughed uneasily. He kept trying to figure out if maybe Jack was trying to insult him somehow. But he decided not.

He took a long drink of the beer. "Anyhow, Jack, I came here to offer you a job. We got two openings for laborers. There was another guy, an Italian, who I promised a spot, and I hired him yesterday. He wanted to bring his brother-in-law on, but personally I didn't like the guy too much. He just rubbed me the wrong way. Tried to be a wise guy. You know the kind? Hey, listen, I don't need any headaches, and I could tell that guy was going to be a pain in the butt. Anyhow, I told the guy I'd hire only him and not his brother-in-law.

"But you know how it is, Jack. I promised you that if I got a regular spot, I'd get in touch. So here I am. I hope you haven't found anything else yet because I'd really like to have you. I mean, if you can, I'd like you to start work Monday. Do you think you can?"

Jack wanted to jump up and kiss Rocco, but he said, instead, "Rocco, I'd start tomorrow, Sunday, if I had to."

Rocco lifted his glass. Jack did the same. They clinked glasses. "Then it's a deal, right, Jack?"

"You're goddamned right it's a deal!"

They drank the two other beers in the bag. Jack was feeling nice by the time Rocco left. He walked him to the corner and decided that rather than go back to the house, he'd make it down to one of the black and tan bars to celebrate his good fortune. And late that night he came home stumbling drunk.

He had been on his construction job two months before Jack made good on his promise, but the Bratchers, he announced one night after dinner, would be moving.

The announcement brought a round of applause from everybody, especially Julie Lee. "Thank you, Jesus," she said.

Julie Lee wanted to move to Harlem, but Jack had found a nice place even farther downtown than where they were. She was disappointed, but couldn't dispute Jack's point that colored people still had too many problems trying to live too close to the white folks in Harlem. "Listen, Julie Lee, I don't want the children to have to face all that so soon. They'll get it soon enough. No, I'm not ready yet for us to go to Harlem. Wait till it gets a little blacker."

The moment she saw the apartment Jack had picked out, Julie Lee felt better. It was a five-story, walk-up frame building. Their apartment was on the third floor. The four rooms were gigantic compared to the old place and every room had at least one window. Julie Lee thought she had died and gone to heaven. Windows. She could have kissed Jack for that. If that new apartment had been a basement, she had planned to sit down in the middle of the floor and cry.

She walked through the freshly painted rooms, thinking about all the pretty curtains she would make. What she could do with a space like that. It didn't even bother her when she leaned out the kitchen window and spied big rats running around in the alley below.

The children ran through the apartment, picking out the rooms they would occupy. There were only three bedrooms and Julie Lee settled the ruckus quickly. George, Jack Jr. and Dexter would share one room. Roxie Kate would have her own room, since she was the girl. The biggest bedroom, the one all the way in the back, would be for Julie Lee and Jack. Lytell would sleep on the couch, since he was out so much anyway or working so late that his coming in would wake everybody else up.

Lena had accompanied them on the visit to the apartment. She was envious, but not so much that she couldn't genuinely wish Julie Lee and Jack all the best in their new home. She was going to miss them something terrible, she said, and she cried on Julie Lee's shoulder when it was time for her to leave. She hated having to go back to the old place after seeing their new apartment. She intended to work on Shimmy that very night. She wanted to move too.

Apparently Lena did a good job, because in less than a month, she and Shimmy had moved, only a few blocks away, on Columbia Street. Julie Lee and Jack's place was on Pitt Street. The apartment Shimmy had found was on the first floor, and Shimmy had swung a deal with the owner. In return for being the superintendent Shimmy would live in the apartment rent-free. As it turned out, however, Lena did most of the supering since Shimmy kept his job at the tailor shop. The only thing Lena didn't do was pull the trash cans out into the street. They were much too heavy. Not having to pay rent was a big saving and it gave Lena a few extra dollars to spend.

Once they were all settled downtown, Julie Lee and Lena sometimes left the children at home, leaving the oldest to look after the younger ones. The two women explored their new community, making sure to note where they could buy the best meat and dry goods for the cheapest prices. They found a yard goods store run by a Jewish merchant who sold very cheap fabric. They scanned the newspapers for ideas on how to decorate their apartments, and since both of them could sew pretty well, they were able to make curtains and bedspreads that rivaled the much more expensive originals.

Julie Lee also found a new church—the Mother Zion African Methodist Episcopal Church on Church Street. The whole family joined, even Jack. He liked both the church and the minister there. Lena was a Baptist, but Julie Lee talked so much about Mother Zion that she decided to join there too.

Julie Lee joined the choir, and for the first time in a long while, didn't feel that she had to offer anyone an explanation about her physical appearance. There were lots of others in Mother Zion who were just like her, light enough to pass for white.

Jack didn't take long to get active in the church either, and much to Julie Lee's surprise and delight, when he wasn't too tired he rehearsed with the men's choir.

At the same time Jack and Lytell became active in the Virginia Society, a group of transplanted Virginians who'd come together to help each other out by providing burial insurance and loans, and to sponsor social events.

Lytell and Jack helped keep the records of the burial insurance payments and the loans, many of which were used to put down payments on homes. Of course, the club provided for others who had come to New York City from Virginia who were just too poor to help themselves. "We just can't let our people go to meet Jesus like they're paupers," Jack always said when he was trying to encourage new people to join.

Julie Lee was pleased by his involvement in the society, but she always wondered why he had joined the Virginia group when he had been born in South Carolina. She asked him about it one day. He answered seriously.

"Julie Lee, girl, don't you understand that when I was in South Carolina, I was a slave, and I know you hate for me to say it, but when I was in South Carolina I was just another nigga on the plantation. But when I was in Virginia with you, Lytell, Hannibal and all, I was free. Don't you know, girl, I was born again in Virginia and that's why I feel that that's my real home?"

After she had settled into her new home and her new neighborhood, Julie Lee babbled on to Amanda about it. She talked about the Jewish synagogue not far from her house and all the different people she had met.

"Lord have mercy, Miss Amanda, all kind of people live down there. You go from one block to the next and you find different people—Jews in one place, Italians in the other and Germans and Irish and, of course, colored folk like us. Every other person you run into comes from a different country."

Amanda knew what Julie Lee was talking about. She and Arnold had moved to Harlem to escape those very immigrants, with their poor English and poverty stricken mentalities. She didn't tell Julie Lee that, however. She didn't want to hurt the poor woman's feelings.

When Julie Lee returned from the park one day, Amanda sprang a pleasant surprise on her.

"Julie Lee, I've decided to tell Arnold that I want to redecorate the house." She swept her arms around the room. "I'm bored with all these things. We've had them since before the children were born, and now I want a change."

Julie Lee was amazed that Amanda thought the furniture was old and boring, since to her mind, it was beautiful and elegant. She was thinking to herself how she would love having such furniture in her own apartment when Amanda said, "When I get my new furniture, I'll give you some of this stuff. Of course, my dear sister will want first choice, but whatever she doesn't want, you can have. All you have to do is to find a way to get whatever I give you down to your apartment."

Julie Lee's mouth fell open. "Oh, don't you worry, miss. If you give me any of the beautiful things, you can be sure that me and Jack will figure out a way to move them. I'll carry some on my back, if I have do."

Amanda's smile was wicked. "I'll talk to Arnold about it tonight." She swirled around and faced Julie Lee. "You know, my dear, that Arnold cannot refuse me anything."

A few weeks later when Jack pulled up in front of their house in the horse and wagon he'd rented to haul the furniture, Lena's mouth fell open.

"Oh, my God. Julie Lee, you mean that white woman is getting rid of all this beautiful stuff? Lord, have mercy. I swear I think sometimes that white folks is wasteful. I mean even if you can afford to buy new furniture every year, I can think of a lot better ways to spend money. Can't you?"

"Lena, I can imagine anything Amanda Clover does. That woman is so damned clever. She reminds me a lot of when I was back on the plantation and watching Miss Whilomene. They're different in a lot of ways, but then again, they are so much alike. Amanda Clover can wrap people around her finger, especially her husband. Sometimes I've been there when her girlfriends have visited, and she even gets *them* to wait on her.

"And lazy? Girl, you haven't seen lazy until you meet Amanda Clover. If it wasn't for me and the woman she has to clean up, the place would be knee-high in trash. The woman won't even pick up a piece of paper when she drops it. And him, Arnold! Girl, he loves that woman, loves her and does for her like she is some kind of queen.''

Lena appeared distressed. ''And here we are working ourselves to death. Oh, there's no doubt our men appreciate it, but girl, we ain't hardly got to be no queens yet.''

''Well, Lena, you just got to understand, our major problem is that we ain't white, and neither is our men. It's a whole different world for us.''

Jack, Shimmy and a friend of theirs named Buster had spent more than two hours unloading the truck. It was empty except for one large piece, a beautiful hutch of dark, gleaming wood.

Lena and Julie Lee were standing shoulder to shoulder. The smile on Lena's face turned into sunshine when Julie Lee said abruptly, ''That's for you, Lena. That's for your house.''

''What you saying, Julie Lee? You saying that you giving me that beautiful thing?''

''That's what I'm saying, Lena.''

Julie Lee was startled when Lena reached up and hugged her tightly around the neck. ''Oh, Julie Lee, I love it, and won't it look real good upside the window in the kitchen next to those pretty yellow curtains I made?''

''That's exactly the spot I had in mind, Lena.''

Lena just beamed.

Chapter 48

Lytell was a hard-working young man. Many nights he almost fell into the apartment, too exhausted to participate in family conversations. How many times had he dozed off to sleep on the couch right in the middle of someone trying to talk to him!

In addition to holding down his job at Pig Foot Sally's, he was going to classes two nights a week studying accounting. He'd always had a good head for figures, and he wanted to develop that talent.

On the nights he didn't attend classes, Lytell hustled extra money as a free-lance bookkeeper for Negro shop owners. There were, contrary to popular opinion, a number of transplanted Southerners who owned small businesses, and while they knew how to do the kind of work that fell into their line, many needed assistance in keeping their financial records straight.

Lytell's reputation for keeping accurate books grew, and before long he was even turning down some people who requested his help simply because he didn't have the time. When that happened, however, he told the owners about some of the other men in his class, and often they ended up getting the work.

He was saving every extra penny he could make to buy his own restaurant, and though it might have been competition for her, Pig Foot Sally encouraged Lytell in his dream to be independent. Her philosophy had always been that there were enough hungry people around for every restaurant owner to get a piece of the action. Besides, she told Lytell, "We colored folks need to stick together. You don't see those Jews arguing about how many businesses each other have. That's how we got to think. Got to pull each other through the eye of the needle."

The boys often teased young Roxie Kate about how she always treated Lytell as if she were his wife or his mother. When he'd fall into the house, she was the first one trying to help him. She would lovingly help him out of his clothes, and she took off his shoes and socks as he propped up his feet. Sometimes when he was particularly tired, she tried to help him relax by brushing his hair.

The fact that Lytell did not have a wife yet, or even a steady woman, had often been a source of discussion between Julie Lee and Jack. Nearly all the young men in their midtwenties had wives already, and if they didn't, most of them had at least one child somewhere. But not Lytell. He seemed much more interested in making money than in making babies.

Each time Lytell brought a new woman home, Julie Lee's heart soared. Maybe this will be the one, she kept thinking. But after one or two visits she never saw them again, and Lytell never bothered to mention them anymore.

Thinking that they had some obligation to help out, Julie Lee and Lena tried introducing Lytell to several of the young women in the church. He was always pleasant to them, but nothing ever came of the friendships. And Lytell was a hot item too since most of the eligible women knew how hard he worked and would have been glad to get a man like him.

Then one Saturday night Lytell arrived at the apartment with a woman Julie Lee and Jack didn't know. Julie Lee had a hunch that there was something different about this one. Maybe it was the way Lytell looked at the girl. His eyes were glowing, and he was smiling more than usual. That was the way Jack had looked at her when they were courting, Julie Lee reflected.

Her name was Henrietta Thomas. She'd come to the city with her aunt from North Carolina only a year earlier. She was nineteen years old and would be twenty in two months, Julie Lee learned. Like Julie Lee, she looked after children for her living.

Lytell had met her after she'd come into Pig Foot Sally's two or three times. She always occupied the same table, by the window, near the door, and every time she came, she was always alone. Lytell wondered what a good-looking woman like her was doing unescorted. Surely, he thought to himself, any man would be proud to take her out. Although it wasn't his job to wait tables, whenever the girl came in, Lytell would jump to it.

One night Henrietta came into the restaurant shortly before Lytell was scheduled to get off work. This, he thought, was a real opportunity. This time, he'd talk to her.

Excusing himself and apologizing for the intrusion, a bold Lytell joined her at the table. She'd seen him around the restaurant, and since he'd served her a few times, she felt as if she knew him and wasn't at all uncomfortable with his presence.

He found he liked just looking at her. She was beautiful and had the longest, prettiest eyelashes he had ever seen, and her waist was tiny. He never had liked big women. As he listened to her voice, his heart soared. It had a lilting quality, and her sweet Southern accent only made it more pleasant to his ear.

On that first meeting, the two fell so deeply into conversation that they hadn't even noticed when nearly all the other customers left.

Candy, one of the waitresses, who had her eye on Lytell herself, impatiently interrupted them. "Is y'all finished yet? I want to go home."

Lytell could tell by the look on Candy's face that she was jealous, but he didn't know why. He had walked her home a few times, but had never been involved with her. After all, Candy already had a husband somewhere and two little babies. Not only did he not care to mix business with pleasure, but he had made up his mind that he wouldn't raise another man's child. Besides, he didn't like the idea of some woman being able to keep an eye on him every minute of the day.

He helped Henrietta into her coat and, given the lateness of the hour, offered to walk her home. She agreed. He felt proud just walking down the street with her and he wished he could run into some of his friends to show her off.

By the time they arrived at her building, which was about five blocks from the restaurant, he felt as if they were old, old friends. He hadn't laughed that much in a long time. She was a funny girl. She told him about the woman she worked for and much about herself, and he in turn told her about himself.

He walked her up the two flights to the apartment she

shared with her aunt, who he had learned was named Lyn. It was, Henrietta explained, short for Gerterlyn. It was an odd name, and no one seemed to know where it came from.

They stood in the hallway talking for several minutes. He ached to kiss her, but he didn't, feeling that she was not the type who would appreciate that. He didn't want to do one little thing to offend her. Something she said caused him to laugh loudly, so loud in fact, that it bounced off the wall and echoed through the quiet hallway, but he stopped laughing abruptly when the door to her apartment swung open. A heavyset, dark-skinned woman stuck her head out. "Henrietta, is that you?"

"Yes ma'am. It's me."

"Girl, what you doing out so late? I been sitting here worrying my head off about you."

"I'm sorry, Auntie Lyn, I just got so involved in this conversation with this young man here that I forgot the time."

The woman came farther out the door. She looked Lytell up and down, and while he appeared to be decent enough, she didn't think it proper for a girl to be standing out in the hall with a man. And since she didn't know him, she wasn't about to tell Henrietta to bring him inside. Instead, she said, "Henrietta, I think you better tell your friend good night. You got to go to work in the morning, and I ain't aiming to be spending all my time trying to drag your butt out the bed."

Lytell hoped her aunt would shut the door, but she didn't. She stayed rooted to the spot, looking from him to Henrietta. Henrietta smiled slyly. "I guess I better go, Lytell. It was real nice talking to you, and thank you for walking me home."

370

"Thank you, Henrietta, for allowing me to."

He was halfway down the first flight and still hadn't heard the door close. Impulsively, he turned around and ran back up the stairs to see if she was still there. She was just standing there with the biggest smile on her face like she was daydreaming.

He found himself stuttering and hoped he didn't look too silly. "Henrietta, you think it would be all right if I came by to pick you up Sunday after church? Maybe we could go to the park or something."

"I'd love to go," she answered quickly. "I'll see you Sunday about two."

He skipped down the stairs and all the way home he kept saying to himself, "That's the one. I'm gonna marry that girl."

The weeks went by quickly. Henrietta was the only woman Lytell was seeing. She turned out to be everything he had expected and more. She was bright and inquisitive and eager to learn. Upon learning of his fondness for numbers, however, she admitted that the subject had never been a favorite of hers. He told her not to worry because under his tutelage she would come to love numbers as much as he did. He was sure she would.

Henrietta passed the toughest inspection too, for everyone in the family liked her, and everybody expected that some day she and Lytell would be married. Even Roxie Kate liked Henrietta, but Julie Lee had noticed that her daughter, young as she was, seemed to be somewhat jealous of Henrietta.

Until Henrietta came along, Roxie Kate thought of herself as the main girl in Lytell's life. After all, he was always telling her that he loved her. Now it seemed that all he talked about was Henrietta.

371

One Saturday morning before he left for work, Roxie Kate decided it was time for the two of them to have a talk. She was a pretty child, and Lytell knew her well enough to know when she had something on her mind, so when the girl asked to talk with him he wasn't surprised.

He sat down on her bed, pulling her close to him. "What's the matter, baby girl? What's the matter?"

She sounded so grown-up that he was a bit surprised when she answered. "Lytell, you love Henrietta? You gonna marry her, I bet."

He looked down at her and smiled. "Roxie Kate, I do love Henrietta, but I don't know about getting married. I haven't asked her yet. She may not want to marry me."

"Oh, yes she will. She'll marry you. I can tell Henrietta loves you too. You think I'm only a little girl but I can see how she looks at you. See I know things. Sometimes I listen when Mama and Lena and their friends be talking, and sometimes I know what they're talking about even though they think I'm too young to understand. But what I wanna know is, can somebody be in love with two people at the same time?"

"Well, I suppose you can be," he said, scratching his head. "I mean, I guess you can be depending on what kind of love it is. See, like the way I love you is different from how I love Henrietta, but I love both of you just the same. Why you ask that kind of question anyway?"

She looked down at her hands and spoke low, apparently shy about what she wanted to say next. "It just seems like since you got Henrietta that maybe you don't love me no more. I mean it seems like you don't hardly got no time to play with me and to go with me to the park. You always taking Henrietta someplace."

He didn't mean to, but he couldn't help laughing at

her seriousness. "Roxie Kate, I'll always love you. You're my little sister. And I know for a fact that Henrietta loves you too. Don't you want me to get married and have children? Maybe one day I'll even have a pretty little girl like you."

She looked up at him again. Her eyes were filled with tears. "I don't know if I want you to get married, Lytell, 'cause then you gonna move away and then I won't be able to see you every day like I do now. I don't want you to move away. Even if you marry Henrietta, why can't you live with us? I mean all both of y'all."

It was getting late and they both knew it. He hated to leave her in the middle of a discussion that was so important to her.

"How about if I make a deal with you, Roxie Kate? When I do ask Henrietta to marry me, if she agrees, you'll be the first person to know. That's behind me and Henrietta, of course. And then when we move into our own apartment, you can come over as much as you want, long as your mama won't mind."

He took a handkerchief out of his pocket and wiped her tears. "Now you stop crying, baby girl. You know I love you."

She felt comforted and after one big, childish blow into the handkerchief, she said, "I know you love me. I know."

On his way out of the room, she blew him a kiss. He jumped back and pretended that he'd felt it touch his face. He giggled and so did she. He thought about Roxie Kate all the way to work, realizing that she was on the verge of becoming what he believed to be the most complicated creature on God's earth—a young woman.

Chapter 49

They were lying in bed. She had her face turned toward the wall and was weeping softly. She was still angry from the argument they'd had earlier.

For the second night that week Jack had come home drunk. She hated it when he was like that. She hated him reeking of alcohol and slurring his words. Jack was a good father and a good provider, but his regular drinking bouts with his coworkers were beginning to become the one big problem in their marriage. How could he spend money in a tavern when they needed it so badly at home? The children were growing so quickly, and every time she turned around, it seemed like somebody needed a new pair of shoes, some new underwear or a new pair of pants. She was doing all she could, buying second-hand clothes and stretching to the limit the dollars, he, she and Lytell brought home. Couldn't Jack see that?

Jack was apologetic. He hated her to be annoyed at him, couldn't stand it when she frowned and wouldn't talk to him for hours. She knew how to make him feel bad, all right.

"Julie Lee," he said tenderly, trying to get her to

turn toward him. "I'm sorry, baby. I promise I won't get drunk no more."

"That's what you said the last time, and they don't mean anything, your promises."

"But, baby, me and the boys was just celebrating. I didn't even get a chance to tell you that—"

"I don't want to hear it, Jack. You got more reasons to celebrate than any man I know. So how come we still struggling like we are?"

She turned toward him and flashes of anger were shooting from her eyes. He felt embarrassed, but listened as she chastised him as if he were a child.

"Don't those other men you work with have families? Don't they have children to feed and clothe?"

"I said I won't do it no more."

She spit back his words at him. "You won't do it no more. You always say that Jack, but you do. It's not good for the children to see you like that, and it's not good for them to see you and me arguing and fussing."

He ignored her coldness and held her close to him. He put mock anger into his voice. "Listen woman, didn't I tell you that I wasn't going to come home drunk no more?"

"I don't believe you, Jack Bratcher. I don't believe you. Now let my arms go, man."

"I ain't," he said playfully. "I'm not going to let you go until I tell you what I was celebrating about."

"I don't want to hear it now, Jack. Let me go."

"I said I ain't." He kissed her all over her neck. "Shut up your mouth, Julie Lee Bratcher, and listen to me, woman."

She stopped struggling, knowing that it was useless anyhow.

"I got a promotion today."

"You what?" she exclaimed wide-eyed.

"I said, I got a promotion. Rocco told me that the boss man was real pleased with how I handled myself in the time I been working there, and he wants me to be a foreman, the first colored foreman they ever had.

" 'Course now I won't be the foreman over the white men, but I'll be over all the colored laborers. And besides that, I'm gonna be making five more dollars a week."

She punched his arm. "What you saying, Jack Bratcher? You telling me that you gonna be a boss Negro?"

"That's what I'm telling you, woman. Now, you still mad at me for getting drunk? Tell me I ain't had nothing to celebrate."

She put her arms around his neck, sorry she'd been so hard on him. If he ever had a reason to celebrate by having a few drinks with his friends, this was it. What a good man he is, she thought, and then she felt his familiar fumbling under the covers.

"I want to love you, woman. I done had my liquor. Now I want my woman."

She pushed his hand away. "I'm too excited, Jack."

"No such thing as too excited, baby."

She laughed. "Oh, Jack, stop talking like some old street man."

"Come over here, girl."

"Oh, Jack."

"Oh, Jack nothing. I'm going to make sweet love to you, woman. You gonna forget all about ever being mad at me."

She never could stay angry with him very long. He was too sweet a man and she loved him more than anything. He worked himself to the bone trying to do right by her and the children.

Her breath grew short as his hands wandered over her body. Soon Jack had carried her to that warm, wet place, just like he always did. The years had not dampened his spirit, and he still knew how to make her holler. Thank God for that, she thought, as she wrapped her legs tightly around him.

Chapter 50

They had been going together for the better part of a year, and Henrietta's aunt was about to drive her insane about Lytell. She kept saying, "Henri, if that boy asks you to marry him, you better get to it, girl. How many colored men you know like Lytell? Working so hard and everything and then going to them classes at night to try to better hisself.

"Child, I'll be so glad to have you write home to tell your mama that you done hooked youself a good man. You marry Lytell and you going to have a good life. Not like me and your mama, just working all the time without getting nowhere. Honey, what every colored woman needs is a good old colored man."

And Aunt Lyn was right. Lytell was a good man, but he sure was taking his time about asking her to marry him.

It was Sunday, and Henrietta was terribly excited. Julie Lee had invited both her and her aunt for dinner after church. That was a good sign as far as Aunt Lyn was concerned. If the boy weren't interested in her niece then his mother certainly wouldn't be inviting them both to dinner.

It was a beautiful day and a beautiful meal. Aunt Lyn had a ball, Henrietta could tell. It seemed that ten different conversations were going on at once when Lytell stopped everyone from talking by hitting on his glass with a spoon.

"Attention. Attention. I've got an announcement to make."

Roxie Kate's heart fell down into her shoes. She knew what was coming. She knew he was going to say that he was going to marry Henrietta and that they were going to move away. He hadn't kept his promise. He promised that he would tell her first thing when he asked Henrietta to marry him, and now he was going to tell everybody all at once. She wanted to cry.

Jack and Julie Lee were sitting next to each other. Unconsciously they put their arms about each other.

All eyes focused on Lytell, who was standing up with a most ridiculous grin on his face.

"Listen, everybody. I want y'all to be the first to know. I've saved me enough money to . . ."

Henrietta wanted to shout out the rest of the sentence. Her knees were knocking under the table. So this was how Lytell was going to propose? He was just going to blurt it out in front of everybody and embarrass her?

"Is everybody listening?" Lytell asked again, stretching out the suspense.

"We listening. We listening," they responded nearly in unison.

"I'm going to open my own restaurant." Lytell spoke so quickly that what he said nearly slipped passed Julie Lee.

"What you say, boy?"

Roxie Kate heard and her heart soared. Henrietta heard and her heart fell. Jack was surprised and Aunt Lyn believed she was going to have a heart attack. Here she was, all ready to make a speech about how glad she was to be welcoming Lytell into her family, and he was talking about opening a restaurant.

"That's right," Lytell continued dramatically. "I'm going to open my own restaurant. And I'm going to call it Bratcher's Food Emporium."

"What?" everyone said, sounding like a chorus.

Jack couldn't help himself. "Lytell, I don't mean to get in your business, and I sure don't mean to sound ignorant, but what in the world is an *emporium*?"

"Aw, Jack, it ain't no big thing. It only means that my restaurant is going to be a place where the food will be all different kinds. You know what I mean? Variety.

"Most Negro restaurants serve Southern food. Well mine is going to be different. I'm going to have Southern food all right, but I'm going to have other things too, like Italian food and things that Irish folk like and even some of that stuff that the Jews eat. You know, that kosher stuff."

Julie Lee stood up now, proud of Lytell. "Well, I do declare. We're going to have our first businessman in the family. I think this calls for a little celebrating, as Jack always says."

She took a decanter from the cabinet, and from it she poured glasses of wine for everyone. She decided that even the children could have a little taste.

Everyone laughed and talked as they sipped, but Jack kept thinking that it didn't taste as good as the cheap whiskey he got down at the tavern. Of course he didn't say anything, not wanting to hurt Julie Lee's feelings or steal her thunder.

"Lytell," Jack asked. "What you know about cooking white folks' food?"

"I don't. I'm going to hire me a white cook."

Jack was sorry, but he couldn't contain himself. "Please tell me, boy. Where you going to find some white person to work for you in *your* restaurant."

Lytell was serious. "The way I figure it, Jack, people are looking for work, and I expect, the way money is so tight, that there is a white person out there who can cook and won't mind working for a Negro as long as that money is green."

"I think you're right about that," Aunt Lyn chimed in. She had gotten over her disappointment, and was now growing as excited as everyone else. He may not have asked to marry Henrietta, but the fact that Lytell was going into business for himself made him an even better catch for her niece. He was obviously just waiting until he was in a better position before asking Henrietta to be his wife. Now to her mind, a woman couldn't do much better than that.

Lytell told them he had already picked the spot where he intended to open for business—Fiftieth Street between Sixth and Seventh Avenues.

"You mean you going to open up in the Tenderloin?" Jack asked.

"That's right. Right up in that terrible Tenderloin. Bratcher's Emporium is going to be the best eating establishment in that place."

"But why do you call it the terrible Tenderloin?" Roxie Kate asked. She had never heard the expression before.

Julie Lee's face flushed. She didn't want Lytell to tell Roxie Kate that the Tenderloin was famous for its red light district, where the prostitutes were so bold that some men said when they went down there they felt as if they could buy beef on the hoof.

The weeks that followed brought a flurry of activity around the opening of Lytell's restaurant. In their free time, everybody helped out, even the children. Julie Lee, Henrietta and Lena shopped for the fabric for the red curtains Lytell wanted, and each took some of the material home to do the sewing. They sat around the table laughing and talking as they hemmed the red tablecloths Lytell decided he wanted. In a way it was funny, Julie Lee thought. It reminded her of those old-fashioned sewing bees where she and some of the other women on the plantation would take scraps of fabric and make blankets for their pallets.

Jack had convinced some of the men from his job to go to the restaurant with him so that they could help out by giving Lytell practical ideas.

Lytell really didn't have much of an idea of what it was going to cost him to open the fancy restaurant he had in mind. Every time he turned around, it looked like he was spending money for one thing or another.

He had three thousand fliers printed up announcing the restaurant's opening, and offering people a free drink with their meal. He paid George and some of his friends to deliver them around the neighborhood where the restaurant was. He even gave Julie Lee a couple of hundred fliers to take to church.

He had red and black pennants made, and he and Henrietta spent two hours passing them through long strings. The day before the restaurant opened, he attached the pennants to the building and then to the street lamp. When they were up, he watched proudly as they flapped gently in the breeze. That would really get attention. He paid a printer a few dollars to make a great big sign to go in the window which read, ''Grand Opening.'' The same printer had also carefully painted the name of the place on the window glass. Jack had him make the letters so large that they could be seen from a block away.

As the opening day neared, Lytell still hadn't been able to get that European cook he wanted, but he had hired two colored ones and two waitresses. And not to leave his loved ones out, he'd coaxed Henrietta to quit her job to come to work for him and he'd offered George a job as the head bus boy. George was delighted. It meant he could make some money so that he could buy some of the things he wanted. Jack was all for it, believing that George wasn't too young to learn something about making a dollar. Julie Lee protested at first, saying that George had to finish his schooling, but she gave in when Lytell promised that he would only work in the evenings after school.

The great day finally arrived. Lytell put on his best suit and George was wearing some white pants his mother had made and a white shirt. At exactly twelve noon, George flung open the doors of Bratcher's Food Emporium. In minutes, every table was filled and Lytell was already out of his jacket and in the kitchen helping the sweaty cooks turn out the meals that had been ordered.

Meanwhile, Henrietta was running from one end of the counter to the other, taking money and taking orders from customers who'd sat down at the bar since they were unable to find a table.

Lytell came to the door of the kitchen and looked around at the crowd he'd attracted. He recognized many Negro Bohemians—poets, writers and artists—who lived mostly on Fifty-third Street. Even Pig Foot Sally stopped by to wish him well. She hugged him affectionately and pinched his cheeks. "Boy, you making me proud. I knew when I laid eyes on you that you was going to be somebody special. If there's ever anything I can do for you, let me know." He kissed Sally on both cheeks, knowing that she meant exactly what she said.

So the grand opening was a grand success, measured not only by the happy faces and the warm compliments of the customers, but by the cash in the till. All told, when he counted it up that night, he had taken in one hundred and seventy-five dollars. Not bad for twelve hours' work, he told Henrietta later on.

Before they shut the door that night, Henrietta watched him as he lovingly ran his fingers over the table tops. The place was beautiful, so beautiful that he could hardly believe it was his.

As they headed hand in hand toward Henrietta's apartment, Lytell's enthusiasm was bubbling over. "Guess what I'm going to open up next?"

"What?" she asked, thinking that the man was moving too fast for her.

"Well me and the boys—I mean the guys I go to school with at night—well, we were thinking about starting a business for colored owners where we would keep their financial records and all.

"It's a good idea, I think, since nearly all of us is doing part-time work anyhow. Well, we kind of thought we could do better if we consolidated our resources."

She pressed his hand. "I think that's a good idea, Lytell, but don't you think you better get the restaurant going first?"

"Oh yeah," he said, appearing to be off on another thought. "I don't mean right now. I mean sometime later."

She laughed to herself. If Lytell said he was going to do it, then he would.

Bratcher's Food Emporium was open two months, and business was still good. Each new day brought new customers and each new day brought back others who had been there before, and whom Lytell now thought of as his regulars. And business was brisk even without a European cook. He didn't know why he was surprised, but his white customers seemed to enjoy the Southern cooking too, even though most of them had come from places where collard greens were hardly a staple.

Henrietta and Lytell were closing for the evening one night when two policemen came in. Lytell was in the back counting the money and was about to tell her how well they had done that day when he saw the two men. He greeted them warmly. Usually, the owners took care of them by giving a free meal or something warm to drink. These two particular policemen, however, were familiar to neither Henrietta nor Lytell.

In a most gracious voice, Lytell informed the two that the kitchen was closed, and that unfortunately, the best he could offer them was something to drink.

"We didn't come for that," one of the men snarled.

Lytell certainly didn't want any trouble from the law.

"Well, what can I do for you gentlemen then?" he asked cordially.

"We want to talk to you about something, but we don't want to talk out here. Let's go in the back," one of the officers said in the same hostile tone.

Henrietta was feeling very uneasy, and she was sorry now that no one else was around but she and Lytell. Even George had gone home. She didn't like the looks of the two men or the way they talked to Lytell.

385

Meanwhile he showed the men into the back room and pulled the curtain behind them. She had washed the same spot on the counter over and over again, straining to hear what was being said in the back.

The three stayed back there for twenty minutes or more. When he finally emerged, Lytell had a strange look on his face. As they headed toward the door, one of the two men gave her a lecherous look and said, "Good night, little lady."

She rushed to lock the door behind them, anxious for Lytell to tell her what had happened. She had never seen Lytell look like that before. Only a half-hour ago he was happy as could be, and now he looked so troubled. "What did they want?"

He acted as if he were far away. "Nothing that you need to worry about."

She knew better than to press him. She didn't want to have an argument and add to his already tense state, but she couldn't help feeling somewhat resentful that he didn't appreciate how concerned she was.

After that, the two policemen came to the restaurant regularly, always near closing time and always on Fridays. They rarely said anything to her. They just went into the back room, spent a few minutes with Lytell and left.

The restaurant continued to boom.

Henrietta tried to forget about the regular visits by the policemen. She was starting to wonder if Lytell was ever going to marry her. Certainly he had enough money now so that they could get married and live comfortably. They had already become intimate and often he told her that he loved her, but still he hadn't asked the big question.

She was getting anxious and worried that Aunt Lyn

might have been right when she'd said that if a man can get the milk for free then he had no reason to buy the cow.

Her concern was unwarranted, however. Lytell had every intention of marrying her, and by the time the end of the month came, he had indeed proposed. Looking back on it later, all she could think about was how unromantic it all was. He was in the back adding up figures when she came into the little room to get something, she couldn't even remember what. He grabbed her by her waist and pulled her down on his lap.

"You looking real pretty, girl. In fact, you always look real pretty. Did I ever tell you that?"

She giggled. "Oh stop that lying, man."

"I swear I'm telling the truth. You look so good I think I'll marry you. Will you marry me, woman?"

She acted as if she was thinking about his offer. "I'm not sure, Mr. Bratcher." She jumped up and ran to the other side of the desk as he chased after her. He caught her in his arms and kissed her. "You better marry me or else."

"Or else what?" she exclaimed, breaking away and beginning to giggle again.

"Or else nothing. You going to marry me and that's all."

She fell into the chair, acting as he were holding her prisoner. "All right. All right. If you're insisting."

The word spread quickly. A few weeks later, Lytell's friends recruited Julie Lee and Jack into a scheme to give Henrietta and Lytell a surprise engagement party.

Even big-mouth Roxie Kate, whom Julie Lee always teased about not being able to hold water in her mouth, kept her lips sealed.

The crowd had gathered in the social hall of the Virginia Society that night. Lytell and Henrietta had been lured to the place under the pretext that Jack was being honored by the society for a big project of his that had brought two hundred dollars into the coffer.

They almost didn't go in, since Lytell wondered why, if there was such a big to-do, all the lights were out. He and Henrietta nearly fell down the steps to the basement in the dark. He fumbled around trying to find a lamp to turn on, and when he did, he nearly fainted when dozens of voices suddenly screamed out, "Surprise!"

It was a great party and it went on until the wee hours of the morning. Henrietta was walking on air. She was so glad to be getting married, especially to a man who was so loved and respected by so many people.

Chapter 51

Julie Lee had passed the point of being tired. She was downright exhausted and glad to be off her feet, which were now blissfully dangling in a pan of hot water. She didn't usually work on Saturdays, but Amanda had begged her to come in and look after the children since her parents were in the city and she wanted to take them out shopping and sightseeing. Amanda had been good to her and Julie Lee felt she could not refuse the request.

Jack was already in bed. He'd fallen out right after dinner. It was hot and muggy, and his working outside in the sun all week was beginning to take its toll. It must be his age, he told Julie Lee, since working in the sun was hardly something new to an old ex-slave like him.

She leaned back in the chair and shut her eyes. She might have dozed off to sleep if it weren't for George suddenly bursting into the apartment. His eyes were bulging out of their sockets and they were red from crying. He was screaming about a fire and talking so fast that she could hardly make out what he was saying. Jack jumped out of the bed and was still in his undershorts when he ran into the living room. He grabbed the hysterical child by his shoulders.

"What's the matter, boy. Why you crying?"

By the time they arrived at the hospital Henrietta and two of Lytell's best friends, Scootie and Jackson, were already there. The moment she saw Julie Lee, Henrietta ran into her arms, sobbing hysterically. Lytell had been burnt badly in the restaurant fire.

Julie Lee massaged Henrietta's back. She was shaking uncontrollably as she spoke. "He's going to die. Lytell going to die, I know it. I just know it."

It seemed the more hysterical Henrietta grew, the calmer Julie Lee became. "Lytell ain't gonna die. Now you stop saying that. He's going to be all right. Just wait and see."

She was saying it, but not believing it even as the words were falling out of her mouth. She patted Henrietta, but kept an eye on Jack. He was pacing up and down in front of the swinging doors marked "Emergency." She watched her husband opening and closing his fists, and she flinched at the pain he must have felt when he unexpectedly slammed his fist into the wall. Scootie and Jackson were talking with him, apparently trying to calm him down, but it was doing no good. Jack's face was a mosaic of grief.

Finally, after they'd been waiting for the better part of an hour, a nurse emerged through the doors. Julie Lee grabbed the woman by the hand. "Please tell me, how is my son? How is my child?" Julie Lee ignored the startled look on the white nurse's face at this white woman hollering about her child when the only patient was a black man.

"He's doing pretty well, miss. As well as can be expected under the circumstances." The nurse was trying to wrest her hand away from Julie Lee, who wouldn't let it go.

She hadn't liked the curtness in the nurse's voice and she didn't believe what she'd been told. "Tell me the truth. How is my child? Is he going to live? If he's going to die, tell me. I've got a right to know."

Now, the nurse grew visibly irritated. She yanked her hand away from Julie Lee. "I said he's going to be all right. The doctors are doing all they can. Now that's all I can tell you."

The nurse rushed down the hall in a huff. She looked around disgustedly at all the Negroes who were now crowding into the waiting room. Jack saw the look on her face. He wanted to slap that woman.

Word of what had happened traveled quickly. Already Pig Foot Sally had swept in accompanied by two men whom neither Julie Lee nor Henrietta recognized. Shimmy came in right behind them, and then came the pastor of Mother Zion, accompanied by the president of the Virginia Society.

The pastor came over and talked with Julie Lee and Henrietta. Jack had paced himself out and was sleeping with his head on Julie Lee's lap. George had dropped off to sleep too, his head balanced on Jack's lap.

The time went by slowly, and still not one doctor had emerged from behind the swinging doors. Even the nurse they had seen earlier never came back down the hall. Julie Lee suspected that the woman had gone into the emergency room via another route hoping to avoid them.

Julie Lee could barely keep her eyes open. It was like a death vigil. She felt angry and disgusted and wondered once again whether their coming to New York City had been a good idea. She kept feeling that bad luck was becoming a mighty close companion of hers and seemed to follow her wherever she went.

An hour later when the first doctor came through the swinging doors, everyone in the waiting room was asleep. The men had sprawled out on benches around the room, and all the women were huddled next to one another on the long bench closest to the emergency room entrance. The doctor assumed from their proximity that they were family.

The doctor tapped Jack on the shoulder gently, not wanting to startle him. As tired as he was, when Jack realized that it was a doctor, he eyes jerked open as if he'd never been to sleep. Soon they were all awake, anxious to hear the medical report.

The doctor was quite young, but obviously had some experience handling a hysterical family. He spoke softly, understating the situation with very little drama in his voice. He found himself standing in the middle of a semi-circle the family had formed around him. He talked to them all, but addressed himself primarily to Jack, whom he assumed was his patient's father.

"He's resting now. I suppose you already know that he was burned pretty badly. We've done all we can for now. If he makes it through until morning and we can break the high fever he has, then I think we'll have a good chance of saving his life. We'll keep a close watch over him.

"He was ranting some when they first brought him in. We gave him something to calm him down."

Henrietta broke away from Julie Lee and stood right in front of the doctor. "What was he saying, Doctor? What was he talking about?"

The doctor searched his memory. "You've got to remember that he was probably hysterical, so you can't put too much stock in what he was saying. Let me see . . . well, yes, I remember now. He asked about Henrietta and if she was all right, and then he said something we couldn't make out too well. Something about somebody deliberately setting the fire. He mentioned two policemen too. I suppose the policemen are friends of his. That's all I can tell you. I can't remember the other things.''

The doctor excused himself and started down the hall. When he turned they were all still standing there. "Oh, by the way. The young man will be asleep for several hours, so I suggest that all of you go home and try to get some rest. You can come back in the morning.''

The doctor's eyes swept the crowd, and he added, "I'm telling you now, he's in no condition to see lots of people, so I will have to limit the visitors tomorrow to immediate family members. When he's stronger, the rest of you can come, but please help us all by giving him some time to regain his strength.''

It was news, but somehow it seemed liked no news. Jack dropped his head and politely thanked the doctor. He led the small procession out of the hospital. They stood talking for a while on the hospital steps and soon headed off in their separate directions. The pastor told Julie Lee that he didn't expect them in church, but said that he would announce what had happened and would have everyone say a special prayer for Lytell. Both she and Jack thanked him.

Henrietta went home with Jack, Julie Lee and George. Julie Lee decided to leave the children at Lena's house since they were probably all asleep anyway. "No need to drag the kids out of their beds in the middle of the night, and if we going back to the hospital in the morning, they're going to have to stay with Lena anyway.''

Jack, however, said that she should go over to Lena's anyway before they left for the hospital. "You've got to tell them something," he explained patiently. "Roxie Kate will die if you don't give her some word. Besides, I guess Lena will be wondering too."

Julie Lee tried to go back to sleep but couldn't. She jumped up during the night to see about Henrietta, who was apparently having a nightmare. After getting up two times, she decided it was useless going back to bed, so she sat up in the chair, keeping one eye on Lena and listening for sounds from the bedrooms where Jack and George were sleeping.

When they arrived back at the hospital the next morning, Lytell had been moved upstairs. They'd put him in a room by himself. The light was not on and the curtains were drawn. The desk nurse informed them that he was still asleep and that they would have to wait before going in. "The doctor said for me to tell you to wait for him to come down. He wants to see the patient first." This nurse was friendly and appeared genuinely concerned and they settled down to wait.

A small group of men assembled in front of what had been Bratcher's Food Emporium. The stink from the fire was still heavy in the air and some of the wood was still smoking.

The word in the street was that Lytell's place had been deliberately burned down because he'd refused the "big boys'" demand for a higher weekly payoff. Word was that two policemen had let it be known that they were going to punish that "uppity nigga" for trying to act like he could do business without greasing their palms.

One man, already a little tipsy even though it was

early Sunday morning, commented, "Them some mean suckers, and they don't play when it comes down to their money. I heard everybody around here is paying them off, even the white owners. When it comes to collecting their money everybody gets treated like a nigga."

Similar incidents had happened before, and always the two policemen, who were well known in the area, had gotten away with them. Some of Lytell's regular customers and neighborhood personalities vowed, however, that this time was different and that they would get their revenge.

Lytell was still in the hospital recuperating three weeks later. Expecting him to be asleep, Henrietta and Julie Lee tiptoed into the room. He was awake, however, and much to both their delight, managed to smile, although the gesture was obviously painful and came off looking something like a grimace.

For the first few days he was in the hospital, Lytell had been in shock. The doctors kept him drugged up just to calm him down. Many of those early nights after the fire he would scream out, just as if he were being burned all over again. It was not an unusual after effect, the doctors said.

Looking at him now, Henrietta's mind went back to the first time she saw him after the fire. She'd nearly fainted when she'd opened the door to his room and had been greeted by the sight of a mummy. His whole head had been wrapped in thick white gauze. Now, only one side of his face remained covered. The side that was exposed was disfigured, and he had already begun to scar in some spots. The puffiness and swelling was something the doctors had told them to expect. They couldn't explain why, but that condition seemed to afflict Negroes more than whites.

The doctors had asked them to refrain from letting him look at himself in the mirror, even if he begged them to. The doctors patiently explained that they had had cases where their patients had threatened suicide after seeing themselves disfigured. And though he had never been a vain man, everyone knew that Lytell had always been proud of what he considered to be his fairly good looks, particularly when he was all dressed up.

He still did not have the use of his hands, and though the bandages had been taken off daily when the nurses exercised his fingers so they would not get stiff, most of the time his hands were kept wrapped, as they were now.

Lytell appeared to be in good spirits, better than he had been at any time since the fire. With laborered words, which caused the face bandage to move up and down, he told them that he'd even gotten up and walked earlier that morning and looked forward to coming home just so he could eat some real food.

They'd been chatting close to an hour before Henrietta placed the day's newspaper on his lap. On the front page with a banner headline there was the story about two policemen in the Tenderloin who'd been ambushed and stabbed to death in an alley on Fifty-first Street. According to the article, which Henrietta read to him, the police were still searching for the assailants, but were having a difficult time since area merchants who might have seen or heard something were not cooperating with the investigation.

When Henrietta finished reading, she searched his face for some reaction, but there was none—not happiness or sadness, nothing. At least not for several minutes. Then from the eye that was visible, two small tears fell.

He was released from the hospital after another month. Surprisingly, Lytell had handled the experience well, and though he had been physically scarred and financially devastated, in Henrietta's eyes he had remained as beautiful as ever. He returned to daily life with as much normality as could be expected. Of course, he was already scheming on his next money-making project and had received great encouragement not only from the family, but from his friends who agreed to put up their own money in whatever project he ultimately decided on. Lytell was no longer interested in doing business directly with the public because of his disfigurement, but there were other ways to make money, he knew.

Lytell and Henrietta were married some time later in a small ceremony at home. Only a few close friends and relatives were in attendance.

Jack and Julie Lee offered to have their adopted son and daughter-in-law live with them until they were able to get on their feet. It seemed like they hadn't been married any time at all when Lytell stood up one evening and announced after dinner that he and Henrietta were expecting. Julie Lee and Jack were beaming as Roxie Kate happily pointed out that they were going to be *grandparents* soon.

Chapter 52

Lytell pampered Henrietta throughout her pregnancy—treated her like royalty was the way other people explained his behavior. He catered to her every whim and would walk blocks in the middle of the night if he had to buy some special food she said she had a craving for. He would massage her legs, her back, her feet, and he constantly told her how beautiful she was and how much he loved her. She teased him and accused him of being terribly romantic. He acted as if they were courting.

Of course, Aunt Lyn came over nearly every evening after work to look after her niece, and the woman never could help reminding Henrietta how fortunate she was to have a man like Lytell.

Henrietta knew that, and she desperately wanted to keep him happy. She wanted so badly to give him a baby son. She knew how he would love that.

One evening while he was massaging her back, she told him about her wish for a male child. He cradled her head in his lap and talked gently. ''Henrietta, I don't care what you have. Boy or girl, I'm gonna love it. I just want a healthy baby. A baby with two ears, two eyes, one mouth and one nose and a pretty face like yours. Don't get your heart set on no boy because you know God has the final say in that.''

With all the pampering, Henrietta had a very difficult pregnancy, and by the seventh month, she was swollen so large that she could barely see her own feet. She dragged her heavy body around, and though she tried to keep a smile on her face, Julie Lee knew the weight she was carrying was almost more than the girl could bear. Julie Lee had had a terrible argument with Henrietta's doctor after telling him that her daughter-in-law was carrying too heavy to be having just one baby. He didn't like the idea of some untrained woman making a diagnosis for him.

"I believe the girl is gonna give birth to twins or maybe even three babies,'' Julie Lee insisted.

In turn he had told her more than once not to confuse Henrietta by telling her that something they could brew up at home would be as effective as medicine he prescribed. She always acted as if she was paying attention, but as soon as they got out of his office, Julie Lee would tell Henrietta to throw those concoctions away, since as far as she was concerned, they were just a waste of money.

Lord, Julie Lee kept thinking, what would the man do if Jeddah were still alive? She laughed at the thought, knowing full well that if he tangled with Jeddah he would be the loser. "Shucks,'' she told Jack one night, "if Jeddah was here, Henrietta wouldn't be going to no doctor at all.''

Financially, Lytell was beginning to get back on his feet. He never talked much anymore about the restaurant or about his losses. He seemed to be too busy figuring out what he was going to do next. Fortunately, many of his former clients, once they found out he was out of the hospital and fully recovered, brought their books and receipts to him at the apartment. He'd even set up an office in one part of the kitchen. He kept all his papers there, and everyone knew better than to touch them without his permission.

Some of his clients, aware that Lytell had a family to support now and that he'd lost everything in the fire, slipped him an extra dollar or two. As far as they were concerned, the additional remuneration was worth it, since Lytell did more for them than merely keep their financial records. He advised them on how to invest their extra income, told them about ways to organize and train their workers to be more productive. He encouraged them to expand when they could afford to and discussed ways that some of them could even merge to their financial advantage. Some said Lytell was just a born businessman. As the word spread, even before Henrietta gave birth, Lytell was considering opening a small office somewhere, since the volume of business could hardly be handled in the already overcrowded apartment. In addition, he wanted to have set hours and have a professional appearance to his operation.

The last two or three weeks before the baby was due, Lytell ordered Henrietta off her feet. If she needed or wanted anything, either he or someone else in the house would get it for her. "Don't want nothing to happen to this baby," he said repeatedly.

As it turned out, Julie Lee was right all along. On a Monday evening, after thirty-six hours of labor, Henrietta gave birth to two beautiful, chocolate-colored girls. Identical twins. Lytell thought he was going to die he was so happy. He couldn't sit still. God, he was so happy for his two beautiful daughters and happy that his wife had come through the ordeal with stamina and grace.

A week later, little Jeddah and Rhetta Bratcher came home from the hospital. Julie Lee put different colored ribbons on each of their necks so that everyone could tell them apart. Sometimes she would lean down into their cradle, closely examining them.

Henrietta was still very weak from her long, hard pregnancy and delivery, but Jack and Julie Lee were only too willing to play the doting grandparents. Jack often teased her about how much his wife was carrying on over the babies. One day he said, "Julie Lee, seem to me that you want another little one yourself. I ain't too old to accommodate, you know."

She laughed. "Man, you must be crazy. I'm all through with that. Been through. Now, I'm just gonna sit back and enjoy my grands."

During the weeks she spent trying to regain her strength, Henrietta often lay in bed listening to Julie Lee talking to Rhetta and Jeddah as if they were already grown-up. She learned a lot about the family by listening. She heard Julie Lee tell the girls stories about her mother, and about Katy and Jeddah and about other people on the plantation. She told them often how proud she was that they had been born free.

Clearly the house was overcrowded, and it became more so once the girls were settled in. Some of the furniture that was considered luxury more than necessity was moved down into the basement of their apartment building. The super was very nice about it, and he told Jack that he wouldn't even charge them anything for storage.

Despite the limited space, the babies did something for that apartment. They brought a new joy, a new happiness.

Often the boys would look at the tiny little girls in awe, and Jack and Julie Lee could hardly wait to get home from work to play with them. Jack, especially. He loved picking them both up and holding one in each arm and demanding that they "burp for Grandpa." Roxie Kate was in her element. She always wanted to change the girls' diapers or do something for them or to them. Some afternoons, Henrietta had to make her go outside and play with the other children her own age. She was practicing being a mama, and everybody agreed that she was doing a good job. She basked in their compliments.

After Henrietta was strong enough and had gone back to work, when the weekends rolled around, Julie Lee and Jack encouraged the new parents to go out and enjoy themselves. That was their excuse for having the babies all to themselves. Jack even took money that he could hardly afford and hired a photographer to come to the apartment to take pictures of the twins.

Jeddah and Rhetta were treated like royalty and soon came to expect it.

Lytell was a wonderful father. Everyone said so. When the girls grew a little older, his biggest joy was letting Henrietta dress them up, and then taking them out into the park or over to visit at one of his friend's apartments. He'd become quite proficient at handling two youngsters at once. He was rarely bothered by those men who kept reminding him that babies were women's business. And he didn't pay too much mind to those that tried to make him feel he was doing something wrong by being good to his wife. One man told him, "You can't be good to no nigga woman. They don't appreciate it. Mine, I keep her in line. I be good, but not too good. Don't want her to get spoiled or nothing."

The man laughed, but Lytell didn't. "First of all, Henrietta is not a 'nigga woman' as you call them, and secondly, those babies are mine as well as hers, and I'm going to do whatever I can to make sure that they know they got a mama and a daddy that cares about them."

He was so serious that he wiped the smile right off the man's face. "Well, I was only kidding," the man explained, embarrassed and shamed by Lytell's response.

When Rhetta and Jeddah were about eleven months old, Jack came in from work one evening dog tired and upon opening the door, he was greeted by a smiling Julie Lee.

"You should have seen them, Jack." He knew from the way she started that she was talking about "her grands."

"This morning Rhetta stood up all by herself and took two steps. Well, you know that jealous little copycat Jeddah. She took one look at her sister and climbed up, holding the table first. Then she let go and came toward me. And guess what? The child took three steps. Got to outdo Rhetta, you know."

Chapter 53

By the turn of the century, the Bratcher clan had grown. Everyone, much to Jack and Julie Lee's delight, had found himself a husband or a wife. In all, there were twenty-two grandchildren, including Lytell and Dexter's. Everytime Julie Lee turned around, someone else was announcing that so-and-so was expecting again.

No one was surprised that Roxie Kate and Jack Jr. were the two who had pursued a higher education. Lytell had made sure that they did. He could very well afford it, having prospered in his accounting business. He was one of the best known Negro businessmen in New York, and he was highly respected among blacks and whites alike. He was also a silent partner in several other businesses and so his income was quite substantial. Primarily though, he was still interested in getting a better toehold in the booming real estate industry. All in all, Lytell had realized his dream of being "somebody special."

He would have paid for Dexter and George to go to college too, but they had their own ideas.

George was interested in running after women and not in running through the pages of a book. His father had helped him get a job in construction. One thing about George, with all his running around, he always kept a job. Besides, the pay in construction was better than most Negroes were making, and it gave him enough to take care of his family in a halfway decent manner and also made it possible for him to have a few extra dollars for his women on the side.

Everybody, including his wife, knew how George loved to run the streets, but there wasn't anything anybody could say to make him do any differently.

A few times he brought women up to Lytell's office. Some of them were good looking and George wanted to show them off. On more than one occasion, Julie Lee had asked Lytell to talk to George about his behavior.

George's response was almost always the same. "I get tired of you always trying to down me for what I do, Lytell. You my brother, and I love you, you know that. But you is you, and I is me. I got to live my life, and you got to live yours."

This sort of reasoning never failed to exasperate Lytell. "George," he would plead, "you have a beautiful wife and beautiful babies. Why can't you be satisfied? Why you got to have so many women and be associating yourself with such low-down people? I swear, they don't mean you no good and they gonna end up getting you in some kind of trouble."

When Lytell started talking like this, George knew it was time for him to go. "Like I said, Lytell, you is you, and I is me."

Dexter didn't have any interest in more schooling either, but he differed from George in many ways. With financial help from Lytell he went into business for himself and opened a restaurant—nothing fancy, but it helped him to turn a dollar, and he earned some additional money at odd jobs, such as helping people to move their furniture. Dexter was more than happy with his life. He didn't want to go to college, though he had always said he didn't believe much in working himself to death to make somebody else rich.

Roxie Kate had her wish. She had grown to be a very pretty woman, and while she was away at school, she met the boy who would become her husband right after graduation. Charlie Rheubottom came from a little town in Maryland by the name of Sykesville. "Way back up in the woods," was the way Charlie described it. His family was poor, too poor to send him to school, and Charlie only got there because the woman for whom his mother had worked for many years liked him and financed his education. Charlie had studied to be a doctor, and he was two years ahead of Roxie Kate. In between having her children, she taught in a number of New York City public schools on a substitute basis. Sometimes she made additional money by tutoring children whose parents could afford to pay. Charlie always teased her about being money hungry, but she never paid him much mind. "All I want is for us to get ahead," was how she would answer him.

Everybody liked Charlie, and it was obvious that he loved Roxie Kate, though she sometimes acted a little snobbish. Sometimes she hurt her mother's feelings deeply, particularly once when she tried to shush Julie Lee for telling Charlie about life back on the plantation.

"Oh, Mama, do you have to talk about those old times so much? We're free now. I get so tired of all that old slavery talk. Seems like I've been hearing it all my life.

"The thing now is education. We Negroes got to get

406

ourselves educated and get some respect from white folks.
And we are never going to get respect if all we talk about
is being slaves. Why some of my white friends say . . ."

She never finished what she had to say. Jack rose up
from his chair and moved menacingly toward his daughter.
He tried not to raise his voice, but he wasn't about to let
her insult her mother. "You know something, girl? If you
grow up to be half the woman your mama is, you'll be
doing something. You getting to sound like so many of
them other Negroes—want to forget where you come from
and what it took to get you where you is. You don't want
to talk about slavery, huh? I guess you want to pretend that
you came over here with the Pilgrims on the Mayflower.

"You educated all right, but you sound ignorant.
Roxie Kate, you are what you are, and we are what we
are. And one of the reasons we aren't slaves anymore is
because of the things your mama is talking about. You
gonna shush your mama? No, you ain't. I ain't gonna let
you. I don't care how educated you get, I'm your father."

Jack was getting too excited and Julie Lee was worried about his heart. He'd already had one mild attack a
year before. "It's all right, Jack. Roxie Kate's just talking.
She don't mean no harm. Do you, baby?"

Charlie had been quiet throughout the exchange. He
knew better than to get in the middle of such an argument.
He understood what Roxie Kate was trying to say and he
understood what her father was saying as well. If he took
either side, he knew he'd be wrong, so he did the best
thing he could: he kept his mouth closed.

For no reason at all, however, Jack started up again.
"By the way, Miss Roxie Kate Bratcher Rheubottom, let
me tell you something else. You went to college and done
got yourself educated. You know that me and your mama

407

didn't have the money to send you to no college. Who sent you? Lytell sent you, and guess what? Whether you like it or not Lytell was once a slave. He just like me and your mama. So don't come in here with all that highfalutin stuff you talking. We done come a mighty long way, but it ain't over yet, not hardly. You better read the newspapers if you think all we colored folks got to do is go to school and make white folks like us."

If Jack Jr. had heard his father then, he would have been proud. These were the kinds of things the two of them often discussed. His father was certainly not militant, but he surely was no fool. Jack Jr. always told his freinds proudly, "My father is not an educated man, but he's got plenty of common sense. Fact is he always says that if sense were so common, everybody would have it."

Jack Jr. was the family's intellectual. He studied the Negro condition in America with a passion, and when he was not at school or at home with his family, he could always be found in one meeting hall or another with other men like himself who were interested in discoursing and debating the condition of their people and what had to be done to change it. Bettering the lot of his people was his passion and his life.

Chapter 54

It was the first week in August of 1900. It was hot, sticky, muggy, so hot it took the life right out of you. It had been the same way throughout most of July, and now it was beginning to look like more of the same. At their ages, Jack and Julie Lee were really suffering. She kept wiping Jack down with cool water. His heart wasn't so strong, and she knew that this kind of weather was especially hard on him. After all those years, she was still taking care of him. That's what he kept saying.

The weather notwithstanding, Lytell thought it a perfect time to host a good, old-fashioned family reunion. They would have it that very Sunday.

Lytell wanted the reunion very badly, not just because he knew they had so much to be thankful for, but because he also knew that Julie Lee and Jack were getting on in years and that there might not be too many more times when they would be well enough to enjoy it.

Ten years had passed and there had only been one death in the family. That in itself was cause for celebration as far as Lytell was concerned, even though the death was a major one. It was Hannibal.

He'd fallen ill only about two weeks before he died. Thank God Julie Lee had been able to get home in time to see him before he passed on. If she hadn't, she didn't think she would have been able to live with herself.

She and Dexter returned to Virginia by themselves, for Jack had been too sick to go. After Hannibal died, however, a New York delegation from the family went down. It consisted of Jack Jr., Roxie Kate and George. Julie Lee felt better once her children had come to her side.

It was so sad, not just the funeral but the whole week leading up to it. Hannibal's wife Cleo looked dazed most of the time. Nearly all her life, Hannibal had taken care of everything. She just couldn't imagine him not being there. She told Julie Lee as much during those evenings when the two sat up and talked about the old days, the way things used to be, when they were young and only seemed to be inching their way toward womanhood.

Talking about those old times brought back a lot of memories for Julie Lee. Of course, Cleo remembered Dancer and little John, but for Julie Lee they were not merely faded memories, and she wondered every once in a while how it might have been if Dancer had lived and they had been married and had more children.

She and Cleo were up talking the night before Hannibal died. They knew his time was near, and already Cleo had begun talking about him as if he were already gone.

"Julie Lee. You know I loved your brother near 'bout my whole life. I never disrespected his home, and I gave him plenty of babies to carry on his name."

Cleo was crying now. Her head had dropped down to her chest and she was staring at her fingers, which were busily wrinkling her skirt. "What I'm gonna do without my Hannibal? What I'm gonna do?"

Cleo's talking made Julie Lee think of Jack. She'd always wished she would go first. She wasn't unlike Cleo in that respect. Although she was a strong woman and had many independent ways, she couldn't imagine what she would do without Jack either.

What could she do except try to be philosophical about it? "Cleo," she said, "me and you and Hannibal and Jack, we done seen a lot in our times, and Lord knows we done come this far by faith."

She got up now and went over to Cleo. "Be thankful. Be thankful for everything that we done had. We done better than many people, and we got lots to be thankful for."

Hannibal was buried in the new colored cemetery that a group of Negro churchmen had bought in Richmond proper. As Julie Lee watched Hannibal's coffin being lowered into the ground, she felt certain that even at that moment he was sitting up there in heaven right next to their mother, waiting for the day when all the family would be together again. She looked up at the sky. It was so pretty and blue.

By three o'clock that Sunday afternoon, the yard of Henrietta and Lytell's brand-new Harlem townhouse was filled with people—babies, teenagers and adults of all shapes, sizes and colors. Some were white looking like Julie Lee and others were as black as Jack.

Lytell had set up a special place in the yard for Jack and Julie Lee—the guests of honor. There were two big, comfortable chairs under a nice shade tree from where they could see all the goings on. And they loved all they saw.

They enjoyed catching up on what everybody was doing and how they were making out in school or with their boyfriends or girlfriends. Julie Lee even made a game of counting their grands and trying to keep track of what children belonged to whom.

It was still hot when the sky got dark, although it was a lot cooler than it had been earlier. The party continued. Henrietta had about two dozen candles just for that reason. She placed them on tables all over the yard. By then, most of the younger children had fallen asleep.

Some of the older folk were tired too. Jack had dozed off in his chair and was now snoring peacefully. Lytell noticed when George slipped out right after it got dark. He'd whispered something hurriedly to his wife, Deborah, and from the look on her face, Lytell knew that he'd probably told her he would be back in a little while. He wouldn't, and he whispered to Henrietta that she ought to fix up some place in the house for Deborah and the children to sleep. If George came back at all it wouldn't be until very late, and if he did come back, Lytell would not let him drag the children out in the middle of the night. No, he told Henrietta, they would just stay until morning.

Since her Aunty Lyn had died, Henrietta had taken Julie Lee almost as her mother, and she had been happy when Lytell decided to ask his parents to move in with them in their big new house in Harlem. Concerned that it might be getting a little too cool for Julie Lee now, Henrietta asked her mother-in-law if she wanted something to throw over her shoulders. Although she hated to see Henrietta working so hard at her own party, Julie Lee couldn't help but admit that she could use a little blanket or something over her arms.

It was nearly eleven o'clock before the party actually

started to break up. The adults had to go to work in the morning and the children had to go to school. George still hadn't come back, and Henrietta was worried because she knew his children would have to miss their classes the next day. There was no way they could go home that late and still get ready for the next day and hold their little eyes open while somebody stood in front of them trying to impart information.

Before everyone had left, Dexter had taken Jack up and put him to bed. Julie Lee was proud of herself. She had strained and struggled but she had kept her tired, old eyes wide open. In fact, she had kissed each and every one of her family before they filed out.

When the house was finally quiet—about an hour later—George still hadn't come back to pick up his family. Lytell led his mother to her bedroom as if she were a child.

Before going in Julie Lee touched Lytell's face gently. Looking at him she was reminded that she wasn't that much older than he. She just felt much older. Even those few years had made such a vast difference in how they had been affected by slavery. He was but a child then, but she could remember it quite well.

"Thank you, son, for giving me and your father this day, and even though Jack went to sleep early, I know he had a good time," she said. "I swear if my good Lord calls on me before morning, I won't be sad because of what happened here today and this night."

She touched his face again, as a blind person would. She felt the lines and the crevices. "If daylight don't hit this old face again, remember boy, I'll see you in Mount Zion."

He kissed her on her cheek. "Mama, don't get dra-

413

matic," he said teasingly, "you ain't hardly ready to die. I'm not going to let you go and Mount Zion will have to wait a little while."

He helped her inside her room, and once she was settled down, closed the door gently behind him. When he backed out into the hallway, Henrietta was standing right behind him. He hadn't even heard her tiptoe up the stairs. He kissed her forehead. He still thought she was the most beautiful woman he had ever seen. "Let's go to bed, baby," she said sweetly. He wrapped his arm around her waist and they walked slowly toward their bedroom.

Chapter 55

Lytell had already left for work, taking Lytell Jr. and Darnell with him.

Both boys had expressed interest in their father's business, and Lytell had promised to let them work with him all summer. It was agreed that they would be paid.

Lytell Jr. was in his second year at Howard University in Washington D.C. and had earned a reputation as one of the best-dressed boys on campus. He wanted to keep it that way when school opened in the fall.

Darnell, who was just turning seventeen, was leaning heavily toward going to Morehouse College in Atlanta, since that was where his best friend had said he intended to go after graduation.

Rhetta and Jeddah had left even before their father and brothers. They were going to Connecticut to spend the weekend with a girlfriend they had met while students at a small, two-year training academy for young Negro women in Bridgeport.

The twins were like peas in a pod. They did most things together, except when it came to dressing. They had had enough of that when they were children and their mother insisted on buying two of everything. Henrietta was delighted that they had made some friends at school since they didn't have many outside girlfriends, preferring each other's company instead.

Roman, the baby boy, had left with his sisters. They promised to drop him off at the church's summer day school on their way to the train station.

So Henrietta and Julie Lee were left sitting at the kitchen table drinking coffee and talking. Mostly, they talked about family, though sometimes the conversation veered off into politics. Julie Lee had not tired of the subject at all, and she kept herself informed, even more than Henrietta did, by reading the daily newspapers and the Negro publications that featured articles by young, articulate black writers and scholars. She was terribly impressed in particular by one W.E.B. Du Bois. She'd read his work on the suppression of the African slave trade, and it had aroused her curiosity and interest in the African part of her history. She clipped and saved so many old newspapers and other pamphlets that Lytell often teased her, saying if the house was ever set afire, her room would be the first to go.

But those clippings, some of which she'd been saving since the Civil War, were her treasure. They were part of the legacy she wanted to be sure to leave for her grandchildren and great-grandchildren. She wanted them to be aware of their history so that they might avoid some of the mistakes of the past. She even dreamed that one day one of her grands might seek some high political office.

Jack Jr. was so proud of his mother, that he held her arm as if she were his girlfriend when the two went down to the YMCA on West Fifty-third Street one night to hear a lecture. In his mind, his mother was a very modern woman.

As she and Henrietta sat talking, they believed Jack was still sleeping upstairs. They never paid too much attention to his sleeping late, as he'd been doing that a lot since his heart condition had worsened. He seemed so lonely and sad after the doctor told him he couldn't work anymore. Jack had worked all his life, and it just didn't sit right with him to be told he had to sit still.

But this morning to their surprise, Jack appeared in the kitchen doorway, fully dressed.

"Well, how you doing this morning, Papa?" Henrietta asked pleasantly.

"You want some breakfast?" Julie Lee asked him.

He came into the room, kissed her on her forehead and patted Henrietta on the shoulder. "No, don't want no breakfast this morning, but I'll have a cup of that coffee."

Julie Lee started to get up, but Henrietta made her sit down. "I'll get it, Mama. You just relax."

He pulled his chair closer to the table. "I'm going downtown today," he announced. "Going to see some of my old buddies. Ain't seen some of them in months."

A worried looked crossed Henrietta's face. "Papa, you aren't going down to the Tenderloin, are you?"

"That's just where I'm going," he said, watching the steam from the coffee form curlicues in the air.

"But Papa, haven't you been reading the papers about all the terrible things happening down there between white folks and Negroes? They say some of those crazy immigrants is snatching colored folk right off the streets and beating them half to death. Say the police aren't even doing anything to stop them."

Jack didn't seem disturbed by his daughter-in-law's

concerns. "Aw, Henrietta, you know how the papers is, always making things seem worse than they are. I know a lot of white folks down in the Tenderloin, and I ain't scared of them. Ain't never been scared of no white man."

"But Papa," she insisted again, her voice rising in frustration. "I'm not talking about the kind of white folk you know. I'm talking about the mobs, the gangs the papers say are roaming the streets since that white cop went and got himself killed by a Negro. Why don't you just wait until Lytell comes home. Then he can go down there with you. I just don't think you should go alone."

Julie Lee had been silent during the exchange. She knew that Jack was as stubborn as a mule. The more somebody told him to stay, the more he was determined to go.

"Henrietta," Jack said, "I been around a long time, and if I was scared of every little thing white folks did, I wouldn't still be around. 'Sides, I'm tired of just sitting here listening to you and Julie Lee talking from morning till night. Lytell, he's always at work. Sometimes a man gets lonely. Needs to talk to other men. I guess you can't understand that because—"

Henrietta cut him off. "Papa, all I'm trying to say is that you should wait until Lytell comes. I'm not saying that you shouldn't visit with your friends. I'm just saying that this is not a good time for any Negro to be wandering around the Tenderloin."

He sat with them for another half-hour before leaving, and he promised that he would be back in time for dinner. Julie Lee asked him several times exactly who he was going to see, but all he gave her was the vague response that she wouldn't know them anyway and that he was going to be moving around. He hated it when Julie Lee and Henrietta ganged up on him and treated him as if he were a child.

Julie Lee didn't begin to get concerned about her husband until four o'clock rolled around and he still hadn't returned.

"Didn't Papa say he'd be home around this time?" Henrietta asked as she cut up vegetables for dinner.

Not wanting to upset Henrietta any more than she apparently was, Julie Lee said calmly, "He be home soon. I know it."

Julie Lee sat reading the newspaper and occasionally glancing out the big window that fronted onto the street. She was looking at the paper, but not really comprehending the words since her mind was on Jack. She kept thinking, Where is that man?

Lytell came in from work. He kissed everybody and as he usually did, he went into the kitchen to see what Henrietta was cooking for dinner. "Where's Daddy?" he asked, suddenly noticing his absence.

After they told him, Lytell said, "He knows he should be home by now—upsetting everybody and everything."

Since Lytell had always insisted, whenever possible, that everyone eat together, he told Henrietta to hold dinner until Jack returned.

After darkness fell Lytell started pacing. "Maybe I'll just put my clothes back on and go out and find him."

"But where you going to look, Lytell?" Henrietta asked sympathetically. "He didn't even tell us who he was going to see."

Julie Lee interrupted. "Now, Lytell, there isn't any need for you to go out there looking for your daddy. If you go, me and Henrietta will have to sit up here and worry about the two of you. He'll be along soon. I know he's hungry by now.''

They were still sitting tensely when Roman burst into the room. ''Where's Papa? I'm hungry. I know everybody else is hungry, so why do we have to wait?''

Before he realized what he was doing, Lytell had leapt up out of his chair and had taken his son by the collar. ''We waiting 'cause I said so. You're getting a little beside yourself, young man.''

Roman was hurt and bewildered. His father was so angry. All he'd done was to say what he knew everybody else was thinking. He looked at his father with a pathetic expression and Lytell came to himself, suddenly realizing that he had perhaps overreacted. He tried to apologize.

''I'm sorry, baby. We're going to eat soon. Just go on upstairs for right now, okay?''

Roman turned to leave the room, and even though his back was to her, Henrietta knew he was crying. Roman was very sensitive, and because he adored his father, he could not stand to be chastised by him.

By the time they sat down to eat it was going on nine o'clock. They'd sat through dinner without talking. The empty chair where Jack usually sat was too much for them all. The tension was palpable.

Lytell put down his fork and announced, ''I'm going out to find Daddy. Don't know where I'm going, but I'm going to find him, and when I do, I'm going to tell him a thing or two.''

He turned his attention to Julie Lee. ''Mama, I know Daddy didn't say exactly where he was going in the Tenderloin, but do you have any ideas?''

She searched her memory. ''Lord, Lytell, I haven't

been down that way in so long visiting people that I don't
even know who lives there anymore. Anyhow, most of
your daddy's friends are people he met at work, so I
wouldn't know them.''

She wanted to hear Jack coming through the door, but
she didn't want Lytell to go out there trying to find him.
She was about to tell him that when a loud knock came at
the door. At first no one moved, but after a few seconds,
Lytell opened it. There were two white policemen standing
there. Henrietta knew one of them. He was a good friend
of Lytell's and often talked to her when she went to the
market.

Julie Lee tried to swallow the bitter taste that was
beginning to form at the back of her throat.

Lytell did not immediately come back from the vestibule, but remained there talking to the men for a few
minutes in hurried whispers. All eyes were plastered to the
spot where Lytell was standing. Each minute's passing
caused the tension to rise.

Julie Lee could hold back no longer. ''What happened? What happened to your daddy?'' she said, advancing
toward Lytell. He took her by both arms and propelled her
toward a chair. ''Sit down, Mama. Sit down.'' She wouldn't
sit, but he collapsed into a chair.

''Mama,'' he said, but actually addressing himself to
them all, ''it's not Daddy.''

Henrietta's mind was racing. ''What do you mean,
it's not Daddy? Who is it and what's the matter?''

Lytell buried his face in his hands and began sobbing.
His voice was very, very low. ''It's George, Mama. It's
George. Somebody done killed George.''

When Jack pushed the door open, he bumped right
into one of the policemen who was still standing there.

What was wrong? When he got into the front room everybody was crying. He was still wondering what had happened when Julie Lee rushed over and threw her arms around his neck.

The family took up nearly half the small church where the funeral was held. Deborah had insisted on having her husband's service in her church, which was just a small storefront.

Julie Lee pressed herself into Jack's arms. She hadn't stopped crying for three days. Her eyes were red, and she looked as if an extra ten years had been added to her age during those seventy-two hours. For a while, she couldn't even believe that it was all real as the people came in and out offering their condolences. Sitting there in that church, she could not fight back her own cries of mourning. Jack tried to control his emotions, but everytime his wife sobbed aloud, more tears streamed from his eyes, which he patted frequently with a large handkerchief.

The minister, Reverend Arthur T. Barrow, Jr., was not a man to lie. He knew George, but only slightly. He knew George's reputation as a womanizer much better. He stood high over the coffin, which was sitting in the middle of the aisle, almost touching Deborah on the front pew. The coffin was draped with a purple shroud and on top of it was a huge floral spray from Deborah and the children.

Reverend Barrow's voice rolled across the church like thunder. He was there to give a message, not to the dead, but to the living. "We come here today to say good-bye to a man. A husband, a father, and a son," he added glancing toward Jack and Julie Lee. "We come here today to say good-bye to a man whose voice we won't hear no more on this side of the River Jordan. We come here today to say that this is God's will, and that where this man, who lies here so still, has gone, we will all be going someday.''

A loud "Amen" came from the back of the church.

The minister continued. "It's never easy when somebody we love dies, but death is part of life. When God moves His mighty hand, we of the flesh cannot escape. We can't run. We can't hide. Now is George's time, but tomorrow it might be our own. That's why we say in the church, you got to live right with God, because you don't know when the sands in the hourglass will run out for you."

Reverend Barrow's voice droned on. Julie Lee could hardly stand it. After another twenty minutes, it was over. The funeral directors opened the top of the coffin again as the choir hummed "Rock of Ages" in the background. One by one the people filed by the open casket and Julie Lee could feel them patting her as they passed the family.

Before she realized it, it was her turn to view the body for the last time. Her knees gave way, and Jack and Lytell helped her up. The tears fell, and then she frightened the whole church when she wailed, "Lord, Lord, why you take my baby? Why you take my child? Lord, you mean I can't see my son no more? Can't see him smile no more? Oh, Lord. Oh, Lord."

She threw herself onto the coffin, and it took everything Jack and Lytell had to keep her from turning it over. Back in her seat, she threw her head back and felt some of the church sisters, all dressed in white, fanning her.

Julie Lee's outburst had caused a ripple, and soon there was shouting and screaming throughout the building. The situation seemed to be getting out of control, and to stop it Reverend Barrow ordered the choir to sing an upbeat song. It was a rousing gospel number, and as the minister knew it would, it restored order.

Lytell and Jack Jr. made a pact with the rest of the family to spare their mother all the details of how George had died. They told her that George had been killed in the street, but actually he had bled to death in a woman's apartment.

After conducting their own investigation, Jack Jr. and Lytell had found out that George had met the woman in a bar, and after a few hours of talking and drinking had taken her home. Some of George's friends who were with him last said that before he left them he winked and promised he would be right back. They just assumed that he was going to "knock off a little piece" and then come back and finish drinking.

He had been gone hardly an hour, one man said, before the police were swarming all over the neighborhood. None of George's friends seemed to know the woman well, since she hadn't been coming long to that bar, but they remembered she had a deep accent, so they figured she wasn't long up South. Her name was Patti. That's really all they knew. After George was killed the woman disappeared, and everyone suspected that she had gone back home.

The police version of what had happened in the apartment was that George and the woman were in bed together when another man came unexpectedly into the apartment and apparently confronted them. The man had a reputation in the streets as a "bad nigga" who carried a big, long knife, which he didn't hesitate to use. Word was that he had slashed a couple of other people, but had never been arrested since his victims had been just too frightened to turn him in.

From that description, Jack Jr. and Lytell could figure out what had happened next. George was no coward, so they knew that when the man went for his knife George had tried to fight him. George carried a knife too, but with his knife being in the other room inside his pants pocket, he was nearly defenseless.

When Jack Jr. and Lytell went to the morgue to identify the body, the attendant said dryly, "Sure did cut that boy up good."

According to the undertaker, George must have been stabbed twenty-five to thirty times. The undertaker said he had quite a time trying to fix George up so he wouldn't look so bad for the viewing.

The police caught George's killer the night after the incident. They found him sitting up in a bar and when they came to take him out, the people in the street said, the man growled, "The nigga deserved to die, messing with my woman. Yeah, I killed the nigga."

Deborah had held up fairly well throughout it all. It had not even occurred to her how she would make it financially now that George was dead.

"That poor woman," everybody muttered under his breath, knowing what kind of man George had been and what kind of suffering he had put his poor wife through.

As bad as Deborah felt, in some ways, George's death brought her some relief. At least now, she wouldn't have to spend nights sitting up worrying about him anymore. The worst had happened. She'd gotten the news she'd been expecting for some time.

Roxie Kate had deliberately separated herself from the main arena of action. Secretly she wished she didn't even have to be there. She was sad that her brother was dead, but she was terribly embarrassed at how he had died. If that wasn't bad enough, they had to go and put it in the newspapers. She told Charlie when they got the news that that was just what white folks liked. The way George died was, in their opinion, how the rowdy Negroes always settled their disputes, not through negotiation or discussion, but with violence. She told Charlie that she didn't even know how she was going to hold her head up.

Julie Lee and Jack really didn't care what anyone thought. George was their son. They had not approved of how he'd conducted his life, and certainly hadn't reared him to be the way he was, but in their hearts they knew that George had been a good man.

Chapter 56

Jack had gotten through the funeral fairly well and he'd provided most of the strength upon which Julie Lee relied during the days immediately following.

But in the ensuing months, he crawled into his shell, a world of silence, a world from which he shut out everyone. His condition had become so pronounced that the doctor was quite concerned. He wasn't eating much and was talking even less. The doctor said it was a delayed reaction to George's murder, which had sent him into shock. He warned them that it was a dangerous condition for a man with Jack's history of heart trouble.

Julie Lee's heart ached for her husband. They had always talked things out, but now there was nothing. She tried to coax something out of him, but only once did he respond. He kept repeating over and over again, "Why he have to kill my boy? Why my boy had to die like that?" He cried like a baby and slumped into her arms.

George's murder seemed to accelerate his father's aging. His hair grew whiter, daily it seemed. His health was deteriorating and sometimes he seemed too weak even to get out of bed. Everyone knew what was happening, but Julie Lee most of all.

Lytell and Jack Jr. found it difficult to cope with their father's condition. He'd always been so strong, so abiding. But since George's death their roles had been reversed—he was the child and they were the men. Roxie Kate stopped by the house almost every night after work to check on her father's condition. She told her mother about some kind of "shock therapy," which might help. But when Julie Lee and Henrietta discussed it with Lytell and Jack Jr., they both agreed that they didn't want anyone experimenting on their father. Dexter felt the same way. So they left things as they were, hoping that Jack would come out of it naturally.

Shimmy and Lena stopped by to visit several times, but after spending an hour or so with Jack not talking back, they always came downstairs dejected. All Shimmy's joking and clowning couldn't break through the invisible barrier that separated the man from them all.

Everyone agreed not to tell Jack when Deborah announced her plans to remarry. George had been dead six months. She explained to Julie Lee, Henrietta and Roxie Kate one afternoon that she just couldn't make it alone. She appreciated all the things Lytell had done for her and her family, but she just couldn't keep on expecting him to raise her family and his own as well.

Calvin Walker was a member of her church—in fact he was the assistant pastor. He and Deborah had gone out to dinner a few times, and one night when they were talking, she broke down and asked Calvin why they shouldn't get married. After all, Deborah said, she was still a young woman who had a lot of life left in her.

"I haven't even told the children yet," she went on.

428

"I didn't want to mention it to them until I talked with all of you." A wrinkle creased her brow. "Fact is, I'm kind of scared to tell them. You know how they felt about their daddy. No matter what he did, they loved their father."

"That's the truth," Henrietta interjected sympathetically.

"I don't want them to think that I'm trying to get Calvin to replace George. I'm not. But I've been so lonely. You know, even when George was alive, he was gone so much of the time. Anyhow, how many men you know are asking women with seven children to marry them? Most of the men are willing to shack up, but they don't want no part of a wife."

Julie Lee asked what she believed was the most important point. "Deborah, do you love this man? Do you think he'll make you happy?"

She was thoughtful before answering, and tried to be as truthful as she could. "I don't know if I love him or not. But, he's very nice, and thoughtful, and of course he's a decent man. He hasn't even tried to kiss me, and he always drops me off at my door. He says he doesn't think it would be right for him to come into the house, at least not right away."

Henrietta and Roxie Kate seemed to be all for it, but Julie Lee was more reserved. Still she wouldn't tell Deborah that. It wouldn't have been fair, she thought, to deny what would make the girl happy. Of course, she was concerned about this man because whether he wanted to be or not, he would act as father to her grandchildren.

When Henrietta told Lytell of the conversation they'd had with Deborah, he hit the ceiling. The veins in his neck throbbed.

"Well, why can't she wait a little longer? Hell, she's

not over there starving or nothing. Ain't we been helping her ever since George died? My brother ain't even cold in the ground yet, and she's already out catting for another man.''

She grabbed his arm. "Lytell, you stop that. You know Deborah is not that kind of woman. You know how George treated her all those years. You used to complain about it yourself—how it was so terrible and all. George is your brother, and I'm probably speaking out of turn, but George wasn't no saint. Look at how he died. That poor woman has had to live with that. Look at how she always held her head up and went on about her business when everybody was talking about her, calling her a fool and looking at her like she was the most pitiful woman in the world. Isn't she entitled to some happiness?'' She knew she had him now. "Isn't she?''

Lytell relented, but he refused to attend the small wedding and reception Deborah and Calvin had at the church. Her children were in attendance, and so were Julie Lee, Roxie Kate, Henrietta, Jack Jr.'s wife, Betty Jane, and Dexter's wife, Laurieanne.

But the men refused to go. They were not yet ready to accept what they viewed as another man trying to take their brother's place.

In time, however, Calvin won everyone over. He was not only good to Deborah, but he was good to George's children as well. He hadn't insisted that any of them call him Daddy, and he respected George's memory. In the years that would follow, Calvin would become an important part of the family, and Julie Lee would come to love him just like one of her own children.

*   *   *

Jack lingered through most of 1901. His health was failing terribly and the doctor made the mistake of suggesting one day that Lytell consider placing him in a nursing home where he could get round-the-clock attention. But Julie Lee and Lytell would have none of that kind of talk.

"No sir, we aren't putting him anywhere," Lytell told the doctor, who, judging by Lytell's reaction, was sorry he'd even mentioned it. "Daddy's gonna stay right here with us until the day he dies. Whatever he needs, we'll get it. In this family, we always take care of our own."

And that's what happened. Jack stayed right in that house until the day he died. On the morning of December 15, 1901, Jack Bratcher, Sr., ex-slave and Civil War veteran, died in his sleep.

Chapter 57

By 1905, the controversy surrounding one of the most powerful Negroes in America, Booker T. Washington, an ex-
Virginia slave, had split the Bratcher family politically.
There were passionate defenders and critics of Washington
among the various branches of the family, although most
of the younger ones leaned toward the more militant position espoused by their Uncle Jack and his intellectual
friends.

The Bratchers were like most literate Negroes of the
time. They were caught up in the war of words that
volleyed between the forces of Washington's machine,
which emanated out of Tuskegee Institute in Alabama, and
the northern intellectuals led by the likes of W.E.B. Du
Bois and Monroe Trotter of Boston, both Harvard men.

Jack agreed with Du Bois and Trotter that Washington was little more than a traitor to the Negro race. Washington advocated a slow, gradual progress for the Negro
and did not think it important to become politically powerful. Phenomena such as the strict segregationist policies of
Jim Crow he deemed irrelevant. To Washington the most
important thing for the masses of Negroes was education,

not merely idle education, but practical education to prepare them for skilled jobs.

It had gotten so that it was nearly impossible for the whole family to get together without a bitter argument breaking out between the rival camps.

"That man. That damned Booker T. Washington. He's a traitor!" Jack bellowed one evening. He was shouting so loud that everyone was sure he could be heard for blocks. "He's sitting up there around rich white folks, riding in fancy train cars, and he dares to tell other Negroes to be still, to wait for the white man to pat them on the head and declare them free. Hell. With that kind of philosophy we all might as well just crawl back up on the damned plantation."

Roxie Kate took the other side, a position she had embraced most of her literate life. "Jack Jr., you're a fool if you think that the Negro is going to overcome all the obstacles against us overnight. We have got to go slow just like Booker T. says. We've got to win the respect of the white man by being able to compete. Then and only then will we really be free."

Her own voice had gotten pretty loud, and she ignored her husband's pulling at her to sit back down.

"Leave me alone, Charlie. Let me speak. Jack Jr. thinks that just because he can scream and yell that he can bully everybody over to his side. Well, he can't bully me.

"Look at our people, Jack. Look at them. They're mostly uneducated, unskilled and unprepared. Every day you open up the newspaper and there's some other story about how a bunch of ignorant Negroes, mostly unemployed, got into a stupid argument and settled their differences with a knife or a gun. Just look around, Jack. The masses of our people aren't ready for what you and your friends want. Not yet. Maybe in time we'll be ready, but we need to learn how to use our heads and our hands. Fact is, I don't even blame some white folks for being scared of the Negro. I'm half scared of them myself, and I'm one of them.''

Jack laughed sarcastically. ''You wouldn't know you were a Negro by listening to you talking. You articulate the white man's arguments better than he does. Why don't you go on down to Tuskegee with your hero and then both of you can be plantation niggas.''

She thundered back. ''Jack, that stuff you and your friends are talking is worthless to the masses. You and your militant friends are good for nothing but talk, talk, talk.''

Now Jack jumped up from his seat, went around the table and confronted his sister face to face. ''Roxie Kate, you're nothing but an accommodationist. Always were and always will be. You been simpering around white folks all your life. You're an educated, well-spoken, docile nigga. Just the kind white folks like. No, they aren't scared of you because there's nothing to be afraid of.''

Jack made a bowing and scraping gesture then and started scratching his head. ''Yeeesssss suh, Mr. and Mrs. White America. I'se just an old-time nigga just awaitin' for you to make me free. Yessss, suh, massa sir, I'll be free whenever you say so.''

Roxie Kate was furious. ''You can put on a performance if you want to, Jack Jr., but you're still not going to win this argument. I know I'm right and I don't care what you say.''

Before he stormed out of the house, Jack turned to his mother and said, ''Mama, did you raise this ignorant Negro over here?''

434

It usually happened that way—Jack would leave the house to keep himself away from Roxie Kate. When she talked the way she had been talking, he had to do everything he could to keep from grabbing her around her neck, choking her and making her children orphans and Charlie a widower.

Lytell and Henrietta were both on the fence, and since the congregating was usually at their house, they decided it best not to take a position.

Whenever they tried to draw her into those stormy debates, Julie Lee backed off. She had definite opinions, but she preferred to express them during calmer moments.

In her heart, Julie Lee was still a militant, but she nonetheless appreciated the way her children and grands debated the issue. She admired their convictions and the ardor with which they defended them, whatever position they took.

That July she wished Jack Jr. well as he set off for Niagara Falls. There he would be participating in a secret meeting that had been called by forces opposed to Washington's philosophy. When Jack came home a few days later, he was even worse than before. Spending night and day with so many other respected intellectuals and scholars had only convinced him even more deeply that his side was the right side.

Chapter 58

It was an April Sunday in 1916 at eleven o'clock. Julie
Lee arrived at the church just in time for the start of the
morning worship services, and as she did every Sunday,
she took her place on the front pew, right up close to
Reverend Satterfield. That pew was reserved for the mothers and fathers of the church, and no one under sixty-five
dared come near it. The choir was beginning to rock the
house in preparation for Reverend Satterfield's entrance by
singing a rousing version of "In My Father's House." She
sang along with them in her voice, which had grown frail
with age. "In my Father's house, there is joy, joy, joy."
She liked that song, but her favorite had always been and
probably always would be "Precious Lord."

Reverend Satterfield preached for about forty-five minutes. Throughout the service small, hand-held fans, in-
scribed with the name of a Negro funeral parlor, sprouted
up in the congregation like spring flowers. Some of the
women, particularly those of large frame, fanned spectacu-
larly, and it seemed as if the more they fanned, the more
sweat poured down their foreheads and from under their
beefy arms.

Julie Lee waited in her seat until most of the crowd had adjourned downstairs for the noon meal. She sat there until one of her great-grands came to escort her down to the basement.

"Grandma ain't able to move as fast as she used to," Julie Lee explained to the boy as he held her hand tight while she negotiated the steep stairway.

This particular Sunday the escort was Rhetta's son, Rupbert Jr. One grand or great-grand was assigned every Sunday to accompany Grandma to church if none of the adults planned on being in attendance.

Rupbert Jr. was the spitting image of his daddy. Everybody said so. And he was a delight to Julie Lee. The child was mannerly and he was patient with her and all her frailties. He never seemed to resent having to give up half his Sunday in church with Grandma. Admittedly, some of the other escorts shared no such delight, and in one way or another, before their sentence was over, they would let Grandma know that they had much more important things to do.

Rhetta had two children, Rupbert Jr. and a pretty girl named Blossom. Her husband was quite a smart man. He'd come to the United States from Barbados to make his fame and fortune.

Rupbert Sr. studied feet. His brother said that from childhood Rupbert had had a peculiar interest in feet, particularly black feet. He often said that colored feet had walked many a long and dusty road and often times without shoes, or with shoes that were ill-fitting. In any case, he treated all kinds of foot problems; pigeon-toes, hammertoes, enlarged heels, fallen arches and the regular, age-old assortment of bunions, calluses and plain old corns.

To his patients Rupbert Sr. was called Rupbert the Foot Doctor. His patients said he could make them feel like they were walking on air.

Some of Rupbert's female patients talked in sexual terms when they tried to described what he did for their feet.

"It's his hands. I swear to God that man's hands on your feet make you feel so good sometimes that you just want to holler. Make you think you died and went to heaven."

Originally he had wanted to be a "real" doctor, as he called it, but had given up on the idea when he realized that he just couldn't stand the sight of so much blood.

Julie Lee had a touch of arthritis that had slowed her down a bit, particularly on days when the weather was bad, but on balance, the doctor said she was in pretty good health for a woman her age.

"I can't say that I'd recommend that you dance the night away, but you're well enough to do nearly everything else you want to do," he would tell her.

Julie Lee was always amazed by the large number of Negroes who had made their homes up in Harlem. True, many were poor and struggling and barely surviving in hovellike apartments vacated by the white immigrants who'd come before them, but the neighborhood was still vibrant and alive, and many of the Negroes were indeed prosperous.

When she and the boy arrived back at the house, about three o'clock that afternoon, Julie Lee was practically knocked off her feet when Rupbert pushed open the door and a loud chorus of voices rang out, "Happy birthday, Mama! Happy birthday."

Henrietta helped her to a comfortable chair. In between tears, Julie Lee kept asking, "Why y'all doing this to an old woman like me? You know at my age I could have a stroke with all this excitement."

Lytell said, "Well, Mama, I think you better get yourself ready for one more surprise. Just wait and see."

At that moment, a man pushed his way through the crowd that had collected in front of her. He stood directly in front of her now, apparently waiting for her to recognize him. Her mind raced, but she couldn't place his face.

"Now why would you be pretending you don't recognize me, Julie Lee?"

"I guess it's because I can't," she answered candidly, which drew a laugh from all the others.

"I'd recognize you anywhere, even after all these years. You are every bit as lovely as I remember you."

He bent down closer to her, allowing her to examine his face. "Look at me, Julie Lee. Don't you know who I am?"

She stared at him for several minutes and then a flicker of recognition crept into her head. "Oh, my God," was all she could say at first.

He must have been in his eighties then. After all, she estimated her own age as the midseventies.

The years had apparently not been quite as kind to Antonio as they had been to her. Of course, he was older than she, but he looked rather frail, she thought. She touched his hand and gently rubbed his face.

"My Lord, Antonio. How many years has it been?"

"Too many," he said, beginning to cry. Tears collected in the deep wrinkles of his face.

Her mind went back to those years when they both had been so young and daring enough to chance death at the end of the hangman's noose rather than be slaves anymore. The corners of her mouth crinkled and she smiled, thinking about Antonio's attempt way back then to make theirs more than merely a friendship.

"All these many years, and you're still pretty as a picture," she heard him say, interrupting her thoughts.

He took both her hands and squeezed them. "My goodness, Julie Lee. I can hardly believe that I'm standing before you. I convinced myself years ago that I'd never see you again. For the longest time I thought that either you were dead or that you had been dragged back to the plantation."

Looking at him now, she realized that it had been many years since she'd really thought about him. For the first few years after they'd been separated in the Baltimore train station, she wondered what had happened to him. Once she'd even tried to track him down through the governmental and church agencies set up after the war to help Negroes find lost relatives and friends.

She probably would have kept up the search had it not been for Jack's lifelong jealousy over any man from her past.

After a while Antonio had become a dim memory that she called upon every once in a while as she lay beside Jack listening to the steady sounds of his breathing.

Now she watched Antonio's eyes moving over the room. He was looking hard at the furniture, the decorations, her family. When he realized that she was watching him, he said quickly, "You've done well, Julie Lee, and you have an attractive family. It is clear how much they love you."

His eyes saddened when he added, "Your son told me that your husband died some time ago."

440

Her voice lowered. "Yes, Jack died in 1901. We'd been married for nearly forty years." And though he did not ask, she added quickly, "We had a good marriage, too. Yes, we did."

But it made her sad to think about Jack and she changed the subject abruptly. "How did they ever find you, Antonio?"

He reached out and touched her arm. "It's a long story. In fact it was largely through coincidence."

He settled back into the chair and began to unfold his tale. "After I lost you in Baltimore, I decided to stay around for a while. At first I tried to find you, but as you already know I didn't have any luck. Well, my short time in Baltimore turned out to be more than fifteen years. I probably would have left sooner, but I met a most enchanting little girl and we ended up getting married."

His eyes misted and he pulled a handkerchief from his pocket to wipe away a tear. "Her name was Matilda. She was such a pretty little thing. Well, Matilda and I married and had three children, two boys and a girl.

"Matilda died twenty years ago. Our two youngest children had already died before their mother passed away. She never quite recovered from the children's deaths. They had some kind of blood disease, the doctors thought, but we never really knew for sure.

"After Matilda died my son, Antonio Jr., and I moved to Boston. Of course, by then nearly everyone I had known had either died or moved away. I had to do something, and I didn't have enough money to go back into business for myself, so I found a job working on the docks, repairing boats."

He turned his hands palms up and offered them for

Julie Lee's inspection. "That's how my hands got so rough."

His tale was interrupted by Henrietta who came over bearing two plates of food. Julie Lee declined. She wasn't hungry after having eaten at the church. He took a plate, however, and gingerly balanced it on his knee. Noticing his plight, Henrietta summoned one of the children to bring the old man a small table from the other side of the room.

Julie Lee was terribly interested in what he had to say, so much so that she'd become oblivious to all the talk and laughter around them.

"So then what happened, Antonio?"

"My son and I lived rather well in Boston. Antonio's a bright boy. I'm very proud of him. He's been to college and studied in Europe for a while."

He reached into his pocket and pulled out a battered leather folding wallet from which he took a small photograph and handed it to her.

"Oh, he is handsome," she said. The young man in the photograph was dressed fashionably and wore a neat part down the middle of his head.

She knew he was waiting for her to say more, so she remarked, "He reminds me a lot of you years ago."

He took the photograph back and looked at it lovingly. "I suppose he does resemble me somewhat but he really favors his mother. Look at that nose. I've never had a tiny nose like that one. Oh, when Matilda was alive, those two were thicker than thieves. I think they used to get together and plot against me. Matilda and I couldn't even pursue a good argument without him interrupting and taking his mother's side. He was a beautiful child, and now he's a beautiful man."

She still wanted to know how Antonio had found his way back into her life. With all they'd talked about, he still hadn't told her.

"Please, tell me, Antonio, how did they find you?"

"I'm getting to that," he said as he patted her hand. "You always were impatient. That's something that hasn't changed about you either. You're still pretty, and you're still impatient."

She laughed. He was right about the impatient part, but she wasn't sure she was so pretty anymore. How could she be? Just a wrinkled up old lady. Here she was, rushing a man who was trying to cover more than forty years of life in a few minutes.

"I'm sorry, Antonio, but I would like to know how you came to be sitting up here in my living room."

"Well," he said, "I found you through my son, Antonio. Or rather I found you through my son and one of your sons. You see Antonio is an activist. He belongs to just about every Negro organization you can name and he's even founded a couple himself. He travels all over the country for these groups. His wife is always complaining about him being away so much.

"As it turns out, some of Antonio's business brings him to New York and on one such trip he met a certain young man. The two struck up a conversation, and lo and behold, the man he met turned out to be your very own son, Jack."

"What!" she exclaimed. "That Jack. He never told me!"

"I know he didn't. They decided to keep it a secret until they could bring the two of us together. I haven't been away from Boston in quite a while, so Antonio decided to bring me down here to see you. It was part of the surprise.''

"But when did they meet?" she asked.

"I think it was about three weeks ago. Antonio came home terribly excited and told me all about it. He'd heard me mention you from time to time all his life and felt like he already knew you. Apparently your son had heard you mention me and how we escaped together enough to be able to put the two together.''

Julie Lee smiled. "Lord have mercy. Don't that beat all. All these years, and our children bring us together."

Her eyes traveled the room, searching for Jack Jr. When she found him, she beckoned him to come over.

"Boy, you are no good, you hear me? Here you been knowing where Antonio was for almost a month and you didn't tell me nothing. Suppose I would have died? Then I would have never known!"

He smiled sheepishly at his mother. "Mama, I knew you weren't going to die." He wrapped his arms around her shoulders and poked at her chin playfully. "Anyhow, how you gonna die and leave us all here? What in the world would we do without you?"

She returned her attention to Antonio. "Where's your son? I'd love to meet the boy."

"He'll be here later on. He's here in New York too. We took the train together. Your son met us at the station and brought me up here while Antonio went off to take care of some business."

A mischievous twinkle appeared in his eyes. "I really don't know what kind of business Antonio could have in New York on a Sunday. I hope it's not monkey business with some woman. If it is, I intend to tell his wife as soon as I get back home."

She hit him on the shoulder and laughed. "Antonio, you wouldn't do that. Would you?"

He never answered.

Antonio stayed with them for an entire week. Henrietta and Lytell were delighted. They hadn't seen Julie Lee laugh so much in years. Some nights Henrietta had to go downstairs to the living room and literally make the two of them go to bed like children. If she didn't, she knew that they would stay up all night gabbing.

The next Sunday, Antonio Jr. came to pick his father up. It was a tearful parting. Julie Lee hated to see him leave, and he really hated to go. They just had so much to talk about. So much to catch up on.

Antonio Jr. promised to bring his father back some time soon. She watched as the son helped the old man down the steps in front of the house, and she waved to them as they walked down the street. She wondered whether she would ever see him again.

She wouldn't. Antonio passed away two weeks after he returned to Boston.

That same year, Julie Lee bade farewell to two of her great-grandsons as they went off to fight in the Great War. It broke her heart to see the boys go. They had so much to live for and now they were going off to some other part of the world to fight in a war in someplace that they knew nothing about.

She suffered through the ensuing war years. When the boys finally came home, both of them safe and sound, she could hardly stop crying.

They had done well in the military, and as members of Harlem's Negro regiment, the 369th, the first

Allied troops to reach key battle sectors in France, her great-grandsons were part of the group of Negro soldiers to be awarded the French Croix de Guerre for their extraordinary valor in battle.

Chapter 59

Charlie eased his body down into the hot, soothing bath water, leaned his head back and cracked his knuckles loudly. It was a habit that Roxie Kate hated and whenever he did it, she told him so.

He could hear her through the door, moving around in the bedroom, dressing for work. Though he'd never watched her in the classroom, more than one of her students had told him that she was the best teacher he'd ever had. If only she were the best wife, he thought as he ran the soapy cloth over his chest.

He had put up with her for so many years, and now he was just plain tired. Tired of her insufferable snobbishness and her petty meanness, tired of her constant harping and nagging.

She'd become such an ungrateful wretch that he wondered what it was he had ever loved about her. The voice that once had sounded like a sweet melody now rang shrill and hollow to him. The body that once had beckoned him lovingly now left him completely cold. He'd stopped making love to her months ago, but she never said anything. She acted as if it really didn't make any difference. How strange she was, he thought. For all the talking she did, there were some things about which she remained oddly silent.

He took the washcloth and squeezed it, letting the water drip down onto his face. He wasn't really sure when the loving had stopped, when it was that he started hating the thought of having to go home. At least when they were younger, he could hide some of his feelings behind his love for the children. He could dote on them and play with them until it was time for them to go to bed. But now the children were grown and gone most of the time, so there were few distractions when the two of them were alone in the house.

He pushed his body down deeper into the tub, letting the water, which was growing tepid, cover his body up to his armpits.

He thought about the many affairs he'd had during their marriage. Mostly, they'd been brief relationships with some of the nurses or clerks at the hospital. Those women usually adored him. After all, he was a doctor, and to many of them, that gave him status. Funny, he thought now, how some people could be satisfied with so little while others demanded so much.

He'd always been able to cut the relationships off before they went too far, before they got more serious than he was interested in. He supposed that he was a coward of sorts. In his heart of hearts, he really didn't want to hurt anyone—not even Roxie Kate. He never wanted his children to hurt. They looked up to and adored him, despite their mother's constant reminders of his inadequacies.

He knew that now he'd come to the end of the road, though. Of course, he realized that Margie had something to do with it.

Margie. He closed his eyes and conjured up her image. He was able to do that. Margie. She was a tiny little thing. Her waist was so small that he could wrap one arm all the way around her body.

Margie worked at the library not far from the hospital. He met her there after going in to pick up a book that Jack suggested he read. When he stepped up to the counter to check the book out, she looked up and their eyes met for the first time, and his heart tripped. Her eyes were dark brown and her complexion was the same color. She must have felt something too because she looked away quickly. Too quickly, he thought.

A few days later he invited her out to lunch. She never asked if he was married and he never said so. Unlike many other married men, he wore no wedding band.

After nearly a year of lunchtime romance and quiet, sensual nights at her tiny apartment on One Hundred Fifty-second Street and Amsterdam Avenue, he believed he had to make his choice. Margie was beginning to pressure him some. He couldn't stand pressure. Still, he couldn't let her go. He had to have her with him, had to know that she was in his corner. He wanted to come home to her after a long day at work, wanted to let her massage his back and kiss him all over. She spoiled him, made him feel whole again. She encouraged him even in the smallest things. She was his oasis on a desert of loneliness. He loved her.

She was so different from his wife. Where Roxie Kate constantly nagged, Margie always tried to build him up. Where Roxie Kate constantly complained, Margie always tried to understand. He couldn't even remember when the two of them had had a serious argument.

He lounged in the tub longer than necessary. He

hoped Roxie Kate would be gone by the time he got out. He didn't feel like talking to her this morning.

He dressed for work as usual, but he knew that he wasn't going straight to the hospital this day. She was gone by the time he exited the bathroom. She hadn't even come in to tell him she was leaving.

It was snowing and bitter when he finally left the house. He pulled his long, woolen coat around him tightly and walked on. As he walked he listened to the sound of the snow crunching under his rubber boots. He was going to talk to his mother-in-law. It was Friday, the perfect day. He knew that Henrietta would be attending the classes she took twice a week at Columbia University. He didn't know what she was studying at her age, but he knew that she was deeply involved in it whatever it was. He wasn't worried about Lytell being at home. He always left early for work.

Julie Lee was sitting in the kitchen, reading the newspaper and sipping on her third cup of coffee when the doorbell rang. It rather startled her, since she wasn't expecting anyone, and Henrietta hadn't told her that a delivery would be made.

"Lord have mercy, Charlie. What you doing here so early in the morning? Aren't you supposed to be working?"

As he always did, he pecked her on the cheek lovingly. He stomped the snow off his boots, then took them off and laid them atop one another on the rug Henrietta had put down in the vestibule.

After he had settled himself in the kitchen with a hot cup of coffee in front of him, he began to talk.

"Mama, I needed to speak with you, and I wanted to do it when we could be by ourselves."

She could tell by the worry lines that creased his

forehead that he was in some kind of trouble. The first thing that came into her mind was that perhaps he and Roxie Kate had gotten in debt and needed some cash. She and Charlie had talked before. He always came to her when he was having serious problems. He was a good man. Like a son, she thought.

"You look so worried. What's on your mind?"

He hesitated, almost afraid to let the words escape his lips. He had thought about it so many times, but saying it out loud was different. He could sense her anxiousness.

"I hate to tell you this, Mama, but I think I've got to go."

She was obviously confused. "What do you mean you have to go? Go where?"

He found it difficult to match her intense gaze. His eyes dropped down to the table and finally fixed on a crumb that had fallen from a sweet roll.

"What I'm trying to say, Mama, is that I'm going to leave Roxie Kate. I just can't take it no more."

He was surprised by the hot tears that welled up in his eyes. He fished a handkerchief out of his pocket and dabbed at the water from his eyes.

She kept looking hard at him. She seemed to be staring right through him. Unexpectedly, she got up from her chair and came around the table and stood behind him. She pressed her hands on his shoulders. Without turning around, he took those fragile hands and patted them gently.

There was a very long pause before either of them spoke. He started to cry again. "I'm sorry, Mama. So sorry."

"Does Roxie Kate know?" he heard her saying.

"No. I haven't told her yet, but I've made up my

mind. I made up my mind a long time ago, but I haven't had the heart to tell her.''

He let her hands go. He was trembling. She went back to her seat across from him. He looked into her face, trying to read what she must have been thinking. There did not seem to be any surprise in her expression. In fact, he couldn't tell what she might be thinking.

He sipped at the coffee, which suddenly tasted bitter. He fumbled around on the table, searching for the sugar bowl. He found it and added two more teaspoons. He stirred the coffee absently, waiting for her to say something.

"How long you been feeling this way, Charlie?"

"Mama, you always seem to know everything that's going on in this family. Couldn't you see that I was suffering? Couldn't you tell when the loving stopped?"

She was nodding her head sadly. "I seen it, son. I seen it a long time ago. In fact, I even tried to talk to Roxie Kate about it. I really hoped that maybe you two would iron it all out. But it seems like you haven't. I'm sorry about that. Really sorry.

"Roxie Kate is my only daughter, and I think I know her better than she knows herself. I won't take up for her when she's wrong, you know that, but I think, Charlie, that maybe you might be putting everything on her when both of you should share the blame. Maybe the two of you never talked enough. Maybe the two of you never shared enough.''

"But Mama," he interrupted.

She put her hand up. "Now son, you came to talk to me, but I've got a few things to say. Let me finish. You know that I won't stand in your way if you really want to leave Roxie Kate. If you really feel that there is nothing the two of you can do to put it back together. But I ask you honestly, son, to think about it. Think about everything. Think about what might have been her fault and what might have been your own. Then, after you've thought about it fully, if you still come to the same decision, I say go.''

He wasn't prepared for her next question. She asked it so matter-of-factly. "Is there another woman, Charlie? Is that why you want to leave my daughter?''

He wondered how he would be able to tell his own mother-in-law that there was indeed a woman other than her daughter. He didn't want to answer the question. He didn't want to hurt anybody. Suddenly Julie Lee had made him feel like he was a boy again and had just gotten caught with his hand in the cookie jar.

His hesitation prompted her to ask the question again, and this time with more urgency. It sounded more like a demand now than a question.

"Talk to me, Charlie. Is it another woman? You've gone this far, you might as well tell me all about it.''

His voice was low, much lower than it was most of the time. "Yes, Mama. There is another woman, and I love her very much. I want to be with her.'' He heard himself repeating it. "I want to be with her. I love her very, *very* much.''

They talked for another two hours. He cried off and on, and she did too. He couldn't help but be amazed by the compassion she had for him. Still, he wasn't sure whether he had done the right thing by dragging her into the whole nasty mess. He believed he had hurt her—the woman who had been so much like his own mother.

"You must be sure, son. You've got to be sure that this is what you want to do. You know words are worse than stones. Once they're said, once they're out in the

453

world, there is nothing that can make them disappear. People do forgive, but few of us ever forget. I've lived a very long time, and I can't tell you how many times I've regretted saying something, especially if they were angry words to people I love.''

The clock was striking noon and Julie Lee insisted that he stay for lunch. He sat there quietly while she puttered around making something for them to eat. She made enough for Henrietta too. She would be home soon and probably starving.

Henrietta was true to her schedule. She came in about a half-hour later, tired, but famished. She was surprised to see Charlie there in the middle of the day.

"How long you been here, Charlie?" she asked, as he helped her out of her coat. She really didn't wait for an answer. "I swear I'm tired as the blazes. I just can't keep up with all those young girls."

Henrietta babbled on, and neither Julie Lee nor Charlie were even sure she'd heard their explanation that Charlie had just stopped by on his lunch hour.

As the three of them ate their lunch, Henrietta talked about family things, and of course, she asked after Roxie Kate. Charlie said she was fine, but even as he spoke, he checked his mother-in-law's expression. It gave away nothing.

"Well, I got to get back to work," he finally announced.

When the cold air hit him, it felt refreshing. He felt good that finally he had gotten some of the misery off his chest.

He walked along briskly, and before he realized it, he was right in front of the library. He hesitated, thinking that he really should go on to the hospital. Instead though, something compelled him to step inside. He checked his watch and knew that Margie was probably back from lunch.

He walked up the steps, and just as he had expected, she was there behind the check-out counter. She was talking with a young boy. He stood out of sight until the conversation had ended and the child had gone past him. Then he walked out from behind the rack. When she looked up and saw him, her face broke into a happy smile. He knew that his own face must have lit up. At his age, he thought, and still blushing like a young boy in short-legged pants.

Margie's assistant relieved her at the desk. She smiled wickedly as she watched the two of them walk down one of the aisles. They sat at a back table right beneath a tall window. The snow was still falling.

She sat next to him on one of the hard, straight-backed chairs. He smiled as she grimaced. "Why in the hell do they make these chairs so damned hard if the point is to have people sit and read?" he said, his voice full of amusement. She laughed nervously, wondering all the time what it was that he had to discuss that was so urgent.

"I got it out," he finally said. "I finally got up the nerve to let it out."

She grabbed his hand. "You mean you told Roxie Kate about us? You told her that you were going to leave her? What did she say when you told her?"

She was talking so fast that her sentences were crawling all over one another. He had to correct her mistaken impression.

He stopped her by putting one finger to her lips. "No, Margie. I haven't told Roxie Kate. I told her mother. I told my mother-in-law this morning."

Her face lapsed into a puzzled expression.

"Why'd you do that?"

"I'm not sure why," he said, suddenly feeling rather stupid. "I guess I wanted someone in the family to be on my side."

She couldn't hide her disappointment. She rubbed his head gently. "Charlie. My poor, poor baby. Whatever made you think that Roxie Kate's mother would be on your side? That's her daughter, you know."

Suddenly, he didn't want to talk anymore. It just wasn't the right time or the right place. Anyhow, he could tell that Margie wasn't very happy with the way in which he'd chosen to deal with the situation. She didn't understand that leaving a wife involved more than leaving just that woman. After all, when people separated, the family was also involved. He was leaving the Bratcher family, and in his mind, since Jack was dead, Julie Lee was the head of the family.

She sat there looking at him. He wondered what she was thinking. Especially, he wondered if she thought him a coward or a fool.

Without saying anything more, he got up from his seat and helped her up from hers.

"You've got to go back to work, and so do I," he said, as they walked back down the aisle toward the front of the library. "I tell you what. Why don't you and me go out tonight and have ourselves a good time. It will be good for us."

But she was afraid that if he went home after work she wouldn't see him that night. It had happened before. He would promise that they would go out and then something would come up at home and he wouldn't be able to get out. He always had a good excuse, and she always told herself when that happened that she shouldn't expect much different. That was the price she had to pay for being in love with a very much married man. But holidays alone, weekends alone, often days off alone—there was an awful lot of loneliness when a woman was in love with a married man. She had wondered from time to time if it was all worth it.

She watched him as he sauntered toward the door. She wasn't sure, but there just seemed to be something in his walk which suggested to her that something had changed in the man, something deep, something basic. She wondered.

Chapter 60

Henrietta died in December 1928 of walking pneumonia. One day she was fine, and the next day she was gone. Didn't even know that she was sick, might never have known, had she not passed out in the street. Right there on One Hundred Twenty-fifth Street too. It was the middle of the afternoon and the street was crowded with shoppers. By the time they got her to the hospital, her temperature registered one hundred and six degrees.

She lay there in the bed. Her skin had turned ashen, and every once in a while her eyes fluttered open. She kept mumbling incoherently. She looked so old.

"That high fever is just no good for a woman her age," the doctor told Lytell before permitting him to go into her room. "We're putting some ice packs on her to try and cool her down."

Her eyes opened when he came and stood near the bed. He wasn't sure that she even recognized him. She never said his name. She kept running her free hand across her chest. "My heart. My heart. It's moving. Please don't let my heart fly away." She fell silent after that, but appeared to be folding her lips over one another. They were chapped and white.

He wanted to keep holding her hand, but a nurse politely asked him to step out of the way. He watched as the woman adjusted one of the tubes that was feeding clear liquids into her arm. "What's that?" he asked.

"It's just an antibiotic. That's all."

Lytell backed out of the room. He cried when he slumped down onto the bench next to Julie Lee.

"Mama, Mama, what can I do? She looks so helpless lying there. Henri can't die. She can't go away and leave me here."

Julie Lee tried to comfort him, but she had no reason to be optimistic. While Lytell was in the room with Henrietta, she had insisted that the doctor tell her what Henrietta's chances were. She wouldn't let go of his hands. The doctor was surprised by the strength in them.

"Tell me. I've got a right to know," she said. "I've got to prepare my child for whatever is God's will."

The doctor looked her straight in the eye. "She's failing, and she's failing fast. If you want to know the honest to God truth, maybe you should pray. I don't have any medicine to help her now. She's just too old to fight this thing."

She released him from her grip and her gaze. "Thank you very much, Doctor. Thank you for telling me the truth."

Lytell had fallen asleep in the waiting room. He jumped up when he felt a hand tapping him on the shoulder. It was Roman. When he looked at his son's face, he knew.

They all left the hospital together. Lytell Jr. and Darnell walked on either side of their father. They were actually holding him up. Lytell's knees kept buckling. Roman walked behind them, between his twin sisters. Julie Lee leaned on Charlie's arm, and Roxie Kate walked beside them. They had turned the corner of the hospital when Jack Jr. and Dexter came rushing up. They didn't need to be told.

Lytell just couldn't seem to accept that Henrietta was gone. "She went so fast. She went so fast," he kept saying during the funeral. "My baby is gone. What am I going to do now?"

He cried and cried. "Henri. Oh, Henrietta baby, why'd you leave me here all by myself? How can I live without you?"

Theirs had been such a good marriage, a solid union. Half of his successes, and there had been many, he attributed to her. She was there, right beside him, through every major crisis in his life. She had given him strength and encouragement when Jack died. After so many years of marriage, it was hard for him to know where he stopped and she began. Sometimes he would talk, and she would finish his sentences.

On the day of the funeral, the doctor came over early. He was worried about Lytell and Julie Lee.

It was cold that day, in the low teens. They took Henrietta to be buried in the family plot Lytell had bought in the Mt. Olive Hill Baptist Cemetery in Westchester County. The ground was so hard that it was a wonder the gravediggers had even been able to do their sorry work.

The fringes on the green awning, under which they all sat on hard, wooden chairs, flapped in the wind. Lytell's coat was wide open. He didn't feel the cold weather, only the coldness that had settled over his heart. The family was sitting, but all the rest were standing, as Henrietta and

460

Lytell's minister, Reverend Richardson, administered the graveside prayer. When he was finished, the undertaker, an old family friend and one of Lytell's clients, broke off flowers from the wreaths and distributed them to the family friends. One by one, they tossed the petals onto the top of the coffin, which was sitting on two wooden slats that had been placed sideways across the grave.

When it came time for the family to stand at the coffin, Lytell wrapped one arm around Julie Lee's waist so tightly that she felt as if he were trying to absorb her into him. Between sobs, he mumbled, "Henri. Henri. Mama, what am I going to do? Henri's done left me here all by myself."

She laid her head on his chest, wanting so to say something that would relieve him. "You're not alone, baby. Henri left you here with us. She knew that we'd take care of you. We love you. I love you, Lytell. I love you, and don't you ever forget that. Dying is a part of living, baby. We've seen death before in this family and God knows it hurts every time, but we all got to walk that road that Henri walked today."

She tried to hold on to him, but Lytell slipped away from her. He got on his knees beside the coffin. His body rocked. Darnell and Roman stood behind their father. They acted as if they were afraid he would jump into the hole. They were both crying bitterly. Darnell said, "Daddy. Daddy, please. Please, get up. Let me help you up."

They made their way down the hill in a tight group. Lytell was in the middle. He turned back to look just in time to see the gravediggers lowering the casket into the ground. Suddenly, he broke away from them and ran back. His three sons followed behind him. When they caught up to him, they were amazed by the amount of strength he exhibited. They could barely hold him.

"Take me back. Take me back," he kept screaming. From where she was standing, Julie Lee signaled to them to let him have his wish. The four of them made their way back to the graveside. Everyone could hear Lytell's screams. "I want to go with my baby. I want to go with Henrietta. Take me now, Lord. Don't make me live without my woman. Oh, God, you've cut my heart out. My life. Henrietta was my life. Oh, God."

Looking on the painful scene, the family shared Lytell's agony. Their collective sobbing filled the cemetery air. Julie Lee felt Roxie Kate slide up next to her. She held on to her mother. "Child. Child, I done seen so much dying in my time on this earth, so much death, and every time, the feeling is just the same. It's so empty. But, God's will has got to be done."

Chapter 61

The liquor prohibition never existed for most folks who really wanted to drink, and in 1929 the liquor flowed in one of Harlem's most popular speakeasies, the Top Cat Club, on One Hundred Forty-fifth Street and Eighth Avenue. The club was owned by white mobsters, everybody knew that, but it was managed and patronized almost exclusively by Harlem's Negro upper class. People who went there never feared a raid because the mobsters had paid off the police and the spot was left alone.

Dexter was a club member. He had paid the twenty-five-dollar dues, and that entitled him to bring his friends so that they could enjoy themselves in an easy, relaxed atmosphere. When the family was trying to decide where to celebrate Lytell's formal retirement, Dexter suggested that they go to the Cat.

When the party of fifteen arrived that Saturday night shortly after eleven o'clock, Vaughn G., the manager, greeted Dexter warmly. His eyes gleamed when he saw Dexter's party. He knew that there was plenty of money to be made from that crowd.

Vaughn escorted them through the rows of tables to a

section he'd cordoned off and held in reserve after Dexter had made the reservation. Already on the tables, which had been set up horseshoe style, were three large ice buckets. In moments, Vaughn would have the waitress fill them with ice and champagne—an expensive brand that the rumrunners had only brought in a week earlier from overseas.

Roxie Kate had never been to a place like the Cat, and to Dexter's surprise, she was impressed.

"It's beautiful in here," she said, eyeing the thick carpeting and the red velvet curtains that hung around the booths lining the walls. "I've heard other people talk about this place, but I didn't know it was this nice."

Charlie butted in. "Oh, Roxie Kate, you don't drink anyway."

"It doesn't matter. The place is still nice."

Everyone in the party was feeling good. It had been a long time since they'd all gotten together to have a party.

"I tried to talk Mama into coming," Jack Jr. said, "but she wouldn't. Mama said that we should all have a good time."

Jeddah added, "Now, Uncle Jack, you know Mama ain't go out nowhere when she got to go to church the next day. 'Sides, Mama's too old to be in a place like this."

Jack Jr. whispered, "Well, exactly how old do you think your father is? He's almost eighty."

"But that's different, Uncle Jack. It's his party."

It was still early for the Cat's regular crowd, and so the club was half empty. Dexter wasn't really much of a drinker, but he loved music and he even fiddled around with a piano a bit. "The band they're gonna have playing tonight is pretty good, but, man, wait till after midnight. Then it gets so hot in here that you can't hardly stand it.

There's this nigga named Preacher that can play his natural ass off. They call him Preacher 'cause when he gets finished with that trumpet of his, everybody wants to stand up and testify.''

As they were being escorted to the table, the band was setting up for the two sets they would play that night. Dexter turned around and waved at one who yelled in his direction, ''What's the word, baby? You gonna sit in with us later on?''

Dexter tried to act nonchalant about the invitation, but every one could tell that he was flattered. ''Don't think so, man. I got my family with me tonight.''

The man responded. ''Well, you got it if you want it.''

''Thanks a lot, sweetheart,'' Dexter said with uncharacteristic bravado.

Everyone at the Bratcher table was talking and sipping champagne, but they stopped in midsentence when Darnell got up and tapped on his glass.

''I want to propose a toast to my daddy.''

He lifted his glass in Lytell's direction. ''Daddy, we love you, old man. After all these years, you done finally decided to move on over and let us young chickens take over.''

Charlie interrupted. ''Hold it. Just hold it, Darnell. Y'all ain't so young, and none of us is that old.''

Everyone laughed.

''That's right,'' Lytell chimed in. He was laughing, and that was good as far as the others were concerned. After Henrietta's death, he'd grown withdrawn and perpetually somber.

Darnell started his toast again. ''Like I said, I'd like to toast my daddy, the best man that I know. Daddy, I

. . ." He stopped and looked around at his brothers and sisters and the rest of the assembled relatives. "I just wanted to tell you that we love you. You've been our father and our friend. To be sure, you were a pain in the butt every once in a while, but all in all, you've been all right."

Darnell's eyes twinkled as he warmed to his subject. He looked around and smiled boyishly. "What I'm trying to say, Daddy, is that you done good. You done real good. Look at us. Look at your children. Ain't we beautiful?"

Lytell had to stop his son. "I don't know if y'all are so beautiful, but if you are, you know where you got it from." Everyone knew what was coming next, and so Darnell quickly tried to change the subject.

"Anyhow, Dad, I just want to say on behalf of all of us that we're gonna do you real proud too. Gonna make that business you started grow. We gonna make that money and keep you a happy man."

They touched glasses. "Hear, hear!" Roman said loudly.

Dexter had been right. After about an hour or so, the club was packed. Smoke and happy laughter filled the air. Everyone who had passed through the Cat's heavy steel door was dressed to the nines. The women, most of them, sported fur coats, and they laughed loudly and sensuously as their equally well-dressed companions whispered whatever in their ears. The band was playing softly in the background, but nearly everyone was concentrating on their drinking and conversations.

Just then, Dexter looked up and spied Preacher coming into the club. As always, dangling from his arm was his axe, as everyone referred to the trumpet Preacher carried everywhere he went.

Dexter's eyes gleamed happily. "Lookahere. Lookahere. It's Preacher, here early. We gonna hear some playing tonight."

Dexter's excited babbling caused everyone at the table to focus on the tall, dark-skinned, bearded man who was now making his way through the tables. As he passed, several people patted him on his shoulder. He was their very own celebrity, and Preacher loved the attention, it was obvious.

Dexter stood up in his seat and signaled for Preacher to come over. Preacher wasn't especially handsome, but his smile was so friendly and infectious that most people forgot he was a little on the homely side.

When he arrived at their tables, he grabbed Dexter's hand and pumped it. "How you doing, man? How you doing?" he said. He turned and nodded to the others at the table.

"This is my family," Dexter said proudly. "Everybody. I want you to meet Preacher, my man, my friend, and the best musician God ever blew breath into. This is the man I been telling you about all night. Come on, Preacher. Sit down and have a drink with us. We're celebrating a little bit tonight. My brother has finally retired."

Preacher declined and explained that he had to get ready for the evening's performance. "I'll take you up on that drink later on though," he said. "Nice meeting you all," he added, as he headed off in the direction of his dressing room.

When Preacher had walked away, Dexter said to no

one in particular, "Ah, it sure is sweet. A toast to the colored man!"

"That's right," Charlie added. He was obviously feeling no pain. "A toast to the colored man," he repeated louder than he usually spoke.

"How about a toast to the colored woman?" Rhetta interjected, to which Jack Jr. added, "Well, what the hell? How about a toast to colored people? That's right. Let's have a toast to the Negro. We done seen some hard times, and we done seen some good, but we're moving on anyhow."

The Bratcher party kept the scantily clad waitress busy. She was back and forth from the table to the bar, bringing them drinks.

Roxie Kate looked on disapprovingly when she saw how Charlie was eyeing the woman. She didn't say anything, though. She had tried to change her ways, and she had apparently been successful; she had saved her rocky marriage. They had worked out most of their problems, and she wasn't about to spoil things now by getting lockjaw, as Charlie called it, about a strange woman, who probably wasn't even thinking about an old man like Charlie.

She wouldn't have seen the forest for the trees had it not been for her mother. She thought about the conversation they'd had five years earlier.

"Now, Roxie Kate," Julie Lee said. "You know I've never meddled in you and Charlie's business, but I'm telling you, if you don't stop acting like you're acting, you're going to lose a good man. And let me tell you something else. A good man is hard to find, honey, especially at your age. You're not exactly a spring chicken, but believe me, it's much easier for an older man to find another woman than it is for an old woman to find somebody, unless she's looking to get hooked up to some young man who only wants her money."

Roxie Kate had the feeling that her mother wasn't just whistling in the wind. She suspected that Charlie might have gone to her and told her something about their problems. She agreed with her mother that she had to work on her personality quirks and stop her incessant denigrations of Charlie's lack of ambition.

She remembered, too, some of what she'd said during that important conversation. "Mama, I don't know. Sometimes I don't even know why I do the things I do and say the things I say. I love Charlie, always have and probably always will, but sometimes I can't keep the hoof out of my mouth."

She giggled in young girl fashion. "I don't even know if Charlie's a good lover or not. He's the only man I've ever had, and I surely don't have anybody to compare him to."

Julie Lee came back, glad that the conversation had lightened some. "I haven't heard you complaining all of these years."

They laughed knowingly, but Roxie Kate didn't tell her mother that it had been a long time since Charlie had even tried to touch her. She knew about Margie, and all the other women as well, but she'd come to realize that Margie must have been something special. One day she'd even gone to the library to get a look at her competition.

Sitting in that noisy club, as she looked over at Charlie's silly-looking face now that he'd had a few drinks, Roxie Kate couldn't help thinking how grateful she was for her mother. She had really helped to save their marriage.

The unexpected quiet that settled over the club made them stop talking and pay attention to the stage up front. The band was playing softly in the background and Vaughn G. was standing out in front of them. He'd loosened his jacket and removed his tie. He was about to assume his other role as master of ceremonies.

His rich baritone voice reached out to everyone in the room. "Ladies and gentlemen," he said, "and all you others who are sitting on the fence, I'd like to welcome you to the Top Cat Club. I'm your host. You can just call me "G," and I hope you're having a good time tonight. Are you?"

The response was a resounding "Yes."

"Tonight, the Cat has got something real special for you. I . . ."

A woman at one of the front tables interrupted Vaughn. "I want another drink. I don't want to listen to you."

Vaughn was polite, a requirement for someone in his position. "Excuse me, ma'am, but I'm on, and you're not, and I'd appreciate it if you'd let me do my job. Just give me a little space, all right, darling?"

The man who was sitting with the woman started talking. "Now, that ain't no way to talk to your mama."

Two menacing-looking bouncers headed for the table where the hecklers were sitting, but Vaughn signaled to them that they should back off. Nonetheless, the couple quieted down when Vaughn put the stare on them. They had seen the bouncers heading for them and had gotten the message quickly.

"Now, as I was saying before these here folks interrupted me, ladies and gentlemen. Would you put your hands together and give a nice, warm, Cat Club round of applause to the one, the only, Georgia's own sweet peach, Miss Dinah Washburn.''

The lights on the stage dimmed, and when they went up again, a red spotlight focused on a woman dressed from head to toe in white. She even wore two white flowers in her hair. She put one foot in front of the other and curtsied graciously, letting the warm applause bathe her.

"Thank you. Thank you so much," she said in a husky way. "How's everybody?"

She began to look around, but not for long. A young man appeared from the sidelines carrying a high stool. He set it in the middle of the stage. "Thank you, darling," Dinah said sweetly. She sat down dantily, ever so gently, tugging at her sequined gown, which glittered under the lights. She turned her head slightly and signaled to the band behind her to strike up the chords for her first number. Initially, some people talked, but in moments, Dinah's sweet voice had hushed them all. All eyes were riveted to the woman on the stage.

After two of Dinah's numbers, Lytell couldn't help himself. He wept softly, thinking about Henrietta and how much she would have loved this night—being with all her children and the rest of the family. Roman, who noticed his father's condition, passed him a handkerchief. He whispered in his ear, "Don't cry, Daddy. Don't cry."

When Dinah finished, there wasn't a dry eye in the club. "I sure wish Mama could have heard her sing," Jack Jr. said.

"Now, Jack Jr., you know Mama ain't coming out to no club, especially where there's liquor being consumed," Roxie Kate said.

"I know. I know, but I just wish Mama could be with

us tonight, having a good time. I guess I wish she wasn't such an old woman."

Lytell stood up a few moments later. He asked for their attention. "Now it's my turn," he said. "I want to toast you—my children, my family. I want you all to know that I am happy tonight. I love each and every one of you. Thank you for this special night. I'll never forget it."

Chapter 62

"You dressed yet, Mama?" Lytell hollered up to Julie Lee.

"I'll be down in a minute. I'm trying to find my straw hat." She pushed some of her mountain of papers to the side. "Darn it, where's that old thing?"

She came down a few minutes later. She was clutching the hat and carrying a big straw bag, filled with what, Lytell could not imagine.

"What in the world are you carrying in that bag, lady?"

She laughed. "It's none of your business what a woman carries in her pocketbook."

"That's not a pocketbook, Mama, that's a sack." He shook his head and smiled. "Jeddah will be here any minute to pick us up," he said, while trying unsuccessfully to pat down the last few strands of hair left atop his head.

Julie Lee sat down in a living room chair. "Whew. I don't know why I'm so tired. I haven't done anything."

Lytell's face took on an air of concern. "Now, Mama, if you don't feel like going, you know we don't have to. I'll just tell Jeddah and them that we'll go another time."

She waved her hand. "What? And miss a day at Coney Island? No sir! All these years I been in New York City, and I've never been to Coney Island. I'm going to have my fun today."

It was a beautiful day for a trip to the beach. The sun was sitting high up in the sky. It was a little past noon when they crossed over the bridge into Brooklyn.

Julie Lee looked out the window of the car. "Just look at that water. It sure looks pretty."

Jeddah said, "Pretty, Mama? That water is so nasty. I bet if somebody fell in there by mistake, they'd die from garbage poison."

"I know it's probably dirty, but it just looks so pretty with the sun shining on it and everything."

"Well, Mama, please don't get no ideas about jumping in until we get out to the Atlantic Ocean," Jeddah said happily.

By the time they pulled up their cars at Surf Avenue, all that could be seen for miles was people, beach and sky.

Arthur said, "Damn, look at that crowd. I knew we should have gotten an earlier start. It's looks like everybody in New York City got the same idea as us. I bet there's not an empty spot on the beach."

"Don't be so down in the mouth, Arthur," Jeddah chided her husband. "You always think the worst." She turned to him and tried to look very serious, but her eyes were teasing.

Jeddah turned her attention to her sons. "All right, now. Don't just sit there, help your grandpa and great grandmother out the car."

"I'll get the food," Arthur said.

"I just bet you will," Jeddah responded.

They headed out toward a vacant spot for them to put down their blankets and baskets. It was along a spit of land that jutted far out into the ocean. Though no one actually said that Negroes could only sit in one part of the beach, they naturally congregated together in certain areas.

Rhetta helped her father and grandmother out of their shoes so they could walk more easily in the sand.

"Mama, why have you got on so many clothes?" she asked when she had lifted up Julie Lee's dress a little and discovered that she had a heavy petticoat on underneath. "It's hot as sin out here."

"Listen, child, I'm not as young as you are. These old bones of mine are brittle, and I get cold when other folks be hot. Ask your daddy. If you ever get to our age, you'll know what I'm talking about."

Arthur and Rupbert lugged the picnic baskets, and Rhetta's twin sons, Mervin and Irving, carried the blankets, while Rhetta and Jeddah helped the old folks down the boardwalk steps and out onto the beachfront. They headed directly to the spot Arthur had pointed out from the boardwalk.

"We gonna get an umbrella, Daddy?" Mervin asked his father.

"Yeah. We're gonna get two of them. Can't have Miss Julie Lee and your grandpa sitting out under all this hot sun all day. Either one of them could have a stroke."

"Can I go and get the umbrellas, Daddy? Can I?" Irving asked eagerly.

"No," Rupbert answered. "Each of you can get one apiece."

Once they'd put everything down and the boys had

returned with the umbrellas, Rhetta and Jeddah began to unpack the sandwiches, fruit and drinks they'd brought.

Jeddah nudged her sister in the side and signaled for her to watch. "You ready to eat, Arthur?" Jeddah asked innocently.

"Don't mind if I do," he answered back. The two women fell out on the blanket with laughter.

"Girl," Rhetta said, "I'm sure glad I don't have to feed that man."

There was a gentle breeze blowing off the ocean. Irving was right in the middle of his sandwich when Julie Lee turned to him. "Would you like to walk an old lady down by the water, son? I'd like to get my feet wet a little bit."

Irving's eyes were fixed on a group of youngsters about his age who were playing with a ball nearby. He started to try to talk his way out of walking with his great grandmother, but the look his mother gave him made him think better of it.

They walked in a zigzag along the water's edge, attempting to avoid the people who were running and playing in the sand and water. Julie Lee felt good. She felt like talking.

"You know, son, when I was a little girl back on the plantation one of my favorite things was playing by the water when all my work was done. The plantation was right by the river, the James River. Me and your Uncle Hannibal. He died before you were born, but Hannibal was my brother. Lord, child, me and Hannibal, we used to love to get some free time so we could go down by the river and stick our feet in."

She looked out at the horizon. "It's pretty," she said. "All that blue sky and ocean. Did you ever wonder what was on the other side of the ocean?"

Irving looked up absently. "Ain't nothing over there."

"Oh no, you wrong, child. There's people and places over there. I bet that right now some other old lady is walking along a beach talking to her great grandson just like I'm talking to you now.

"Now, like I was saying, when I was little girl, I used to—"

He interrupted her. "You were a slave, weren't you?"

"Yes I was, and your grandpa Lytell, he was too, and so was your great-grandpa Jack, my husband. We were all slaves a long, long time ago."

Irving was interested in talking now. "We studied about slavery some in school. It was hard, wasn't it? I mean being a slave. You couldn't go where you wanted to go or do what you wanted to do unless the master said it was all right. I wonder what it would feel like for somebody to own me."

She looked away from the boy. "Don't wonder, child. It's the worst thing that could happen to a man or a woman. I don't wish slavery on nobody. It was a terrible, terrible thing. I wouldn't ever want the young people of your generation to suffer like we did down on those old plantations."

He held her hand more tightly. "Was you a house slave or a field slave, Grandma?"

"What you know about house slaves and field slaves, child?"

"Well, our teacher said that in slavery time, some slaves was a little bit freer than others. She said the slaves who worked in the house were treated real good and that they cried when slavery time was over."

She stopped walking now and looked at the boy.

"Your teacher told you that? Is your teacher colored or white?"

"She's white."

"I thought so. Well, child, I did work in the house most of the time, but don't let nobody tell you that a house slave was like a free person. Because it's not true. And honey child, didn't none of us cry when slavery time was over. Fact, I escaped before it ended. Listen, a slave is a slave, don't matter if you were in the house or the field, you were still just a piece of property all the same, and the master could sell you any time he wanted to."

They sat down now, right in the sand where they'd been standing. They let their feet hang in the surf, which ebbed in and out and tickled their toes.

"If I ask you something, Grandma, would you get mad?"

" 'Course not, son. What you want to know?"

He hesitated. "What I want to know is . . ."

She urged him to ask his question.

"Well, what I want know is, how come you look so white like that?"

She was surprised not only by the question, but the intensity with which it had been asked. She thought before speaking. "I look this way, I guess, because I was one of the accidents of the slavery system."

His eyes had even more questions in them now. "What you mean, you were an accident?"

"What I'm trying to say, child, is that there were a lot of other slaves who looked just like me. You see, my daddy was a white man. In fact, my daddy was the old massa's son."

Irving made absent traces in the sand. "But how

come Grandpa and Daddy and Mama ain't white like you?''

"I guess your mama never told you and your brother the story of our family, but you see, me and your grandpa Lytell, we ain't really blood kin. I mean, he's not really my son, and I'm not really his mother."

Irving was really confused now. "But why does he call you Mama?"

"Well, it was like this. Your grandpa Lytell and me, we were both slaves on the Johnson plantation back in Henrico County. He was just a little boy at the time, and when I escaped he came along with us. He wasn't really my son—I'm not old enough to be his blood mother—but I raised him up just like he was my child, and over the years, I just never made no difference between him and the children I gave birth to."

"Mama never told me that," the boy said, amazement written all over his face.

"I guess she didn't just because it's not really important. After all, in this family we never did make no separation between each other. Kinfolk is kinfolk, and as long as you live, child, don't forget that when things get real rough, family is all you got. That's why you always see me trying to make sure that our family sticks together through the thick and the thin."

She rubbed the boy on his head as he helped her up and walked back toward the blanket. A thought crossed her mind. "Irving, you're not ashamed of us because we were slaves, are you?"

He smiled up at her. "I don't think so, Grandma. Should I be ashamed?"

She looked down at him. "No, child. You haven't got anything to be ashamed about. A whole lot of people died so we wouldn't have to be slaves no more. They were brave and strong and proud.''

It was after six by the time they packed up their things and headed back to the cars. Both Lytell and Julie Lee had fallen asleep two or three times during the course of the afternoon. Mervin and Irving were exhausted from running and playing with some of the boys and girls they'd met on the beach. Arthur had stuffed himself, and now there were nothing but crumbs in the bottom of the baskets.

Rupbert helped Rhetta fold up their blanket. He kissed her on the cheek unexpectedly. ''Did you have a good time, baby?''

''Do you have to ask? I had a great time. It was nice getting out of the city for a day.'' She looked over at her father and Julie Lee. ''And I think they had a good time, too, don't you?''

Jeddah walked over to where they were standing. ''You two should be ashamed of yourselves, out here smooching like teenagers. If you're not careful somebody might think you all are still in love.''

''We are,'' Rupbert said playfully. He patted Rhetta on her behind. ''Aren't we?''

She smiled at him.

Chapter 63

Julie Lee didn't start coughing until later on that evening, several hours after they'd returned home from Coney Island.

"Oh Lord, Mama, it seems like you done went and caught yourself a cold. Maybe it wasn't such a good idea for us to go out to the beach."

"Lytell, please. It's nothing but a little cold. I've have so many colds in my life that I don't know how many. Don't go getting worried about me."

They both went to bed and the house was quiet. Lytell woke up suddenly when he heard the sounds of a racking cough coming from her room. He got up and moved as quickly as he could down the hall. He pushed open the door and went inside.

"Mama? Mama, wake up. Are you all right?"

Now she was startled. "What's the matter, Lytell?"

"I heard you coughing all the way down in my room." He touched her head. It was hot.

"I'm all right. Bring me some of that cough medicine out of the medicine cabinet. I guess I did get a little cold. Maybe it was that ocean air."

When he suggested that she get up and let him take her to the hospital, she protested.

"Lord, Lytell, I told you that I'm all right. Don't go making such a fuss about a little sniffle. Besides, I'm not up to that Harlem Hospital emergency room tonight. I swear I'm not. I'll go to the doctor tomorrow."

Not long after he had given her the cough syrup she fell back to sleep. He sat by the bed for a while, but went back to his own room once he was convinced that she was resting comfortably. He lay in the bed with his eyes open, keeping an ear out for the sounds of her coughing. He heard none. In less than a half-hour he had also fallen back to sleep.

He dreamed that night about Henrietta, only this time, the dream was a little different than the usual. In it, Henrietta was not still and cold, lying in her coffin. In this dream Henrietta was alive and she was young. They were both young. She was smiling and he was smiling back at her.

He balled up his pillow and caressed it. It was Henrietta to him and he squeezed her tight. "I love you, Henri. I love you."

By the time morning had come, Julie Lee had gotten worse, but she still refused to allow him to take her to the hospital. She had cough syrup several more times, but it wasn't doing any good.

"You've got to go, Mama. That's all there is to it," Jack finally said when he arrived later that afternoon.

"But I've got to go to my own doctor," she insisted.

Jack said, "There's no need for you to argue with me. You're going to the hospital, and that's it."

"But I want to go to my own doctor," she protested again.

482

"Damn that private doctor. I'm taking you over to Harlem Hospital now."

She relented. She felt too weak to fight. He helped her back upstairs to her room.

"All right, son, give me my green dress over there in the back of the closet."

He pulled out an emerald green dress and started to hand it to her.

"No, that's not the one," she said petulantly.

"Mama, you're not going to a fashion show, you're going to the hospital. Now stop stalling." He had to laugh at her. At her age she was still trying to be clever.

She sat up straight on the bed and said in the strongest sounding voice she could muster, "Who's the mama here? I'm your mama, and I said I want to wear my green dress. If you don't get it for me, then I'm not going anywhere."

He took another dress out of the closet, the right one this time. "Oh, you're going to the hospital, little lady, even if I have to pick you up and carry you over there naked."

Julie Lee was admitted quickly after Jack Jr. and Lytell brought her in. The emergency room doctor said that they had been wise to get her to the hospital as soon as they had. When she opened her eyes, they were all huddled around the bed. She could tell by their expressions that she must be pretty ill, though she didn't feel that bad.

"What's wrong with y'all? You look like you're attending a funeral or something. I'm not dead yet, you know. Ya'll looking at me like I'm a ghost or something."

Jack stepped forward first. He kissed her on her forehead. "How do you feel, Mama? You've been sleeping for hours."

She started to answer him and while attempting to sit up, she saw that an intravenous bottle was swinging over her head. The bottle was attached to a tube that ran into her arm. The arrangement reminded her of when Henrietta had been sick before she died.

She was concentrating on the bottle and the tube when Lytell leaned down over the bars on the side of the bed where he was standing. "How you feel, Mama?"

"Well," she answered, trying to sound strong, "if you're asking me if I'm hurting, I'm not. If you're asking me if I feel like going to a party, I don't."

"That's good. That's good," he said absently, patting her on the arm softly.

She looked around at them all and said, "I thought the hospital had rules about how many people were allowed in a hospital room at one time. How come they let all of you in here?"

"We've got connections," Jeddah sassed back.

One by one the assemblage broke up, so that each could have a turn kissing her and asking her how she felt. She got through the night with few problems. For the next two days it was much the same.

On the fourth day, however, a doctor stopped Lytell and Jack Jr. on their way up the hall to her room.

"I'd like to talk with you before you go in to see your mother," the doctor said. His manner was grave.

"What's the matter, Doctor?" Lytell asked anxiously.

The doctor ushered them into a nearby examination room.

"What about our mother, Doctor?" Jack Jr. said.

"I'd like to give you some good news, but I can't. I want to suggest that you get in touch with everyone in

484

your family just in case somebody lives out of town and has to travel. Your mother took a bad turn this morning and we think that, given her age and general state of health, she doesn't have long to live."

Lytell unconsciously hit his hand against the wall. "Age. Age. That's it, isn't it, Doctor? It's almost like age kills people instead of disease."

"I'm sorry," the doctor said, "but I just wanted you to know the truth of the situation. The fact is that your mother is a very old woman, and her body has slowed down. Truthfully, age *is* a killer. The longer we live, the fewer reserves we have to fight off sickness, even a common cold like your mother started off with."

A lump of foul-tasting bile settled itself in Lytell's throat. He was reliving it all over again. It had been less than a year since he'd buried Henrietta, and now Julie Lee was going.

"Damn, damn," he cried.

Jack Jr. held him tightly around his shoulders. "Come on, Lytell. Pull yourself together. Come on now. You don't want Mama to see you crying. She'll know she's really sick."

"Huh. If I know Mama, I bet she's done already made her peace with God."

The doctor was touched by the scene of the two men embracing so warmly. It was something that he did not see often.

"Your mother must be a wonderful woman. I've got to go on my rounds, but I'm glad that I had this opportunity to talk with you."

"Thank you very much, Doctor," Jack said. "She was, I mean she *is* a very beautiful woman."

They walked toward the room together, but Jack stopped midway down the hall. "You go in to see Mama, Lytell. I'm going to try to round everybody up."

Lytell was alone with her in the room. He had asked the attending nurse if she would mind leaving him and his mother alone.

"How you feel, Mama?"

Her voice was so weak and low that he had to put his ear right next to her mouth to hear what she was saying. She was still trying to put up a good front.

"I'm all right, I guess, but I don't feel as good as I did the day before yesterday. I'm getting weaker. I guess I'm tired, Lytell. Real tired. But promise me something. When I die, please don't let everyone fall out and cry. I've lived a long, long time and to tell you the truth, I'm about ready to check out of this old world."

He could feel the tears filling up in his eyes, but he tried to hold them back. He held her hand tightly.

Over the course of the next two hours, family members filed into the room, one and two at a time. Roxie Kate rushed to her mother's bedside.

"Mama, it's me. It's Roxie Kate. I'm here, Mama. How you feel?"

She wanted to answer Roxie Kate, and she even opened her mouth to talk, but her voice had gone.

"Can you hear me, Mama? I'm here, Mama."

She couldn't speak, but she tapped her daughter on the hand. She wanted her to know that she knew that she was there.

Roxie Kate was about ready to become hysterical and might have had Charlie not taken her by her arms and moved her away from the bed.